Soulwalkers

Soulwalkers

to Dawn,

 BOOK ONE

THE RIVEN CHRONICLES

CASSIDY THOMAS

LITTLE BIG BOOKS

First paperback edition 2019

Cover design by eBook Launch

ISBN 978-1-7334271-0-4

Little Big Books
Houston, TX

www.cassidythomas.com

for mom,
thank you for passing along your dreams

"What can you ever really know of other people's souls—of their temptations, their opportunities, their struggles? One soul in the whole creation you do know: and it is the only one whose fate is placed in your hands."
-C.S. Lewis

1

"**Y**OU'RE GETTING OLD."

Kia and Katelyn LaStrauss were sitting in Kia's car, staring at their school for the first time since classes ended last year.

"Kia, are you even listening?" her sister asked. "You're a senior now and in a couple of months you will be 18, and in precisely nine months, you will be graduating high school, never to return to this place." She gestured around the car and toward the school. They both turned back and looked at the building, and together, almost as if it was planned, they tilted their heads to the right and sighed.

"Old." It was meant as a question, but when it came out it sounded like Kia was agreeing with Katelyn.

"Yup. Should we go in?" Katelyn asked.

Kia's hands gripped the wheel slightly. "I guess so."

But neither sister got out of the old Jeep Wrangler. The knuckles on Kia's hands turned white as she gripped the wheel tighter.

"What's wrong?" Katelyn asked, her eyes on the steering wheel and Kia's hands.

Kia let go, and blinked, still staring at the school. "I had the dream again."

Katelyn's mouth formed a little *oh*, but no sound came out.

Outside, the bell signaling the start of class was ringing.

Kia shook her head, trying to clear out the dream from her head. "Sorry, what?" She hadn't been listening to whatever Katelyn was saying.

"I said…" Katelyn drawled out, "we better go in."

✤✤✤

Kia hated the first day of school. Going over the syllabus—which no one paid attention to—filling out a contact information sheet, playing those pointless "Get to Know You" games. She hated it all. She knew that it was for the teacher's benefit, but she couldn't help but be frustrated hearing the same things repeatedly.

In English, the teacher's game of choice was Two Truths and a Lie. Kia groaned. She *hated* that game.

After they had gone over the syllabus and played the game, they still had 30 minutes left of the 90-minute period. It was officially going to be the longest day ever.

"Every morning we're going to start the class off with a journal entry," Mrs. Cavanaugh said. Kia groaned again. She had hated that about her English class last year, partly because prompts were always something stupid, but mostly because she didn't normally like other people to read the things she had written. On the overhead projector, the teacher put up their prompt.

All of you are starting your senior year, no doubt already making plans about what you'll be doing and where you'll be next year. But as you're almost two decades into your life, have you stopped to think about what you could accomplish in the next two decades? Please spend the remainder of the class writing about your "twenty-year plan." Don't hold back. Dream big.

Kia had to laugh to herself. What Katelyn had said in the car that morning was starting to feel more and more true. Saying she was 17 years old didn't make her sound old, but when you thought about it as two decades—well, almost two decades—suddenly the amount of time she had spent on the earth seemed so much greater.

She picked up her pen and started to write. *My twenty-year plan. What is my twenty-year plan?* She had always been one to write whatever popped into her mind. The paper was a sacred place where she didn't have to filter her thoughts like she did when she spoke out loud. Katelyn was the one with word vomit, not her.

College, I guess. Her parents had gone to Louisiana State University— that was where they met—but she was never much into the Tigers and the die-hard fandom that came along with that. Maybe someplace out of state. No, she could never leave her sister alone.

Kia had spent the summer volunteering in different departments of the hospital that her mother worked at. Marie LaStrauss was head of cardiothoracic and had pulled some strings—well, one string, Marie had said—and got Kia accepted into the volunteer program. Summer hits hard in New Orleans. Escaping the high heat and humidity outdoors, and the monotony of staying home every day, was what drew her to working in the hospital in the first place. She wasn't even sure if medicine was a path she wanted to follow, though she couldn't help but find joy in the small things she was able to help with in the hospital, and her mom was ecstatic at the slight interest Kia showed.

Pre-med? She wrote.

She leaned over to look at how much the person next to her had written. It was a lot. She looked down at her four sentences and suddenly felt sad that she hadn't thought about what her life would look like in twenty years. *Whatever*, she thought. That's what college is for, deciding what you want to do with the rest of your life. Plus, Katelyn was being ridiculous, and so was she for agreeing with her. She wasn't getting old.

Kia was saved from having to write anymore by the bell ringing. She stood and headed to the cafeteria for lunch.

It was small, just big enough to hold the few girls in each lunch period. There were three lunches: one for elementary girls, one for junior high, and one for high school. Kia liked it that way since she got to eat lunch with her sister and their friends.

Light streamed in from the school's old windows illuminating the tables. Kia sat down at the same moment that Katelyn got there. "So," Katelyn began, slamming her impressively large literature book on the table, "there are rumors."

"Here we go." Kia opened a bag of chips.

"About the boy's lacrosse team. Don't you tune out so quickly! I see you rolling your eyes, Kia!"

Kia laughed. She didn't even realize she was doing it. Their school, like most private schools in the area, had a brother school. The boy version of theirs. That was one of the things that Kia hated about the genders being separated. Everything was a rumor, and her sister loved the rumor mill. "Well Ms. Cliffhanger, are you going to tell us?"

"Sarah's brother told Sarah, who told Ashley, who told me..."

Kia rolled her eyes again.

"That there are some new guys on the team, and that they are in peak physical condition." She raised her eyebrows suggestively.

One of the girls at the table, Jackie weighed in. "Sarah's brother actually commented on the attractiveness of the lacrosse team?"

Kia laughed.

"Well maybe he didn't use those words exactly, but it was basically the same thing."

"Uh huh," Kia and Jackie said together.

After Kia had been to Economics, English, and Calculus, all she had left was French, which was one of her favorite classes. She was in Advanced Placement French IV this year and had Madam Arson again, the same teacher she'd had for French since freshman year.

"*Bon après-midi, Mademoiselle LaStrauss, comment s'est passé votre été?*" Madam Arson asked as Kia walked into the classroom.

"*Bonjour Madam Arson.* My summer was good, but unfortunately, my French is a little out of practice."

Madam Arson laughed and gestured for Kia to take a seat. When the bell rang and everyone had quieted down, Madam Arson welcomed the class and started going over the syllabus. Kia tried listening to Madam Arson, but that it was fruitless this late on her first day back, especially with how tired she was.

She hardly ever had the dream two nights in a row and hoped she would sleep better tonight.

Madam Arson talked for almost the entire 90-minute period. Kia only caught bits and pieces of what she was saying. The native speaker's French was too fast for Kia's ears. Luckily, the bell signaling the end of class came before Madam Arson started asking any questions.

"Please complete this homework assignment, so I can gauge how much your French suffered over the summer," Madam Arson said in English. The class groaned. This was the only homework assignment Kia had gotten all day.

The other students had packed up their backpacks during the last couple of minutes of class, but Kia hadn't been paying attention to the time, so she still needed to get her things together. She was one of the last students to get up and head out.

Madam Arson passed out the homework assignment at the door as the students left the classroom. "Kia, I am glad that you decided to take another year of French. You are one of my best students, even if you have forgotten some of your *Français*," Madam Arson said, winking. They both laughed as she handed Kia the homework assignment and put her hand out to shake Kia's.

Kia's smile faded as her hand came in contact with Madam Arson's. She could hear wind roaring, but not in her ears, under her skin. It pushed and pulled her body, twisting and sucking. Was she screaming? She heard screams but couldn't feel any sound escaping her lips. Her vision went black.

And then so many images passed before her.

Someone's funeral. Going to the very back of the closet to find the only black dress she owned. Another funeral. Looking up at the Arc de Triomphe. Red roses.

The wind died, and Kia slipped back into reality with the taste of chocolate éclairs in her mouth and the air knocked from her. Her hand fell from Madam Arson's as she struggled to catch her breath.

It must not have lasted longer than a second because Madam Arson didn't seem to notice that anything had happened at all. Kia mumbled goodbye, left the room and stumbled her way to the women's bathroom, nausea welling up inside of her.

There were a few women inside, chatting about nothing and everything in the way that teenage girls always seem to do. Kia hesitated for a moment, but she could taste bile on her tongue and darted into a stall, vomiting into the toilet.

She heard a gag from one of the girls, as another one said, "Ew!" They all started laughing and left the bathroom, as Kia heaved again.

This can't be happening again, Kia thought, as she rested her head on her arm. The dream she had last night was no coincidence then.

The dream was an ever-present companion in Kia's bed. It had popped back up every few months since she was eight years old. It was the dream that kept coming back like the stray cat you fed one time. The dream that wasn't a dream at all. The dream that was actually a memory.

Her parents fighting. A suitcase. The front door held wide open. Rain. Heavy Rain. Their dad blowing kisses to her as he got into the car. The car door closing right when she reached it. Her mother screaming at her father. Tears running down her face mixing with the rainwater. The silhouette of her Dad as the car faded from sight. Rain.

It had been almost nine years since the moment of the memory, but really, memory was a loose term. While she did, in fact, have that memory, it came in two forms.

First, the time she saw it in her head.

And second, the time she saw it in real life.

Kia had been playing that silly reflex game with her sister. Her hands were suspended over Katelyn's, their palms facing each other's. Kia was concentrating hard, trying to feel for when her sister moved. The moment when their hands touched, just for a split-second, she was pulled into the rain, into watching her father leave them. When it stopped, her vision went black, and she fainted.

It took her a long time to tell anyone about it. Even at eight years old she knew that having visions wasn't necessarily normal. But once she had the vision, she couldn't get it to stop appearing repeatedly in her dreams. So, she told her sister.

The very next day their father left them. She had been prepared. It was why she told Katelyn in the first place. She had seen the signs. The yelling and fighting. But her future changed, because instead of running after her dad as she had seen, Kia stood at the door and watched him blow kisses to Katelyn as she stood on the steps crying. Kia would never forget the look in her sister's eyes, rain mixing indistinguishably with angry, sad tears, as Katelyn stared into Kia's dry eyes. At that moment, Kia felt it in her soul that Katelyn believed her.

"Oh god," Kia said out loud. Her stomach muscles contracted, and she moved over the toilet in case she was sick again. But nothing happened. Slowly, she got up and went to the sink to rinse her mouth. What the hell was happening to her?

In her pocket, her phone vibrated. No doubt an angry text from her sister asking where she was. She rinsed her mouth one more time and went to meet Katelyn in the courtyard.

Kia barely said a word, but that didn't stop Katelyn from chattering on about the rest of her first day back at school. "...and Michelle apparently got her license last week and drove her brand-new BMW that 'daddy' got her for her birthday to school today. She was pretending to know about cars and spitting out all this pointless information about horsepower and GPS. Like any of us care, seriously, this is an all-girl school. No one cares. No, that's sexist, maybe someone cares. Just not me."

Kia tried to look interested in what Katelyn was saying. She nodded and "mmhmm-ed" in all the right places, but Katelyn wasn't buying it.

"Kia, hello! Are you still in the dream or something?" Katelyn asked as they got into the Jeep.

"Yeah...or something." Kia started the Jeep and headed home.

When they got home, Kia sat on her bed staring at the wall trying to figure out what exactly had happened, or more importantly why it was happening again.

She remembered that the first incident happened when her hands touched Katelyn's during the game, and then today it happened when she shook hands with Madam Arson. *It happens when I touch someone*, Kia realized. Maybe she could not touch anyone again. Wear gloves and long sleeves at all times. She immediately nixed that idea since living in New Orleans was like constantly living above a giant bowl of hot soup—humid, hot, and sticky. Long sleeves would never work during the summer.

Kia laid back on her bed and grabbed one of her many pillows to hold. She sighed as she ran through the possibilities of what had happened.

One: It was just her imagination. But Kia had never even been to a funeral. She had also never been to Paris, but it's possible being in French class jogged her memory so maybe that made her subconscious think of the pictures she had seen of the Arc de Triomphe.

Unlikely but possible. Next option.

Two: Maybe this was her future. Funerals and...chocolate éclairs? She saw what would eventually happen with her parents during the first incident. Kia saw herself running out the door, but when it actually happened, Katelyn was the one running out in the rain. It was Katelyn's future, not hers.

"Katelyn's future!" Kia yelled out.

If it was Katelyn's future that she saw eight years ago, then today she must have seen Madam Arson's future. She suddenly felt sad for Madam Arson. There was so much death there.

Kia was pondering the chocolate éclairs when Katelyn knocked and opened her bedroom door. Katelyn's head peeked through the opening.

"Hey...so, are you okay?" Katelyn asked.

"How did you guess?" She said with a grin. Kia was suddenly in a better mood since she had kind of, sort of, maybe figured out what had happened. And besides, it was too hard to be anything but nice to Katelyn when she had that look on her face. She was like a little lost puppy.

Katelyn smiled back, shoved the door open, ran and jumped on the bed. Kia and Katelyn told each other everything. They were closer than any other sisters they knew, even though they were two years apart. After their parents divorced and their dad moved away, there were never many adults in the house. Their mother worked long hours at the hospital. Katelyn was young during the divorce, and though Kia wasn't much older, she had had to grow up fast to help take care of Katelyn.

But still, Kia was very careful in how she told Katelyn what happened in French class. Her sister listened closely, but her eyes grew and grew with each passing second.

"You have to try and do it again," she said when Kia had finished her story.

"I'm sorry, but what?" She stared, open-mouthed at her sister.

"The future thing. You have to try and do it again. Here take my hands." Katelyn thrust her hands into hers, but Kia recoiled quickly.

She looked at her sister for any sign that she was messing around or making fun of her, but there was nothing. "You're serious?"

Katelyn threw her hands in the air, exasperated. "Of course, I'm serious! It's not every day that you find out your sister can see the future. Now, grab my hands." She shoved her hands back into Kia's.

Kia reluctantly held her sister's hands and closed her eyes. Katelyn grasped hers tightly as if that would somehow help the bond, but Kia had no idea what she was doing. Her heart beat solidly against her chest. She peeked out from under her eyelid to see her sister staring at her unblinkingly.

"Anything?" Katelyn asked.

Kia shook her head.

"Well, you're probably not trying hard enough."

Kia shut her eyes again but rolled them under her closed lids. Her sister was so persistent. This was not something Kia wanted to be doing, but Katelyn was super into it. So, as Kia did so many times in her life, she did what her little sister wanted.

She sat for what felt like forever, but not once did she feel that pull that she had felt with Madam Arson. She sighed and opened her eyes.

Katelyn nodded and said, "Don't worry. We'll try again tomorrow." Her sister got up and walked out of the room before Kia could say anything else.

Again?

Tomorrow?

Kia threw her pillow across the room, but it wasn't enough to ease her frustration.

Katelyn didn't mention anything about seeing the future at all the next day, but whenever Kia saw her sister in the halls or at lunch, she saw a gleam in her eye. One that said, you'd better be ready. Problem was, Kia wasn't ready. She didn't want to ever be ready. All she wanted was to live a normal life and never have another future-seeing-incident again.

In fact, she was probably crazy. All of it, a figment of her imagination. And Katelyn was just as crazy for believing her.

Yes, that sounds right.

But there was no stopping Katelyn once she set her mind to something. So, Kia decided to put countermeasures in place and invited Jackie over to study.

"Do you have dance after school today?" Kia asked Katelyn before their last period class.

"Yes!" She said, excitement written all over her face. Katelyn loved to dance. "But then I'm coming straight home." Translated: you'd better be ready.

The sisters went their separate ways after school. Katelyn promised to get a ride home from a friend, and Jackie hopped in the car with Kia to head over to her house.

They tried to study. Really, they did. Only...not studying was so much better.

"I get my SAT results back next week," Jackie said in between the sour cream chips she was shoveling into her mouth.

"How many times have you taken it now?"

"Three."

Kia sighed. She hadn't even taken it once. In fact, she hadn't even signed up yet to take it. She should probably do that soon.

They continued to chat, with an open book nearby, to give the illusion of studying. Even if the illusion was just for themselves. Katelyn busted through the door not long after the sun had started to dip below the buildings, casting a slanted light across the hardwood floors. "Kia! Let's do this!" she said first thing through the door.

Katelyn walked in the living room and stopped in her tracks looking at Jackie. "Do what?" Jackie asked.

Kia smiled as her sister narrowed her eyes and shot her a death glare. But out loud Katelyn said, "Ice cream. We need it. Now."

Kia looked at the empty snack bowls in front of her and Jackie and shrugged. It wasn't like her mother would be coming home anytime soon to cook dinner. Most of the time, Marie left money on the counter for the girls to grab something with. Although, Kia didn't know why she even did that. The American Express in her wallet had a limit high enough to buy dinner. And a pair of Christian Louboutins, or four.

The ice cream parlor was within walking distance, as was almost everything else in the French Quarter, where the LaStrausses lived. It was the oldest neighborhood in New Orleans, and the most famous. Kia loved the fact that everything was a walk away: great food, jazz, a cup of coffee. Sleep during Mardi Gras was nonexistent, but with a cup of caffeine only minutes away, who cared?

"I'll have a triple scoop. Cookies 'n cream, mint chocolate chip, and cookie dough please," Katelyn told the worker behind the counter.

"I don't understand how your sister can eat like that and still look the way she does," Jackie remarked as she handed over money for her ice cream.

"It's a gift," Katelyn said, not even looking over, paying for her triple scoop.

"It's ballet," Kia said.

They laughed and walked to the outside tables to eat their ice cream. Even though it would melt in minutes in the hot summer heat, they always sat outside when they ate there. It was a tradition.

They sat quietly for a couple of minutes, all enjoying their ice cream, so refreshingly cool on the hot day. But then Katelyn whispered, "Don't look now, but some guy is staring over here, from that other café."

Instinctively, Kia and Jackie both turned around and looked behind them at who Katelyn was talking about. "Or do. You know, whatever," Katelyn said.

He was far enough down the street that she couldn't quite make out his features, though she could tell it wasn't anyone she knew. He was tall, but not gangly, with muscle to build out his tall frame. He had long dark hair that hung around his face. He *was* looking their way. She could feel his eyes on them. Kia quickly turned back around. Jackie was still looking, and Kia lightly hit her on her arm.

"He's not even looking away," Jackie said.

Slowly, Kia turned around again. Jackie was right. The guy was leaning against the side of the café across the street. He had his leg propped up underneath him, his arms crossed over his chest, and he was unmistakably staring at them with a smirk on his face.

"He's cute," Katelyn said. "Maybe I should go ask him what it is he finds so amusing about us."

Katelyn got up from the table, leaving her now empty ice cream bowl, but Kia quickly pulled her sister back down. "Absolutely not!"

Katelyn reluctantly sat back down. "You're not any fun."

"I've got to go anyways." Jackie threw her bowl in the trash can. "My brother is picking me up from your house in like 10 minutes."

They got up and headed home, which was in the opposite direction of the guy. But before they turned the corner, Kia looked back one more time to see him still standing there, watching them walk away.

Ian Stalbaum did not know what he was doing spying on Kia. He knew he shouldn't have been, though he was smart enough to know that he needed to keep a pretty precise distance. Too close, and she would ask questions. Too far, and she wouldn't be able to notice him. And notice him she did.

He pushed himself away from the wall that he had been leaning against and pulled out his phone. Into the Instagram app he typed Kia's full name into the search bar. There was only one Kia LaStrauss. Her profile was open, and he scrolled through her artsy photos of New Orleans. Hardly any of the photos were of herself, and none of them showed her face. Smart girl. It wasn't the first time or even the first time that day that he had scrolled through the photos. He pushed the lock button on his phone, once again feeling creepy.

"You are not creepy," he told himself. A passerby on the road turned and looked at him slightly confused.

He knew it was a risk having followed her to the ice cream shop. Eugene had told him to wait, that he wasn't officially assigned to her yet. But if he was honest with himself for once, he was finally excited about something again. In his pocket, he rolled a small coin chip around his fingers. The official assignment would come Friday. He could wait to talk to her until then.

2

"YOU DID THAT on purpose," Katelyn said the moment Jackie walked out the door.

"Did what?" Kia asked jokingly, trying to lighten her sister's mood. She knew that Katelyn was mad. Katelyn stood, blocking the doorway, an immovable embodiment of female rage.

"Are you freaking kidding me?" Katelyn screamed. Her heels clacked across the hardwood floor, and she seemed to stomp harder with each step, emphasizing her point. She was a great actress, sitting and eating her ice cream looking perfectly content. Even Kia had almost believed she had bypassed her sister's wrath.

Kia crossed her arms over her chest. "We had to study for class."

"That's bullshit and you know it!" Katelyn threw her arms up in the air. "I don't know why this isn't a big deal to you! You saw the freaking future! Again! Either you apply to the Xavier School or pack your bags to go to a mental institution."

Kia's face drained of color. *I am not crazy.* She turned around and started walking toward the stairs, but Katelyn kept talking.

"I believe you, of course. But how many other people will? Don't you think that a demonstration would be the best way to convince someone? And how exactly are you going to give them one if you don't know how to control it?"

Kia stopped in her tracks. All the questions Katelyn was asking were ones that Kia had been asking herself all day. Granted, she didn't know if she would ever want to tell anyone. That didn't work out so well for the X-Men. What she could do—if she could actually do it—wasn't some parlor trick for her to join the circus with. But nevertheless...

"Fine," Kia acquiesced and turned around.

Instantly, Katelyn's whole demeanor changed. She relaxed her shoulders, and the little crease she got in between her brows when mad smoothed out. "Oh good!" She said in her sing-song voice, clapping her hands together. She ran up to Kia, grabbing her by the arm.

"Oh, now?" Kia asked. It was already dark outside, and Kia had still yet to do her homework.

"Yes, of course now!" Katelyn dragged Kia over to the kitchen table. The sisters sat across from each other, hand in hand.

The next few hours passed excruciatingly slow. Kia did everything she could think of to try and make the incident happen again. But she only failed. By the end of the night, when they couldn't hold their eyes open anymore, Kia repeated the same thing over and over to herself.

I am not crazy.

I am not crazy.

I am not crazy.

I. Am. Not. Crazy.

Kia sighed in exasperation, not for the first time that day. "Do you think it was just my imagination? I mean, if it wasn't, something would have happened by now, don't you think?"

She tried every day for the rest of the week to make the incident happen again. At school she would bump into her friends or gently touch their skin without them knowing, concentrating on what she knew about their life, trying to make the scenes fill her head. Nothing ever happened. At night, she would try with her sister, sitting in front of her, holding her hands, staring into her eyes. But still, nothing.

"Your imagination? Doubtful," Katelyn said, bringing her back to the present. "Besides, Rome wasn't built in a day."

Kia wasn't entirely sure that was the right analogy. "Maybe we should give it up." Kia thought back to that day in French class, only five days ago. This strange and oddly remarkable thing happened to her, and she couldn't make it happen again. Waiting for it to happen again, hoping it would happen again, was driving her crazy.

"Why would you say that?" her sister asked.

"Because this is stupid. Maybe I should tell Mom to take me to a shrink because I am seeing...saw...things." Kia sat herself down on the floor, pulling a pillow into her lap. She was whining, but she couldn't help herself.

"No!" Katelyn's voice was almost screaming. "We promised. No matter what we don't tell Mom or Dad. Okay?"

Kia flinched, unprepared for Katelyn's tone. She might have slightly overreacted, but she was right. "Yeah. Okay." Kia sighed again. "I am going to go and do some homework."

Katelyn raised an eyebrow at her sister. "Homework? On a Friday? You are a freak." She paused for one moment. "So, *Gilmore Girls* in like an hour?"

Kia smiled and nodded as she went upstairs. Her room was one of three bedrooms upstairs. It was also the bedroom that her mom christened to be the room where family and guests stay when they visit, which was completely ridiculous considering the house had a separate guest room.

Her room was a little messy, but she located her laptop easily. After grabbing it, everything after was like a reflex. Google Chrome. Facebook. Email.

Spam. Spam. Coupons from Victoria Secret. Email from Dad.

She contemplated deleting it before she even read it. Her dad had been oddly absent from their lives for the past couple of years. Well, he wasn't around a whole lot since the divorce in the first place, but recently it's been only birthdays and Christmases only, with the occasional email and phone call. As she opened the email, a text ping from her cell phone grabbed her attention.

The phone number was one she didn't recognize, but it was a local area code.

Hi, Kia, it said.

Kia texted back quickly. Hey, who's this? Sorry, don't have your number stored.

Three typing bubbles appeared immediately. *My name is Ian.*

Kia didn't know anyone named Ian. The typing bubbles appeared again.

Ian: Stop trying to figure out if you know me. You don't.

"Okay, well that's creepy." Kia put her phone down. It's best to not reply. It pinged again.

Ian: But I can help you understand what you saw and what's happening. Meet me at Royal Street Coffee at 7:00 tonight. -Ian Stalbaum

Kia read the text again to make sure she read it correctly. First of all, he said his name was Ian, he didn't need to sign off a text like you did a letter. And second, *help you understand what you saw.* Her finger hovered over the delete button. This had to be a scam, someone playing a joke on her, but how was it possible that someone else knew about her incidents?

It wasn't. Only her sister knew what had happened. They had promised each other not to tell anyone. The text was probably some new phishing scam. She learned in school that people will do about anything to get you to reply to an email so they can steal your passwords, bank accounts, or identity. This text was probably a new age version of that, and completely unrelated to the incident.

She looked down at her watch. 6:14.

"Definitely some crazy dude trying to steal my life," she said aloud as she deleted the text.

Kia pulled out her Advanced Calculus book to get a head start on the homework her teacher had assigned for over the weekend. She hated math and was only taking the class to try and impress colleges.

Numbers filled Kia's mind. But not the numbers on her homework, the numbers on her watch.

6:27.

She couldn't shake the feeling that this Ian person actually knew what happened, considering he said *I can help you understand what happened.* It couldn't get any clearer than that.

6:42.

But it was the 21st century and people made careers out of hacking into computers and government databases. People could find out almost anything on the internet through Facebook. *Facebook!*

6:48.

Kia clicked back over to her Facebook tab and typed out Ian's name. Nothing. Not a single profile. How was that possible? Everyone had a Facebook. She closed the window in frustration and stared at the wall. Maybe Instagram? Opening the app on her phone, she searched his name. One profile! But the profile was private, and the profile photo was a photo of a large sword. Weird.

She *could* just go to Royal Street Coffee and scope the place out. Unless she held a sign that said IAN STALBAUM like the chauffeurs at the airport, she highly doubted he would know who she was.

6:52. There was still time to go.

Since all she had planned was marathoning *Gilmore Girls* with her sister, Kia didn't feel too bad about throwing some clothes on, running a brush through her hair, and running down the stairs to tell Katelyn she was going out.

"Out? I thought we were hanging out here?" Katelyn turned off the TV and turned around to face Kia.

"I know, but something came up." Kia thought she should probably tell her sister where she was going in case this Ian person turned out to be a psycho killer, but she didn't want her sister tagging along, which she inevitably would. She was sort of embarrassed to even entertain the idea that someone else out there could help her. She would tell her sister everything if there was anything to tell, once she got home. "Tell mom I will be home before 10." *Not that she will be home before I am.*

Kia didn't like the long hours her mom worked when she was younger, always having babysitters and going to after-school programs, but now that she was older, not having her around seemed to be a good thing.

The coffee shop was a five-minute walk away. Kia glanced at the clock as she walked out the door. 6:57. She would probably be there on time if she powerwalked. The sun was on its way down, but it was still high enough in the sky that the temperature hadn't dropped any from the afternoon. The second she walked out the door Kia was already sweating. She felt her shirt sticking to her back as she turned onto Royal Street and almost tripped over a person sitting on the stoop of the shop on the corner.

"I'm so sorry!" Kia muttered, backing up around the corner to the street she had come from. Her chest tightened as her heart beat against her rib cage, threatening to escape. She leaned against the window of the shop. Inside were paintings from local artists, imagery of the city evident in all of them: *fleur de lis*, masquerade masks, Mardi Gras beads, a blue dog. The shop was an explosion of purples and golds.

She pushed off the wall, turning back toward her house instead of the coffee shop. This was insane. But then again, so was the idea that she could see the future.

"What am I doing?" Kia said aloud.

A passerby, beads hanging around his neck, said, "Not drinking, that's for sure. Here, have this." He shoved a large white cup into her hand, half-full of a reddish cocktail. "Did you know you can just walk around with alcohol?" He walked away, his cry of "I love this city!" fading as he turned the corner.

Kia laughed; her anxiety forgotten for a moment. People were not strangers in this city for long. Taking a deep breath, she turned back around, walking onto Royal Street.

As the coffee shop's sign came into view, Kia hesitated one more time. This couldn't possibly end well. She looked down at her watch. 7:11. She hated being late to places. Punctuality, she thought, was always one of her strong suits. But in this case, maybe it was better that she was a little late.

Now Ian would probably already be there, and she wouldn't have to wait at a table by herself looking for someone who she didn't even know.

Here goes nothing.

To get to the actual entrance of Royal Street Coffee, you had to first go through a breezeway and a courtyard. Kia figured that Ian would be sitting inside instead of out in the courtyard because of the heat. But the minute she walked through the breezeway she knew exactly where Ian was sitting. He didn't stand out by his looks or clothes or have a sign with her name on it. She could *feel* where he. It felt like she was attached to a string that has suddenly pulled tight. She knew he felt it too because she saw him look up and smile when she came in. She didn't know how it was possible, but they felt exactly where each other was. The connection was as strong and reassuring as iron.

Well, there goes my "scope it out" plan, she thought and walked over to the table and pulled out a chair. She stood hovering uncertainly.

"Hello, Kia," Ian said. He sounded as if they were old friends catching up over a cup of coffee, rather than two complete strangers meeting for the first time. "I'm Ian. But you probably already guessed that."

All of Kia's questions slipped from her mind as she stared into Ian's face. He looked like a normal guy, albeit an extremely attractive normal guy, but not the psycho killer she had been afraid of. His dark brown hair fell in waves that he pushed back out of his eyes. He had enough stubble to looked laid-back but not lazy, a strong, straight jawline, and striking blue eyes. Kia had only seen eyes that blue in one other person—herself.

Ian's eyes stood out, but his eyes were blue in a different way than Kia's. Where her eyes were all indigos and royals, his were sky blue. A brilliant, sky blue.

People had always told Kia and Katelyn that they looked so much alike they could be twins. Kia couldn't disagree more. Katelyn was already as tall as Kia, and she was sure that Katelyn would continue growing until she reached that perfect 5'10" model height, while remaining a size 2—all while eating everything she wanted. Kia's body held slightly more curves and the toned legs of a runner. Katelyn's brown hair always had the perfect amount of volume and curl, and Kia was only good at growing hers long. But Kia did have something she admired about herself more than she admired in Katelyn; she had blue eyes. Katelyn's were brown and blended in with her pupils, while Kia's stood out. They were her favorite thing about herself. She imagined her eyes standing out like the waters in the Caribbean do on a satellite image.

"While standing is good for the legs and all, sitting is the normal custom for conversation." The look on his face told Kia that she must have been standing for longer than she realized.

Ian's voice brought Kia back to reality, and questions flooded her mind, her mouth struggling to form a coherent thought. "What—How...," Kia blanched at the smug look on Ian's face. She sighed, finally sat down, and said, "How do you know who I am?" She looked around, lowering her voice. "And what I can do?"

Ian looked around too. Kia couldn't tell if he was mocking her or being serious, but he leaned in close, his face inches from hers. "Because I can do it too." He smiled and leaned back in his chair, slinging his arm casually over the back of the chair next to his.

Kia found herself leaning further over the table. "And what is *it* exactly?"

"You're asking the wrong questions." Ian smiled a smile that said he had something good to say. Kia sincerely hoped that was the case. "I think I should probably start at the beginning."

"Start in the middle, beginning, or end. I don't particularly care." She was starting to think that maybe this guy was just wasting her time. He knew something. She wasn't sure how, but she could tell that it wasn't going to be easy to get it out of him. "But you asked me to come here. You said you could help me, you said you know what's going on...well?"

"Okay, right to it then. You are a member of an elite group of people. You were born with this gift so that you could do something great with it. I, for example, have it so I can seduce women after convincing them I can see their future." His smile—full of perfectly white teeth—told Kia what she needed to know. *Sarcasm.*

"Well, this was a waste of my time." She stood up to leave but Ian's grabbed her hand. The muscles in his arm were taunt, but the hold he had on her was gentle.

"Kia, wait." His face suddenly became very serious. "If you leave, you will never understand who you are or what to do with your gift." He dropped his hand, and a smile spread across his face again. "And you will probably end up going crazy."

"I don't even know you!" She knew she sounded like a child throwing a tantrum, but she couldn't stop herself. "I can't sit here and listen to this nonsense. There is something going on with me—" Her voice broke, and she sat back down in her chair, trying to regain herself. "You know what it is, but why should I stay if you won't tell me?"

"I thought my charm, wit, personality, and extremely good looks would make you want to stay." His blue eyes twinkled under the lights.

Kia couldn't help but laugh. A narcissist. Awesome. "Look, Ian, is it? Do you want to help me or not?"

Ian's chest expanded as he took a large breath. "You are a Soulwalker, just like I am."

She searched his face for a sign that he was lying or being sarcastic in any way, but she found none. "I'm sorry, a what?"

"A Soulwalker."

Kia eyed Ian as he took a drink of his coffee, still unsure if he was messing around with her. "A Soulwalker? Am I supposed to know what that is?"

"No, probably not. We tend to keep it a secret. But the basic idea is that you have a sixth sense, per se. We can look into people's souls and see the fiber of that person's being. Their memories, past and future—although that is not always set in stone—smells, tastes, feelings. Everything that makes that person who they are is housed within their soul...and we can see it."

Kia thought back to the other day with Madam Arson. She replayed the images that she had committed to memory through her mind.

Funeral. Dress. Funeral. Arc de Triomphe. White roses. Chocolate éclairs.

Funeral. Dress. Funeral. Arc de Triomphe. White roses. Chocolate éclairs.

Funeral. Dress. Funeral. Arc de Triomphe. White roses. Chocolate éclairs. Something clicked inside her mind the third time she replayed the images, and she understood that they were memories of Madam Arson's. The taste of the éclairs finally made sense. It was a taste that reminded Madam Arson of her home—France.

"You're getting it aren't you?" Ian cocked his head to the side. "I can see you working through it in your mind. The things you saw in your Walk." He continued before Kia could even say a word. "A Walk being that moment when you enter someone's soul."

Kia nodded, still processing. "Can this be possible? I mean...how can it be possible?"

She thought of the old Sherlock quote: *once you eliminate the impossible, whatever remains, no matter how improbable, must be the truth.* She still couldn't quite believe it was true, and yet, it felt true. Just the word *Soulwalker* was a puzzle piece fitting into place where nothing had fit before.

"Well, no one really knows when it started." Ian picked up and took a sip of a cup of coffee that had been sitting on the table between them. "Since the beginning is my guess, but we didn't start keeping records until the early 1600s. So, before that is a mystery."

"But how did I—" A loud group of people walked into the café and sat at the table next to Kia and Ian interrupting her train of thought. "Wait a second. How did you know about me?" Kia had been so caught up in finding out what was going on with her and what Ian could tell her, she never stopped to think about how he even knew about the incidents in the first place.

"All Soulwalkers have a connection with each other. That is how you knew where I was when you walked in. Since you're new, the range you can feel is not very wide. Mine still isn't very big—a mile maybe—but there are some very powerful Soulwalkers who could feel every Soulwalker it the city." He leaned forward, clasping his hands around his coffee mug. "So, how many times did you turn back toward your house, only to turn back around to meet me?"

Kia blushed. If this string that connected her to Ian was something he could feel up to a mile away then, of course, he could feel her turn back and forth. She chose not to answer, and instead asked, "How many are there...Soulwalkers?"

"In New Orleans, somewhere between 20 and 30. When I told you earlier you were a member of an elite group of people, I wasn't lying. There aren't many of us around the world."

Kia imagined a man sitting cross-legged on the floor monitoring the movements of every Soulwalker in the city. The thought of having more than twenty strings that Kia had felt pulling when she walked in the café was overwhelming.

Ian continued, "So when you had your First Walk earlier this week, Samson—he's our Finder—felt you pop up on his map, so to speak. Some other people tracked you down and here we are."

"Here we are." Kia paused. "Wait, so you've known about me all week long? Why are you just now meeting me?"

Ian shrugged. "I do what I'm told. Although," he smiled, "I don't approve of your choice in ice cream flavor. We'll have to fix that too."

Kia's face scrunched in confusion, but then ironed out as she finally realized where she recognized Ian from. "You were the creepy guy staring at us the other day!"

"Creepy? No. Mysterious, yes. But I'm never creepy."

Kia laughed. "You were totally creepy. Why didn't you come up to me?"

He made a noncommittal noise and lifted his shoulders. "Samson said I need to give you some time to process after your First Walk. It's a lot on a person, or so he says."

"Yeah." Kia nodded, wondering if she should tell him about the incident with her sister when she was a kid. "But that wasn't the first time."

Ian's eyebrows peaked. "What wasn't the first time?"

"You said, 'when you had your First Walk earlier this week,'" She lowered her voice, imitating his, but he didn't find it funny. His face was lined with concern. She continued, but lightly, as if she was unsure about each word. "I had my First Walk when I was 9."

Ian shook his head ever so slightly, then his face became a mask, hiding any traces of concern and worry it had held moments before. He took another drink of his coffee. "Now this is interesting."

"Interesting isn't really the word I would use."

Ian just nodded and laughed.

After a couple of seconds of staring at each other, he finally spoke again. "Look, I know you have a lot of questions, which is why I am here. I am your mentor to help you with these first couple of months. Show you how to do things, what not to do, that sort of thing."

"And how did I get so lucky?" Kia said, her voice dripping with sarcasm.

"I would ask myself that every day if I were you, Kia," Ian said. Then he winked.

Really, a wink? Kia thought. A real charmer, this one.

3

KIA STAYED and talked to Ian for a while, but was home, as promised, before 10. After answering way fewer questions than she would have liked, Ian said he wanted to know more about her and for her to know more about him, since apparently, they would be spending a lot of time together.

"So, what kinds of things do you like to do?" he asked.

"What, your people can't find that kind of stuff out too? I was beginning to think that y'all's stalker capabilities were endless."

"Oh, never underestimate *our* stalker capabilities. But I would like to know more than what I read on paper." His subtle emphasis on *our* wasn't so subtle.

"Can't you read my soul? That should tell you about everything." Kia regretted saying it the moment it came out of her mouth. She didn't want a person who she just met looking into the corners of her soul. He would probably learn more about her than she even knew herself.

Ian smiled as if the idea excited him, but replied, "It doesn't really work like that. Well, it does, but Soulwalkers don't like to Walk other Soulwalkers. It gets very confusing because of a lot of times the Walks that we go on impact our lives enough to be seen in another Walk. Headaches and dizziness ensue. So, we tend to steer clear of doing that."

"Oh." The muscles in Kia's jaw unclenched as her anxiety at the thought of Ian looking into her soul abated. "Well...I like to watch movies, hang out with my sister and my friends. Pretty normal." *You never realize how boring you are until someone asks you what your hobbies are*, Kia thought. *Don't we all just watch Netflix?*

As if he was reading her thoughts, he said, suddenly serious, "Looks like I'm going to have to break my personal rule to never hang out with boring people." A small smile tugged at his lips.

"Oh, thanks."

He laughed, and Kia decided it was a laugh she could get used to hearing. "Anything else?"

She smiled, evading his question. "So, what about you? Tell me about yourself."

He leaned back in his chair, crossing his arms behind his head. "My favorite subject. Well, my first Walk was when I was 15—young by Walker's standards. But apparently not by yours." He paused. "We are going to have to talk to someone about that by the way. And now I am here, four years later, doing something I never thought I would be." A new emotion—sadness maybe?—that Kia had not seen that night showed on his face. But after an instant, it was gone, and the cool, confident exterior was back up. What did Ian have to be sad about?

Kia took a second to make sure her math was correct. As basic as it was, she didn't believe that she was right. "Four years? That means you're 19?"

"Yeah. I turned 19 this summer."

Kia had already thought about how old Ian was. When she first saw him, she figured he was around her age, but after having been talking to him she noticed things that made her think he was older. The lines she saw when he smiled didn't go away after it had faded. When he pushed his hair out of his eyes, Kia could spot a few gray hairs growing close to his hairline. But 19? She would have never guessed that. Nineteen was only a couple of years older than her.

He walked her to the end of the block before saying goodnight and turned in the opposite direction of Kia's house. Once he was out of her sight, she sprinted the two blocks home.

Katelyn was already asleep when Kia got home. She fell asleep with the TV on ever since they were little kids. Kia could always hear her sister's TV coming through the walls at nighttime growing up. Tonight was no different. The screen saver for Netflix was looping through on the TV.

Kia thought about waking her sister. It was why she had run the width of half the French Quarter home, but how exactly do you tell someone about the conversation she had. *Yes, hi. I am a Soulwalker.* Apparently, some kind of mythical creature, like a unicorn or a pot of gold at the end of a rainbow. Not that a pot of gold is a creature, it is an object, but mythical, nonetheless.

No, it wasn't exactly the easiest of conversations. And besides, she didn't even believe it herself. Kia took a deep breath. That was a lie. She did believe it. She felt it in the way her blood had rushed through her veins at the mention of the word *Soulwalker*, in the iron tether that connected her to Ian when he was near. There was no denying this, and no real evidence to explain it either. She had to tell her sister.

"Katelyn...wake up." She patted her sister on the back to try soothingly. "I'll sleep here."

"No, come on wake up. I have to tell you something."

"Ughhh" Katelyn muttered as she pulled her blanket over her head.

Kia yanked the blanket off her sister's head and threw it over the back on the couch. "Katy, seriously. You're going to want to wake up to hear what I have to tell you."

"Jesus!" Katelyn's eyes flew open, wide and angry. "What!"

Deep breath, she told herself. "I met someone...someone like me." Kia didn't know how to begin telling Katelyn about Ian or about being a Soulwalker or how to even explain what a Soulwalker was.

"What? Someone who has a squeaky voice when they get excited or someone who likes to annoy their little sisters by waking them when they were having an incredibly good dream? Kia, really...that is fan-freaking-tastic." She pulled the blanket back down over her head.

Kia picked up a pillow that had fallen to the floor, no doubt from Katelyn tossing around on the couch after she fell asleep and threw it at her sister. "HA HA funny. No, I met someone with my...abilities."

That woke Katelyn up.

Katelyn threw the pillow and the blanket off her and sat up. "You mean...?

"Yeah. His name is Ian."

"His?" She smiled slightly. "We'll come back to that. And what exactly did he say?"

Katelyn had always been boy crazy, so Kia wasn't surprised that what Katelyn was most interested in was Ian. "That I am a Soulwalker." Kia began the long story, telling her sister about everything that she and Ian had talked about that night in excruciating detail.

"Am I going to get to meet your mentor-man Ian?" Katelyn asked as soon as Kia was done telling the night's story.

"Yes, definitely. He says that pretty soon you and I will be sick of him."

"If he looks the way you say he does I highly doubt it."

Kia smiled, not entirely disagreeing with her sister. "He is going to teach me how to control and use my gift, and the only way to do that is practice. And you're the only one that I am telling, so you get to be the guinea pig."

"Oh, joy! When's the first practice?"

"Sunday."

They both fell into silence as the gravity of the conversation lingered between them.

Katelyn finally whispered, "You're totally freaking out, aren't you?"

"One hundred percent," Kia answered.

Kia woke up on Saturday morning earlier than usual. The sound—and smell—of her mother making coffee downstairs woke her. But instead of rolling over, pulling a pillow over her head and falling back asleep, she laid in bed running her mind over the last week.

People had souls. And not in a figurative "feel it in your heart and soul" way, in an actual "sell your soul to the Devil" way. And then people—Soulwalkers—could see into souls. And she was one of them. It was hard for her to wrap her head around it.

What did this mean for her life? She didn't know what she wanted to do or be. But was this interrupting her so-called plans? Ian seemed to be enjoying life fine.

And then there was Ian. She didn't know what to think of him.

Cocky: yes.

Sarcastic: yes.

Attractive: definitely. She tried to remember the way his hair fell across his face or the color of his eyes, but her mind couldn't get it right. But that didn't particularly matter. He was her mentor. There to teach her things. His sculpted muscles, perfect skin, and flawless smile was of no relevance. Although having someone that's around that was easy on the eyes never hurt anyone.

Kia giggled as she kicked off her comforter and got out of bed.

In the kitchen, there was a note on the counter from her mom.

> *Kia and Katy,*
> *I'm on call tonight, so here is some money for dinner. Order in or go out. But make sure y'all are home by curfew. Lock the doors. Love you.*
> *-mom*

Parenting from a note. How nice. Marie tried so hard to be a good mom, but some people were just not good at it, and she was one of them. It wasn't her fault. She was good at healing, but not so much at nurturing.

"Ugghhh. What is that awful noise?" Katelyn murmured as she stumbled down the stairs.

Kia looked around the kitchen, holding a spoonful of cereal in midair, searching for the "awful noise" Katelyn was talking about. "Uhh...New Orleans?"

"Make it stop."

Kia slid the box of Lucky Charms toward her sister in an effort to quiet her complaining.

"Mom's on call again," Kia said.

"Shocker." Katelyn poured herself a bowl of cereal.

They sat there for the rest of the morning letting the sounds of their city linger between them. Already they could hear the Fresh Quarter full of people, cars honking as they navigated the narrow streets.

The day passed in a whirl of popcorn and Netflix. The marathon scheduled for the night before was rescheduled. Katelyn complained about having to watch some of the episodes over again, but Kia knew that she didn't mind, and they both fell asleep mid-episode.

"Kia! Someone is at the door!"

Kia woke up and at first didn't know where she was. She had fallen asleep on the couch, something she never does, and slept so hard that she never woke up to sleep in her bed.

Katelyn was yelling from upstairs, her words lost as they sank through the walls and floors. Then she heard it. A knock on the front door. That must have been what woke her, that or Katelyn's piercing voice.

Still half asleep, Kia dragged herself to the door and looked through the peephole. And there standing on her porch was Ian. After she saw him through the peephole, she realized she didn't have to do that. Through the pull of the connection between them, she could feel it was him. But she looked through the hole again regardless. Was he holding a box of donuts?

Kia looked down at what she was wearing. Cherry-patterned boxer shorts and a red tank top. No bra. *Well, at least I match*, she thought.

Ian knocked again, and Kia stood in a sort of limbo, looking down at herself and then back at the door. Herself. Door. Herself.

"KIA! Door!"

Door. Kia slowly opened the door and tried to hide her braless chest behind it. Ian was indeed holding a box of donuts.

"Morning, kid," Ian said. "I brought donuts." He opened the box, full of every flavor of donuts the store had.

"Hi," Kia said, her voice flat.

Ian frowned, "If you're not excited to see me, you should at least be excited about the donuts."

"Kia, aren't you going to invite the gentleman in?" Katelyn had appeared out of nowhere, dressed, makeup on, and hair brushed and curled. Kia hated her sister at that moment.

"Donuts? Thank you!" Katelyn plucked the box out of Ian's hands and pranced off to the kitchen, the sound of her heels clacking behind her.

"You didn't have to get all dolled up for me," Ian said as he came in and closed the door.

Speech was apparently impossible at this point

They stood in the foyer for what seemed like forever. Kia blushing and Ian looking...clean.

"It's early," Kia finally said.

"She speaks!"

"Food first. Words later."

Ian bowed. "After you, kid."

Thankfully, on the way to the kitchen was the coat closet where Kia kept a couple of sweatshirts. She grabbed one as they passed by to put on over her tank top.

In the minutes since Katelyn had run off into the kitchen, she had been busy. On the island in the middle of the kitchen were all the donuts laid out on plates. Chocolates on one. Glazed on another. And one of random assortment. There had to be at least two dozen. Milk and orange juice were in glass pitchers. Plates and napkins. Fruit.

Kia leaned over the counter and whispered to Katelyn, "Who are you?" Her sister was less of a morning person than she was, and this morning she had apparently woken up early, showered, got dressed and now spread out a breakfast feast. This was not normal.

"Well, I thought we should have something nice for our guest." She put the last piece of silverware on the counter.

"Uh, okay. Ian, this is my sister Katelyn. Katelyn, Ian."

Katelyn stuck out her hand to shake his, but Ian grabbed her hand and kissed it instead. Katelyn's face turned bright red. Kia started laughing and soon Ian and Katelyn were laughing with her.

No one mentioned souls or Soulwalkers the entire breakfast. Kia was nervous when Ian showed up at the door but the conversation, donuts, and the laughter had put her at ease. Maybe this first lesson wouldn't be so hard. She was a Soulwalker after all. She already had the gift.

Kia could tell that Katelyn was completely in love with Ian already. She hung on every word he said and laughed at everything, even the things that were not supposed to be funny. Homeless people. Laugh. Stealing a kid's lunch money. Laugh.

Eventually, the donuts and juice ran out, and Kia's heart started pounding with anticipation again. She looked at Ian and then over at Katelyn. They were talking about how people from New Orleans and the South are portrayed in movies. Ian thought it was a complete misrepresentation. Katelyn thought that they played on the stereotypes, but that movies did that for every group of people.

"But come on. Seriously, we don't sound like that," Ian said.

Katelyn burst out laughing, "I think you sound just like *that*."

Ian joined Katelyn in laughter after he realized that he had exaggerated and ended up sounding how the movies portray them. Kia could hear everything that Ian and Katelyn were saying, but her mind was focused on the lesson that was bound to begin any minute. Now all that she could focus on was her heart pounding out of her chest and the sweat pooling in her palms. She needed a moment to calm down.

Kia stood up from the island, and her barstool scraped across the tile floor. Ian and Katelyn slowly came out of their laughing fit to look over at Kia.

"I am going to go change," Kia said, already halfway out of the kitchen.

Up in her room, Kia could think a little clearer. Her pounding heart didn't sound like she was sitting right in front of a drum line anymore. She pulled out jeans and her favorite worn-down Saints t-shirt. She played with the hole at the bottom of the shirt before putting it on. The shirt had ripped when it got caught in a chain-link fence that she was hopping over when she was a kid. Even though the shirt was now old and ragged, she didn't want to throw it away. Her dad had given it to her.

She pulled the shirt over her head as there was a knock at her bedroom door.

The old door squeaked open and Ian poked his head in, "All dressed?"

Kia stood in front of her full-length mirror and stared at herself. She imagined that instead of the nervous, teenage girl reflecting, a confident Soulwalker stared back at her. Kia laughed to herself. She tried hard to be the person she pictured, but she wasn't ready.

Kia saw Ian's head poke a little further out the door through his reflection in the mirror. He looked her up and down—presumably to make sure she was dressed—and then pushed the door all the way open

"Looks like it," Ian said.

"And if I hadn't been?"

"Well, there was only a little left up to my imagination with that tank top this morning. So, I guess I would see if I was imagining correctly."

Kia was still staring at his reflection, and she saw that half-smile of his. She realized that since she was seeing him through the mirror, that he was probably seeing her through the mirror as well and could see that her face was the color that her tank top had been earlier. A dark red. To try and cover up her embarrassment, Kia grabbed her brush that was sitting on her dresser and threw it at Ian. But he was quick and caught it like he had been anticipating her throwing it the whole time, which he could have possibly been.

Instead of throwing the brush back or putting it on the bedside table, Ian used the brush to flatten his hair. He ran the brush through his hair several times, stopped and examined it and then threw it on top of the bed.

"Now that my hair is back to perfection," he ran a hand over his head, "shall we begin?"

Kia stood in the middle of her room staring at Ian. One second he is undressing her with his eyes, the next he is all business, but instead of trying to figure him out, Kia plopped herself down on the floor and sat cross-legged.

Ian sat down on the floor in front of Kia, mirroring her. He scooted closer, closer, closer until his knees were grazing hers. Not really touching, just the hint of a touch. He closed his eyes and sat there.

"And what exactly are we doing?" She asked, growing frustrated.

"Breathing." He peaked out from under one eyelid, but quickly closed it.

"I think I do that well enough on my own, thanks."

"Are you sure? Because you have been holding your breath since I sat down." Ian said, his eyes still closed.

Kia hadn't realized she was holding her breath until then. She sighed and closed her eyes to join Ian in breathing. Her breaths were labored at first, coinciding with her frustration. But the longer she sat, the longer and slower her breaths got, spilling out a little anxiety with each breath.

She uncrossed her arms and lowered her hands down to rest on her knees. Her eyes popped open when Ian grabbed her hands and held them in his. She went stiff and her breath staggered again. But she didn't pull her hands away. What was he doing? Ian still sat, unmoving, eyes closed, breathing.

Kia closed her eyes again and soon their breaths matched. Inhale for inhale. Exhale for exhale. Kia's mind cleared and before long she felt like she did during breakfast—calm and content.

"Okay," Ian said, bringing Kia out of her mediation. "I like to start by clearing the mind. It helps me make room for what I am about to fill it with."

All Kia could do was nod. The seriousness in Ian's voice quieted Kia like a father telling his child to *shhh*.

"I'm going to go get Katelyn," Ian said, standing up. "I told her to wait downstairs."

Nod, again.

Kia barely had time to pop a piece of gum in her mouth—she didn't have time to brush her teeth—before Katelyn was kicking off her heels and sitting next to her.

"This is going to be fun!" Katelyn squealed.

"Well now that we have a willing participant, we should start," Ian said. "You guys sit on the floor like you and I were earlier, Kia."

Kia had to maneuver Katelyn to get her in the right position and once she did, Katelyn looked at Ian then back at Kia and raised an eyebrow.

Kia ignoring Katelyn's inquiring eyebrow said, "And now what?"

"Now, hold her hands in yours—"

"Ian, this isn't going to work. We've tried this a thousand times, and nothing has ever happened."

"Patience, young grasshopper. You'll see."

Kia huffed in protest but grabbed Katelyn's hands and closed her eyes. She slowed her breathing back to how it was during her meditation with Ian. She imagined what she would see and feel inside Katelyn's soul.

Nothing happened.

Sigh.

Nothing.

Kia opened her eyes to peek at Katelyn and Ian. Katelyn had her eyes squeezed shut creating a line in between her eyebrows. Ian was sitting on the side of her bed, watching her intently.

"Kia, you can do this. It's instinct." His voice was soft, encouraging. "Just clear your mind and let it come."

So, she did. Kia closed her eyes and let every thought slowly trickle out of her head. The reality of her situation. How all of this was happening so fast. That they were able to do this in her house because her mom was not home. How her mom was never home. How she hasn't seen her father in eight months. How Katelyn had been saying for the past five months she doesn't want to see him. Senior year. English quiz.

Every thought ran through her mind on its way out. And once her head was clear, she took two deep breaths and knew it was about to happen. Her body felt overly small in an overly large room. Wind blew beneath her skin. There was a gentle tug first at her chest, then everywhere all at once. It wasn't pulling her in any particular direction, rather *inward*. She let it pull her down, down, down. Down into her sister's soul.

She saw more than images of Katelyn's past. With each image came feelings so strong that Kia felt as if they had once been her own. Again, most images passed before she could even register what they were, pictures and emotions rolling and crashing through her mind and heart. She was caught in a riptide, catching her breath only to have another wave crash down. Goosebumps erupted across her arms and legs. Some images she saw clearer than others. Everything she saw was happening to her, but a thought tickled at the back of her mind reminding her that this was Katelyn's soul, so everything was from her perspective.

Katelyn riding a bike for the first time. Her first crush. Crying in her room after their dad had left. Her first day of high school and how scared she was.

But then the scenes changed from moments that Kia recognized to ones she didn't.

Katelyn taking the driving test for her driver's license. Her first kiss. Her first drink of alcohol. She looked down her body, laid down on a table, her midriff exposed. A needle in gloved hands hovered above her navel. "Ready?" a man asked. She nodded her head. The needle moved, a small prick at first, but then popped out the other side of her skin and…

Kia gasped from the pain and came back into the present time.

She instantly felt hands on her. How many hands she didn't know. She opened her eyes and saw through her blurred vision that it was only Katelyn and Ian. Why did it feel like so many hands?

Katelyn's hands on her shoulders—when did she move behind her?—Ian's hands holding her face between his hands—when did *he* move in front of her?—and her hands clutching at her stomach.

Six hands, all prodding and poking to make sure she was okay.

"Kia! Kia!" Katelyn pleaded.

Kia's vision finally cleared and the ringing in her ears stopped.

"I think I swallowed my gum," Kia said, looking around the floor as if she might find the gum somewhere next to her.

Both Ian and Katelyn let out the breath that they had been holding. Kia stopped the fruitless search for her gum and looked up into expectant faces.

"You get your bellybutton pierced. It hurts like hell," Kia said flatly. And then, all the thoughts that she had pushed out of her mind in the moments before the Walk had rushed back, and her shoulders slumped down with the weight of it all.

Ian dropped his hands from Kia's face and slumped back against the bed. His mind raced through all the Walks he had been on in his years as a Soulwalker. He remembered every detail of each one. Smells stuck with him the most. Chocolate chip cookies. Sweat. Perfume of a loved one.

He had once Walked a soldier back fresh from Iraq. Michael had been a close friend of Ian's before he had enlisted. The Army and war had changed him. He suppressed memories and feelings, creating a new person from the memories of war. Ian worked for days to reach the deep parts of his soul and help Michael remember who he was.

Only, to get there Ian had to go through the war. Michael had been one of the too many soldiers injured in roadside bombs. 55% of the right side of Michael's body was covered in burns.

The pain had been very real.

The only thing that had kept Ian going was the thought that once he left the Walk and was back on the Outside, the pain would be gone.

The smell of burnt flesh would stay with him forever.

"My belly button? God, Kia! I thought you were dying or something. Your eyes turned white. It was freaky!" Katelyn shrieked at her sister, hitting her on the shoulder as she stood up.

Ian looked from Katelyn to Kia. "The eye thing. That's normal. It means that Kia is on the Inside."

Ignoring Ian's comment, Kia said, "Seriously, Katy. It hurts. Don't do it." Kia held her stomach on top of her sweatshirt. There was a slight tingle above her navel where the piercing had happened in the Walk. It was more the shock at feeling it as if it was happening to herself than actually painful. The tingling was already going away.

"Whatever. I need some water," Katelyn said as she walked out the door.

Kia sighed and lay back on the floor. She rubbed her finger on her shirt above her belly button, certain she was going to find a newly pierced hole later when she could look. "It feels so real."

"I know," he paused, seemingly to collect his thoughts. "Because it is real. You are really experiencing what she did, or in this case, maybe will." He paused and looked out into the hallway where Katelyn disappeared to. "I've been there. Walking people as they go through pain. It isn't fun, but the pain goes away once you're out of the Walk."

Kia was quiet for a moment, thinking. Gone once she left the Walk? She felt her belly button again. It was still sore. She decided to ignore it and asked, "Why do I see a lot of images and scenes? And a lot of the future?"

"You're still an infant. New in your abilities. The scenes, they are the easiest to see. Emotions, smells, tastes—those things come later," he paused. "As for the future. That's pretty normal. But some of the things you might think are the future actually aren't. Like with your French teacher."

"Oh."

"But you have to be careful with that. We aren't psychics or Seers. What we see are events that will or could shape a person's life. And it definitely isn't set in stone."

Katelyn walked into the room with three bottles of water. She threw one to Ian, which he gracefully caught without even looking, and handed the other to Kia. All three of them sat in silence, drinking their water.

After a couple of minutes, Kia put the cap back on her water and said, "Again."

4

SUNDAY WAS EXHILARATING. Over and over again Kia dived into Katelyn's soul. Mostly she saw the same things every time, with little variance. But she was doing it, actually soul Walking. The belly button piercing didn't bring her out of the Walk anymore, since she was prepared for what was happening, although it was still a shock. And later when she discovered that she had a hole in her belly button, she decided to bring that up some other time. Her and Ian were getting along so well, and she didn't want to disrupt their playful banter with that worried scowl he sometimes got.

Every day for the rest of the week, Ian came over to Kia's house. Every day he helped her learn more and more. Katelyn was the only person that she got to practice on.

"For now," Ian said, taking a bite out of an apple. He had made himself at home very quickly in their house. He ate from their pantry, not bothering to ask. He lounged on furniture, claiming it as his own the way a cat would. The side of Kia's mouth twitched in a smile before she remembered the matter at hand.

"How long?" She asked.

"When I decide you're ready. Besides, it's not like you can just go up to a random person on the street and tell them what you are. I could, because I have this." He smiled seductively, gesturing to his expression. "But you, kid, would probably make a fool of yourself."

Kia scowled then, looking for something to throw at him, but there was nothing around.

Katelyn didn't seem bothered by Kia Walking her one bit. Not the fact that Kia was learning things about her that she probably didn't want anyone knowing—like the time that she had an accident in the second grade, but never told anyone about it—or that Kia was experiencing some of the emotions that came with memories that Katelyn held dear. She was enjoying the attention. That was Katelyn in a nutshell—all legs and attention-loving.

Ian always left minutes before Marie came home. It couldn't have been timed more perfectly since Kia had no idea when she would be home. She never did.

A week and a half after their first lesson, when Ian was about to walk out the door to leave, he turned around and said, "You did good today, kid." He smiled, almost shyly, not looking at her.

Kia felt her cheeks warm. "Thank you. It's getting easier." Already she learned that she could navigate her way during the Walk.

Ian nodded and said, "I'm really proud of you."

Kia's face burned hot then, but before she could reply, Ian said, "Tomorrow, you join The Network." Then he walked out of the door.

Kia had no idea what The Network was—the network of Soulwalkers?—but why she wasn't already in it, she didn't know.

After he left, Kia sat in the living room, concentrating on the connection. As always it felt as solid as iron, reassuring in its strength. She followed it and could feel exactly where Ian was, and then feel as the connection faded and eventually snapped off. Ian didn't get very far before she couldn't feel him anymore, 25 or 30 feet maybe. Kia smiled at the idea that one day, maybe, possibly, she could feel all the Soulwalkers in the city. Already, she was connected to Ian further and further. But the smile quickly faded, because every time he left, she suddenly felt so alone.

"36 hours is a *long* time to be at work," Marie said, plopping down on the couch next to Kia, minutes after Ian had left.

It wasn't like Kia didn't like her mom. She loved her, but she was frustrated by her. She was always so detached from their lives, and after their dad left it got worse. Marie couldn't even see all the emotions that were playing on Kia's face—the smile pulling at her lips, the anticipation in her eyes, and...the touch of loneliness. People that barely knew Kia could probably tell that she was excited about something, but not her mom. She could never tell.

Kia looked over at Marie, who had taken her shoes off and was rubbing the bottoms of her feet. "Yeah, sorry." Her mother's return had tainted the day with a bruise that only Marie could inflict.

Marie looked at Kia with a cocked head. "There's something different about you." She paused. "We haven't seen each other in...God, has it been over a week? You doing okay, sweetie?"

Kia was shocked. Maybe her mom could *see* her. "Things have been..."

But Marie wasn't listening. She was staring at Kia, her eyes glazed over in deep thought. When she spoke, her voice was quiet like she was talking to herself. Kia had to strain to listen. "But it couldn't be..." She shook her head. "I'm tired. I'm off my game." She got up off the couch and walked toward her room, turning around once, shaking her head again briefly before disappearing from Kia's view.

When Ian got the text from Ellie saying that Marie LaStrauss was leaving the Ochsner Medical Center, he knew that meant he had somewhere in between 15-30 minutes before she got home, depending on traffic. He would eventually have to meet Marie and tell her the same lie he told everyone else: "Hi, I'm Ian Stalbaum, I am studying at Tulane, nice to meet you too." But for these first few weeks, it was easier to avoid her altogether.

Ian had no idea how Ellie got a lot of the information she did. He knew she could hack into almost any computer or database, but knowing when a person leaves work? She must track her phone or swipe a keycard. It was impressive, even he had to admit.

Ellie was The Network's technology guru. The girl was barely even in high school, and she could probably hack into government websites if she wanted. She was too smart for her own good. Ellie had tried to show Ian how to do a simple background check once, but he failed miserably. She had made fun of him for days afterward. He was always good at everything he tried, so not being able to do something that a 13-year-old could do was embarrassing. Nevertheless, he was glad she worked for The Network. She was a Soulwalker with an impressive talent which he was thankful for whenever he needed any kind of information.

With every step he took on the walk back to his car—stupid French Quarter parking—Ian could feel the connection between him and Kia abate. The thread that connected her to him felt unlike any other Soulwalker's. It flowed over him like water, engulfing him in her presence. But he could also feel at least two other Soulwalkers within the vicinity walking around, standing still, driving, going about their daily activities. Each connection he felt with another Soulwalker was unique and identifiable. He knew that the two other Soulwalkers in the Quarter were

36

Stefan Thibodeaux, The Network's accountant, and Anna Williams, another Mentor. His connection with Stefan pulsed slightly, like a speaker with a lot of bass. Anna's was softer and smooth as marble. Ian always felt weird knowing where the other Soulwalkers were, or that they knew where he was. He felt it was an invasion of privacy. But as long as they didn't go poking around in his thoughts like the Telepaths, he was fine.

That was why he had moved out of Metairie, a suburb of New Orleans. Three other Soulwalkers lived within a couple of blocks of him. How was that even possible? Two dozen or so Soulwalkers in a city of well over one million people and three lived near to him. He decided that was a little too crowded for his taste.

So last week when he found out he was going to be mentoring Kia, he moved a few miles from her in the French Quarter to the Lower Garden District. He hurried home. There was so much to do for the party tomorrow.

Ian was already outside Kia's house when she pulled up after school the next day. He was leaning against the back of a silver Toyota Prius, a "My kid is on the Honor Roll" sticker on the bumper. He was parked in her driveway, if you could even call it a driveway at all, more of an alley beside her French Quarter home. And really, she was lucky to have that.

Kia pulled up behind him and got out. Thankfully, Katelyn had gone over to a friend's house to work on a project. "You're taking up the whole drive—" Kia was interrupted by Ian popping open the trunk of his Prius and pulling out a black garment bag with White House | Black Market written on it.

"For you." Ian unzipped the bag and hanging inside was a dress. It was simple, but elegant: a wrap-around dress, black with white polka dots, and soft ruffles around the neck and bottom.

"This is for me?" Kia asked, fingering the ruffles around the neck. It was chiffon. "But why?" Then she looked over at Ian, who she realized for the first time was not wearing jeans and a t-shirt like usual, but instead sported black slacks, a white dress shirt, and a black skinny tie. The boy cleaned up well.

"We're going to meet the family and we can't have you wearing that." He pointed toward her school uniform.

Kia looked down at herself. Her school uniform wasn't exactly flattering: a plaid skirt and a white button down with the school logo embroidered on the left side of her chest.

"Now, pip pip! Go inside and change." Ian smirked and handed Kia the garment bag, along with another White House | Black Market bag and ushered her toward the door. She looked back at her Jeep sticking halfway out into the road and ran inside to change.

Inside her bathroom, looking into the mirror, she unbraided her hair. She was running late for school that morning so instead of blow drying it like she normally would she French braided it down her back, the end resting below her bra strap. Now, unbraiding it, she was shocked at how well it held the shape of the braid. The waves made her layers fall perfectly on to each other, framing her face. She pushed her grown out bangs behind her ears and was glad that at least she wouldn't have to do anything about her hair.

She rummaged through the bag that Ian had given her, exploring the goodies inside. She opened the make-up powder and dabbed a little on her face. Her usual routine consisted of a little foundation, mascara, and the eyebrow pencil that Katelyn painstakingly showed her how to use.

She slid out of her skirt and shirt and put on the dress, wrapping it around and tying it securely around her waist. It fit perfectly. It was maybe a little shorter than she was used to, probably from years of wearing uniform skirts that came down to her knees, but her butt wasn't hanging out or anything. Still, she decided to keep the black tights that she wore with her school uniform on.

The bag also had a box of shoes to go along with the dress. Just like the garment bag, the shoe box had the same White House | Black Market logo printed on it. The shoes inside looked like something that Katelyn would kill for. Her sister loved shoes and, on most days, could be found in a pair of heels. These ones had a white leather V-shaped strap, a 4" heel with a hidden platform, and a glossy black patent toe. She turned the shoe over to check the size. 7 ½—of course, her size. How did Ian know her sizes?

She reached into her backpack and pulled out her cherry Chapstick and put it on. Not quite red, not quite pink. The perfect in-between.

There, she thought, staring into the mirror. *All ready.*

5

KIA AND IAN pulled up to park on the street, outside an office building on St. Charles Avenue. The building was tall; she started to count the floors but lost her place after she reached fifteen. The street level was filled with shops and a bank, with a glass tower rising into the sky from atop its back. She looked around; the street was busy with people and cars, going home after the workday, which was probably the only reason they found a parking spot.

She'd passed by the buildings in this part of town many times, but never been inside. Somewhere in there were the other New Orleans Soulwalkers. Her hands were suddenly sweaty.

Ian was several steps toward the door already. "Come on kid, let's go enjoy your party."

In the elevator, Kia's heart pounded faster with each rising floor. Everything was happening so fast. The Walk with Madam Arson, finding out about Soulwalkers, Ian, training. Now, meeting all the Soulwalkers in the city. While the only two people in there, the elevator suddenly felt very small, and Kia longed to go back outside.

Neither of them said anything as the elevator continued to rise, giving it an eerie calmness. She silently cursed herself for leaving everything in Ian's car, her phone, wallet, everything. She didn't have a purse to put it in, so she thought it made sense to leave her things in her backpack, but now she felt like having something to hold on to would give her a little piece of security. Without anything to hold, she clenched and unclenched her fists at her side, hoping it would calm her nerves.

She focused on her hands: the way her knuckles went white and spread apart when her fists were clenched, how the polish on her right index fingernail was chipped. *Open. Close. Open. Close. Open—*

A hand slid into hers and held on tightly. Her chest rattled with a sharp intake of breath. She looked over at Ian, who was looking back at her. His face looked different somehow. His eyes wider. His smile lines almost completely faded into his skin. "I'll be right here the whole time," he said.

Kia nodded and let go of his hand as the elevator opened. They walked out, and she followed Ian around the corner, stopping with him in front of the only door on the floor. The door was entirely frosted glass, except for where the name of the company was etched in.

"Eugene Broussard Inc.," Kia read. Through the clear writing, she could see a room full of people, all gathered together and talking. "This is where the party is?" It was a stupid question for her to ask. Even if Ian hadn't stopped in front of the door, she would have known this was exactly where the party was. On the other side of the door were 15 Soulwalkers.

Having so far only felt the connection between her and Ian. She was surprised to feel 16 different threads connecting her to the Soulwalkers nearby. One felt as cold as ice, another as warm as the sun on her skin. Each one completely unique as the next.

"Yes. And *shhh*, it's a surprise. Remember?" Ian grabbed the door handle, but before he opened it, he turned around to face Kia. His hands were still clasped on the door handle behind his back. "Can you feel them?" he asked. Kia nodded. "How many?"

"Fifteen," said Kia, a little excitement creeping into her voice. It was like she was at school and the teacher handed out a pop-quiz. But she wasn't worried, because she knew all the answers.

Ian pulled a hand around from behind his back and patted her on the head. Kia glared at him, though she was pleased at herself. "Good girl," he said and opened the door.

Kia didn't know what she was expecting when she walked in, for the music to stop and for everyone to turn and yell "surprise," but that didn't happen. What did happen was a small group of Soulwalkers welcoming her and Ian at the door, with warm smiles on their faces. It was the man standing at the front that had the warmest smile of them all.

He was tall, well over six feet, with a bald or shaved head, she couldn't tell. His skin was the color of dark chocolate, rich and warm and without any imperfections. He said something to the woman next to him and walked forward to where Kia and Ian were standing, dismissing the welcoming party behind him.

"Welcome, my friend," the man said to Ian.

Ian nodded and shook the man's hand. "Kia, this is Samson."

"The Finder?" She said, remembering the name Ian had mentioned the night they met. "It is nice to meet you." Up this close, Kia could see that his chocolate skin wasn't nearly as perfect as she thought it was. It was lighter in some places, and he had a scar on his cheek below his left eye. *His eyes.* They were blue. Not all one color like Ian's, but they had flecks of white and a darker blue, like the deep ocean. She had never seen a person with skin as dark as Samson's with blue eyes. It had a chilling effect, but Kia couldn't look away.

"Finder, yes. I see that Ian here has been doing his job properly," Samson replied, chuckling under his breath. "We were worried that he might get a little...distracted."

Kia looked over at Ian. The blood rushed to her face fast, making her blush. Ian looked like he didn't even hear what Samson had said. He had that same nonchalant look on his face that he had at Royal Street Coffee, the first time she met him. Maybe she misunderstood Samson. It was probably conceited of her to think that Samson meant that *she* could be the distraction.

"Kia, come by my office later. There are some things that I would like to show you," Samson said, jolting Kia out of her thoughts. "Now, please go enjoy the party."

Kia looked around. The room they were in looked very much like the reception area of every office in the city. A row of chairs was up against one wall with a magazine-covered coffee table between them. There was a desk with a computer and one of those desktop calendars on it next to the door that Ian and Kia had walked in. The room even had some of those stock paintings that could be bought at Ikea or World Market.

She moved to explore around a little bit, but Ian dragged her in a different direction toward the rest of the people in the room. Most of them had acknowledged their presence in some way and were slowing making their way over to meet her one or two at a time. *To not to overwhelm you,* Ian had whispered. Each person she met she tried to notice something about them to pair with their name, otherwise, she would never remember anyone. *Forget it,* she thought. *There is no way I am going to remember them.*

"IAN!" A small girl yelled over the room of people and pushed her way over to them. The lady they had been talking to—Anna?—laughed and walked away.

The closer the girl got, Kia could tell that she wasn't walking—or running, for as fast as she was going—but rolling toward them. Kia glanced down at her feet and saw that she was standing on a skateboard. In boots. The skateboard rattled across the hardwood floor, people moving out of the girl's way as she came close.

"Ellie, still skateboarding on the hardwood even though Eugene asked you not to? Good girl," Ian said with a wink as she finally stopped in front of them and kicked her skateboard up into her hand. Ian was beaming. "Kia, this is Ellie Kobayashi, youngest Soulwalker in the city." Ian put his arm around Ellie, securing her in a headlock.

"And smartest." She added.

Ellie was tiny. *Really* tiny. Kia was average height, and she stood a good six inches above her. She was wearing a skirt, her pencil legs sticking out beneath it. She had her black hair in a high ponytail on her head. And slightly hidden beneath her bangs were her almond-shaped eyes. Her eyes, a color that could only be described as Tiffany box blue, matched the ribbons in her hair.

Blue? Kia looked around the room. It was then that she realized what she had thought was strange about everyone there. Everyone had blue eyes. Anna Williams, the tall blond with rings on all her fingers: cerulean. Hunter Jamison, the plump man with milky-white skin: azure. Quentin Russell, the black man with tattoos up his arms: cobalt. It was strange seeing all these people in the same room, all with distinctively different colors of blue eyes.

She looked over at Ian with his sky-blue eyes. He was immersed in conversation with Ellie. He must have said something funny or exciting, because she was bouncing up and down, her ponytail bouncing against her shoulders.

"You must be the guest of honor," boomed a deep voice behind her. Kia turned around to see who the voice was coming from, her mind still filled with wonder and shades of blue. And there in front of her was another shade, although Kia had to look up to see them. The man's eyes were the least blue of all the people in the room, almost a blue gray. "I'm Eugene."

Kia shook Eugene's outstretched hand. "Kia. It's a pleasure."

Ian finally turned around, his arm still around Ellie. Kia watched as Ellie tried to hide her skateboard behind her legs. Kia didn't think that she would be able to hide a Matchbox car behind her legs, as thin as they were, much less her skateboard.

"*Frère de mon âme*," Eugene said to Ian, laying a hand on his shoulder.

"*Votre lumière brille*," Ian responded. The French flowed out of his mouth and sounded beautiful on his lips. She translated quickly in her head. Brother of my soul. Your light shines brightly.

Seeing the bewildered look on Kia's face, Eugene turned to her and asked, "Ian must have not taught you the traditional Soulwalker greeting. Come, let's go to Samson's office. We have much to talk about."

Samson's office was through the closed door on the right side of the lobby area, where the party was underway. His office didn't look anything like Kia thought it would. One wall was lined with bookshelves, filled to the brim. The shelves were made of a light color and contrasted nicely with the dark wood that the desk and round table were made of. The desk had a glass top and gave the room an overall warm feel. Samson was sitting at his desk looking over some papers. He wasn't sitting on a pillow in the middle of a dark, candle-lit room, as Kia had imagined, monitoring the movements of the Soulwalkers.

There was, however, a large map of New Orleans and the surrounding areas on one of the walls. The map had colored thumbtacks stuck in it in various places. Red, blue, yellow, green. What did they all mean? Maybe representing Soulwalkers? Kia walked over to the map, to try and find her house and see if there was a thumbtack stuck there, but her attention was drawn away by a large book in a glass case sitting on the table under the map. The book was old, and it looked like it had been read many times and had had a good life. But the more Kia looked at it, she realized it wasn't a book to read, but a record book. The writing was in elegant script and hard to read, like *The Declaration of Independence*.

"Ah yes. The Book of Souls," Eugene was standing behind her, looking over her shoulder at the book. "It lists every Soulwalker. This is the old one of course. We haven't used it since 1890. It now rotates between The Network cities—here, Paris, and Beijing. These days, each city has its own Book of Souls to write its names in."

"Is my name in one?" Kia asked, turning around. Samson was still sitting at his desk, but he had put away the papers and was paying attention to her and Eugene. Ian was laying down on the couch, not paying attention to anyone.

Eugene put a smile on his face. "Not yet. Today, you will officially join The Network by writing your name and the date of your first Walk in the Book of Souls."

"But first," Samson joined in, "we have some things to talk about. Have a seat." He gestured toward the round table that was in the corner by the bookshelves.

"So, tell us about yourself," Eugene asked while they were walking toward the table.

This again, Kia thought. She knew that Eugene and Samson already knew everything about her just like Ian did when they first met. She didn't know what to tell them. Not her age, or about school. Who her parents are, what she wants to be when she grows up—not that she knew that herself. She decided on her basic interests. "I like movies and…Mexican food."

"I also love some good *fajitas* every now and then," Eugene said. "What else?"

Kia's eyes scanned the room, trying to think of a way to change the subject. The table was scattered with books and papers, all with the same letterhead at the top. Eugene Broussard Inc.

"'Eugene Broussard Inc.?' Is this your company?" Kia asked.

Eugene nodded, but it was Ian that answered, though he was still lying down and had his eyes closed. "Eugene is The Authority of this city—the head of The Network here. He runs the show, hands out the paychecks…and the whippings." Ian peeked out of one eye and smiled.

"Each Network city," Eugene took over, "has an Authority. And as Ian so delicately put it, we run the show. The Authorities work together, but no one Authority is higher than the other."

Kia looked over one of the letters on the table, hoping it would give her some insight on to what the company was. It didn't. "So, what exactly is Eugene Broussard Inc.?"

"The company is a front, of sorts. A way to keep the IRS off our backs. We don't want the government to think that the money which the Soulwalkers are paid with is drug money." Eugene paused to smile at his joke. "Everyone has a legitimate job here. But usually, the job they actually do is rather different." He chuckled.

"Like Finder, or a Mentor?" Kia asked, glancing over at Ian.

"Exactly," Samson began. "my job as a Finder is to keep track of the existing Soulwalkers within my field, or my area of connectivity, and to notify Eugene if and when any new Soulwalker pops up."

"He is also Eugene's right-hand man," Ian said, eyes still closed.

It was starting to all make sense to Kia. The structure and how it was so fast that Ian had gotten in contact with her. Samson's field couldn't encompass the whole country. Was it a coincidence that she happened to live in one of The Network cities? "What about the Soulwalkers that don't live here? What if I had lived in…I don't know? Wyoming or something?" She said, voicing her concern.

Sampson smiled, seemingly pleased. "Soulwalkers live across the world. Usually, new Soulwalkers are found within the first couple of months, if they don't live close to another Soulwalker. People travel, you see, and will eventually enter another person's field. And then that Soulwalker contacts me." He paused. "There are, of course, gray areas, and people do fall through the cracks." The sadness in Samson's voice was mirrored on his face.

Kia paused. There was something she had been wanting to ask since she found out she was a Soulwalker but was always too afraid to. "I—I still don't understand what the point to all of it is." Kia's eyes flickered between Samson and Eugene, hoping that they would understand what she was trying to ask. Being a superhero and saving people from burning buildings she could understand, but having the power to see into people's souls, she couldn't understand for what good it could be used.

It was Eugene that spoke first. "The point to what, dear?"

Kia searched for the right words. She didn't want to offend anyone. "To…of being a Soulwalker. Why have the abilities?"

"A fair question. A fair question, indeed." Samson murmured. "Well, it is different for each person. You might have been graced with the gift to change one person's life…or many. We never know why we were chosen. Until we know."

"Because *that* makes sense," Ian said. If he hadn't spoken, Kia would have thought that he had fallen asleep on the couch. But now, he seemed interested in the conversation. He was still lying down, but his eyes were open, and he was turned toward them.

Kia thought about Samson's answer. "But how are we chosen? And by who?"

"God, The Powers That Be, Higher Beings –"

"Morgan Freeman," Ian said, interrupting Samson.

Samson continued as if he didn't hear Ian or Kia's stifled laughter that followed. "How you have the Gift or who gave it to you," he sneered at Ian, "doesn't matter. What matters is what you do with it."

After Kia had run out of questions, she didn't know what to say. Samson and Eugene talked lightly amongst themselves, but their conversation didn't involve Kia, so she let her mind wander. Through the door, she could hear the party still going on. Ellie's skateboard was rolling back and forth across the hardwood floor. She must not have been talking to anyone there. The closest people to her age were Kia and Ian, and they were in Samson's office. Ellie was skateboarding from one end of the office to the other. She would go to the window on one side, stand still, and then skate to the other side, and back again. Kia could feel every time Ellie moved. In fact, she could feel every time any of the Soulwalkers moved.

"It is a little distracting at first," Samson said. She hadn't realized that he had been watching her and her eyes moving across the wall, back and forth like she was watching a pendulum swing. "You'll learn to ignore it when you need to."

The image of Samson sitting on a pillow rose again to Kia's mind. Although she now knew that was ridiculous, she couldn't help thinking of Samson meditating, if only to block out every move that the Soulwalkers made. It could drive a person crazy.

Ian finally sat up, yawning. "Well, shall we get this show on the road?"

"Indeed, we shall!" Eugene said, already moving toward the glass case where the Book of Souls was. He pulled a set of keys from his pocket and unlocked a drawer in the table. Kia hadn't noticed the drawer earlier, but then again, her eyes had been locked on the book and map above it.

The book that he pulled out of the drawer was smaller than Kia expected. She thought it was going to be the size of the old one in the glass case, but this one was about was about the size of a hardback novel. It was bound in dark brown leather, with gold-rimmed page edges. Eugene was carrying it with the utmost care, like it was a baby in his arms.

He sat it down on the table, flipping to a page. When Kia looked down, she saw a list of names and dates. On one side, a list encompassed the whole page, while on the other side the list ended about a third of the way down the page, where she was to write in her name.

Ian had come over to the table from the couch and sat down next to her. His hair was pushed up in the back from where he had been lying on it. Kia itched to push it down, anything to distract her from her heart pounding in her chest. Eugene slid the book over to her and sat an elegant looking pen down on top of it.

"All you have to do is sign your name—legibly of course," Eugene said, smiling. "And then the date of your First Walk next to that."

Kia looked down at the space where her name was supposed to go. Suddenly, this simple task of writing her name seemed daunting. Her eyes scanned the list of names above the empty space. Ellie's was the last name and Ian's two above hers. She saw the names of all the Soulwalkers in the room. The names on the opposite page were names that she didn't know, and next to them were two dates, not just one like Ellie's or Ian's.

Alexander Donaver   *March 11, 1979 - May 23, 1997*
James Sasson   *November 7, 1980 - August 1,1996*
Jessica Costa   *January 3,1982- June24, 1999*

These second dates didn't make any sense. She scanned the rest of the names that had two dates written and none of them were longer than twenty years after the first. Kia's eyes followed the column up to the top, hoping there would be an explanation about what it was. There was something written at the top, but once Kia saw it, she would have traded anything to unsee what was written there. Maybe if she didn't know, it would make it not true. Not possible.

The hand that held the pen started shaking. Her pen fell as she reached to point to the words at the top of the column.

"Th – this date," her voice cracked.

Eugene and Samson both looked at her with sad eyes. Eugene spoke first. His voice was quiet, solemn, "That is the date of death."

It was possible then. Kia continued flipping through the book, silently doing math in her head. Every name and every page confirmed what she was dreading. Every Soulwalker dies within twenty years of their First Walk.

6

THE WIND RIPPED through Kia's hair, stinging her eyes. Her legs had carried her out of the office faster than she would have thought possible. She heard her name being called as she rushed out but ignored it. Outside, she could breathe. She could think.

She willed herself not to cry, using deep breaths as a buffer. Each full breath in and out without tears motivated her for the next breath until the harsh wind betrayed her and tore a tear from her eye. Once that one tear fell, it opened the gates for the rest, and she couldn't stop them from falling. If she had anything in her stomach that probably would have been on the sidewalk along with her tears, but she didn't, so that was a plus.

This couldn't be happening. A couple of weeks ago, she and Katelyn were joking around about her getting old. She thought she had her whole life ahead of her. A good 60 or 70 years. But now those numbers were mocking her and her 20 years. What could she accomplish in 20 years? A family, yes. But see her children grow? No. Probably not.

20 years from her First Walk was not enough. Her First Walk, that was last week. *Wait a second,* she thought. *That was not—*

"Kia," a voice from behind her said. It was quiet and almost got lost in the wind. Of course it was Ian who had come after her. He was supposed to teach her, take care of her. How had he *forgotten* to mention something like this?

"Kia," he said again. She wasn't responding. She didn't even want to turn around to face him. No doubt, her mascara and eyeliner were all over her face. "I should have...it was my job to..." He started. He was so close to her now that she could feel his words warm on the back of her neck. "I am so sorry," he said, his voice thick with sympathy.

Finally, she turned around and buried herself into his body, the top of her head resting on his collarbone. His arms folded protectively around her, and he nuzzled his face against her hair, saying "*shh*" under his breath. She knew that her makeup was probably staining his white shirt. The black running down her face, running down his shirt as well, but she couldn't bring herself to pull away.

Soon she would have to pull herself together and go home. Katelyn couldn't see her like this. She was always strong for Katelyn. When their dad left, when their cat got run over. She was strong. If she saw her crying, she would ask questions. And Katelyn could never know this. Never.

"She can't—" Kia tried to tell him, but her words were lost in tears.

"*Shh*, it's okay." Ian untangled his fingers from her hair and started stroking her face. "I was supposed to tell you. But I couldn't. Not since—" but he didn't get to finish. They dropped their arms from around each other as they both felt the tug of a Soulwalkers presence, simultaneously turning to see Eugene standing in the doorway.

Eugene had his hands in his pockets and a miserable expression on his face. This had to be the hardest part of his job, but this was his life too. It wasn't like he just dealt the bad news, he lived it.

Kia and Ian made their way over to Eugene. She wiped the last of her tears away, trying to remove the evidence of her breakdown.

"Let's head back up," was all Eugene said.

Upstairs, the party was still going on as if nothing had happened. But, Kia guessed, that nothing really did happen. All these people already knew the dark side of being a Soulwalker, and apparently had accepted it, since no one seemed to be running out of the room crying as she had. Anna and Stefan were fighting over who would go to the Super Bowl this year. Anna said the Saints; Stefan said the Patriots. Ellie was eating a slice of cake that Kia hadn't even known was there.

Seeing the cake, Kia suddenly felt how empty her stomach was. Outside, she was glad for the emptiness. Now, all she could think about was how much it ached. And waffles. Waffles sounded pretty good right about then.

She was ushered back into Samson's office, wishing that the oblivious room of Soulwalkers would turn and see her. Whisper something to her, something to keep her from running back down to the street. But no one turned and the door shut behind her. The office was empty. Samson must have been out in the main room, but Kia hadn't noticed him out there.

"It's been a while since we've had that kind of reaction," Eugene began. "Not since my first year or so." He looked around the room as if some invisible person was going to confirm the story for the rest of them.

"I'm glad I could be the entertainment for the evening," Kia snapped.

Ian, who was standing in the corner, shot Eugene a venomous look.

"Oh no, no, no! I didn't mean harm. I am sorry, Kia. It is hard for me to remember what it was like thinking you had the rest of your life ahead of you." He paused and turned to Ian, who still hadn't relaxed. "Ian, would you mind letting Kia and I talk alone?"

"Yes. I absolutely mind." He huffed, as if the request was an outrageous one, as if Eugene asked Ian to let him perform a lobotomy on her or something.

Eugene turned toward Kia. "Well then, maybe my question should be, Kia, would you mind talking? Just you and I?"

Kia looked over at Ian. His reaction had kind of scared her. Why didn't he want to let them talk by themselves? Was there more bad news? She saw her answer in his eyes. *Worry.* They were looking right at her, pleading for her to let him stay. He didn't want to leave her if she wasn't okay, that much she could tell.

She looked back at Ian and hesitated at first, but said, "Sure. That is fine." Ian's face changed instantly, and she realized why he had looked different in the elevator when he grabbed her hand. His face was unguarded. The expressions he normally wore to guard himself against the world, hadn't been there. Now they were back.

"Whatever. I wanted cake anyways," he said as he walked out the door, letting it slam behind him.

It hurt her to send Ian away, but whatever Eugene wanted to talk to her about without him there, she wanted to know. "What do you want to talk about?"

Eugene sighed. "I am in my eighteenth year. Every time that I kiss my wife and kids goodnight, it could be my last. But every night I think about all the Walks I've been on, all the lives that I have helped or changed, and it all seems worth it."

Kia hoped that was true, that it could also be true for her life as well. Her path was figured out for her. Now, all she had to do was walk it.

The cake was probably good. It was chocolate and white swirl, with chocolate icing, and it was still warm. Megan, Hunter Jamison's wife, probably made it. She was always baking things that he would bring into the office. Ian couldn't taste it as he shoveled it down his throat. He said he wanted cake, so he ate cake. His mind was too much in other places to enjoy it.

Ian imagined that this day couldn't get much worse. He shoved his free hand in his pocket, grabbing the small coin that went everywhere with him. It pressed hard into his palm. It was the reassurance he needed.

The way Kia found out about a Soulwalker's life span, it was all his fault. Eugene had told him countless times that it should be one of the first things he tells Kia. He kept putting it off. He didn't even remember that the dates were in the Book until he saw Kia staring at it, wide-eyed and scared. He cursed himself as he watched her run out the door. Now at least she knew, and she could come to terms with it in her own way, like everyone before her. Hopefully, she would find a more creative outlet than Ian did. The little white scars that dotted across the crook of his arms weren't as easy to cover up as his internal ones. Those he could hide with words and smiles. He pressed the coin into his palm deeper.

Ian threw away his paper plate, as his stomach rumbled. He reached for another piece of cake but stopped when Kia and Eugene walked out. He was hesitant to go up to her after she had kicked him out. Was she mad at him? As he got closer, he could see she was smiling. Her and Eugene's heads were lowered, and they were whispering and laughing. When she looked up, Ian saw that all her tears and the mascara that she had aimlessly tried wiping away were gone.

"Talking about me?" Ian said when they stopped next to him.

"And what would make you think that?" Eugene asked.

"The only thing that could elicit that smile," he pointed to Kia, "after all of that would be a conversation about *moi*."

Kia rolled her eyes and tried to hit Ian on the arm, but he was faster and caught her hand in mid-air. Using her caught hand as leverage, he spun her around until her back was toward him and her arm was pinned behind her. "Got to be faster than that, kid," he whispered into her ear, releasing her.

Kia stumbled to regain her balance after Ian let go of her, but he reached out again and steadied her. Her feet were starting to hurt after wearing heels for the past few hours, not to mention the frantic run she made to the ground level.

"So..." Ian began. "Everything good-to-go now?"

Good-to-go? Kia thought. Why yes, every person in the room will be dead within the next two decades, many sooner. But sure, we're good-to-go. Instead, she said, "I signed my name if that's what you mean."

In the office, Eugene had talked to Kia, calming her down. She had signed her name in the Book. The Walk eight years ago. That is the date she wrote for her First Walk. She told Eugene all about what had happened that day, and he decided that is when she should write down. She couldn't remember the exact day, but Eugene said that the month and year were enough. As for an explanation on why she had her Walk then but was never connected to any other Soulwalker until her Walk last week, he didn't know. *I'll contact the other Authorities, see if they've heard anything like this before,* he had said. A big help he was.

Out in the main room, Eugene put a hand on Kia's shoulder. "There are some matters that I need to discuss with Samson. You two enjoy the rest of the party," Eugene said as he walked away.

Kia was left with Ian who was staring right at her.

"I'm hungry," he said.

"Well, there's cake you know."

"I know. Let's go." He started walking to the door, not stopping to see if she was following him or not.

Kia stood there a moment, trying to decide whether she should at least put up a fight. This was her party after all. But he was her ride. She had to jog a little to keep up with him. "Where are we going?"

He pushed the down button on the elevator. "Out to eat."

These short answers were starting to annoy her, and she thought putting up a fight started to seem like a good idea again, but they were already in the elevator. The pain in her feet reminded her of what she was wearing. "I am all dressed up."

He looked at her, as if for the first time that night, his eyes sliding slowly up and down her body. "Isn't that what you're supposed to do on a date?"

Kia looked at Ian and started to laugh, but his voice had been completely serious. "We're not going on a date."

"Why did you get all dressed up then?" He asked, cocking his head to the side.

"You bought me this dress!"

"Technicalities."

Kia sighed. She wasn't going to be able to win this battle. "Waffles."

"Waffles?" Ian raised an eyebrow, intrigued.

"If you're going to take me out to eat, I want waffles."

A smile broke out on Ian's face that stretched all the way to his eyes. "Waffles it is then."

Kia was grateful that they had parked on the street outside the building. She didn't know whether she would have been able to walk to the parking garage that was attached on the side. Her feet were throbbing, and she felt like her pace was measurable to that of a snail. *And in a surprising turn of events,* she thought, *Ian hasn't commented on it once.* Once in the car, Kia immediately traded her heels for the ballet flats that she had shoved in her backpack.

Kia lived less than five miles away from the office building but now they were heading in the opposite direction. She was glad for the space put between her and her house. Between her and her sister. She wasn't ready to go home. Outside, it was already dark, and Kia could only vaguely tell where they were going. There weren't many streetlamps and the ones that were working were dimly lit.

"Ian..." Kia began. She wanted to explain to him about how she didn't want to tell Katelyn about a Soulwalker's life. It was a new notion for her, keeping things from Katelyn. If she knew, Katelyn would want her to stop being one, and it wasn't like she could just stop— "What if I don't want this life?"

His face was unreadable as they finally turned off a side street and onto the highway. They were heading toward the Mississippi River. They passed a streetlight and it illuminated his face. It was Serious-Ian again. "Unfortunately, we don't choose this life. It chooses us."

"There's no way out?"

He laughed. "Out? Of course, there are ways out, but only if you want to kill yourself." He paused for a moment, but if there was something in his expression that would have alerted Kia to anything, it was gone the instant it appeared. Now his flawless smile was back on his face. "But if you want to live, then no. There is no way out."

Kia wasn't expecting Ian to bring up suicide. She would have never even thought of that. She had been taught that suicide is never the right choice, no matter how bad your life is because it will always get better. Before she could even reply, he said "Now, I have heard of Warlocks transferring a Soulwalker's power. But you know how Warlocks are, they love to, ah, *embellish,* their stories, so there can't be much truth in that," he laughed as if it was absurd.

Kia didn't know how Warlocks were, much less that they even existed. If she had the ability to see into a person's soul, then why shouldn't magic exist? Maybe all the fairy tales were true. This conversation has taken a strange turn. She decided to get it back on track. "Katelyn can't know."

Ian had apparently not gotten back on track. "About Warlocks? Why not? There are some perfectly nice ones. I know one that lives on the East Bank who likes to turn eggs into—"

"No, you idiot. About how I have a lot less life than I thought left." Ian's moods changed so quickly it was giving Kia whiplash. One second he was talking about suicide and the next he is blabbering on about turning eggs into God knows what.

She was expecting him to make a snarky remark back or protest what she wanted, especially after she called him an idiot. But his mood changed again and all he said was "I agree."

Kia didn't realize they had pulled into a parking lot in front of a building until she saw a bright light in front of her. In the window flashed a neon sign, changing color with every flash. Blue. Green. Yellow. Red. Orange. Open 24 hours, it said. The building itself looked like it might blow over in one of this season's hurricanes.

"Um... *this* is where we're eating?" Kia asked skeptically.

Ian glanced sideways at her. "This place has the best breakfast in the city."

On their way toward the door, Kia finally saw something that made her recognize this place as a restaurant. On the door was "Not Your Grandmother's Pancakes" in yellow paint. Kia had loved her Maw maw's pancakes when she was alive, so she thought that the name of the restaurant was a little off-putting.

"You're going to love this place," Ian said, holding the door open for her.

Inside, there were too many things to take in at once. One wall was covered in a rust-colored stone, one wall was painted maroon and another one orange, and the ceiling was painted a dark green. The fourth wall was made entirely of windows. Outside, Kia could see the Mississippi River, boats floating up and down it. On the other side, downtown glittered in the distance. Not one table or chair matched another. Each one looked like it had a whole history and story before it came to be here.

A waitress, wearing jeans and a t-shirt printed with the same yellow writing as the front door, grabbed some menus and took them to a table in the corner by the window-wall. The top of the table was wooden and was etched and marked with people's names and dates.

The waitress, who informed them her name was Sally, handed them the menus. It was one-sided and had only two sections: "Breakfast" and "Not-Breakfast." Kia perused the short menu before deciding on the Belgian waffle and a side of bacon. Ian ordered the Grandmother's special: four pancakes, eggs, bacon, sausage, and home-style hash browns. It was the largest item on the menu, and didn't quite make sense to Kia, calling it the "Grandmother's special," since it was "not your Grandmother's pancakes." She chose to ignore the irony and focus on the chocolate milk that Sally had just brought.

They were the only people in the restaurant and the silence that lingered between them made Kia feel awkward. She said the first thing that came to her mind. "So...was the day you joined The Network as bad as mine?" She tried to laugh as she spoke, but it didn't feel real.

His face darkened, and he crossed his arms over his chest, holding onto his forearms. The waitress walked up at that exact moment, and the tension that Ian held in his body released. "Oh, look our food!" he said.

When he moved his hand from his arms, right below where he had rolled his sleeve up to, Kia saw little scars scattered across his skin which she had never noticed before. She didn't get a chance to think about them before Sally set the biggest waffle she had ever seen in front of her. It was close to a foot in diameter, spilling over the edges of the plate. Ian's pancakes were even bigger.

As if on cue, her stomach rumbled, and she pulled out her fork to dig into the waffle. Ian was right, she *did* love this place. The food was delicious, and the view was amazing. Although, it did look like the roof might collapse in at any moment, but the thought was pushed from her mind by the cozy feel of the interior.

Kia didn't know how she had never heard of this place before, and how she spent almost eighteen years of her life without these waffles. *Well, at least I have another ten years or so to enjoy them.* Every time she thought about being a Soulwalker and the life that came with that, a new question popped into her head. "So, what is the deal with the short life?" she asked, taking a bite of her untouched bacon.

Ian's eyebrow rose at her nonchalant manner, but he didn't question her change in attitude. "The legend is that we live lives fuller than the normal person, because of all the Walks we go on." He shoved a fork-full of hash browns into his mouth, "but who knows?"

"And how old is everyone? Eugene, Samson, Ellie?"

"Eugene is somewhere in his late forties, I think. His First Walk was fairly late. He had a wife and kid, a whole life before he even knew he was a Soulwalker." He paused to put more food in his mouth.

Kia thought about Eugene: his white-gray hair, age spots. He looked closer to 60 than 50.

Ian swallowed and continued. "Samson is 32 and Ellie is 13. Everyone else somewhere in between Ellie and Eugene."

Kia broke off a piece of her bacon. "What causes the different First Walk dates?"

"Whoa, slow down and let a man eat. You had your First Walk, what...a week ago? There is plenty of time to learn the histories."

"Try eight years ago."

Ian almost spewed sweet tea out of his mouth. "What?"

"Remember? I told you. I Walked my sister when I was nine." *That was only like a week ago, your memory can't be that bad*, she wanted to add.

"Of course, I remember, but—"

Kia shrugged her shoulders. She couldn't place the tone in Ian's voice. It was somewhere between anger and worry. "After talking about it with Eugene, he said that is the date that I should write down.

"But that couldn't possibly have counted!" Ian said frantically. "How could you not have been spotted until last week? You've lived here, right under Samson's nose this whole time." It sounded like he was talking to himself. "We have the best Finder in the world, and he couldn't even find you."

"Well, that is the date that Eugene made me write in the Book of Souls." Kia thought this was obvious.

"But, you didn't...maybe since..." he struggled for his words, and his brow furrowed. Kia had never seen him stumble over his words before, granted she hadn't known him for very long, but he had always been quick with words. Then, so soft, barely a whisper, "It's not enough time." He paused and then let out a breath that Kia hadn't known he was holding. It wasn't quite a sigh, but she saw his chest contract and his shoulders drop. Suddenly he sat upright. His face was amused but his voice bitter. "I'm in the presence of my elder. Please teach me everything you know. In fact, why don't you be the Mentor?"

"Lesson number one. Etiquette." Kia snapped. She liked it better when he was stumbling over his words. "You sure do know how to make a girl feel loved."

"Love? This is only the first date, but maybe if it goes well, you'll get lucky." He made an exaggerated wink.

Kia threw her hands up in exasperation. She got up but remembered she still had one piece of bacon left. She would be damned if she left that bacon on her plate, so she grabbed it and went to wait outside by the car.

Kia's phone buzzed not 30 seconds after Ian had started the car. She had two new text messages. The first was from her mom from earlier that afternoon: "Emergency surgery, be home late...or early. Lol." *Ugh*, Kia hated when her mom said "lol." The second message was from Katelyn: "Where are you?!"

"Didn't anyone ever tell you not to text and drive?" Ian asked, looking over at Kia.

"Why yes, but since I'm not driving..." she left the sentence unfinished held up her phone and texted Katelyn back.

It was getting late. It was almost ten o'clock and they still had to get back to their side of the river, and she had homework. Luckily, there wasn't much traffic so it shouldn't take too long.

There also wasn't much conversation. Ian tried several attempts to lower her agitation at him. He told her what that Warlock turned eggs into, and Kia wished he hadn't, but he never actually apologized, so Kia stayed quiet. She wasn't even mad at him. She was mad at herself for letting him affect her so much. Her side of the car was quiet until they pulled up outside her house.

She moved to get out and saw Ian put the car in park and turn it off. "This is a no-parking zone," she said, but now he was giving her the silent treatment and didn't reply, getting out of the car instead.

He came around to her side of the car as she was putting on her backpack. Kia stared at him, wondering what he was doing. Why didn't he drop her off and drive away? He was probably going to get a ticket or towed if he came in. Not that she would let him.

He stared. Kia stared back. Finally, she said, "Goodnight," and walked toward the door, but Ian grabbed her hand and pulled her back around. His touch was gentle, but his hand clasped her in a way that said he wasn't letting go.

"Kia, wait." She felt déjà-vu, back to the coffee shop where they had met. Back to before she understood his habitual sarcasm. Back when she wanted to leave the moment he started using it. *This is it*, she thought, *he is going to apologize.*

But, instead, he said, "You have syrup in your hair." She looked down and indeed she did have syrup in her hair. It never failed, every time she ate something with syrup on it, she always got it in her hair.

She reached up and tried to pull the syrup out, but Ian's hand was already there trying to do the same thing. Their hands touched, and she tried to pull it away, but he had clasped his around hers. She let out a little gasp of surprise and looked up from their embraced hands to his face, which was inches away from hers.

He was Unguarded-Ian. Kia instantly forgot her anger, or why she was mad in the first place. All that mattered was what caused the worried expression on his face. She didn't get to ask, because as she opened her mouth to ask what was wrong, Ian's lips pressed against hers. They were soft and pleading. Asking her lips to move along with his. And they did. *Oh*, they did.

The hand that had that been in hers on her hair was now taking off her backpack and setting it on the ground. He pressed harder against her until her back was against his car. The engine was warm beneath the hood.

What had once been a soft and gentle kiss was becoming more and more desperate. She could feel the faintest bit of stubble above his lip as their lips moved together. She felt the rest of the world slipping away from her, as if none of it mattered. Wind picked up beneath her skin. It was all slipping.

If their eyes had been open, Ian would have seen Kia's eyes change from their turquoise-blue glory to pale white.

7

KIA FELT A CRAVING, one like she had never felt before. A small pinch in the crook of her left arm and within seconds the craving was gone.

Ian didn't know what came over him. Okay, he did know. But normally he would have never acted on it. He was a professional. A Mentor. But now, kissing Kia, he couldn't stop.

He could no longer feel her connection to him, which had scared him at first. He realized that because their bodies were pressed so close together, that they no longer seemed like two Soulwalkers, but one. One connection. One body.

He almost couldn't help himself as he lifted her up onto the hood of the car.

The feeling of being lifted off the ground brought Kia out of her Walk. She yelped in surprise, one, from the Walk, and two, from the swift movement by Ian.

His lips were still pressed to hers—had she been kissing him during the Walk. His body stiffened as he said, "Oh I'm sorry! I didn't mean—"

"No, no it's okay." Kia cursed herself. How had she lost her grip and fallen into his soul? After being reassured that what he did didn't upset her, Ian's hands came down and rested at her hips. Her legs were going numb, maybe from sitting on the hood of car. Her toes tingled, but in a feel good kind of way.

Should I tell him? She debated with herself. She leaned forward and rested her forehead on his chest. Her mouth was so dry. She let her hands fall from his neck and slid them down his arms, clutching his elbows. She swirled her thumbs around his skin, thankful for the moment of silence to clear her thoughts. Before she knew it, she was rubbing the little scars on his arms that she had seen earlier.

Then it all made sense to her. The scars. The Walk. "What are these from?" she asked, leaning back away from him.

"What are what from?" he said, leaning his forehead against hers. It was a gesture that Kia had seen a thousand times in movies. She always thought it was more romantic than kissing. Her heart swelled and then ached for what she was about to ask. "These scars. Are you...did you...?"

Ian's hold instantly dropped from her and he backed away. "Did I what?"

Without Ian's arms on her, Kia slipped off the hood of the car. She stumbled to the ground, and Ian made no move to steady her step.

"Did I what?" His voice was loud now, rigid.

She took a deep breath and the question rushed out, "Did you used to do drugs?"

Even in the dark, she could see his normally olive skin go pale. "Drugs?" He paused. "Why yes, Kia. Didn't you know that I have a whole crop of marijuana back at my house."

Not catching his sarcasm, she said, "Weed? But that isn't what I saw." Her hand shot up to cover her mouth. *Crap! I shouldn't have said that. I shouldn't have said that.*

"Saw?" The confusion on his face quickly turned to fury. "YOU WALKED ME?"

Suddenly a feeling of pure euphoria spilled over Kia, and the words erupting from Ian's mouth were lost in the wind, and she laughed, not caring enough to reach out and catch them. "It was an accident," her voice was calm. She didn't understand why Ian was so upset.

The look on his face told Kia that she was supposed to be upset at what she had done, but strangely she couldn't muster the feelings. Any other time, the things Ian was saying would probably have brought her to tears. Now, all she felt was satisfaction. She was becoming a great Soulwalker, she could Walk without even trying. After only a few lessons! Ian should be proud. She was.

"Aren't you proud of me? You said that Soulwalkers couldn't Walk one another."

"No," he said firmly. "I said 'wouldn't', not 'couldn't'."

She didn't remember Ian making that distinction. "Now I know more about you."

"No...you know nothing about me, kid." He was no longer yelling. His voice sounded sad.

"Why won't you share it with me?"

"You're the last person I would ever want to share my past with." He turned and briskly walked to the driver's side. He left, leaving Kia standing on the sidewalk smiling.

Ian's words finally made an impact on Kia around two in the morning when she jolted awake. She had gone straight to her bed and promptly fallen asleep. But now, she couldn't sleep. She didn't know why she said the things she did to him. Or what she felt? She had been proud! Now all she felt was disgusted. Disgusted with herself for breaking into Ian's soul. Because that is what she had done. Broken in. He didn't give her permission, and she wouldn't have felt comfortable doing it even if he had.

The look on his face when he realized that she had Walked him was imprinted on the back of her eyelids. Fury. And shame.

When the chills started, Kia thought that they were because she was upset. Then there was the nausea. This was no time for her to get sick. She had to make things right with Ian tomorrow.

She ran into the bathroom before she got sick all over her bedroom floor but ended up holding her stomach and writhing in pain on the bathroom tiles. She pulled her knees to her chest and hugged them tight to try and get warm. Her teeth were chattering so hard she could hear every time they hit.

She pulled the floor rug on top of her. She had to get warm.

"Stupid Grandma's pancakes," she said, thinking that it was the dinner she had that had gotten her sick. She would get food poisoning from some run-down, hole-in-the-wall restaurant. Then again, this didn't quite feel like the last time she had food poisoning. It didn't quite feel like anything she had ever been sick with before. Having a doctor for a mom sometimes had its advantages. Kia had quickly learned the difference between a common cold and the full-on flu. Her mom had taught her how to recognize the symptoms. Using the same trick, she cataloged the symptoms she was having now to try and figure out if it was anything she had before.

Chills, nausea, and sweat on the back of her palm after she wiped it across her forehead. She never experienced them before, at least not altogether.

She had seen something like it before. But no, it couldn't be. The only place she had seen someone like this was the rehab centers her mom had made her volunteer at when she was younger.

Withdrawals. That is what she had seen. People crying out for the drug that they were craving. Their body telling them that they needed it to live. Withdrawals could only come from a high and—*oh my God, I was high.*

Ian hadn't heard from Kia in two days. This was the longest he had gone without hearing from her. Granted, he hadn't known her for very long. For Christ's sake, they kissed! No, not just kissed. They had a moment, and then...

Why did she have to go and Walk him? She was too new in her abilities. She probably thought that he was mad at her—which he was—and that he didn't want to talk to her—which he didn't—but that didn't mean he still wasn't her mentor. He had an obligation to teach her.

He walked to her house from where he parked his car, cursing the parking in the French Quarter. He didn't care if Mrs. LaStrauss was home or not. He rang the doorbell several times, hoping it would be Kia that answered but knowing it wouldn't be. She was probably hiding, making Katelyn do her dirty work for her.

As he thought, it was Katelyn who answered.

"Ian." She looked tired. There was no makeup hiding the dark circles under her eyes. No smile. No twinkle. "What are you doing here?"

"Mentor." He pointed to himself. "Student," he said pointing up in the vicinity of where Kia's room was.

"Kia's not well," she said.

"Not well?" At least that cleared up why she hadn't called. Unless Katelyn was lying of course. A likely explanation.

"Yes. Not well. Something you probably know *all* about." Katelyn cocked an eyebrow at Ian's confused face, but said, "You should go."

Not one to have a little girl tell him what to do, he swiftly pushed past Katelyn and walked up the stairs, taking two at a time, heading toward Kia's room. Katelyn was running up behind him yelling, "Wait! Wait!" He didn't hesitate in pushing open Kia's door and going in.

Next to the bed was a small trash can, empty of the bag. The bed sheets and pillow around Kia's head were soaked through with sweat. A damp rag laid across her forehead. One leg out of the covers, one in.

Apparently, she was actually sick.

"Ian?" Kia's eyes poked out from underneath the washcloth, even from across the room he could see that they had lost their shine. The blues had faded, her pupils dilated, and her normal pearlescent skin around them had turned a dark gray.

She was really sick.

"Well, she *was* sleeping. Way to go, Bucko." Katelyn said. She was standing behind Ian in the doorway. He didn't take his eyes off Kia to look at her, but he felt Katelyn shooting lasers into his back.

Kia sat up, clutching her stomach. "It was the Walk," she said. Her voice didn't sound as weak as she looked.

"The Walk?" What was the Walk? She was probably delirious from fever. Ian walked to her bedside, reached down and gently put the back of his hand to her forehead. Before he could feel if there was a fever, she pulled his hand back down and held it in hers.

"The Walk. Remember the one I went on the other night?" There was a playful tone in her voice, but it quickly disappeared. "Somehow, what I saw...it did this to me."

Ian looked around the room and back to Kia. The scene in the room was all too familiar to him. But he didn't understand. How was this happening to her? Nothing from a Walk is supposed to manifest itself outside but looking at Kia he knew she could only be sick from one thing.

She was in withdrawal from heroin.

Behind him Katelyn was making *huffing* noises, clearly impatient. "Can I talk to you in the hall for a second?" She spit out.

Reluctantly, Ian followed her out into the hall, shutting the door behind him.

"Look. I don't know why you're here now. She's been like this for the past two days, ever since she went out with you the other night. I don't know what happened, I don't care. She won't tell me. But you need to fix her. And fix her *now*."

"Your mom—?" He asked

"Doesn't know. Kia made me promise not to tell." It was clear that Katelyn didn't like the fact that they were keeping this from their mother, but he also knew that if Kia asked Katelyn not to do something, she wouldn't break her sister's trust.

Ian's mind raced back to the withdrawal and the treatment. And the relapse. And the cycle over again. Only major users had withdrawals like the one Kia was having. If the hit that Kia had taken during the Walk manifested itself outside the Walk, then this would be her first hit and she shouldn't be having this reaction.

Then again, Ian was once a major user, and she was living his memory. That had to be it. He didn't know how, but how it happened didn't matter anymore.

Ian touched the coin in his pocket. One year sober. He steeled himself and walked back into the room, sinking to the floor next to Kia's bed. "I am so sorry." This was the second time in a couple of days that Ian had done something to hurt Kia. He would never forgive himself.

"Why didn't you tell me?" She asked.

"I didn't know it would happen. I don't know how it happened. This...this kind of thing...it's never happened before."

"No. You didn't tell me you were a—a" Her eyes gently closed as she spoke.

"A drug addict." He pushed a piece of wet hair out of her face, tucking it gently behind her ear. "You never asked."

"I—" her voice cracked, and she reached for the glass of water on her bedside table. Ian grabbed it for her first, gently tilting it to her mouth. "I'm asking now," she finished.

Behind him, Katelyn was tapping her foot on the floor apparently expecting Ian to wave a magic wand and make Kia feel better, but his eyes were glued to Kia. She sat up, and he thought she looked a little stronger somehow. Not as deteriorated. "Some other day. Okay, kid?"

He got up and walked back out to the hall with Katelyn. She could be scary sometimes.

"Well, can you fix her or not?"

"Honestly, Katelyn, do I look like a doctor?" Yes, it was his fault she was like this, and now, unfortunately, Katelyn knew it, but that doesn't mean he could fix it. She stared at him. "No. No one can really. She will be better in a day or two," he said with a sigh. "We need to keep her hydrated."

"And how do you know this?"

"Because I—I have had what she has before." *Many times*, he added to himself.

"And what exactly is it that she has?"

"You know what they say. Always wait 30 minutes after you eat before you soul walk."

Katelyn threw her hands up in exasperation and turned to leave but changed her mind and turned back around. She didn't say anything but looked at Ian, eyes full of sadness and desperation. He knew exactly what it meant: *I feel so helpless.*

He wanted to say, "me too," but he nodded and walked back into Kia's room.

Soon after Ian arrived at her house, Kia was able to sleep more. For the last two days, she had gotten a combined total of three or four hours, but the insomnia was wearing off and she could sleep in longer chunks.

During the times she was awake, Ian was always there. In her reading chair, bringing her water, noisily rummaging through her things. What he could possibly be looking for she didn't know. She didn't have the strength to tell him to stop.

Her phone buzzed from text messages and calls a lot those first few days. Friends at school wondering where she was. Jackie called five times in a row at one point. They eventually stopped calling, whether from the lack of an answer or from Katelyn explaining while at school, she didn't know.

Ian never left, or at least she assumed he didn't, because he never seemed to be wearing anything different. Then again it was always jeans and a white t-shirt. He probably owned a hundred white shirts.

Kia opened her eyes to see Ian looking at some photos on her wall.

"What are you looking at?" She asked.

Ian turned around and looked at her, and she noticed for the hundredth time how tired he looked. the circles under his eyes made his sky-blue eyes stand out like a patch of blue sky shining through a storm. She itched to reach out and touch them. "Is this your father?" he asked.

Kia got out of bed, grabbing onto furniture to keep her balance as she walked toward him. He pointed to a photo of her and her dad. She remembered the exact moment that the photo was taken. It was her eighth birthday, back before Kia had, what she now knew was, a Walk with Katelyn. Her dad had gotten her a cake with Woody and Jessie on it from Toy Story 2. She had been so obsessed with them. To this day, it has been one of the best things her dad has ever given her.

She made a noise of acknowledgment deep in her throat and leaned against him.

He sighed and put his arm around her. "You should get back in bed."

Kia tried not to bring up anything about the night she walked him, but she wondered if his presence was an acceptance of an unspoken apology. The thought that he still might be mad at her plagued her for days.

"I'm sorry," she finally said. Ian was dozing off in her reading chair, but she knew he wasn't asleep yet. He looked at her through slit eyes. "For Walking you. I am so sorry."

He jumped out of the chair and reached the bedside in two strides. "There is no reason for you to apologize." He sat down on the edge of the bed. It was the closest he had been to her since their kiss. She felt his connection to her, bringing an electric feel to their closeness. The past few days, his connection had been a constant in her life. If he left now, Kia felt it would be like losing a part of her.

"I just lost control," she felt the blood rush to her face at the memory of their kiss.

"Again, there is no reason to apologize."

She scooted over in the bed, trying to make a little room for him. He saw what she was doing, and his eyes lit up. They were bluer than they had been in days. The color of the sky on a perfect summer day. He laid down next to her, and she moved to rest her head on his chest. Beneath her head, his chest rose and fell steadily, but she could hear his rapidly beating heart.

After a few seconds, his arms closed around her, and she could see the scars that freckled his forearms. She rubbed her fingers over them, trying to picture the Ian that she knew crouched in a corner shooting the drug into his arms.

"I was in a car accident not long after I joined The Network. And my parents..." Ian paused. Kia dared not move or say anything lest she scare him off. This was the most he had told her about himself so far. "Well, I had a lot of pain after the accident, and it was all too easy to.... become addicted."

Kia still didn't speak. What had he been about to say about his parents?

"I don't...not anymore," he said, breaking the silence that hung between them.

"But you still want to." It wasn't a question.

"Every day."

"Will I be like that?" She didn't think she could handle the cravings. Not if it was like what she felt in the Walk.

"I don't know," was all he said.

8

KIA WOKE UP on Saturday morning feeling better. Friday was the first day she was able to keep anything down, and the food and water gave her strength back. With it, she longed to be outside.

She rolled over in bed and jumped at the sight of Ian lying next to her sleeping. He was hugging a pillow and facing her, still in his jeans and t-shirt. They must have accidentally fallen asleep. It looked like he hadn't shaved in a week. The hair on his face was no longer stubble but practically a beard. *He should go home*, she thought.

As quietly as she could, Kia got out of bed and took a shower. It felt good to stand in the shower, letting the hot water run over her body. She felt like she was washing away the last week.

Ian was still sleeping after she got out and dressed. She didn't want to wake him. He probably had as much sleep as she had in the past few days. So, she left him and went downstairs.

In the kitchen was her mom, standing by the coffee machine waiting for it to finish.

"Well, hello stranger," Marie said as she walked into the room. She was wearing her work scrubs. *Just home or just leaving,* Kia wondered.

"Good morning," Kia replied.

"I hope you finished that research paper of yours, I was starting to miss you."

Research paper? That must have been what Katelyn had told her to keep her from coming up into her room. "Yeah, yeah." She nodded. "Thanks for the peace and quiet," Kia added as an afterthought.

"You're welcome. Katelyn said you were in a grouchy mood and probably would be until you were finished. So, I figured I would leave you alone. What are your plans for the day now that you're finished?"

"Umm..." Kia thought. Suddenly she remembered the sleeping boy up in her room. She blushed.

"Oh, I see," her mom said with a wink. "I know it's not cool to talk about your love life with your mom. I have work today, but maybe I will get to meet him soon?"

Her face turned so red and hot that Kia thought that she had a fever again. "*Mom.*"

"Okay, okay. I'll see you later." She patted Kia on her burning red cheek and walked out the door.

She kind of felt bad for ignoring her mom for the past few days but trying to explain it all to her would have been harder. What she felt worse about was ignoring her friends. She pulled her cell phone out and finally texted back the people who had checked up on her. Immediately, she got responses, and she smiled that at least she didn't ruin things there. Her relationship with her mother would take more than a text message to get back on track.

It took Kia about two seconds of rummaging through the pantry to realize that there was not anything worth eating for breakfast in the house. It was still early. Katelyn was probably still sleeping like Ian, so she decided to go out and get some breakfast to bring back for them.

"It's the least I can do for them," she said aloud. Both barely left her side for the last week. Katelyn even missed two days of school before Ian got there. She said she didn't want to leave Kia by herself, but with Ian there, Kia guessed she felt comfortable enough to leave.

She didn't want to drive anywhere for breakfast, so she would have to settle for something in the French Quarter that she could walk to. Instantly she knew what she wanted. Café Du Monde.

The French Quarter was home to the original Café Du Monde. Most of the time, Kia avoided it because it is a popular tourist stop and always crowded. The line for their legendary *beignets* was always long, but she had a craving for the powdered sugar covered fried dough.

The morning was already hot, but that didn't stop the outdoor restaurant from having an extremely long line. There were all kinds of people there. Students on school field trips, all wearing the same shirt, an elderly couple having a *café au lait,* families eating breakfast together.

With a sigh, Kia got in the back of the line. It was then that she felt it. A slight tug, almost as if the wind was pulling her toward something. She looked around the room to the point where she felt the end of the connection. Another Soulwalker.

He was sitting at a table, underneath one of the fans. *Prime seating,* Kia thought. All she could see of him was the back of his head. He had blonde hair, cropped close to his head. He was with a group of friends talking and eating *beignets.* He wasn't far away. Even a new Soulwalker like herself would be able to feel her at this close range. She thought she saw him stiffen slightly, but he didn't look over.

She knew it was no one that she had met before. The connection felt different, weaker than normal. As the line moved forward, she kept thinking that he would feel her and look over. He never did.

The line moved forward again, and she was right next to his table, standing behind him. Finally, she worked up enough courage, tapped him on the shoulder, and said, *"Frère de mon âme,"* remembering what Eugene had said to Ian. *The traditional Soulwalker greeting,* he had called it. Brother of my soul.

The boy's friends stopped talking and stared at Kia. They didn't know then. She must look crazy to them, speaking French to a stranger, but she knew he would understand.

Finally, the boy turned around, and her heart skipped a beat. She had gotten used to the striking eyes of all the Soulwalkers. Each person's a different shade of blue, but not this boy's. The eyes that stared back at her were not Soulwalker eyes. They were brown with flecks of gold.

"Excuse me?" the boy said.

Kia couldn't get over her mistake. Yet she knew it wasn't a mistake. He was a Soulwalker. She felt it. *"Frère de mon âme,"* she said again.

"I'm sorry, I don't speak French," the boy looked at her like she was a tourist trying to find directions to Jackson Square.

"I don't understand," Kia said.

"I don't understand you either."

The boy's friends started laughing at her. There was no way for her to not look stupid now. "I'm Kia," she blurted out, as she spoke her hand shot out from her side and rested inches from the boy.

He turned around and looked at his friends, who were now laughing hysterically. "Ha ha, you guys. Funny joke."

"We didn't do this," one of them laughed.

The boy turned back to Kia, as she lowered her hand. "Kia, I'm very sorry for my friends here. But you see, I won't be in need of your services. Thank you," and he turned back and hit one of his friends on the arm.

"Excuse me?"

Another one of the brown-eyed boy's friends said, "I don't know Riley, whoever got you this birthday present is a much better friend than we are."

Kia blurted out, "Do you think I am some kind of prostitute?"

"I think you better talk to her Riley," the friend who he punched said.

Kia had lost her place in line, the impatient people behind her pushing her out. She didn't care. "Could I talk to you over there for a minute?" Kia asked. She knew if she got him away from his friends, he would talk to her. He probably didn't want his friends to know about him being a Soulwalker.

Another one of his friends tipped Riley's chair forward so that he fell out of it, regaining his step before he crashed into Kia. Riley turned around and shot his friend an angry glare but followed Kia out onto the sidewalk.

"Why are you pretending you don't know me?" Kia was furious.

He looked at her like she had just escaped from a mental hospital. "Because I *don't* know you."

"I know you don't *know* me, but you know me. I am like you. Can't you feel me?" She took a step toward him.

He moved back a couple of steps, holding up his hands. "No disrespect ma'am. But I have never seen you before in my life."

For a minute they both stared at each other. Kia found herself examining the features of his face. How one side of his smile lifted further up than the other side. How his nose was slightly too big for his face, in a charming sort of way. How the gold in his eyes reflected the sun.

"But—" Kia stammered. She didn't understand. Was there a secret code that no one told her about where you pretend to not know another Soulwalker on the street? Or did he actually not know?

"Have a nice day, ma'am."

Before she could say anything more, he turned around and walked back to his friends—who were still laughing. The back of his shirt said "Hewitt" and had a big "17" underneath it. She recognized it as a Brother Martin, one of the all-boys private schools, lacrosse team shirts.

Kia ran back to her house and up the stairs to her room. Ian was still sleeping when she got there but jumped awake after she swung open the door.

"Goodness gracious woman, didn't anyone ever teach you how to wake a man properly?" He sat up and stretched. His hair was a little messy, but besides that, he didn't look like he had been sleeping at all. "Scratch their back, whisper sweet nothings into their ears. That is the proper way."

Kia turned the light on in the room, and Ian shrank away from it, his eyes not yet adjusted. Once he opened his eyes again, he looked at Kia. Something in her manner must have alarmed him because his tone turned suddenly serious, and he said, "What happened? Is everything alright, kid?"

He rose out of the bed and again, his swiftness shocked Kia because he was by her side in seconds. He brought his hand up and cupped her face.

"Everything is fine. Is there a Soulwalker named Riley in the city?"

He relaxed but seemed reluctant to let go of her face. "Never heard of her."

"Not a *her*, a *him*. I met him at Café du Monde."

"Café du Monde? Did you get *beignets*?" He yawned and sat back down on the bed, clearly not seeing the issue as Kia did.

"Must you think about food all the time?"

"I am man," he said, pounding his chest.

"Could you listen to me for a moment?"

Ian waved his hand in a gesture that meant "go on."

"I went to Café du Monde to get breakfast, and before you say anything, no I didn't get any *beignets*. I felt the connection of another Soulwalker. But, when I tried talking to him, he didn't seem to know that I was a Soulwalker. He thought I was a prostitute."

"It is a little early for call girls." Ian finally looked intrigued. "And you don't seem to be in proper uniform."

"That is beside the point. Even after I pulled him aside from his friends, he still didn't act like he knew. He must be new right?" Kia's brain finally caught up with her. "Wait, proper uniform?"

Ian smirked, sitting quietly for a moment. Kia sat down on the floor. The run back to the house had tired her out.

"And he had brown eyes," she said, mostly to herself.

Ian closed his eyes and focused on his surroundings. Café du Monde was not even a mile away. If there was a new Soulwalker there he would be able to tell. The only connection he felt was Kia's. The new Soulwalker must have left already.

"What did you say his name was?" he asked.

"Riley Hewitt."

"Riley Hewitt?" he paused, stretched again, and said, "Guess it's time to go see Samson."

"Okay good, but we better get something to eat on the way. I am starving."

Ian's eyebrows shot up. "You're starving? You're the one that didn't get any *beignets*."

Kia's eyes narrowed in answer.

"A lot of good you are." He looked at Kia sitting on the floor. She was looking better. The circles under her eyes had almost disappeared. "How are you feeling?"

"Better." She smiled. "But...I probably shouldn't have run home."

"Probably not." He handed her the glass of water that had become a permanent resident to her bedside table. "You also shouldn't come with me to see Samson."

Ian watched as the smile on her face melted off. Her eyebrows knitted together in frustration. It was the cutest thing he had ever seen. "What? Of course, I'm going. I'm the one who discovered him!"

"Discovered? I wouldn't say that. Embarrassed yourself is probably more like it." He smiled to himself, picturing her talking to Riley. "But you're just feeling better, so sorry, kid, but I don't think you should push it."

"Who are you, my mother? I'm going!" She stood up to make her point.

"No. You're not." He wasn't lying. He wanted her to take it easy, but Samson would be able to tell that Kia had been sick the past couple of days. Sampson always said he was just good at reading people, but Ian thought he had a weird sixth sense. Ian would have to explain what had happened, which he wasn't ready to do.

Kia's face twisted again, and her frustrated look turned into a doe-eyed plead. "Ian, please. I have to know."

"And you will. As soon as I get back." He brought his hand up and brushed her hair out of her eyes. "And I will be back, I promise."

This time she stepped back out of his reach, and Ian's hand dropped from her face. "I know you'll come back, but I still want to go."

"Kia, can't you listen to me this once?"

"This once? When have I ever not listened to what you've said?"

Ian rolled his eyes, but in the end said, "Fine. You can come."

Kia jumped up and down and clapped her hands in excitement. It was the first time that Ian had seen her do anything remotely teenage-girlish.

Kia was surprised when they pulled up to the office building on St. Charles Avenue. She figured they would be going to Samson's house, considering it was a Saturday. He must be a man devoted to his work. That or it was a better meeting spot. Miraculously, they found parking on the street again.

They found Samson sitting at his desk pouring over a map of the North shore of Lake Pontchartrain. There were yellow dot stickers all over the map. Kia wondered briefly what they were indicating when Samson looked up and smiled.

"Kia. Ian. I'm so glad you've come," he said, as he got up from his desk and gestured toward the table in the corner. "Please sit down."

They sat, and Kia wondered if Ian had told Samson what they came to talk about. Her silent question was answered when Samson said, "Ian told me what you said happened this morning. Would you mind telling me the story yourself?"

She nodded, taking a moment to organize her thoughts. How did she want to start? "Well, I was at Café Du Monde, and I felt the connection you feel with another Soulwalker." She paused and looked to Ian who smiled encouragingly. "I thought that maybe he just wasn't at the party on Monday, so I didn't meet him. The connection was weaker than normal, maybe because I didn't know him?"

Samson nodded, "Maybe."

"I went up to him and said, '*frère de mon âme*', but he had no idea what I was talking about."

"His friends laughed. She was quite traumatized," Ian said, patting her head like she was a puppy.

Kia shrugged him off and continued her story. "I asked him to talk to me away from his friends. I figured he would admit it to me then. But he still had no idea. I realized he must be a new Soulwalker and not know yet."

"It would be strange for us to get a new Soulwalker so soon after you, but not unheard of. I have been monitoring the area since I heard from Ian." He paused and looked from Kia to Ian and back. "But there haven't been any new Soulwalkers."

"You must be mistaken. Riley is a Soulwalker. I know he is."

"I'm sorry—" Samson began.

"Kid, maybe you still weren't feeling very good. You probably made a mistake," Ian said.

Traitor, she thought. Ian was supposed to be on her side. She gritted her teeth. "I'm feeling just fine."

"You're welcome to look over my notes from the morning if you want. I charted the locations of all the Soulwalkers in the city." Samson looked apologetic, like he was truly sorry for the mistake that Kia made. But it wasn't a mistake. She knew what she'd felt, like she knew that Ian and Samson were standing next to her.

"That's okay." She would figure something out. Some way to show them that Riley was a Soulwalker.

"While you're here Kia, I wanted to talk to you about something," Sampson said.

"And that's my cue. I'm going to my 'office'" Ian said, making air quotes as he spoke. He left and closed the door behind him.

Kia stared at Ian's phone that he left on the table when Samson began talking. "How are things going? I know you had a rough time the other night."

"Oh, I'm good." She said, not paying attention once Samson started talking again. She was too busy looking at Ian's phone. The minute that Samson turned his head she furtively snatched it, making up a plan as she went along.

All her attention was focused on the phone. Surprised that Ian didn't keep it passcode locked, she scrolled through the contact names, knowing exactly who she was looking for.

Ellie Kobayashi.

Kia remembered Ian talking about Ellie when they were eating at the restaurant on Monday night. He said that she was great with computers and could do amazing things on the internet. Ellie was the one who had gotten all of Kia's information for Ian—her email address, her home address, school transcripts, any paperwork ever written on her or by her, like her sophomore year English research paper. If Ian wanted it, Ellie got it.

Kia smiled. She remembered the twinge of jealousy she'd felt hearing Ian boast about Ellie like that. Not now. Now she was all business.

Kia clicked on Ellie's name, saying her number over and over in her head until she had committed it to memory. She slid the phone back onto the table, picking the conversation back up with Samson. He was pouring over the maps that he had been looking at when they came in.

"—more Soulwalkers have been moving to the North shore. It is a little out of my range, but I am expanding."

Ian walked in, eating a bag of chips. "You two all chatted out?"

Kia nodded. She had no idea what Samson had been talking about these last couple of minutes, but she wasn't going to let Ian know that.

"Oh well, you two enjoy your Saturday," Samson said.

Kia barely managed a bye before Ian ushered her out the door.

"never wanna hear you sayyy. I want it that way–"

Kia hit the button that turned the radio off. She was trying to figure out the whole Riley situation, and she couldn't concentrate with Ian singing The Backstreet Boys.

"Hey. I like that song." Ian pouted. His bottom lip protruded over his top lip. Kia stole a glance down at his lips and was instantly reminded of the way they fit perfectly around hers, how they moved in synchronized harmony. She felt the heat rise on her cheeks and turned her blushing face away from him. "Picturing me in my underwear?" He asked.

"What?" Kia whipped her head around toward him, her red face betraying her.

"Well, I would be if I were you." He shrugged.

"Wow, Ian. Do you ever think about anyone but yourself?" She tried to sound teasing but instantly regretted saying it at all. He had been with her every minute for the last few days, always helping her. "I'm sorry. I didn't mean that."

"Yes, you did." His voice was quiet.

They had pulled up next to her house in the no-parking zone. Kia thought that meant that the conversation was over, unless for some reason they started making out on the hood of his car again. This time she didn't get out and neither did he. She looked over at him. He had his hands still gripped on the steering wheel at ten and two. His face was expressionless, staring out into the void.

Kia pried one of his hands off the steering wheel, pulling it towards her in the hope that he would turn with it. When he finally did turn, there was a silent fury in his eyes. He looked at her like he didn't care at all. Not about her, not about Soulwalking, not about anything.

"What?" He snapped.

Kia was still holding his hand in hers and although his voice was rigid, his hand was soft in hers. "I didn't mean it. I was just teasing."

"Kia—"

"No. Let me finish. I don't think I could have gotten through this week, or last week for that matter, without you." She meant every word she said. "I'm glad you're here with me."

75

The tension melted off his face, and as it did, he leaned across the center console and ever so lightly, kissed her.

9

THE AIR FELT so good on Kia's face. It wasn't exactly cold; it was too early in the season for that. But a cool front had blown in overnight, making it in the high eighties rather than the hundreds. She ran against the wind, letting it blow wisps of hair out of her ponytail.

It was the first time she had been able to exercise since she was sick. Her friend Jackie was supposed to join her but bailed at the last minute. She didn't mind though, running by herself was better anyways.

She spent all last week catching up on schoolwork. Well, she was throwing herself in schoolwork so that she didn't have to talk to Ian. She could still feel his kiss on her lips when she thought about it. Soft and tender. It was the familiarity that scared her, it was like it was something he had done every day and would continue doing each day after. And, if she was honest with herself, it scared the hell out of her. Better to avoid it altogether. Kia needed a little time to focus on something other than Ian and his blue eyes and the way they devoured her, or that one chunk of hair that was constantly falling in his face, or how she could see his muscles move beneath his—

Kia grunted out loud. She needed to focus on something else. Like her Soulwalker purpose. Or the mystery that was Riley.

Every day for the past week, she picked up the phone to call Ellie to have her find out about Riley. She couldn't help but feel like a creeper and a little bit guilty about going behind Ian's back. So, she kept putting the phone back down.

She was glad for the weekend. For the time to forget everything. All her conflicting emotions about Ian and her lingering thoughts of Riley would fade away as she ran.

Finally pushing the thoughts of boys from her mind, she turned a corner and ran out from the cover of trees into a sun patch. She slowed down to stretch her muscles, soaking up the sunlight. It was a nice day to go to the park, and she saw that she wasn't the only one taking advantage of the nice weather. In a clearing ahead of her there was a group of people playing ultimate Frisbee. A tall figure ran down the field to catch a Frisbee with a dog bounding along beside him. He caught it and immediately threw it to another teammate, taking off running again. Only this time the dog didn't run with him.

Kia started running again and could make out the scene more clearly the closer she got. One team had just made a touchdown and was celebrating in the end zone. The dog had his nose up in the air sniffing.

Suddenly the dog took off running, not toward the celebrating team but toward Kia. He was upon her so fast that she barely had time to move. She bent down to him, but he jumped up on her and licked her face. Kia didn't normally have any kind of aversion toward dogs, but this one was covered in mud, and his breath smelt like French Quarter trash.

She let out a high-pitched scream and was immediately embarrassed because a couple of the guys turned to look at her.

"Caesar! Come, boy!" One of the guys called.

But he didn't come. Caesar circled Kia, smelling every inch of her. His owner came running over apologizing. "I'm so sorry," he said. "Normally he never jumps on people. He must really like—hey you're that girl! The French girl."

"What?" Kia asked. She looked at the boy and thought he looked vaguely familiar. Then she realized that the boy was one of Riley's friends that was at the restaurant last week. That must mean—

She looked across the field and sure enough, there was Riley.

"Yeah. The girl that was speaking French to Riley." He turned around toward the group of people behind him. "Riley! Brad! Come here!"

"Uhh…" She stuttered. What was she supposed to say? Yeah, that was me. The crazy girl making a fool of herself.

"We've been talking about it all week. It was one of the funniest pranks we've seen in a while. Still don't know who put you up to it though. But it doesn't matter, poor Riley will never live it down." He finally grabbed a hold of Caesar, pulling him away from sniffing Kia's crotch. "I'm Oliver by the way. You're Kia, right?"

"Ummm… hi." Kia wasn't paying any attention to Oliver or Caesar anymore. She was focused on Riley. He and Brad left the Frisbee game and were walking toward her. When Riley got close enough to recognize Kia, he looked suddenly embarrassed and tried to turn around, but Brad pulled him along with him.

"I think I better go," Kia said, looking down at her non-existent watch. She wanted to sink into the sidewalk, but her intrigue was getting the best of her and even she heard the doubt in her voice.

"No, no. Don't go yet."

Before she could reply, something hit her like a hurricane force wind. It was Riley. Or rather, his connection to her.

"Ah-ha!" she said aloud. She knew she wasn't imagining things. While the connection had hit her all at once, it still didn't quite feel exactly like what she felt with the other Soulwalkers. It was more jagged and cut.

Oliver gave her a puzzled look, but said, "Riley has been wanting to talk to you again."

Riley was close enough to hear, and his face turned beet red. "I have not," he said shyly.

"*Bonjour,* Kia!" Brad said, breaking the ice. He walked up to Kia and kissed her on both cheeks. She didn't know what to do, so she stood there, still as a statue with both hands at her side. Did these guys actually think she was French?

"I told you she wasn't French, Brad," Riley said, shaking his head at his friend. "Kia, again I have to apologize for my friends."

"W-what are you doing here?" She mentally slapped herself in the face. *What are you doing here? Seriously, Kia?*

"Didn't you know?" Brad said. "Riley has been stalking you."

Riley shot Brad a look full of anger and embarrassment. He wasn't happy with his friends for picking on him. "Half of our team is over here. Why don't y'all two go back?" he said.

"But, I wa—"

Oliver was immediately cut off by Riley. "Why don't y'all two go back?" He said it without any hate or anger but gave them a stern look.

"Fine," they both said in unison. They walked—or stalked—back toward the game. Oliver had to drag Caesar away by his collar. He was still trying to get back to Kia.

"Caesar seems to really like you," Riley said. He had that same smile on his face that she had seen at the café. The one that was a little higher on one side than the other.

"I'm sorry about that. Asking 'what are you doing here?'" Kia looked down at the sidewalk as she spoke, trying to hide the hint of blush on her face. "I've been recovering from being sick and I don't think my verbal filter has come back yet."

"Oh, no worries," he shrugged. "But," he said, looking her up and down, "glad you're feeling better."

Kia looked down at herself and could only imagine how she looked. The front of her shirt was covered in mud from where Caesar had jumped on her. She had no makeup on and could feel her hair plastered to her neck with sweat. "Oh. Um...thanks." She tried to tuck a piece of sweat-soaked hair behind her ear.

They stood together a little awkwardly, staring at each other. "Well..." Riley said, starting to back away to go back to his friends.

Kia didn't want him to leave. She had to figure out why she felt a connection with him but no one else did. She said the first thing that popped into her head. "Can we start over?"

He turned back and looked at her, his eyes squinting in the sun.

"I'm Kia." She stuck her hand out to shake his, and thankfully this time he shook her hand instead of staring at it.

"Riley," he said, smiling. "It's a pleasure to meet you, ma'am."

"Do you go to school around here?" She asked, even though she already knew the answer. She remembered the school name from the back of his shirt.

"Yeah, yeah. I go to Brother Martin. It's my first year. I just moved here."

"And how is the city treating you?"

He looked up, his eyes meeting hers for the first time. Kia was once again shocked to see that their color was not blue, but brown. They twinkled, the gold around his irises reflecting the sun. "Oh, it's treating me just fine."

Kia smiled at his Southern drawl. He wasn't from around here. Texas. Mississippi maybe. "Texas?" she asked.

He smiled, picking up her meaning. "Mississippi."

"That was my next guess." Over Riley's shoulder, she could see Brad and Oliver staring at them, occasionally nudging the other with their elbows. She figured they wanted him to come back to the game and tell them everything that she and Riley had said. She sighed, knowing that she should probably end the conversation. She stuck her hand out again, turning the charm up to eleven. "It was nice to meet you, Riley from Mississippi."

"You too, Kia from...yet to be discovered." His charm was turned up too. "Maybe I'll see you around?"

Kia started walking away, smiling. "Maybe."

Second time's the charm, she thought, after she started running down the path again. *Now, all I have to do is not trip.*

✤ ✤ ✤

Kia almost ran right past Katelyn when she got home. She was sitting on the couch watching television, but Kia was in such a hurry to shower that she didn't even notice her sister. She had to skid to a stop when Katelyn started talking.

"Ian came by," Katelyn said over her shoulder.

Kia let out a sigh. She had completely forgotten about Ian. She was supposed to call him once she got home from running, but her mind had been so focused on calling Ellie.

Katelyn pushed the mute button on the TV and turned to Kia. "That boy gets more attractive every time I see him."

Kia had to laugh and nod at that. It was true. Every day that she saw Ian, it was like he changed a fraction and always for the better.

"There isn't anything going on between you two, is there?" Katelyn asked.

"W—what? No! Of course not!" *But that wasn't exactly true, was it?* She thought. She didn't know why those words had come out of her mouth so quickly.

"Really? Because the way he was talking today it sure sounded like it." She raised her eyebrows, begging Kia to tell her she was wrong.

Kia wanted to ask what he had said that made her sister think that, but then that would only prove she cared that he said anything about her at all. Instead she said, "He talks like that about everyone. It's no big deal." She needed to change the subject before Katelyn could tell she was lying. "Want to go somewhere with me?"

"Yes. We haven't hung out in forever. I was starting to think you found a new sister to love and let borrow your shoes."

"What?" Kia looked down at Katelyn's feet. She was wiggling them in the air, showing off the high-heeled shoes that Ian had bought Kia. She laughed. "Sure, you can borrow those."

"Thanks, big sister!"

"Okay, I'm going to shower. Then we'll go."

Kia darted up the stairs and into her room. She closed the distance to her bedside table in two strides. In the bottom drawer, she found the piece of paper where she had written Ellie's number when she had gotten back from the Network's office last week.

She was about to dial Ellie's number when she noticed a slip of paper taped to her mirror across the room.

You can't ignore me forever. The handwriting was distinctly male. Ian. Of course, he had left her a note when he came by earlier.

This time Kia didn't hang up when she dialed Ellie's number.

"So, where exactly are we going?" Katelyn asked, looking down at the Google map directions on her phone.

"I'm pretty sure that is what a navigator is supposed to know." She pointed to herself, "Driver." She pointed to Katelyn. "Navigator." Sighing she said, "Warwick Court."

"Right!" Katelyn looked back down. "So, this Ellie person, she's another Soulwalker? Take a right, here."

Kia turned, as per Katelyn's instructions. "Yes."

"And why are we going to see her?"

"I told you. Because she knows computers well, and she can look up information about someone for me."

"Okay. It's there." Katelyn pointed to a house not far down the street. "The house on the left."

Kia pulled into the driveway of a small white brick house. There were no cars in the driveway and the blinds were all closed. "Doesn't look like anyone's home," Katelyn said.

Kia had to agree. She shrugged. "She said she would be here," she said as she got out of the car. Katelyn hopped out after her.

They walked up to the front door in silence. Kia pulled her jacket closer around her. The sun was going down and it was starting to get cool. She reached out to push the doorbell, but Katelyn grabbed her hand.

"Wait a second. I feel like we are about to get Texas-chainsaw-massacred." Katelyn looked around like she expected the boogeyman to jump out.

"You're so dramatic," Kia said, as she shook off Katelyn's grip and rang the doorbell. She already knew that Ellie was inside. The connection with Ellie was light and airy, and it tingled a bit. Almost immediately, a young Japanese boy answered the door.

"It's for me!" they heard someone call from inside. The little boy ducked back behind the door as Ellie moved into place. "Hey! Come on in."

"Ellie, this is my sister Katelyn."

"Hey! Cute shoes!" She said looking down at Katelyn's feet. "Let's go to my room."

Ellie walked down the hallway, and Katelyn and Kia followed her. They passed the little boy who answered the door, whom Kia assumed was

Ellie's little brother. He stood silently by as they walked further into the house.

They reached a room at the end of the hall that had police caution tape strung across it. Ellie pulled out a set of keys from...somewhere. Kia looked down at what Ellie was wearing. She had on black boots that went up to her knees and laced all the way up the back, purple tights, and a black tutu. So where exactly she pulled the keys out from, Kia didn't know.

"Little brothers," Ellie said, rolling her eyes, as if that explained everything. Then she unlocked the deadbolt on her door. "Come on in."

Kia wasn't shocked at what Ellie's room looked like. She almost expected it. About every inch of her walls was covered with posters and pictures. Bands, movies, famous paintings. It was all there. In the corner of her room was a desk bigger than her bed. Three computer screens sat on it, all of them with a program running.

"So, what is it that I can help you with?" Ellie asked, sitting down in her desk chair.

Kia glanced over at Katelyn who was pretending to be looking at the pictures taped to Ellie's mirror, but instead actually listening to what Kia was about to say. Why wouldn't she? Kia hadn't told her why they were at Ellie's. The truth was, she was a little embarrassed. She didn't want to be a stalker, even though, she guessed she was kind of being a stalker by having Ellie look up information about him. Yeah, she was definitely being a stalker.

"Well..." she started. "There is this guy, and—"

"No need to explain!" Ellie squealed. "Name?"

"Riley Hewitt," Kia told her. Ellie turned around to the second set of computer screens and quickly typed his name in.

"Riley James Hewitt. Born in Jackson, Mississippi," Ellie rattled off. "Went to Jackson Academy and has played on the varsity lacrosse team since freshman year. Moved to New Orleans in June. Goes to Brother Martin, plays on varsity lacrosse. 3.989 GPA. Who is this guy?"

"Well," Kia started, "I'm pretty sure he's a new Soulwalker."

"Got a picture?" asked Katelyn, who had abandoned all pretenses of looking at the pictures on the mirror and was now peering over Ellie's shoulder.

Ellie clicked around a couple of times and then a picture of Riley from his Instagram popped up, filling the entire screen.

Silence filled the room as all three girls stared at the picture of Riley.

"It's not a very good—"

"*Shh,*" Katelyn interrupted. "I think I just fell in love."

"And what else is new?" Kia said. She playfully pushed her sister, making her release her gaze of the picture on the screen. "Seriously Katelyn, you fall in love with any guy who is remotely good looking. First Ian, now Riley."

"You fell in love with Ian?" Ellie laughed.

"I wouldn't call them remotely good looking. I would call them smoking hot!" Katelyn bounced on the balls of her feet and let out a little wail. "*ow-owww!*"

"You do pick a particularly good crowd to hang around with," Ellie said, now clicking through Riley's Facebook pictures.

"I'm not exactly hanging out with him. We only met a couple of times," Kia said shyly.

"Good then I can have him," Katelyn said, nudging her sister back.

Ellie laughed. "And Ian. Well...let's say I wish he was my mentor." Kia felt her face turn red, the heat creeping up her neck all the way to her ears. "But," Ellie continued, "There hasn't been any new Soulwalker activity in the city." She pulled up a new webpage. "Samson's email," she explained. Kia was shocked, Ellie actually could get into everything. "He always emails the other Authorities when there is a new Soulwalker in the city, even if they are visiting. But he hasn't mentioned anything. Sorry Kia, I don't think your guy is a Soulwalker."

A photo of Riley was still on the screen. His eyes were staring at her. The picture didn't do them justice. You couldn't see the different shades of brown, how they got lighter toward the center, the flecks of gold around the iris. He was a mystery, and she was going to solve it.

Kia was lying in bed, twirling the piece of paper with Riley's phone number on it around her fingers. It was too late yesterday when she got home from Ellie's house to do anything about calling Riley. But today, she couldn't bring herself to call him. Instead, she played with his phone number. Twirling it around, putting it down to go do something else, only to pick it right back up again. Call? Don't call? Call? Text? Don't text?

How would she explain how she had gotten his number? Hi Riley. It's Kia. My 13-year-old friend hacked into God-knows-what database and got your phone number. And your credit card number. And your medical history records. Sorry about that broken leg last year. Glad to see it has healed up well.

Kia sat up and put the piece of paper on her bedside table. Don't call, she decided.

Across the room, the Post-it note that Ian had written on was still stuck to her mirror. *You can't ignore me forever. It's very ominous,* she thought. Of course, he was right, she couldn't ignore him forever. She was also pretty sure she was being an idiot for doing it at all.

She picked up her phone, wanting to dial the number that was on the piece of paper next to her bed, but instead, she scrolled to Ian's name in her address book and hit call.

He picked up before it had even rung three times. "Kia," he said. It wasn't a question. Just an acknowledgment of the fact that she was calling.

"I got your note," she said.

"You know, normally when I'm in a girl's bedroom she wouldn't have to be asked twice to be there with me."

Kia sighed. "I'm sorry, it's been—"

"Save your excuses. I don't need to know your reasons for ignoring me," he interrupted her. When he spoke, his voice was laced with a false hurt, but Kia had to wonder whether it was really false or not. "Tomorrow, whether you want to or not, we are having a lesson. Finish whatever *homework* you have tonight." Kia could almost hear him do air quotes around the word "homework."

"What time?" Kia asked, trying to sound excited.

"Right after school."

"Sounds good! See you then."

10

KIA LOOKED UP at the giant standing in front of her. Her line of sight was no higher than the giant's knees. She looked around the room filled with giant things. Giant tables. Giant chairs. Giant people. And a giant dog coming right for her, snapping his jaws.

Kia pulled herself out of the Walk, how she wasn't sure, but she managed to come back to reality before the dog got to her. She let go of the little kid's hand that she had been holding. "He's adorable," she said to the mother, a little out of breath. Coming out of a Walk felt like a kick to the chest. It was as if all her air had escaped her body, and she was left gasping, trying to fill her lungs with the oxygen that her body craved.

"Thank you," the mother began, starting a story about some "major" accomplishment that the little boy had made. Kia just smiled and nodded, trying to focus her breathing back to normal. She looked down at the little boy standing next to his mother. He had lines of scars running down the left side of his face.

Kia was starting to notice a trend of the Walks she was going on. A lot of the things that made people who they are were tragic things. Dog bites, abuse, car accidents...and overdoses. Maybe that was why she had this ability. Maybe she was supposed to learn things about people. How they work. Save people's lives.

"Or maybe you're supposed to find out the secret recipe to Bush's Beans and tell the whole world," Ian said when she brought it up. "Next up." He had pulled her away from the scarred little boy and his mother. He always changed the subject quickly when she brought up the purpose of Soulalkers. He must not know his purpose either. She wondered if he was as scared about it as she was.

The LaStrauss sisters met Ian in the French Quarter after school for her lesson. They didn't know what they would be doing, so Katelyn decided to come along. Turns out, Katelyn didn't need to be there, but she didn't show any interest in going home.

Ian was trying to teach her control. "Don't want what happened while we were you know what to happen again," he said. Ian's face was perfectly composed, if she hadn't known, Kia would have no idea that he was talking about their hood-of-the-car-make out session. Kia blushed, trying to hide her face from Katelyn. Hopefully, she hadn't heard. Kia did agree though. She needed to learn control. So, they were walking around the French Quarter, and she would touch people. Maybe a slight bump here, a handshake there, and sometimes she would Walk them and sometimes she wouldn't. Ian had devised a code to let her know if he wanted her to dive in or if he didn't want her doing anything. A hand on the small of her back meant she was supposed to Walk whoever was approaching. If he didn't touch her at all, she would still try and come in contact with as many people as possible, but she wouldn't look into their soul. It was evasive, and she wasn't sure she liked it, but it's not like she could go around telling people about what she was.

"Well?" Ian asked. After every Walk, he wanted to know what she had seen.

"It's a sad one." Kia looked in a boutique shop window that they were passing. *Fall in love* was written on the window. Fall colored leaves mixed with small confetti hearts were scattered all around the mannequins. "He was attacked by a neighbor's dog. It bit him right in the face."

Ian turned back around as if he could see the little boy again, but they were long gone. When he turned back to face her and spoke, it was so quiet that Kia had to lean toward him to hear. "It's always a sad one."

Kia took a deep breath. She was getting tired, with each Walk her body was feeling weaker and weaker. Every step was a huge effort. She looked over at Ian. His aviator sunglasses gleamed in the setting sun. She saw his eyes flicker toward her, and she looked away quickly, hoping he didn't notice her staring. She couldn't help but think about the way his lips felt on hers when she looked at him. She knew that under those sunglasses and blue eyes, Ian held a lot of secrets, locked away beneath so many walls that she didn't know if she would ever be able to see what was hidden. He wasn't only keeping things about himself from her, she knew that for whatever reason, he was keeping things from her that she had a right to know. His body tensed every time she came out of a Walk, his eyes darting up and down her body as if checking her for wounds. He wouldn't explain to her what had happened when they kissed. How whatever she had seen had happened to her. Maybe he didn't know why it happened, and that scared her more than the alternative.

And then there was Riley. He was a mystery to her, and she planned on figuring him out.

"Was that all?" Ian asked.

She turned toward him, letting the force full of his gaze settle upon her. It was as if he had been reading her thoughts. Was that all that was bothering her? "Was what all?"

"The boy and the dog? Was that all you got?"

Oh. "Oh." She started walking again. "Yeah. Yeah, that was all."

Ian grabbed at her arm. She felt his rough callused hands through the thin material of her shirt. "It's time you went deeper. You need to find more." He watched as she closed her eyes, resting them for one moment. "You're tired?" He asked.

Kia nodded, but behind him, Katelyn shouted, "Yes!"

Next to them was a small bakery that Ian inclined his head toward. "Here, let's sit for a bit."

The bakery was a little place that sold crepes and other sweets. Kia was partial to the cafe au lait at Cafe Du Monde, but theirs wasn't terrible. She ordered a cup and sat down in a small wire chair with a heart-shaped back. Katelyn was still looking over the dessert menu at the counter, but Ian took a seat next to her with a cup of black coffee in his hand. "How are you feeling, kid?" he asked.

Automatically, she said, "I'm fine, thank you," because that's what you say. Because most people don't actually want to know how you are doing. Inside those people are screaming, *just say fine, please don't say what is really wrong,* but Ian wasn't most people.

He raised an eyebrow. "Fine? Wow, must be nice to be so fine." His sarcasm was tangible. "I mean, don't get me wrong, I am fine all the time, though I usually like to use the term ridiculously sexy."

Kia rolled her eyes. Behind Ian, Katelyn was walking up, and Kia saw her mouth, "Oh yes you are," which caused Kia to roll her eyes again. Katelyn sat down and suddenly Ian was all business again.

"When the waitress comes to bring you your coffee, I want you to Walk her. But this time, push your limits. Try and see more. *Feel* more."

Kia nodded. The waitress was heading toward them.

"Glasses." Quickly, Katelyn slid Kia's sunglasses over to her. She had been wearing them to cover her eyes. She didn't want people catching flashes of pure white in between flashes of blue. Even though they were inside, Kia slid them on as the waitress walked up.

"Here you are, sweetie," she said as she held out the hot cup of coffee. Kia put one hand under the saucer, gently covering the waitress'. She had a brief fear of the coffee spilling all over her during the Walk, but she still let it pull her under. Ian was right, it was easier now.

The world was spinning, spinning, spinning. Around her, Kia heard laughing and screams. And the smells, oh the smells. Popcorn. Cotton candy. Spilled sodas.

A carnival. She was at a carnival. A hand slipped into hers, and she looked up at her mother. A smile spread across her face, and Kia knew that it mirrored her own.

The scene changed and Kia was left staring at herself in the mirror. Only it wasn't her, it was the waitress. She was tall, but not obnoxiously. Her brown hair fell in ringlets to her shoulders. She was standing in her bra and panties, mascara and tears running down her face. She turned slightly so that the reflection showed her back. She saw long, red burn scars running down the length of her back onto the top of her thighs.

And suddenly, she was standing in a church. She still felt tears running down her face, but this time she was happy.

"I do."

Smoke started billowing in the room. Thick, black, and angry. She wasn't in the church anymore, but in a barn, horses neighing in fear as a fire roared behind them. She was hastily unhooking latches, letting the horses run out to safety. She breathed in. She knew she shouldn't have, but she couldn't help it. Her body needed oxygen. Smoke filled her lungs.

She felt someone pounding on her back, though there was no one behind her.

"God, Kia, choking on your own spit?" It was Katelyn's voice.

Kia coughed out the smoke that was undoubtedly in her lungs. She could feel it rolling around, burning and rotting her insides. Ian stood up from his chair, and not for the first time, Kia had that feeling that he was a jaguar, muscles taut, ready to move at a moment's notice. His face held that same look of concern that she had seen on every Walk she had been on that day. Kia continued to cough as the waitress walked away, looking back over her shoulder. Once she was out of earshot, Ian said, "Kia, what happened?"

She knew that he was asking her what happened *inside*, not if she had indeed choked on her own spit. She took a deep breath, filling her lungs with the clean air of the cafe. "I don't understand," she finally said.

"What?" Ian and Katelyn said in unison.

Kia's memories of the Walk played again in her head. The burn. The wedding. The fire. It was all wrong, it was like—

"It was out of order."

A small smile played at Ian's lips, though Katelyn looked confused. "Ah, to be young again," Ian said, slightly sing-songy.

Now it was Kia's turn to look confused.

"It takes a little while to get used to things," Ian began. "Sometimes it doesn't come in order. Past. Present. Future. It's a bit jumbled." Kia started organizing the timeline in her mind while Ian continued. "After more practice, you'll be able to sort it out. It will come more linearly. There is a point you reach where you'll know what is what."

It made sense. Sometimes it was hard for her to even lock in on a memory, a feeling, smell, taste. Anything. She was getting better, but she needed more practice. "Okay. Let's do some more." The coffee helped her get a bit of energy, and she was ready to get back to the lesson. "But first, I have a question."

Ian had stood up, ready to go, but sat back down as Kia continued.

"We keep talking about the future, and you've said it isn't set in stone," she said, trying to sort out her thoughts. Ian nodded. "Does that mean we can change it?"

Katelyn leaned forward, interested.

Kia continued. "Because I've always thought that changing the future was bad. You know, killing butterflies and things."

Ian didn't reply right away. He had his *thinking* face on. "That is a story. In reality, changing the future isn't bad, it's difficult. You don't know what you have to do to change it." A flash of darkness covered Ian's face, and Kia wondered if he had tried it in the past and failed. She changed the subject before the darkness lingered.

"Gotcha, another lesson for another day. Let's finish this one first."

Back in the French Quarter, a man who looked to be in his thirties was walking by. He had on a pair of jeans and a black shirt that said "ARMY" across the front. Beneath the collar, she could see what looked like a chain that dog tags hung on. Winding down his right arm were black tattoos. The closer he came toward her, Kia could tell that they weren't just black lines, but words. Words forming shapes and patterns that spiraled down his arm.

She knew that Ian was going to do it even before he did it. He gave her a slight nudge, his hand on the small of her back, hoping for her to gently touch the man, have her Walk him and apologize while they moved on. That is not what happened. Not even in the least.

Ian's nudge sent Kia's footing awry, and one of her shoes got caught on a piece of cobblestone. It sent her flying into the Army man, arms spread wide. The man moved to catch her fall.

All day she had been practicing how to control her Walks. To choose when to make them and when to not. She knew that Ian wanted her to make one now, but as things had it, she didn't have a choice. Her hand slammed into the man's muscled arm, closing around his spiraling tattoos. Immediately she was thrown into the Walk.

She looked around the room she was in. A little boy's room. The walls were covered in blue paint with clouds painted toward the top. In her arms was a teddy bear. Its head was wet. She was crying. Her tears fell endlessly down onto the top of the bear's head, coating it in salty wetness.

She looked up as she heard glass shatter in another room. "I can't stay here anymore!" a woman's voice screamed.

"And where will you go? To your brother's?" a man said.

The first voice sounded slightly muffled. "I don't know."

"Go if you want, I won't stop you, but take Caleb with you. I don't want anything to do with him anymore."

They were talking about her...him. She heard a soft sob.

The man spoke again. "You'll come back here. You always do."

Kia heard the definite sound of a hand slapping someone's face. She briefly wondered who had hit who before it changed.

Kia looked up at the sun blazing down on her. She blinked, trying to adjust her eyes. When she opened them wide enough, she took in the scene in front of her. She stood in front of a road with a few abandoned buildings behind it, a roadblock set up to their right. Stretched out behind them were miles and miles of desert. A car was parked in front of her and men in camouflage uniforms were examining it. One went around the bottom with a mirror attached to a long pole, looking underneath. Another one walked a German Shepherd around the car, pointing at nooks and crannies. She stood with four other men beside the road, watching the perimeter and gazing back into the city. She felt sweat dripping down her back.

Kia looked down into her arms and saw that she was carrying a giant gun. She didn't know what it was or how to use it, but she knew that Caleb did. A moment later, she heard gunfire in the distance. A couple of men next to her pulled their guns up and looked in the direction of the noise. The sound grew closer and instinctively, Kia pulled her gun up to her shoulder, trying to find the source of the sounds.

She saw it too late. They were upon them. Agony ripped through her arm.

"Careful there," Caleb said.

Kia's vision wasn't quite clear yet, but she knew that she wasn't in the Walk anymore. "I'm so sorry sir!" She managed to stutter out.

"That's quite alright ma'am," he said with a smile. Turning to Ian he said, "Better keep an eye on her, you'll want to be there next time she falls."

The man helped Kia right herself, gave a nod, and walked away.

"Really, Kia? You should seriously learn a little balance," Katelyn said, linking arms with her. "I thought you were a runner. Aren't they supposed to be like, super coordinated?"

Kia looked down at her right arm entwined with Katelyn's. It was a friendly gesture, and they used to do it all the time when they were younger. She looked up and smiled.

"Kia...what...what is that?" Katelyn asked, pointing to Kia's upper arm.

She looked back down. There, staining her white shirt, was fresh blood, streaming down her arm.

Ian was walking behind Katelyn and Kia, so he couldn't see what they were pointing at. Katelyn was dramatic. There was probably a bug on them or something. They stopped walking, and Ian stopped abruptly behind them, careful not to run into Kia. He didn't need to touch her more than he needed to. Already things were getting...*complicated.* He watched as Kia hastily unlinked her arm from Katelyn's and touched her arm. The look on Katelyn's face said it was more than a bug. Quickly, he walked around to see what was going on.

Kia pulled her hand away from her arm. It was shaking, her fingers spread apart wide. The tips of her index and middle fingers were covered with blood.

Ian closed the gap between them and grabbed her shaking hand, steadying it. He was about to ask where the blood was coming from when he noticed the large pool of it forming on her shirt sleeve. "Kia," he said, as he slowly pulled her face away from her blood-soaked shirt to his eyes. He saw the panic in them. "What happened?" He was careful to keep his voice calm.

"I—I got shot." A single tear slid down her face.

Ian turned around, looking back down the road to the man that Kia had Walked. The Army man. He hadn't heard a gunshot. No. This didn't happen here. It happened in the Walk. Ian's mind raced with different thoughts, each one battling to be the one on top. How was Kia different? How could they stop it? What if they couldn't? But most of all, with every question that formed in his mind, was terror. Kia was hurt.

"While you just stand there Ian, I think I'm going to take Kia to the hospital," Katelyn said, turning Kia back toward the direction their car.

Kia let out a whimper of pain and Ian's heart broke. Why was all of this happening to her?

"No!" Kia yelled. "Mom is at the hospital. We can't go there."

"Kia, darling. Don't be silly. You've been shot, you need medical care," Katelyn said. She was holding Kia's arm, making sure she didn't move it. Her voice sounded calm as she talked to her sister, but when she turned toward him and said, "Ian. Come on!" he saw his own fear mirrored on Katelyn's face.

"Hold on a minute. I need to think," he said. He turned to look at Kia. Her eyes were closed, her eyebrows knitted together. He counted her breaths as her chest rose and fell. One. Two. Three. She opened her eyes and looked straight into his. Her normally blue eyes had glassed over, appearing almost gray. Words started pouring out of his mouth. "There is a Warlock I know. He can help."

11

KATELYN GLARED at Ian through the rear-view mirror. A Warlock? Seriously? Of course, they would go to a Warlock. Only a Warlock could heal a magical gunshot wound made from a magical gun during a magical situation. Maybe after they saw the Warlock, they could go have cookies with the freaking Keebler Elves. She *did* love their cookies.

Katelyn sighed as she looked over at Kia. Somehow, Katelyn and Ian managed to get the rapidly tiring Kia into the back of Ian's car. Luckily, he wasn't parked too far away so they didn't attract too much attention. A girl profusely bleeding from her arm would cause a scene, even in New Orleans. Once in the car, Katelyn demanded Ian hand over his belt, and she swiftly used it as a tourniquet on the uppermost part of Kia's arm. She used her cardigan to help staunch the bleeding, but it was still getting all over Ian's car seats. *Humph*, serves him right. She smiled. This was somehow his fault. Katelyn looked back up at Ian through the rear-view mirror and hoped that if looks could kill, hers would.

"How is she doing?" Ian asked, trying to turn around and look.

"Keep your eyes on the road, mister," Katelyn said.

"And don't talk about me like I'm not here," Kia added. Her voice was weak, but it sounded like she was trying hard to make it sound normal. "I'm doing okay. I'm just so...tired."

Katelyn and Ian's eyes met in the mirror. His blue eyes stared back at her, pleading. Pleading her? *Her!* As if she didn't know what was at stake. He was ridiculous. What did he have to lose? A girl that he had known for a couple of weeks? She had everything to lose. *Everything.*

"This Warlock of yours better be able to help her," Katelyn snapped.

94

He brought his eyes back up to meet hers. "We're here."

Katelyn looked up to see a house made completely of glass. Okay, well half-made of glass, the rest of it was wood paneling. It looked like one of the houses that she had seen in the architectural magazines that the dentist offices have floating around in the waiting room: cold and modern. Standing on the porch was a man with his arms clasped behind his back.

Slowly, she unbuckled her seatbelt and got out of the car. Ian was already out and was in the process of trying to get Kia's hurt arm from around the seatbelt without moving it too much. Once he succeeded, he picked her up as if she was as light as a feather and carried her all romantic-like up to the house.

"Dominik," Ian began. He didn't even sound out of breath from carrying Kia. *Figures.* "We need your help."

Dominik was a tall man. A very tall man. His skin was darker than anybody's she had ever seen. His head was shaved, but he had a goatee. Despite all of Hollywood's notions about wizards and Warlocks and pointy hats and robes, Dominik wore a perfectly tailored suit.

"I know why you are here," he said. His voice was deep and smooth, and Katelyn thought he should narrate audio books, or Planet Earth shows, or something. "Jeanine told me you were practically shouting on your way down the drive. Please, come in."

Shouting? Ian hadn't said a word. This situation was about to get a whole lot weirder.

Katelyn followed them into the house and to the kitchen. Dominik cleared off the few papers that were on the dining room table and gestured for Ian to lay Kia on it.

Ian made his way over to the table and over his shoulder, Katelyn saw that Kia's eyes had closed. He gently laid Kia down, taking care to make sure her injured arm did not moved. Even so, Kia still winced as her body touched the table. Though it was Kia who was in pain, the looked that crossed Ian's face was one that made Katelyn think he was hurting even more.

Dominik took a step toward Kia, and Ian moved to get out of his way. He leaned down and examined the wound, showing no signs of his findings in his expression. Kia was silent the whole time, her eyes closed, though Katelyn didn't know if it was because she didn't want to see, or if she had passed out from the pain. Slowly, Dominik picked up her arm and looked at the back side. "The bullet went straight through. It doesn't seem to have hit bone or any major arteries."

"That's good. So, you can patch her up and make her all shiny and new?" Katelyn said with a hint of sarcasm in her tone.

"Ian," came a voice from the hall. "Your friend here doubts."

Katelyn turned around to see who the voice came from. Standing in the doorway to the kitchen was an African American woman with dreadlocks down to her shoulders. Her face was covered in freckles, but it was her eyes that stood out. They were a pale gold, pure and unblemished.

"Jeanine," Ian said.

"It's good to see you, Ian, even under these circumstances." She put a hand on his shoulder, and he pulled her into a hug. "Now, what seems to be the problem?"

"Asking questions that you already know the answer to, my love?" Dominik asked, still examining Kia's wound.

Both Ian and Jeanine smiled, apparently in on some secret. "Umm... what's going on here?" Katelyn asked.

"Jeanine is...well she can—" Ian began.

"I'm a Telepath, dear," she said, giving Katelyn a smile that brought tiny wrinkles at the corners of her eyes.

"A Telepath and a Warlock. Of course," Katelyn said. This was too much. She could feel the tears begin to well in her eyes, but she pushed them back. Not here. Not now. Taking a deep breath, she said, "Now Mr. Warlock man, could you please tell me if you can heal my sister?"

Dominik smiled and said, "How exactly did she get this wound?"

"I've been asking myself that since it happened," Katelyn answered. She looked over at Ian, hoping he would be able to explain.

"Hmm...interesting," Jeanine said, nodding her head at Ian. *Okay, now that is weird*, Katelyn thought.

Not even pausing at Jeanine's remark he began, "We were having a lesson. And in the Walk, she...he... got shot."

"I see," Dominik mumbled.

"But how it actually happened, I have no idea," Ian began. "I always thought that what happens in the Walk stays in the Walk."

"Well clearly, just like Vegas. That isn't the case," Katelyn said.

"And something like this has happened before?" Jeanine asked.

Ian looked down when he answered, "Yes."

All of this was over Katelyn's head. Warlocks. Telepaths. Soulwalkers. All she knew was that ever since Kia had been introduced into this strange magical world, she was constantly getting hurt. Sick, shot, and who knows what next.

"Indeed, this is something new," Dominik said. He left Kia's side and went to a drawer in the kitchen. He pulled out a pair of scissors.

Jeanine looked at Dominik and nodded. "Why don't we go wait in the living room?"

"Excuse me, but I think I'll stay right here by my sister," Katelyn said, crossing her arms. "Especially since you just pulled out what one could call a weapon." She gestured toward the scissors.

Dominik held up the ordinary pair of kitchen scissors. "These are to cut your sister's long sleeve shirt off."

Katelyn looked at Ian expecting him to say some smart-ass remark about getting naked, but he kept his mouth shut. Smart man.

"Katelyn, I really think that we should wait in the living room," Ian said, beckoning Katelyn toward the doorway.

He obviously didn't know her very well. She *was* going to stay here with Kia. Quickly, she grabbed a chair from the table and sat down on it. She once saw a girl in a movie wrap her ankles around the chair legs and grab the seat when she didn't want to leave. The situation seemed appropriate, so Katelyn did the same, thankful that today she was wearing her Tory Burch flats instead of heels. They would have gotten in the way. She clamped her hands down on the sides of the seat, securing herself to the chair and gave everyone in the room a "now try and make me go" look.

Ian rolled his eyes.

Katelyn sneered and locked her eyes on a vase of white roses, trying to ignore everyone in the room. Before she even realized what he was doing, Ian had picked up her chair and carried her into the living room.

Well, so much for that, Katelyn thought. She glanced back over her shoulders to see Jeanine give Dominik a grave look and close the door that led into the kitchen. Katelyn let out a grunt when Ian plopped her down on the ground. Resigned, but still angry, she stayed stubbornly in the chair.

The sensation of being pulled into a Walk is what brought Kia to. *Not now*, she thought, quickly stopping it. Her eyes shot open and she looked up at a ceiling she had never seen before. It wasn't the fact that she was in a strange room that frightened her though, nor the pain that shot through her arm, but the unfamiliar face that was staring back at her.

"Hello," the man said.

Kia fought to sit up, to get away from the man, to figure out where she was, but more importantly to see what was causing the ripping pain through her arm. It felt like her muscles had been ripped apart. She caught a brief glimpse of blood, but the man in front of her put his hands on both sides of her face, pulling her gaze back toward him. She tried to escape the intimate gesture, but he held fast.

"My name is Dominik." Despite the fear she knew resided in her, his voice seemed to calm her. "Tell me, Kia, what is the last thing you remember?"

It was as if the question brought all the memories back to her. They flooded into her mind, as hard and as fast as the pain did the moment she saw the blood.

"I was shot."

But not really. It was difficult to explain. She had been another person while she was shot. No, that didn't make sense either.

The Warlock, because she now remembered that that is who he was, ran his hands over her arm, never quite touching her skin. His knitted his eyebrows together, his brown eyes darting back and forth, up and down her body. "This was done on the *inside*," he said finally.

She nodded her head. Yes, on the inside. She was on a Walk. She was in the desert. She was in the Army.

"This has happened before." It wasn't a question. She didn't know how, but he could tell. Maybe it was his magic, maybe it was the scared look on her face, but either way, he knew. She nodded again. "Tell me."

So, she told him. She told him about the time with Ian, she told him about Katelyn and her belly-button ring, and how now Kia had a hole perfect for fitting one into. Dominik nodded along, and when she was done, he removed his hand from her arm. Instantly, the pain returned. She hadn't realized it, but while she was talking, she couldn't feel the wound in her arm.

"How very...peculiar. But then again, so are you." He picked up a vase of white roses and brought them over to the table. "Now, this might be a bit uncomfortable."

There were times that Ian felt uncomfortable around Jeanine. He knew a handful of Warlocks, a hell of a lot of Soulwalkers, and even a few Seers, but Jeanine was the only Telepath that he had ever come across. It was a rare gift, and although sometimes he thought he did, it wasn't one he would want for himself.

He looked out of the corner of his eye toward the Telepath. He knew she could *hear* him, but she gave no inclination that she was listening. He turned his gaze upon Katelyn, who still sat sitting with her feet wrapped around the legs of the chair. The LaStrauss girls were a handful. Each one stubborn in her own way.

A feminine voice floated through the door from the kitchen, and all at once, the three people in the living room turned their heads toward the door. Katelyn jumped up out of her chair, knocking it over in the process. Ian flew up after her. "Oh no you don't," he said. He grabbed her arm, preventing her from knocking open the swinging door separating the two rooms.

She looked back behind her, first at Ian's hand on her, then up into his eyes. *"Let. Go. Now,"* she hissed. The venom in her voice poisoned the air around them. She could hate him. He didn't care, but he wouldn't let her through that door.

"You need to wait," he shot back. He could feel Jeanine move silently behind him.

Katelyn jerked her arm away. "*You* don't get to tell me what to do. *You* have no authority over me. You may over Kia, though God only knows why. But let's get one thing straight, if you ever grab me like that again, if you ever prevent me from seeing my sister, I can promise you that I'll be the one standing over you."

Jeanine clapped her hands to get their attention. "Okay, now." Her voice was sing-songy, it cut through the room and penetrated whatever had come over Katelyn. Ian watched as the hate slipped away from her face, the shallow girl returning.

"There's no problem," Katelyn said, a true smile on her face.

Ian was still shocked. He had no idea what to say. Jeanine spoke before he had the chance. "My husband needs the quiet. You'll have to wait here. He will come get us when he's done."

Katelyn looked back at the door before sitting in her chair. Ian thought he heard her mutter something under her breath, but he couldn't be sure.

In the other room, he heard Kia talking.

"Dad?"

Standing in front of Kia was her father. He was in a suit, but that wasn't anything new to her. He was an attorney, and most of her life she had seen him in a suit. Though this one looked different, more tailored, more expensive.

He nodded at her and clasped his hands behind his back.

"What are you doing here?" This couldn't be right. Kia was just at Dominik's house. She had been shot.

"You're dreaming," he said, echoing the thoughts that had come to her.

She then realized that she hadn't seen her dad in almost a year. Not that she saw much of him since he left anyway, but he usually made an appearance around the major holidays. He didn't even show up for her or Katelyn's birthdays last year. "It's only in my dreams that I get to see you then?" She meant to say it firmer, harsher, but it came out sounding like a sad question. Still, it had the effect she wanted. Gabriel winced.

"I'm sorry I haven't been around, baby girl." He took a step toward her.

She didn't step away, though she wanted to. "I'm not your baby girl anymore. So much has happened. I'm not..." If this was a dream, then she could tell him everything. "Dad, I'm not human." She closed the gap between them. He folded her in his arms like she was a little girl again.

"Of course, you're human," he said, wiping tears from her face. "You're just a different kind. A better kind."

She looked up into his eyes. He knew. Those eyes said he knew.

But this was only a dream.

Katelyn looked around the room, and for the first time noticed how amazing this place was decorated. Jeanine had great taste. Everything fit perfectly together, but the room had an eclectic feel. There were traces of different influences from around the world. African, Spanish, Chinese, and of course, New Orleans. Everywhere throughout this room were roses upon roses. All white and placed in a dozen different places around the room.

Ignoring the couples' rose obsession, she turned her attention back to the kitchen and to Kia. "Is this going to take very long?" She asked, impatient to know what was going on.

"Shouldn't be long now," Jeanine said. She was standing on the opposite side of the room, staring out of one of the room's numerous windows.

Katelyn looked over at Ian. He was sitting on a couch, with one arm flung over the back like he was hanging out watching some TV. It's not like Kia was in the other room with a hole in her arm or anything. Men could be so thick sometimes.

They had heard Kia and Dominik talking not long ago. She thought about making a dash for the kitchen again, but she was afraid the mind-reader would give her away. Jeanine looked at her with a face that said, *don't even try it.* So she hadn't.

Now the silence stretched between them, and it was worse than being able to hear her sister's voice.

What was going on in there? Katelyn had never seen magic before, she didn't know how it worked. All she knew was the crazy things that voodoo queens did. If she saw a chicken head, she would be out of there faster than you could even say the word magic.

"That's an old type of practice," Jeanine said, still looking out of the window.

"That's not creepy at all."

Jeanine turned around slowly. "I'm sorry, I forget that you are not used to my gifts. I usually try to stay quiet, but you're shouting so loudly."

"So pretty much like when she talks out loud then," Ian said.

Just then the door to the kitchen opened and Dominik walked out. "She is healed," he said.

Katelyn flew out of her chair, darted past Dominik and into the kitchen. Kia was still lying on the table, now with a blanket pulled up over her. Katelyn walked to her side and grabbed her hand, thankful she was okay. Her sister was asleep.

She sat down in a chair next to the table and noticed that the vase that had been on the countertop earlier was now next to Kia's head. All the beautiful white roses that had been in it were now dead and brown.

"It's from the magic," Jeanine said, reading her thoughts again. Everyone was now in the kitchen, and Katelyn could see the relief on Ian's face. "This is how it is practiced now."

She looked back and forth between the couple, not understanding.

"The magic I already have, but the life, the energy, well, it has to come from somewhere," Dominik explained.

She looked back at the roses and touched one of the dead petals, watching as it detached itself from the bud and fell lifelessly to the table.

12

WHEN KIA WOKE up, she was back in her bed. She wished that she had imagined everything that had happened yesterday, but she knew she hadn't. All the Walks. Caleb. Iraq. The gunfire. She rolled over onto her back so that she could reach over to feel where the bullet had hit. No doubt there would probably be a large bandage. Which probably meant she would have a gunshot scar once the wound healed. *Ugh, those are the worst. I can't pull that off,* Kia thought. When she felt her arm, there was nothing there. No bandage. No bullet holes. Nothing. Maybe she *had* imagined it.

She reached over to her bedside table and turned on her lamp. Stifling a scream, she stared into the face of a woman. She was sitting in a chair by Kia's bed, sleeping. Who was she? As quietly as she could, Kia scooted to the other side of the bed and tried to get out. What she was going to do after that, she didn't know. Because to get out of the room she was going to have to go right past the woman in the chair. The woman didn't look scary, per se. Although she did have a head full of dreadlocks, which, at least to Kia, made her pretty hardcore. The fact that there was an unidentified person in her room was scary enough. Kia thought briefly about the odds of her incapacitating this woman if she tried to attack her. Not good, probably.

She stepped out of bed and right on to a creaky board. "Damn it," she hissed.

The woman in the chair stirred and opened her eyes, blinking to adjust to the light from the bedside lamp. "Ah, you're awake," she said.

Without hesitation, Kia ran around the bed and out the door, slamming it behind her. What now? Before she could decide on whether to run downstairs or into Katelyn's room, her door opened, showing the woman with a slightly amused look on her face. She was faster than Kia would have given her credit for.

"My dear, you don't need to run. I'm a friend." She extended a hand in what was clearly a friendly gesture. She would have to forgive Kia if she didn't quite believe her. She'd been shot for goodness sake! Kia started to slowly back down the hallway, still facing the woman. Seeing what she was doing, the woman sighed and said, "Kia, please lie back down, you need rest." When she continued backing down the hall, the woman added, "Ian asked me to be here."

Ian? This woman knew Ian? How? She wasn't a Soulwalker. Kia would have known immediately because of their connection. She must have been someone he trusted if he sent her here.

As if reading her thoughts, the woman said, "My husband and I are friends of Ian's. He brought you to us after your accident."

Kia hesitated but spoke for the first time since she'd seen the woman. "So, I didn't imagine it? I figured since there was nothing here..." Kia looked down at her healed arm. "Well, I thought I might have just dreamt it all. I was having this dream about my dad, but..."

The woman held her hand out again, gesturing Kia back inside her room. "No, my dear, you didn't imagine it. Dominik, my husband, he healed you."

Slowly, it all came back to Kia. A vague memory of Ian: *There's a Warlock I know, he can help.* Dominik saying, *this might be a bit uncomfortable.* A smile emerged on the woman's face. Kia didn't remember her at all. She couldn't even think of her name.

"My name's Jeanine," she said.

It was like Jeanine was reading her thoughts. Was she—?

"A Telepath. Yes."

Kia sat back down on her bed and let out a breath. Her life was getting so complicated.

"That tends to happen," said Jeanine, sitting back down in the chair next to the bed.

Okay, that was weird, Kia thought.

Jeanine laughed. "That is exactly what your sister thought."

At the mention of her sister, all thoughts of Warlocks and Telepaths left her mind. "Where's Katelyn? Is she okay?"

"Considering you were the one shot, I think I should be asking you that." Both Kia and Jeanine's heads snapped to the doorway where Katelyn was standing. "Miss me?"

A smile spread across Katelyn's face, and she ran into the room, her bare feet padding across the hardwood floor. She launched herself into Kia's arms, hugging her sister tightly before letting go. "Kia, you were shot." Katelyn was there, and she still sounded shocked.

"So it seems," Kia answered.

"And a wizard healed you."

A laugh erupted from behind them, and Jeanine said, "Don't let Dominik hear you call him that. I can't imagine he would be too keen on that name. He's never been one for a beard."

"Okay. Warlock. Whatever." Katelyn finally let go of Kia.

Kia laughed. "I would have loved to see you ask him where his wand was," she bumped playfully into her sister's shoulder.

"Believe me, I wanted to. But he's a little scary. No offense," Katelyn said to Jeanine. Jeanine held her hands up in return. "Ian didn't even give me much of a chance to say anything. He literally carried me out of the room."

Kia smiled. "That sounds like him." But her smile quickly faded as her thoughts turned to Ian. Why wasn't he here? And why did he send Jeanine to babysit her? She turned her eyes to the Telepath, expecting her to answer her thoughts, but she showed no signs of speaking. "Where is Ian?" She asked finally.

"Who knows?" Katelyn said, lying back on the bed. "He made this huge deal about having to leave when we were at the odd couple's house. But apparently, by leave, he meant only himself, because he took off in that stupid little car of his and made Jeanine take us home. I seriously hope you stained the back seat of his car with all the blood of yours. I mean, for real? You got shot. The least he could do was drive you home. That's one strange boy you got there, sister."

Kia felt blood rush to her face at Katelyn's nonchalant mention of Ian being "her boy." Hopefully it didn't look like they were *together* together. Were they *together* together? Kia didn't think so. But maybe she wanted...

She laid back on the bed next to her sister and sighed. Ian taking off like that didn't sound like him. She turned her head toward Jeanine, again hoping that she would provide more information.

This time the Telepath came through. "Ian went to talk to Eugene. He wanted to see if your Authority has heard of anything like the situation that happened to you earlier today."

So, Ian had gone to Eugene's. That made more sense than him bailing. He's not the run-away-from-a-bad-situation type. Kia looked at Jeanine. Apparently, Ian *was* the send-a-babysitter type. Sitting back up, she asked,

"Why are you here, Jeanine?" before she could comment on Kia calling her a babysitter...twice.

"Well, obviously Ian would be here if he wasn't doing something else. That boy adores you," Katelyn answered before Jeanine could.

"One minute he is abandoning me and the next he adores me? You sure can't make up your mind about him, can you, Katy?"

Katelyn sat up and stared into Kia's eyes. "Can *you*, sister?" For a moment, both sisters stared at each other—Katelyn's look full of inquisition, and Kia's full of hurt...and self-realization. Katelyn was right.

It lasted only a moment before Katelyn flopped back down on her bed, putting her hands behind her head. All traces of seriousness gone. "It doesn't matter what I think or don't think. Ian would cross oceans for you."

Whatever.

"She's right," Jeanine finally spoke up. "Ian would be here if he didn't have other business to attend to. Since he can't be here himself, he kindly asked me to stay until you woke up."

"How kind of him," Kia said, probably a little too bitterly. "Well, I'm awake now."

"Indeed." The Telepath nodded her head and crossed her arms. "But before I go, there's something I want to talk to you about."

Ian checked his watch before ringing the doorbell.

12:17...AM.

Eugene had little kids, and it was a school night. Not that kids their age would be awake past midnight on a non-school night. Ian didn't want to wake everyone up. Especially not at this time of night.

He could just call him. *Way to go, Ian, why didn't you think of that ten minutes ago before you started pacing the porch?* He pulled out his phone, scrolling through his numbers to find Eugene's.

Ring. Ring.

"Come on. Pick up."

Ring. Ring.

"Hello?" A groggy voice said.

"Eugene! It's Ian."

"Ian," Eugene paused. "Why are you standing on my porch?"

"Kia...she was shot." Ian knew that she was fine, that the threat had passed, but he still heard the desperation in his voice.

Another pause. "Veronica, turn on the light. Ian, I'll be right down." The line disconnected, but Ian didn't move the phone from his ear. He stood, rooted in place until the front door opened.

Eugene hastily tied his robe and stepped aside to let Ian in. Once the door closed, The Authority laid a hand on Ian's shoulder and asked, "Did she—"

"She's fine now," Ian interrupted before Eugene could say the word *die*. He couldn't hear that word used in the same sentence with Kia.

Eugene sighed in relief. "Let's go sit in the living room. Veronica is making coffee."

Ian followed, the shock of the night wearing off slightly with the smell of coffee. He always liked Eugene's house. It was exactly what a family's home should look like. It was *inviting*.

"Tell me what happened," Eugene said, as they sat down. "Kia was shot?"

"No...well, yes," Ian tried to explain.

"Is she okay?" Veronica asked, as she brought in coffee and a plate of blueberry muffins and sat them on the coffee table. She proceeded to stand behind Eugene with her hand on his shoulder. That was one thing that Ian always noticed when around the Broussard's. They were always touching. A hand on a shoulder here. A foot wrapped around a leg there. When you knew your days were extremely numbered, you did everything you could to be with the person you loved.

"Yes, ma'am. She's fine now. I took her to Dominik."

"Dominik? Why did you take her there if she was shot? Isn't her mother a doctor?"

"Yes, but it's complicated."

"Complicated? How?" Eugene asked.

"Well, that's kind of why I'm here. I don't know what happened, and I was hoping you would be able to tell me." Ian knew it was a long shot. If this kind of thing was common among the Soulwalkers, he was sure that Eugene would have heard about it before.

"I don't know how I can help." Eugene finally took a sip of the cup of coffee he had been holding.

Ian was picking at his muffin. Veronica made amazing muffins, but he had no appetite. "The thing is..." How could he explain this? "Kia wasn't really shot."

"Now I really don't understand."

"*Shhh*...let the boy talk," Veronica said.

Eugene looked up at his wife and smiled, grabbing her hand which still rested on his shoulder. "I'm sorry. Go ahead."

Ian paused to gather his thoughts. Trying to explain this was going to be harder than he'd thought. "It was in a Walk." He waited to see if Eugene would speak, but he didn't, so Ian continued. "She was shot in a Walk. Not her, but the person she was Walking. But then, when she came out...she was... also shot."

Eugene waited a moment before he spoke. "That's not how it works, Ian." There was no doubt in his voice. It was like he was telling a child that money didn't grow on trees.

"I'm aware of how it works, *Eugene*." Ian sat his plate down on the table and stared at his Authority.

Eugene sighed. "Are you sure it was the Walk? There wasn't any gunfire around you?"

Ian's temper was quickly rising. "Of course I'm sure! Don't you think I would have noticed if someone was shooting at me? At *Kia*?"

"Yes, of course, you would have." Eugene ran his hand tiredly through his hair. "It's just...I don't know how it would have happened. Things from the Inside don't manifest on the Outside. It's not possible. You must be mistaken."

Ian didn't know what to say. He looked at his Authority. He had so much faith in this man. He had to. His whole life rode on him. Now looking at him, with Eugene doubting him, his faith began to crack.

"There has to be another explanation." Eugene looked at Ian with his blue-gray eyes, almost pleading.

"Another explanation?" Ian was trying hard to keep his anger at bay. Tears threatened the corners of his eyes, but he pushed them back.

"Yes. Let's be rational about this, Ian."

Ian could tell that Eugene was tired. That he didn't want to be having this conversation in the middle of the night, but this was his job. He was the Authority. That didn't mean only between the hours of nine and five.

Before his tears could betray him, he stood up and walked toward the front door.

"Ian, wait!" He heard Veronica call after him. If it had been Eugene he would have kept going, but he stayed out of courtesy for her. He stopped in the foyer and slumped against the wall. In the other room, he could hear the whispers of the couple. Veronica's frustrated voice carried.

"Why don't you listen to him?"

"I *was* listening, V. But this is not something that happens. It just doesn't." Eugene shot back.

"There was a time when you would listen to everything that boy had to say. A time when you treated him as a son."

"I still would. Still do. But you don't understand what he is suggesting. It would change everything."

Ian didn't wait to hear anymore. He didn't need to. He walked out the front door, not caring enough to make sure it didn't slam behind him. He heard the door close, only to open again seconds later. He didn't have to turn around to know who it was. The connection with his Authority had always crackled with electricity. Ian didn't know if it was because of his anger, but he could feel it singeing his skin.

"Ian, listen—"

Now he turned around. "No, *you* listen." Ian stumbled over his words as he saw the look on Eugene's face. He had never talked to Eugene this way. Not even when he was young and rebellious. Now, not unlike his teenage years, his anger was taking control again. "I know *exactly* what this would mean. For you. Me. For all the Soulwalkers. But I especially know what this would mean for Kia. Because I've seen it. I've been there when she was suffering." He was yelling now, unable to control how loud he was speaking. "And no one, not even you will tell me that it isn't real." He pointed a finger wildly at Eugene.

Eugene stood there on the porch, staring. Ian could tell that he wasn't mad at him for yelling, but that maybe, just maybe, he was starting to believe him. Behind him, Veronica walked out of the door and down the steps to where Ian was standing.

She put her hand on his arm. "Why don't you come back in and tell us everything? Start from the beginning."

"I don't understand." Kia listened to what Jeanine was saying, but none of it was making any sense. "You have to remember, I'm new to all of this."

"This, being the magical world," Katelyn explained. "I'm not even a part of this, so *I'm* extremely confused."

Jeanine had been talking...mostly *at* Kia and Katelyn for the past half hour, and still, none of it was sinking in.

Jeanine sighed. Kia almost felt sorry for her. It had to be hard trying to explain magic to two teenage girls, who weren't...well, magic. "I have the ability to read people."

"Well obviously, you're a mind reader," Katelyn said, stating the obvious.

Jeanine continued, disregarding Katelyn's input. "It's because I can read minds that I can tell a certain something about a person. Sense auras. Things like that."

"And you sensed something about me?" Okay, maybe this she could understand.

"Yes. Normally Soulwalkers all *feel* the same, and they all feel different from, let's say a Telepath."

"But Kia doesn't feel normal?" Katelyn asked, cocking her head to the side. "Why do I feel dirty when I say that?"

"Katelyn!"

"What? I'm just staying." She shrugged.

"Aside from Katelyn's colorful way of putting it, that is exactly what I mean." Jeanine sat back in her chair, and Kia could visibly see the muscles in her shoulders relax.

Not normal? Nothing in Kia's life was normal anymore; it just made sense that she didn't *feel* normal. "But what does that mean?"

"I'm not sure, but I do know that there is something different about you."

Of course, there is something different about me, she thought. I can freaking see into people's souls.

Jeanine grabbed Kia's hands and held them in hers. "Don't lie to yourself. Open your heart to try and see what is going on. It's more than Soulwalking. Try to *see*."

Kia stared at the woman. She was right. All this stuff that was going on in her life had something more to it. Something that she hadn't figured out yet. Something that she needed to. The thought of why she was a Soulwalker in the first place was always in the back of her mind.

"That was something I thought about a lot growing up too," Jeanine said, reading her thoughts again. "I don't know why Soulwalkers feel the need to constantly search for their purpose. Why was anyone given the gifts that they are? Why can I read your thoughts? Or Dominik use magic? We use what we were given in our lives. You could have just as easily been given an artistic ability, and with it, you would create art. You were given something that not many people are, so use it, without questioning why every time."

Kia nodded, letting her words sink in.

"But now, my dear, it's time for you to rest." Jeanine's eyes flickered over to the clock on Kia's bedside table. "Three AM. Your mother will be home soon, and you have to wake up for school in a couple of hours. This is where I take my leave." She stood up, still holding Kia's hands in her own. "I hope to see you again soon." She leaned down and kissed Kia on the forehead. "And you too my dear," she said to Katelyn, doing the same. "Goodnight."

Then she was gone. Out the door and out of the house like she came and went all the time. The sisters sat in the bed and stared out of Kia's door as if they expected Jeanine to pop back in again at any moment.

But she didn't, and after a while, Katelyn said with a smile on her face, "School? I think you could make up a good reason to skip school tomorrow. You were shot. You need to rest."

"You're right about one thing."

"Oh yeah?" Katelyn asked, raising an eyebrow. "Just one?"

"I do need to rest. As for school, I have to go tomorrow."

"Suit yourself, sister. But if I were you, I would milk getting shot for as long as possible."

And then Katelyn was gone, and Kia was left in her room with nothing but her thoughts.

Ian spent the rest of the night talking to Eugene and Veronica. He did exactly what she had asked and started from the beginning. He told them everything, leaving out only a few things. Although, he didn't think anything got past Veronica, including his feelings for Kia. He could see the knowing look in her eyes as he carefully chose his words.

The interrogation started when he finished. "What did she see when she Walked you? What symptoms did she show?" Eugene asked.

Ian sighed. "All of them, and I'm..." he paused, "I'm not sure what else she saw." He didn't want to know. There were a hundred things from his life she could have seen. Most of them things he wouldn't want her knowing. Not now. Not ever.

"Has Kia shown any...other abilities?" Eugene asked.

"Abilities?" Ian asked incredulously. "I'm not sure I would call getting shot or opioid withdrawal an *ability.* Maybe a side effect."

Eugene ran a hand through his hair. "You can call it what you'd like, Ian, but I need to know if she has or not."

"No, she hasn't," Ian said through gritted teeth.

Eugene nodded. "Has she done anything that would seem...untrustworthy?" He paused for a fraction of a second before he said it. He had to have known how Ian would react.

It was Veronica who spoke first, cutting Ian off. "Eugene Broussard. That girl is one of your own, and you will protect her like you would any of the others."

One side of Ian's mouth twitched.

Finally, Eugene said, "This isn't possible." He looked at his wife as he spoke.

"Here we go again," Ian moaned.

Eugene quickly recovered and turned to Ian. "No, I mean. I don't know how this is possible. But I believe you, and I'm very sorry for doubting you earlier."

Ian didn't quite believe the tone in Eugene's voice, but they nodded at each other, a silent acknowledgment of each other's wrongs.

Shifting the conversation quickly, Veronica said, "Ian, you're probably too tired to drive. Please make yourself comfortable in our guest room and stay for what is left of the night."

"Thank you," Eugene said, but Ian could tell his thoughts were already somewhere else. "We can speak with Samson once we all get some rest."

Veronica walked Ian to the guest room, showing him where the towels, an extra toothbrush, and extra pillows and blankets were. Not that she needed to show him. He probably spent more time here than his foster house when he was in high school, but that was Veronica. Always helping. Always caring.

She was turning down the bed when she said, "I'm sorry about Eugene earlier."

"You don't need to apologize for him. Plus, we made up." Ian tried to finish the turndown, but she would have nothing of it.

Laughing, she said, "I saw. A nod. But that wasn't enough. Not from him, and not from you either." She turned to look at him.

"Yes, well," Ian said, helping to turn the bed down anyways. "We're not about to hug it out."

"Maybe you should. I think you need a little more affection in your life."

Ian kicked off his shoes and jumped into the bed. "That's why I prowl the streets at night. Looking for love."

Veronica slapped the bottom of Ian's foot, causing it to uncross from the other. "Ian Christopher Stalbaum."

He shrugged and laid back in the bed, closing his eyes.

"Maybe this Kia girl will be good for you," Veronica said. She walked toward the door but hesitated before she asked, "When was your last meeting?"

Ian knew she wasn't asking about a meeting with The Network, that she was asking about Narcotic Anonymous. "After...it happened with Kia."

Veronica nodded. "Good. Go to another soon." And then she walked out and shut the door.

13

"**B**ONJOUR LA CLASSE. *Je m'appelle Madam Coffey.*"
Kia stared at the woman standing in front of the class. A substitute. Her school hardly ever had subs, especially in Madam Arson's class. Three years Kia had been in her French class and the teacher hadn't missed a single day.

"I will be substituting while your teacher is away," Madam Coffey said.

"Where did she go?" A girl in the back of the room asked. Apparently, Kia wasn't the only one who was shocked there was a sub.

"Madam Arson had a family emergency and had to fly to France." The teacher turned back to the board in an attempt to begin class.

"For a funeral?" Kia blurted out before she could stop herself. She had seen so many funerals in her Walk with Madam Arson.

The entire class turned to look at Kia, then back at the substitute, waiting expectantly for an answer. "Yes, I believe that is why. *Nous allons commencer la classe.*"

The sub began speaking rapidly in French, ignoring the protests of the students, but Kia wasn't listening. She was lost in her thoughts. She really had seen Madam Arson's future.

Jackie leaned over and asked, "How did you know Mrs. A was at a funeral?"

"Um...she told me that one of her family members was sick last week." Kia wasn't a very good liar, but she hoped Jackie wouldn't ask further.

"That's so sad," Jackie said, then quickly changed the subject. "I hope the sub is good." She nodded her head toward the teacher. "Otherwise we're going to have to have extra study sessions." Kia smiled at her friend.

Their study sessions always ended in ice-cream. Jackie smiled back before they both turned toward the substitute.

Kia's eyelids started to droop. She was bored with the sub's monotone voice and rapid French. Mostly she was tired from last night. She had gone to school, just like she told Katelyn she would. But she was starting to regret that decision. Her bed was sounding very nice right about now. It was the last class of the day. Maybe she would be able to take a nap when she got home. She deserved it. After all, she was shot.

Kia paid little attention to the rest of the class and half-heartedly participated during the discussion. 2:20 came fast, and so did the bell signaling the end of the school day.

In the hallway, Katelyn was talking to a couple of girls in her grade. "I haven't decided what to be yet." Kia heard her say when she walked up.

"Be for what?" Kia asked.

"Halloween," one girl said.

"Trick-or-treating," another one said.

Kia laughed and started to walk toward the parking lot. Katelyn bid her friends a hasty goodbye and ran after her. Once out of earshot from the other girls, Kia said to Katelyn, "I can't believe you're going trick-or-treating."

Katelyn looked at Kia like she had told her that Santa wasn't real. Actually, it was the exact same look as when Kia told her Santa wasn't real. "I can't believe you're not."

Kia laughed. Katelyn was always surprising her. "Well, it's only a couple of days away. You better figure out what you're going to wear."

The talk of clothes always brought a smile to Katelyn's face. "Ah, I know!" She said excitedly. "We're going with James and Ryan and the like to run from house to house. Actually run."

"Heels are out then," Kia said.

"True." They stopped so Katelyn could grab some books out of her locker. "But hey, I heard there was a sub in French today. That Madam Arson is in France?"

"Yeah, weird right? Come on, let's go." Kia wanted that nap.

Katelyn zipped up her backpack and they headed for the parking lot. "I wonder how long this sub will last. Remember when Mrs. Stark was out two years ago? I think we went through about a dozen subs before the headmistress begged her to come back from maternity leave. I bet the sub you had today isn't there when I have French tomorrow."

"Catholic schoolgirls. A substitutes' worst nightmare." Kia and Katelyn laughed as they walked out the door to the parking lot. But then Kia felt it. Very lightly. A Soulwalker's connection.

"What's going on over there?" Katelyn asked, gesturing toward a group of younger girls giggling. "Must be a boy. Only way to get those bitchy junior high girls to smile. I wonder who it is."

Kia already knew who it was, and it wasn't the boy she had expected to show up in the parking lot. The junior high girls finally made their way toward the cars, leaving the boy unattended.

"Isn't that...?" Katelyn asked, recognizing him from his photos.

"Yeah," Kia answered, as confused as her sister. "Riley."

"And the plot thickens!" Katelyn stopped walking and stood next to Kia.

"*Shh,* he's not here to see me. He probably has a little sister here or something." That was the reason Kia hoped that he was there, but deep down she knew that wasn't true. Even though they were still a good 20 yards from where Riley was standing, she could see that he was staring at her. Only at her.

"He's looking at you." Katelyn wasn't convinced with her sister's theory either.

"Yes, I see that."

"Now he's waving at you."

Kia looked over at Riley and sure enough, he was waving at her. It was a little wave, almost like he wasn't sure if he should even do it at all. "Yes, I see that, too." How did he even know where she went to school? Should she be freaked out about this?

Kia could see Katelyn looking back and forth between her and Riley out of the corner of her eye. "Well, you'd better go talk to him before I do. His pictures didn't do him justice," Katelyn said, eyeing him.

Kia slowly made her way over to where Riley was standing. This was way more awkward than running into him at the park. That had been a complete coincidence. This was intentional...at least on his part.

"Riley...what are you doing here?" She mentally slapped herself in the face for saying the same thing she had in the park. Quickly, she recovered. "This is an all girls' school, you know." She put on a smile and hoped that her flushed face didn't give away her embarrassment.

A smile spread across Riley's face, reaching all the way to his eyes. "Yeah, I can see that," he said looking around at the few girls still wandering out from inside the school.

Kia laughed and hugged her French book to her chest. She waited for him to say something else. She assumed he had something to say, considering he had shown up at her school. They stood there and stared at each other, letting the tension rise between them. Kia looked behind her at her sister. Katelyn was still standing where she had left her, but now she was talking to a girl Kia didn't recognize.

Riley scratched the back of his neck and sighed. "This wasn't as awkward when I planned it in my head."

"You planned this out?"

"Yes," said Riley, sounding a little unsure of whether he should speak at all.

Before he could say anything else, Kia asked, "Want to get some coffee?" Yes, it was a little forward, but she wanted the chance to sit down and talk with him. She had to find out why she had the same connection she felt with the other Soulwalkers with him, but no one else did.

There was that smile on his face again. This one way bigger than the last. "Yeah. I would like that."

"Okay well, I have to take my sister home and then change." She gestured over her shoulder toward Katelyn. "You can follow me to my house though…if you want."

"That sounds good," he said as he put his hands in the pockets of his jeans.

Katelyn must have been listening, because she pranced over, her heeled boots making hardly any noise on the pavement. "Riley, this is my sister, Katelyn."

"Nice to meet you, ma'am," he said, shaking her hand.

"Oh! I love when a man calls me ma'am. Especially a cute one like you." Katelyn threw her arm through Riley's and steered him toward the parking lot. "Now, tell me where you got that accent of yours."

"Oh. My. God. Kia! How is it possible that you have two men fawning over you and I have none?" Katelyn blurted out as soon as they shut the doors to her Jeep. "I know you have those pretty blue eyes, but come on, have you *seen* my hair?" She did a classic hair flip and turned her head batting her eyelashes at Kia.

They both laughed as Kia pulled out of the parking lot. "But seriously sister. Pick one, and then give me the other." She sounded serious, but Kia detected mocking undertones.

"First of all, I don't have two men *fawning* over me. And second...well, I don't have two men fawning over me." She hoped not.

"Good, then I'll take Riley" Katelyn leaned her chair back and propped her feet up on the dashboard.

"Uh-huh." Kia didn't have the time or the energy to think about boys right now. She needed to talk to Ian about what Jeanine had said about her mind. How it was different. And she needed to talk to Riley about the connection. Okay, maybe she *did* have time to think about boys, but only in a strictly non-romantic way.

She looked in her rear-view mirror to make sure Riley was still behind her, not that she needed to. Through their connection, she could tell he was about ten yards behind her. It still felt a little different than all the others, but it was still there. He was driving a huge truck. It looked like he had driven it right off the farm that morning.

"Too bad I'm not invited to have coffee with y'all," Katelyn said. Subtlety wasn't really one of Katelyn's strengths.

Kia glanced at her sister. "It *is* too bad, isn't it?"

Katelyn huffed in response.

"Oh, crap." Kia pulled into her driveway and saw her mother's car parked in its normal spot. Behind her, Riley was pulling into her driveway as well. The back end of his truck stuck out into the street.

Katelyn looked at their mother's car and then back at Riley, laughing. "This is karma for not inviting me." She hopped out of the car, her backpack swinging at her side, and walked into the house.

Riley was already out of his car staring up at Kia's house in awe. "*This is where you live?*"

Kia looked back up at her house. She knew it was a nice house, but because she had lived in it her whole life, it didn't think about it. It looked like almost every other building in the French Quarter, with its wrought iron balcony and Spanish finishes. The house had been in her family for generations, passed down on her mother's side. "It's not much," Kia said, hitching on a smile, "but I call it home."

They walked in the backdoor, leading to the kitchen. Katelyn was sitting on the island countertop talking to—

"Marie," Kia whispered.

Kia's mom turned around. She was wearing her scrubs; actually, she was always wearing her scrubs. Kia didn't think she saw her mother out of scrubs except for Christmas and Thanksgiving. That is if she wasn't at the hospital on those days.

"Hey, sweetie," Marie said. No matter how many spelling bees or dance recitals that her mom missed, she always insisted on calling Kia and Katelyn "sweeties," like she was the perfect mother or something. "And who's this?" She asked, looking at Riley.

Riley took a step forward and stuck his hand out, "I'm Riley Hewitt, a friend of Kia's."

Marie shook Riley's hand. "Any friend of Kia is welcome here anytime. Make yourself at home, Riley."

"Actually, we were going to go get some coffee." Kia grabbed Riley's hand and dragged him toward the stairs. He jumped at her touch, but then he wrapped his hand around hers. Kia looked down at their intertwined hands while she pulled him up the steps. His hand almost completely covered hers. It wasn't like Ian's hands, slender and strong. Riley's were large and callused, but his hold on her was gentle. Once at the top of the stairs, Kia let go.

They walked into her room, and she shut the door behind them. "I need to change really quick. You can hang out in here." She grabbed some clothes—jeans, a black V-neck shirt, and a purple cashmere cardigan—and rushed into the bathroom to change. After running a brush through her hair, she put her black flats back on that she had worn to school and went back out into her room.

Riley was looking at the pictures on her wall, and she felt a huge sense of déjà-vu. During the week that she was sick and in withdrawal when she had woken up to find Ian looking at the same photos.

Kia remembered how she felt a shiver down her spine at Ian's touch. But not only that one touch, every touch. Touching Ian was like catching a ray of sun on a cold day. Something everyone hoped for.

"So," Riley said, bringing her out of her reverie. "Where are we going?"

The elevator wasn't going fast enough for Ian. He tapped his foot, impatient for his floor to arrive. He hadn't seen Kia since Jeanine took her home last night, and he was eager to see how she was doing. Not to mention, he had also planned something different for their lesson tonight.

Samson was waiting for Ian outside the elevator when the doors opened. He was wearing a tweed suit despite the hot weather outside. "There is a cold front coming in tonight," Samson said.

Ian stepped out of the elevator and into the hall. "Oh no, not you too. I spent most of last night with a Telepath. Don't you start reading minds too."

Samson laughed. "I am merely observant. I saw you staring at my suit, and I know you well enough to know what you were thinking. Not," he said, turning around, "that *you* should be giving fashion advice."

Ian looked down at his dark jeans and white t-shirt. "What you put on isn't important, it's who takes it off."

Samson opened the door to the office and let Ian walk in ahead of him. "I'm going to choose to ignore that comment."

"You choose to ignore most of my comments."

Eugene walked out of his office. "And he will continue to do so until you say something of class," he said with a smile.

Ian smiled back at his Authority. It was always like this between him and Eugene. No matter what kind of fight they got in, they always made up and were back to joking with each other in no time. "*Frère de mon âme.*"

"*Votre lumière brille,*" Eugene answered back. "We have a little while to talk with Samson about what you told me last night before the others get here."

"The others?" Ian wasn't quite sure he wanted the rest of the Soulwalkers in the city to know about Kia's...side effects.

Samson ushered them into his office, and Ian briefly wondered why they were always meeting in Samson's office instead of anyone else's. Probably because he has the comfy chairs. Samson sat behind his desk and looked down at the same maps that Ian remembered he had been looking at on the night of Kia's induction into The Network. "We are having a family meeting. There are some things that we need to discuss."

Eugene sat down next to Ian on the couch. "We decided—Samson and I—that it would probably be best if Kia didn't attend this meeting, considering what she went through last night. But I assume that you are meeting with her tonight?"

What is this meeting going to be about? He wondered, but simply said, "Yes."

"Then you can update her on the goings on."

Samson shuffled the papers around on his desk, pushing them to the side. "Can you tell me exactly what happened last night?"

Ian knew that was the reason why he was here but going through the whole story again would be...well, a bore. "Hasn't Eugene told you?"

"No, he has saved that job for you."

Ian sighed and launched into a retelling of the events since Kia's Walk with him. He talked for almost twenty minutes straight and Samson—or Eugene—didn't interrupt him once. When he finished, Samson didn't have much to say. In fact, he didn't say anything at all. He sat and rubbed his bald head.

Ian looked from Samson to Eugene and back again. "Speak up, good men!"

The room stayed quiet as Ian's anxiety rose.

"Samson," Eugene prompted. "Is this something you've heard of before?"

Samson didn't move to speak. He didn't really move at all, except to continue scratching his head. Finally, he said, "No. In all my years, I haven't heard anything like that."

Ian slumped back in his chair. He didn't have a lot of hope, but what little he did have was gone with Samson's words. If someone, *anyone*, knew about this type of situation, it would have been Samson, with his extensive knowledge of Soulwalker history and lore.

Ian had been burned, shot, and beaten in Walks. If Kia couldn't stop it...

Eugene stood up and started pacing back and forth. "We need to see it."

"Absolutely not." Ian stared at Eugene. How could he even suggest something like that? To deliberately put her in danger? "She's not some little toy that you can play with."

"Eugene is right," Samson began. "If we saw it happen..." He left the rest of the sentence unspoken. Ian knew why. Because if they saw it happen, then what? Nothing, that's what. They still wouldn't know what to do.

"You must bring her here tonight." Eugene's tone was final. It wasn't often that he demanded something be done. He was more of a friendly let's-make-this-big-decision-together kind of person. But he was the Authority. And his word was law.

Ian stared at the map of New Orleans on the wall. He couldn't face either one of them. He spoke through gritted teeth. "I have a lesson with Kia tonight."

Everyone turned toward the lobby as they heard the door open and felt a Soulwalker come in. Eugene got up and walked toward the door. "You two will come here after it then." He paused with his hand on the doorknob, and Ian thought he was about to say something else. Something more like himself, but all he said was, "Everyone is arriving. I will see you in the meeting room."

Silence filled the room once Eugene shut the door. Ian couldn't believe this. For the past four years, he had put everything into The Network. He gave up his whole life to be a Soulwalker, to help people. Not to poke around inside them to deliberately hurt them.

Samson started packing up his maps to get ready for the meeting. "We should go," he said. His voice was solemn, as though he sympathized with Ian and Kia, but not enough to stop what Eugene wanted.

Ian stayed glued to his chair. "She's not some girl to turn into a lab rat, Sam."

Samson put a hand on Ian's rigid shoulder. "I know. We won't treat her like one. She's a part of the family, as you are."

"Is that right? Then tell me why exactly she wasn't invited to the meeting?"

Samson said nothing. He picked up his stack of papers and went to the door. "I'll see you in there." And then he was gone, and Ian was alone. "Damn it." He didn't even know if Kia would ever want to Walk again after last night. Now he was going to have to tell her she was being forced to go through someone else's awful experiences. *No.* He wouldn't make her do that. He would figure out a way to stall Eugene on this one.

The meeting room was full by the time Ian got there. He had waited a while to go in, trying to figure out a way to tell Samson why there was now a large hole in the wall of his office. *Screw it*, he decided. Sam was a smart man. He'd figure it out after one glance at Ian's bloody hand.

Eugene didn't waste any time once Ian sat down. "I'm sorry to call everyone in here on such short notice, but there is a pressing matter which we need to discuss." He turned toward Samson. "Will you begin?"

The Finder stood up and pulled out his maps. "The surrounding districts and I have been charting some...peculiar occurrences these last few months."

Ian racked his brain to think of who the Finders in the nearest districts were. He only half paid attention when his mentor told him. District 2, Mandeville and Madisonville, was Delilah...Delilah—

"Delilah Morgan has informed us—"

"Morgan!" Ian whispered.

Eugene shot Ian a withering look. "What was that, Ian?"

"I was just commenting on how pretty Anna looked today." He looked over at the Soulwalker sitting across from him and winked.

"Maybe when you're done flirting, we could get back to the meeting," Stefan said.

Stefan, Ian thought, *he's never liked me.* "By all means, don't let me hold you up, Sam."

Samson shook his head. "But Districts 4, 6, and 7 also reported—"

"Come on, Samson. Get on with it." Stefan shuffled in his seat, clearly impatient.

Samson paused, a look of pain crossing over his face. "Soulwalkers in the surrounding districts have been going missing."

Gasps and "what's" and "how can it be's" filled the room. Ian looked around, taking a mental roll call of his city's Soulwalkers. All were there but one.

Kia.

Ian quickly pulled out his cell phone and sent Kia a text while Samson cleared his throat to bring the, by the looks on their faces, confused Soulwalkers back to his attention. "The other Finders and I have been charting these disappearances."

"What do you mean by *disappeared*?" Someone asked.

"The Finders in the districts do a lot of the same things that I do. They keep track of their district's Soulwalkers. But some of their districts are larger than ours, so while I don't have to travel around to be connected to you if you're in the city, they might need to." He held up a map of Southern Mississippi, District 4 Ian remembered.

"The Finder here travels throughout his district to check in on the Soulwalkers. Only, every time he went to visit some, he couldn't feel their connections."

The room was quiet as they all stared at the map that Samson was holding up. Ian figured that feeling no connection didn't mean they disappeared, merely away from their home. Someone else in the room was thinking the same thing. "If the Finder never actually went to their house, then these *disappearances* mean nothing."

Samson nodded and continued to pull out other maps with large red X's on them. "Two gone from District 2, three from District 4, and one each from District 6 and 7. And yes, the Finders did go to their houses, called them, their relatives…"

Ian's phone buzzed in his pocket. It was a text from Kia. Ian's shoulders relaxed slightly as he was able to breathe and think again. All that mattered right now was that Kia was alright. Okay, maybe the missing Soulwalkers mattered too.

Eugene stood up to talk for the first time since scolding Ian. "I already had a scheduled meeting in Paris this week, so I am flying to meet with the other Authorities tomorrow. Until we can figure out what is happening. Please keep yourselves safe."

"What do you suggest?" Anna asked.

It wasn't Eugene who answered, but Quentin, their lawyer, or as Ian liked to call him the Enforcer. "Use general caution when going places, and until further notice, call or text to check in with Samson every night."

Quentin weighed in at 220 pounds, pure muscle. If anyone could wrestle whoever was making these Soulwalkers disappear using only his bare hands, it would be Quentin. Ian, on the other hand, liked to carry a little protection. He thought of the dagger back home in his apartment. It was one of many blades that his father had owned, and the dagger always been Ian's favorite. It was the one he always brought to his *Kali* training, a weapon-based Filipino martial art. He made a mental note to stop by his apartment to get it before going to meet Kia. Ian looked up as he heard Eugene calling his name several times. "You summoned?"

"I believe it is time for you to go. You have your lesson, and you don't want to be out after dark."

Ian looked at the time. Almost five o'clock. Eugene was right, he should get going.

"Okay, so that whole showing up at your school thing..." Riley began.

Kia smiled. "Was a little weird."

Riley laughed a big hearty laugh, almost spilling his cup of coffee that he was holding. "Yeah, I guess it was."

Somehow Kia and Riley had managed to get out of her house without running into her mom. Maybe she had gone back to the hospital. Kia didn't care. As long as she wasn't going to have to explain how she and Riley had met. Now, they were in an almost empty café, and Kia had her favorite coffee drink in hand.

"I just—" He began. He sighed and set down his cup of coffee, sitting up straight and looked Kia right in the eyes. "I had to see you again. And yeah, I know that sounds weird too."

"No, not too weird." *Because I needed to do the same thing.* Kia had been wanting to try and ask Riley again about the possibility of him being a Soulwalker, because, well, why else would she feel that connection she only felt to other Soulwalkers? But she didn't know how to without freaking him out. What was it that Ian had said when she first met him? *You are a member of an elite group of people.* God, he had smiled so big after that. Though Kia thought he was being sarcastic and lying, that smile was her first look at who Ian was. His blue eyes seemed so—*stop it.* She had to stop thinking about Ian. She had other things to focus on.

Here goes nothing. "Riley, have you—"

"Wait, I want to explain." He paused, taking a drink of his coffee. "That day in Café du Monde, *can't you feel it*, you said. I was so freaked out. And then in the park, it was like I would have known exactly where you were even if my eyes were closed." He put his head in his hands. "God, I know this sounds so crazy."

Kia reached up and pulled down his hands. It was almost too good to be true what he was saying. "It doesn't. Go on." She needed him to say something about having Walks...not that he would know what they were. Then she could know for sure. And well, she didn't hate to say I told you so.

"I feel...connected to you. I know that sounds creepy because I don't even know you. I mean, I had to ask like a dozen guys at school to try and find out something about you."

So, that is how he found out where she went to school. Guess he didn't have a super hacker friend like she did.

Before she could say anything in return, her phone went off in her purse. It was a text from Ian: "Are you okay, kid?" She smiled and quickly she sent a text back saying, that yes, she was indeed okay.

She turned her attention back to Riley. He still hadn't mentioned anything about Walking, but he felt the connection. Maybe he wasn't ready to tell. He was right. They didn't know each other. "Well, maybe you could get to know me. Then you don't have to feel like a creeper," she said with a smile.

He smiled back that crooked smile of his. "Yeah. I'd like that," he replied, but Kia had a feeling he meant it quite differently than she did.

They talked for a while about nothing in particular. Kia didn't bring up Soulwalking. She wasn't exactly qualified for that, so she figured she would leave it to the most experienced Soulwalkers. She still didn't understand why they both felt the connection, but none of the other Soulwalkers did. She would have to bring Riley to Samson. Show him in person.

Ian called while they were talking, but Kia didn't answer and let it go to voicemail.

"I'm sorry again for showing up all stalker-boy at your school today," Riley said. He reached up to grab his hair, something Kia was starting to recognize as a nervous habit. She wondered if he had longer hair and recently cut it down to the buzz cut it was now.

"I can't say I wasn't surprised, but it was nice." It saved her from having to call him.

He paused but clearly wanted to say something. After a deep breath, he said, "How about tomorrow I take you on a real date?"

Her phone started buzzing again, distracting her before she could properly answer and apologize to him for giving him the wrong impression. Riley only smiled and walked back to his truck.

Kia sighed. It's not like she didn't see it coming. She figured feeling that kind of connection to a person and not knowing what it was could be confusing.

She answered her still buzzing phone, "Katelyn, hi." She didn't let her sister get very far before she said, "I'll call you later," and hung up. She didn't have time to hash through her conversation with Riley to her sister right now. Then she looked through her missed messages.

14

TWO MISSED CALLS, two new voicemails, and six text messages. All from Ian. The first voicemail was him asking her to meet him at St. Louis Cemetery #1 at 5:30. She looked down at her watch. It was already 5:45. *Oops.* Guess it couldn't wait. The second voicemail was an irate Ian asking why Kia wasn't already at the cemetery and preaching about the dangers of the night. The text messages followed in a similar fashion.

She sent a text message saying that she was on her way. The cemetery was right across the edge of the French Quarter over North Rampart Street, not a very far walk from her house. It wasn't necessarily the safest place for her to be walking. Alone. At night. But she was meeting Ian once she got there, so she figured it'd be okay.

Kia pulled her cardigan tighter around her body. The sun had almost set, and it was getting cold. She wished she had thought to grab a jacket from her house but hearing Ian's angry voicemail made her hurry.

Once the cemetery was in view, she felt Ian's iron connection snap into place and knew that he was pacing back and forth right inside the entrance. Kia had a love/hate relationship with New Orleans' cemeteries. For one, all the bodies had to be buried above ground. Because the city was beneath sea level, bodies buried underground would float up when it flooded, which it inevitably did. Each coffin was put inside vaults or tombs. Entire families could be buried together inside them, making the tomb their final family home. It was creepy.

The old cemeteries, like the one Kia was going to, were beautiful and scary. Visitors to New Orleans spent a lot of money touring of the cities of the dead, but each tour guide always warned to never go at night. Kia was starting to rethink her decision to meet Ian so late.

Ian stopped pacing as soon as Kia walked up. "Nice of you to show your pretty face."

"Well, I see only one predator of the night here." Kia looked around in mock exaggeration only to land her gaze on Ian.

He grabbed her hand in his. "Don't joke, kid. There are a lot of things you still need to learn."

The seriousness in his voice startled Kia. If there were dangers, why were they out at night? "Ian, what are we doing here?"

Ian pulled Kia by the hand into the maze of tombs. "Have you heard of Marie Laveau?"

"That's what this is about? Everyone knows the Voodoo Queen. She is rumored to be buried here." Ian's grip on her hand was strong and his pace fast. She had to walk quickly to keep from being dragged.

"No. Not rumored." After walking past a couple of tombs, Ian took a sharp left, turning down one of the alleys. He stopped in front of a tomb, finally letting go of Kia's hand. The setting sun cast a golden light, causing the normally stark white tomb to appear bronze.

Drawn all over the tomb were X's of all different sizes, and down in the bottom left corner was a plaque. "Marie Laveau," Kia read. "This Creek Revival Tomb is reputed burial of this notorious 'voodoo queen'."

She looked over at Ian as he pulled out a camping lantern from a bag that she hadn't realized he was carrying. He turned it on as the last bit of sunlight faded from the tomb. "I still don't understand what we're doing here," she said.

Ian turned to her and gently rubbed the place where she had been shot only the night before. It already seemed like a hundred years ago. She could feel the warmth of his hand through her cardigan. "How are you feeling?" He asked. The anger that she'd heard in his voicemail was gone, along with the sense of urgency she felt during the drag over here. He dropped his hand from her arm and once again that spot was cold like the rest of her body.

Kia noticed that Ian had on his usual personal uniform: jeans and a white V-neck tee. Today, he also had on a black leather jacket to shield himself from the cool air. "I'm fine," she said, trying to catch his eye. But he looked away, back into the bag he had brought along. If only she could see his eyes, then maybe she could figure out what this was all about. No matter what came out of his mouth, he always carried truth in those blue eyes of his.

"Good. Well since you chose to be late to our lesson, you get the turkey sandwich instead of the chicken salad." Sticking his hands into his bag, he pulled out two sandwiches and handed one to Kia wordlessly.

She stood there staring back and forth between the sandwich and Ian, who was now sitting down with his back propped against the tomb. "Excuse me if I'm wrong, but maybe this isn't such a good time to be taking a dinner break. We are in the middle of a cemetery you know. And you— you're leaning against," she lowered her voice to a whisper, "a Voodoo Queen's tomb."

"One thing you've got to learn, kid, hunger will stop for nothing." He took an impressively large bite of his chicken salad sandwich, making sure Kia heard the *mmm's* and *ahh's* that came after it. "As for Marie here," he patted the tomb, "she won't be any kind of trouble. Will you Marie?"

Kia expected thunder to roll across the sky and lighting to strike down at Ian for talking that way to the grave of someone as legendarily powerful as Marie Laveau. But the sky stayed the same dark color, so Kia sat down to eat her sandwich, though she sat further away from the tomb.

"Why exactly are we having a picnic in a graveyard?" She asked.

Ian shoved the last bit of his sandwich into his mouth, then pulled out a bottle of water and gulped down half of it before speaking. At least he had some manners. "I thought you might like a little history of magic lesson after last night, and well, where better to start than our very own Voodoo Queen?"

He was right. Kia was interested in what had happened last night, and how. She nodded hoping that she wouldn't have to say much for Ian to launch into his usual dramatic storytelling. She didn't want to have to stay in the graveyard much longer. It was giving her the creeps.

Ian began to talk. "Just as there have always been Soulwalkers, there has always been magical folk. Warlocks, witches, and the like. But, unlike Soulwalking, magic seems to run in the blood. A parent passing it down to a son or daughter and so on." He paused, obviously for dramatic effect. "We are chosen. They are made."

Kia's interest piqued. "But where does Voodoo play into it?"

"Voodoo is magic. What they are doing, or did, is real. Let's say they're taking the scenic route, while people like Dominik take the expressway."

Kia thought about the things that she had learned over the years about Voodoo—turning pictures upside down and cutting up dead husband's shoes—and decided that Ian's metaphor sounded accurate.

"The magic is done by drawing energy and life from the things around the practitioner. It takes a lot of energy to perform any kind of magical act,

128

even more if touch isn't involved." He paused and looked into Kia's face. "Got it?"

"Yeah. Sure," she said with only a mild amount of sarcasm. "Warlocks, Telepaths, Soulwalkers...any other mythical people I should know about? Fairies, maybe?"

"Don't be ridiculous. Fairies aren't real." Ian laughed. "But there is a slew of other humans that have supernatural abilities. There are people whose sole purpose is to keep the balance of good and evil in the world. And while some like to stay hidden, everyone is always known to The Riven."

"The Riven?" Kia had heard the word in her SAT vocabulary before, but never as a noun.

Ian picked up a small stick from the ground and drew three circles in the dirt, all intersecting each other. A Venn diagram. In one circle he wrote Soulwalkers, in the second he wrote Warlocks, and in the third he wrote, Seers.

"This circle," he pointed to Seers, "is made up of a couple of different people. Their abilities are all slightly different...reading minds or seeing the future, but their purpose is all the same."

He drew small circles near the outside of the large ones and left them unlabeled. "These are the outlining groups. The ones that stay hidden. Most don't even know about the existence of the other groups."

In the middle section, where all three large circles intersecting, he wrote, The Riven. "There is a council made up of Soulwalkers, Warlocks, and Seers. They are The Riven. But," he drew one more circle, this time encompassing his entire drawing, "most people call this The Riven."

"So, it has two meanings?" Kia asked.

"Yes." He looked down at his drawing, thinking. "There have always been complex relationships within The Riven. Friendship between Soulwalkers and Warlocks. Rivalry between Soulwalkers and Seers. Everyone is always trying to get the upper hand. As of now, no one has it. All three groups are equal in The Riven."

Kia sat quietly, letting all the information sink in. When she looked up at Ian, he wasn't looking at her, but at his drawing. Suddenly, he wiped it away, removing any evidence that it was ever there.

"Any more questions?" He asked.

Umm, yeah. She had about a thousand questions about magic and related things, but she had more pressing questions that she wanted to be answered. "Ian..." she began. "How—why is this happening to me?" She didn't need to explain what she meant by *this*.

Even in the dim light, Kia could see Ian's muscles tense up, but his voice was as light as always. "I always say it's best not to question why you're alone with a man as criminally handsome as I am."

Everything was always a joke with him. Smoke and mirrors. Just a way to distract her from what he was feeling. "Yes, while a date in a cemetery is incredibly romantic, you actually aren't what I was talking about. Shocking, I know."

"We're on a date?" Ian asked, raising an eyebrow.

"What? No." She shook her head.

He leaned back against the tomb, stretching his legs out and putting his hands behind his head. "I do believe you called this a date. You know, if you want to go on a real date with me all you have to do is ask. First, you con me into a date by getting all dressed up and asking for waffles, and now you casually mention how a shared tomb in the dark qualifies as a date. Not to mention the several occasions in which you kissed me. Looks like you have the hots for me and you're too afraid to say anything." He continued even through Kia's protests. "It's okay, nothing to be embarrassed about. It's not anything I haven't experienced before."

There was that phrase was again. Real date. "Kissed you? Kissed *you!*" Kia said as she got up and walked around the other side of the tomb. She had been wanting to check out a couple of other ones close by and doing it now and stalking off from Ian just seemed like killing two birds with one stone. As she rounded the corner, she heard Ian say something about her missing dessert.

Ian pulled out a cookie from the container in his bag. Chocolate chip with M&Ms, his favorite. When he was younger, he used to make them all the time with his mom. She would let him drop the M&Ms into the batter and watch while she swirled and swirled the little pieces of chocolate around. He didn't have homemade ones now. Not anymore.

Ian heard Kia's feet crunching on the gravel on the other side of the tomb. "Don't go too far, kid," he said. Kia gave an *mhmm* in response. Satisfied, he got up and brushed the dirt off his jeans to look around a little bit himself. The tomb right next to the Glapion, Marie Laveau's, tomb was short, only large enough to fit one coffin inside. The lantern's light didn't reach much further than that.

He sighed and leaned back against the marble, waiting for Kia to come back around. He heard more foot crunching, but not from the direction that it should have come. Across the alley, over on the next row of tombs someone was walking. He knew it was a risk to bring her here so close to dark, but he had thought they'd be out by now. If she hadn't been late… "Kia," he whispered. "I think it's time to go."

Kia walked from around the corner. She stopped and put her hand on her hip. "Oh, so now you want to leave?" She said with a smile.

Before he could say anything, the smile slid from her face. Her eyes widened as she stared over his shoulder. Then he heard it. The crunching noise was now right behind him.

Ian tried to turn around, but Kia's scream forced his head back toward her. He wanted to run to her, to get her out of here, but the man was already on Ian.

He had his arm clamped around Ian's throat cutting off his airway. Ian coughed once before his adrenaline kicked in and he was able to think clearly again. He stepped back with his right foot putting it behind the man before Ian threw him over his leg.

Ian spun around to face the man who attacked him. He figured it was a homeless man, angry about his prime cemetery real estate spot being occupied, but now looking at him, Ian could tell that this man was no homeless person.

It wasn't only his clothes, which were tailored perfectly, that gave him away, but his build. He was taller than Ian's own six-foot frame and looked like he spent every spare moment at the gym. He didn't quite look like a juiced-up bodybuilder, but he looked like he could take a man down with a punch. Clearly, he knew this as well, because seconds after Ian spun around the man was charging at him.

But Ian was trained for things like this. His father had made sure. Using the man's momentum, Ian grabbed him by the shoulders, kneeing him in the face, and then, thinking the tomb might make a nice resting place, threw the man into the one behind them. The guy's head hit the marble with a crack and when he got up Ian could see blood trickling down his face.

Ian vaguely thought back to the meeting that was held in the Soulwalker's offices earlier that afternoon. It seemed so far away. And here he was now, possibly facing the person who had been wreaking so much havoc on his world. He was glad he did, in fact, stop by his apartment to get his dagger. "And why, may I ask, have we joined in this little dance?" Ian said, as they circled around each other. Both Ian and the man had their fists up, ready to strike when an opportunity presented itself.

The man just stared back at Ian, smiling. By now the blood had spilled over into his mouth and the little light that the lantern emitted was turning his teeth an eerie red black.

A shadow crossed over the man's face and his eyes shifted away from Ian. Ian saw his opportunity to get in a hit, but then he realized exactly what it was that the man was looking at.

Kia.

Ian felt anger rising inside of him, growing hotter with each moment that this man was staring at her. He clenched his fist, and as hard as he could, hit the man square in the jaw. His head snapped back with the force of the blow, causing him to stagger back a couple of steps.

"Kia. I think this might be a good time for you to go find my car," Ian said through clenched teeth, all the while never taking his eyes off the man.

Out of the corner of his eye, he saw her hesitate, then turn around and take off running.

The cemetery was a maze. The tombs weren't stacked in nice little neat rows like suburban houses. They were angled and crooked and pushed so close together in some places that you couldn't fit in between them.

Earlier it was funny when she joked with Ian about predators of the night. It wasn't so funny now.

She ran, hard and fast, through the maze trying to find her way out. To find someone. To get help. But it was dark and too many of the tombs looked alike. She turned corners only to come to a dead end and have to turn back again.

After yet another dead end, Kia turned a corner and saw light filtering from around the tombs. It wasn't much, but it was something. Following the light the best she could, she found herself back where she started. In the alleyway, by the Glapion tomb with Ian's lantern light shining next to it. Beside it, Ian and his attacker were still trying to hit each other, although it looked like they both had got a few punches in. Both men had blood dripping down their faces.

From where she was standing, she couldn't make out many of the features of the man, except that he was big. Really big. Ian probably wouldn't be able to keep up with what he was doing much longer.

She was right. Ian was down on the ground, and the man kicked and stomped him.

Kia could hear the cries from Ian every time the man sent out another forceful blow, but it was like she was glued to her spot. She couldn't move. She couldn't speak or cry out for help. All she could do was watch as Ian was being beaten to death.

She felt a tear escape her eye and slide down her face. It was cool on her flushed skin. Her eyes met Ian's and she saw him mouth one word.

Run.

The pain in his chest was unbearable. Every time Ian thought he would be able to take a breath, another blow struck him in the chest. In the face. In the stomach.

And he couldn't...

Breathe.

His vision was starting to blacken, and he knew that if he didn't do something, get up, or roll over, then he would lose consciousness. Rolling over would be easier. Then he would be able to grab the dagger that was in a sheath under his jacket.

He heard a voice. It sounded familiar, but like it was a thousand miles away. "Hey, you...you, big dumb man!"

Kia. Why was she still here? He told her to run. Why couldn't she listen to him, just this one time?

Ian needed to do something now. He wouldn't let this man hurt her.

He heard Kia grunt and saw something fly across the air hitting the man in the face. A rock fell next to him.

It was the distraction he needed.

As the man's attention was on Kia, Ian grabbed his leg, yanking it with as much strength as he had left toward his chest. The man lost balance and started to topple down. For good measure, Ian hit him in the back of the knee, sending him flying forward onto his knees.

Ian scrambled up off the ground, pulling his dagger out of its sheath. But he wasn't fast enough, because the man grabbed Ian and threw him back against a tomb.

Ian fell into the jagged corner of the rock, crying out as he felt the flesh of his side tear open.

"You've been a tough one, Soulwalker," the man whispered into Ian's ear. "The others didn't put up much of a fight."

Ian was having a hard time breathing with the man's arm pressed against his throat, but he managed to say, "I bet the others didn't have a knife either."

133

A look of fear crossed the man's face as Ian used his last bit of strength to push the man off him. He held tight onto his dagger as he sliced across the man's face, all the way from his jaw up to his hairline.

The man's hands flew up to cover the gash down his face. His screams were deafening, but Ian wasn't done with him.

He may have fought most of this fight with his hands, but he learned through many years of training that his legs were more powerful. Leaning back, Ian brought his leg up, and kicked the man right in the chest, sending him flying onto his back.

The man let out one little whimper, before getting up and running off into the night.

It didn't take long for the pain to return and for Ian to crumple to his knees. Every breath in and every breath out was like trying to lift an eighteen-wheeler off his chest.

"Ian!" It was Kia's voice again. He was suddenly grateful for her stubbornness and her inability to listen to anything he said.

Her small hand came up and touched his face. It felt cold like she had been holding ice in her hand.

"Oh my God," she said. "Oh my God."

"Come on," he coughed. "I don't look that bad." But he didn't even put much effort into the quip because he knew he did look that bad.

Kia's hand slid from his face down to his shoulders. He wanted to tell her to put it back. That he needed it, but the pain when he spoke was too much.

Slowly, Kia began to take off his jacket, sliding it down his arms. As a hiss escaped his lips, she whispered, "Easy."

Once the jacket was almost off, Kia said, "You know, it's too bad you're bruised and bleeding."

Ian winced as she pulled off the other sleeve. "Why's that?"

"Because this would be the perfect time to make some joke about getting naked."

Ian smiled. "My girl really knows how to make me feel better."

His girl? Did he actually call her that? He might have a concussion. Whatever it was, Kia didn't seem to notice.

"You need to go to the hospital," she said, examining the cuts and bruises on his face. "You probably have a couple of broken ribs," she said.

"No." Ian tried to stand up, and when Kia noticed what he was doing, stood to help. "I just want to get home."

"Ian, I don't think that's a good idea. You need to see a doctor."

He tried to take a few steps by himself but couldn't. Kia draped his arm over her and gently held him in place. "You didn't want to go to the hospital yesterday. I didn't ask questions. I said okay and thought of a new plan. So, today, when I say no hospitals. I mean no hospitals."

"Okay," she said, sounding a little hurt. "No hospitals." She looked down at Ian's stomach and he followed her gaze. Half of the left side of his shirt was stained red with blood. "Let's get you back to my house. I can clean you up there."

15

KIA DIDN'T THINK that taking the time to walk to Ian's car and sit in the French Quarter traffic was worth the time. It would be much quicker to walk the ten minutes to her house.

Ian, of course, had other ideas. "Kia, my car. *Please.*"

She felt bad. She knew that every step that they were taking was causing him a great amount of pain. She could see it in his face, in the soft sounds that escaped his lips, but going to the car... "It will take too long. I'm sorry."

He was quiet after that, letting Kia practically drag him down the street. He could barely walk, *hell*, he could barely stand. Thank God no one paid them any attention.

Finally, Kia could see the flags that adorned her house's second-floor balcony. She pulled out her keys, letting Ian go for a second, but it was a second too long and he slumped to the ground. She didn't have enough strength to pull him to his feet after the walk home, so she pulled out her cell phone and called her sister.

"Hello," Katelyn said after she picked up.

Kia wasted no time in niceties. "Katy, come downstairs quick please."

"Downstairs? Are you calling me from on your phone from downstairs? Wow, that is an extremely lazy thing—"

"Katelyn! Come down! Now!" She yelled, hanging up the phone.

Kia looked back down at Ian; his eyes were closed. "Ian, you can't go to sleep. Not yet." Gently, she put her hand on his face and stroked her thumb over his bruised skin.

"*Mmmm,*" he cooed.

A moment later, Katelyn threw open the front door with an annoyed look on her face. "And why exactly did—oh my God! What the hell?" She stood staring, open-mouthed, at Ian's bloody face.

"Help me get him inside. And please tell me, mom's not home."

Katelyn kicked off her heels and came outside to Ian's other side. Together, they picked him up. "No, she's not."

At least she wouldn't have to worry about that. Although, it might have been nice to have an actual doctor in the house to help, but it wasn't worth having to explain everything...at least probably not. "Let's take him to the kitchen."

Kia cleaned off the kitchen island with one hand, the contents clanking as they hit the floor. They gently laid Ian down on it. His eyes opened as his body touched the cold marble countertop. Panic filled his beautiful blue eyes as he struggled to figure out where he was. Kia grabbed his hands before he tried to sit up. "Ian," she said in what she thought was her most soothing voice. "We're going to take care of you."

The terror left his face, and he closed his eyes again. Kia turned to her sister. "Stay here with him while I go and try and find some things to help him."

Ian wished he had enough energy to open his eyes. Enough energy to tell Kia to not go, to please stay with him. But he didn't. He was devoting all his energy to breathing. And just for a split second, he wished he didn't have enough energy to do that, because breathing hurt like hell.

He heard Katelyn moving around the kitchen doing things. Washing her hands, rolling up a towel and placing it under his head, running other towels under the water and wringing them out. She did all of this wordlessly. Maybe she was too scared to say anything, like the doctors at the hospital that day. *I'm so sorry, Ian.* Sorry for what? But they didn't have to say. Their silence said everything.

Maybe that was why she wasn't saying anything now. Because what could she say to make his injuries go away, to make him feel better?

"Okay, I think I found the stuff we're going to need," Kia said as she came back into the room. Ian opened his eyes to look. She was carrying a load of stuff: gauze pads, rubbing alcohol, other things in those sterile blue packages that they have at the hospitals. She set everything down on the counter and surveyed her loot.

Katelyn stood staring as well. "Kia, you can't be serious." She lowered her voice to a whisper. "*Look at him*. He needs a doctor." She put her hand on Kia's arm, but Kia shrugged it off.

He couldn't be sure, but he thought that he saw a tear shining on Kia's face, but her voice gave away no hint of crying. "If you don't want to help, then you can leave now."

"Of course, I want to help, but—"

"Then shut the hell up and start helping."

Katelyn sighed and grabbed one of the wet towels and started to dab at Ian's face. Of course, the daughters of a doctor were used to this type of thing. Katelyn didn't flinch one bit.

Ian's eyes were heavy. He could feel them closing with every moment that passed, but the second they finally closed, he snapped them back open as the feeling of cold metal touched him above his pant line.

Scissors.

Kia's eyes were cast down, focusing on the job she held at hand. When she glanced up at Ian's wondering eyes she merely said, "I'll buy you another shirt."

There was something calculating beneath her bright blue eyes, like she was unsure of whether he'd be upset that she was cutting off his shirt. "I'd say this isn't the best situation I've been in where someone takes off my clothes, but it isn't the worst either." His voice didn't sound right to him. It was hoarse and scratchy. Speaking hurt, but it was worth it. Even from the angle, he was at he could see that Kia was smiling.

Ian heard the last snip of the scissors at his collar and closed his eyes again. He didn't like being unable to see when sharp objects were around his skin. Kia started peeling away his shirt, taking extra care around where he had hit the sharp part of the tomb. His shirt had already begun sticking to the wound and pulling it apart was making fresh blood spill out. Ian could feel it slide down his side and under his back.

Beside him, Kia's hands started to shake slightly. The slight vibrations were tickling his skin. She finally pulled his shirt all the way off. He realized it was the first time she was seeing him without a shirt on. He had taken special care to not let that happen, because if she did, she would see the thick, red scar running down the length of his sternum. Quickly, he threw his arm across his chest, trying to block as much of it as he could.

Ian coughed a bit, trying to help his voice return to normal. "What's the prognosis, doc?"

He peeked out from under his eyelids to study Kia's face. Her eyebrows were scrunched together in determination, but her eyes kept flickering back and forth between the cut on his side and his stomach. Not his chest. His abs.

Ian smiled.

Kia couldn't help it, and Ian knew it. That's why he had that stupid grin on his face. Of course, she'd seen some pretty nice bodies, but his looked like it was straight out of a magazine, even with it covered in dirt and blood. She shook the thoughts of rubbing her hand across his abs from her mind. "Better wipe that smile off your face. You're going to need some stitches."

Ian's already exhausted body seemed to slump even further. "Stitches? Really?"

"Yes really." Kia stopped, trying to decide whether to continue. "What you did what stupid. You have to know that, right?"

Ian moaned beneath her touch. What kind of moan it was exactly she couldn't tell.

"And what was it exactly that you did?" Katelyn asked.

Of course, Katelyn would ask what happened. How could she not? What, with a bloody man lying on their counter and all. But it wasn't the right time and she should know that. Kia shut her up with a glare full of daggers.

Kia put her mind back to the cut in Ian's side. "I can do the stitches for you, but they won't be very good. You're going to have a scar."

"Good," Ian said. Kia knew that speaking was hard for him. Each breath he took didn't fill his lungs as it should have. He probably had some broken ribs. But pain wouldn't stop Ian from making jokes. "I'll tell all the ladies I cage diving with sharks, and one got through."

Kia shook her head and picked up Ian's arm to look at the rest of his injuries. He struggled with her for a moment before finally relinquishing and letting her move it. As she peeled his arm away, she saw what he was hiding beneath it.

A long red scar ran down the length of his chest, positioned right above his sternum. Kia sucked in a breath of air. She knew what that scar was from. Her mother gave one to people almost every day. Only a surgery that required opening the chest cavity caused something like that.

She reached down and touched the very end of it. Ian's eyes clenched down together, almost as if her touch was causing him pain. She drew her hand back immediately, and he visibly relaxed. He wasn't saying anything about it. And although she knew she shouldn't ask, she couldn't help it. "Ian, what—"

He interrupted before she could even get her question out. "So, stitches?"

Kia sighed and decided to breach the subject at another time. She turned back toward the counter and looked through the medical supplies she had brought down. If only she could find—

"Here it is." Kia held up the pill bottle in her hands. "Vicodin. It won't be as good as a local anesthetic, but it'll help enough."

Ian's eyes flew open, wide and dilated. "No."

"No?" Both Kia and Katelyn asked at the same time.

"No," he repeated.

Kia's head cocked to side involuntarily. "Ian, but—"

A wave of anger flashed beneath Ian's eyes, darkening them, but in a split second it was gone, and the bruised and broken face returned. "I don't want to take any painkillers."

Kia stared at Ian. He was starting to act idiotically. She looked to her sister for help, but Katelyn held up her hands and backed away. "If you're trying to be some sort of hero," she said *hero* in quotes, "then you need to stop right now. You played hero once already tonight and I think it's time to put your glasses back on."

"Ha! Like Superman!" Katelyn exclaimed from the opposite side of the room. Both Kia and Ian turned and looked at her. "What? Oh, shut up." Katelyn said and walked out.

Once she had left, Kia said, "Please, Ian. Take them. You've got to be in a lot of pain already. I really don't want to cause any more."

Ian grabbed her hand and held on with more strength than he should have had. "Listen to me very closely." He spoke slowly, as to let each word sink in. "I'm not trying to be any kind of hero. I've been sober for one year and if I took...I just can't." His voice was so sad, almost like he thought he was a disappointment, and Kia hated anyone who had ever made him think he was.

"I'm so stupid," she said, almost in a whisper. "I didn't even think. I'm so sorry."

"Don't be. It was my fault." He let go of her hand and closed his eyes. "Now, let's get this show on the road, doc."

It took a lot for Ian to say no to her for anything, even more, to say no to what she was offering him. The truth was, each day was a battle. No one

140

knew. Especially not Kia. She never would. If it had been up to him, he would have never told her about his...*addiction* in the first place, but it wasn't up to him. Somehow, she had wiggled her way into his secret, into the thing he keeps hidden from everyone. His past. He couldn't change the fact that she knew, but he didn't have to talk about it.

Ian hissed as he felt an ice-cold liquid hit his skin. The smell of rubbing alcohol filled his nostrils as Kia poured it over his side. He arched his back off the table as she poured again and felt the alcohol curl around his body and pool underneath his lower back.

Ian closed his eyes again. Maybe if they were closed it would hurt less.

Probably not.

Definitely not.

He felt someone beside him and peeked out from under his lashes to find that Katelyn had come back in the room. She was shooting daggers at her sister, apparently trying to communicate her disapproval wordlessly. Kia's back was turned so she couldn't see, but Ian smiled, nonetheless.

When Kia turned back around, she was holding a needle that was curved slightly. She sat down on a stool next to him, and Ian's muscles involuntarily contracted at the thought of it piercing his skin.

He looked at her and noticed that her hand was shaking slightly. He grabbed her gently. "It's okay," he whispered. "I trust you."

She took a deep breath, and Ian clenched his eyes closed.

The needle piercing him was nothing he hadn't felt before, but it still took his breath away. It was bearable only for that second in between each stitch where his mind said, *one more, make it through one more.*

But Kia had just started.

Katelyn was beside them, mopping up the blood that Ian felt trickle down his side and onto the table.

One more.

"How did you learn how to do this?" Ian said through clenched teeth.

"Uh, what?" Kia asked.

One more. "Kid, you're shoving a needle into my skin repeatedly without any kind of medicine. Throw a guy a bone and distract me."

She paused for a second before continuing the assault on his flesh. "Well, our mom was always adamant about us knowing first aid, like super crazy about it. *You need to know how to heal someone when they get hurt.*" Kia's tone dropped a little deeper, in what Ian assumed was an imitation of her mother's. He had never heard Marie's voice before, so he wondered how close her imitation was to the real thing. By Katelyn's laugh, he guessed it was spot on.

"She taught us all kinds of things," Kia continued. "We were suturing bananas by our tenth birthdays."

"Sounds very..." Ian winced, "educational."

"It was mostly, but I don't know if I plan to become a doctor so I'm not sure why I need to know the exact place of the carotid artery or how it connects to other vessels." Ian could feel her arms rise slightly in a shrug.

"It's coming in handy today."

Ian felt her tie off one more. "All done."

"Thank God," said Ian as he laid his head back and let the darkness take him.

"No, no, no," Kia said as she gently cupped Ian's face. "No sleeping."

Ian's eyes fluttered open. "But, *puh-lease,*" he whined mockingly.

Kia smiled at this playful Ian, who by all accounts should be crying in pain. "I'm so sorry to have to do this," she said, helping him sit up. "But I think I need to take you home."

Ian grunted, and she hurried to explain. "My mom's been kind of inquisitive lately. I don't want to have to explain a half-naked boy, who's been beaten up, and why he's sleeping in my bed."

"I could put on a shirt," Ian answered.

"There's no need for that," Katelyn said in the background.

Kia and Ian both looked over at her, but while Kia was gaping at her sister's word vomit, Ian said, "Her, I like."

Kia shook her head and said, "I think it would be best if I took you back to your house."

Ian nodded and, with the help of Kia and her sister, eased himself off the counter. He needed their help to walk, but Kia wasn't having to prop his whole body up on her like she was before.

They got into the car with no problem, but as Ian's eyes started to close once more, she realized she had no idea where he lived. "Um, Ian," she said as she pulled out of her driveway. "Which way to your house?"

His eyes fluttered open. He didn't say anything but raised his hand and pointed to the right. And that's how the entire car ride went. Ian pointed, and Kia turned. She didn't try to talk to him, although she wanted desperately to do so. She wanted to ask him what that was all about in the cemetery. How did that guy know they were Soulwalkers? Would he come after them again? But she kept her mouth shut and followed his pointing.

When they finally pulled up at his apartment complex, Ian said, "I'm on the top floor."

Kia looked up at the concrete steps, winding back and forth several times before stopping at the third story. She sighed as she got out of the car. She was going to have to help Ian up the whole way.

She wrapped an arm around him as he got out of the car, careful not to touch his bruises or stitches. She was fully aware of each move they made and her arm as it slid over the hardened muscles of Ian's back.

"I don't know about you, but I want a shower," Ian said as he pulled out his keys when they reached the top of the landing.

Kia smiled. They were both covered in sweat from the ascent, and Ian was covered in dirt and grime from his tumble across the cemetery floor. A shower sounded nice. But as Ian opened the door, Kia's mind went into a panic. She didn't know if he lived alone. What if he had a roommate? Or what if this was his parent's house? Why had he never mentioned where he lived before? Her concerns tumbled out of her mouth. "Do you have a roommate? Is this your parent's house?"

Ian paused opening the door. A crack of light spilled out from the opening and illuminated his face. His jaw was clenched, and his nostrils flared with each breath. "No." He pushed the door open the rest of the way and went in, holding himself up for support on the entryway wall.

Kia followed, shutting the door behind her and looked around Ian's home. Strewn across the living room were all kinds of workout equipment. Weight machines, punching dummies, a strange wooden thing. There wasn't anything in the room that said *living room*. No couch or chair. He had a television, but it was pushed to the corner, and Kia couldn't tell if it was even plugged in or not. She wondered briefly how he had gotten all the equipment up the three flights of stairs. "Um, work out much?" Kia said mockingly.

Ian was standing at the refrigerator drinking water out of a jug. He wiped his mouth with the back of his hand. "No. Those are for show. I look this sexy naturally."

Kia's eyes flickered involuntarily to his sculpted stomach. She looked away quickly, but he already saw. Her face grew hot as his grin grew wider.

Ian walked over to her and put his hand on her face. It was warm against her. Out of the corner of her eye, she saw dried blood on his knuckles. "I—I should probably go now," she said, feeling a little bit uncomfortable at his proximity. Her heart beat faster.

Ian's hand dropped, and he backed up immediately, a concerned look on his face. "There's no way in hell you're going anywhere."

Kia was taken aback at his answer. "Excuse me?"

His concerned look quickly shifted to anger. "Could you be any more naive?" Kia winced at his harshness, but he continued. "We were attacked by some crazy man, and you want to go out in the dark, by yourself? Like I said, there's no way in hell."

He grabbed her arm, and Kia was surprised to see he still had so much strength in his grip. He pulled her into his bedroom, where he sat her on the bed. "You. Sit. Don't move." He stormed off into the bathroom that was attached to his room and slammed the door behind him.

Kia heard the shower start running and sighed. Guess she would be staying there. She pulled her cellphone out of her pocket and sent a quick text to Katelyn telling her so. She looked down at her jeans, dirty and ripped from her fall, then over at Ian's closet. She smiled and walked over to it, opening the doors.

Inside, she expected to see an arsenal of V-neck t-shirts, but Ian had a full wardrobe inside. Most of the stuff she had never seen him wear. She flipped through a couple of things, recognizing the suit that Ian had worn to the party at the Network's office. On a shelf above his hanging clothes were a couple of plain shirts. She pulled one down and quickly took off her shirt and slipped it over her head. It covered her to her mid-thigh, so she peeled her pants off as well.

Not knowing what to do with her dirty clothes, she walked over to the side of the bed and put them in a neat pile next to a box on the floor. Kia hesitated for a moment, looking at the box. Being inside Ian's apartment was an opportunity to glimpse into his life, one that she wouldn't get even if she asked him for answers. The water was still running in the shower. Feeling a little guilty, she opened the box and looked inside.

There didn't seem to be much in it. Some papers, a trophy. But then, Kia found a stack of photos and started looking through them. They were obviously pictures of Ian from when he was younger. He stood next to a man, both in martial arts robes. The older man had a black belt around his waist, and Ian had on a brown one. In his hand, he was holding a black belt and a huge grin stretched across his face.

"What are you doing?"

Kia's head whipped around and some of the photos fell out of her hand. She didn't hear the water stop or Ian come out of the bathroom, but there he was standing in front of her, with just a towel around his waist.

The scar along his chest stood out bright, so red next to the paleness of his skin. Kia again fought the urge to ask him about it.

Ian bent down to pick up one of the photos and immediately froze. "Where did you get this?" His voice was hard.

"They were in that box," Kia answered. She stood up and backed away, pulling at the hem of the shirt as she did.

"You shouldn't have done that." Ian picked up all the photos and gently laid them back in the box, closing the lid. Once he finished, he walked past her into the living room, running a hand through his hair as he did.

Kia followed him out. "I'm sorry?" She didn't mean it to come out as a question, it just had.

Ian turned around and faced her. Fury shown on his face, and it was as if a storm brewed in his eyes. "You can't go through people's things, touching things that aren't yours!"

Anger boiled up in Kia as his voice grew louder. Her not touch his things? She remembered back to that week she had laid in bed sick. Flashes of Ian rifling through her things, touching everything in sight. Then an image of him caressing her face popped up in her mind and her face grew hot in embarrassment. She said the first thing she could think of. "You're always touching things that aren't yours!"

The anger washed from his face, the storm quieted, replaced with no expression at all. He took a step back. "Oh," he said. "Oh, I see."

It was plain to her what he thought. That *she* was the thing he shouldn't touch.

"No, no that's not—" she tried to explain, but he cut her off.

"Well, you can rest assured that won't ever happen again." He turned on his heel and walked back into his bedroom, closing the door with an eerie calm behind him.

Kia stared at the closed door, open-mouthed. Ian's moods changed so quickly. She couldn't keep up anymore. "Fine! I'll just go!" She screamed at the door. She made it halfway to the front door before tears started running down her face and another two steps before she realized her keys were in Ian's room...in her pants.

She sat down on the floor next to the front door and let her tears fall freely. She was so tired. Tired of this constant fighting and making up with Ian, of training, of thinking about how short her life had become, of not knowing whether what happened in a Walk was going to kill her, of people attacking her.

She was tired of it all.

16

WHEN KIA WOKE, she was no longer on the floor. She looked up to see Ian eyes glowing in the moonlight. He was carrying her from the living room into the bedroom. He must not have noticed that she was awake, because he didn't say anything. And really, she was too tired to say anything either, so she let him silently carry her.

As he laid her down on the bed, he noticed her eyes open and sat down next to her at the foot of the bed. "I'm sorry, I didn't mean to wake you," he said. His voice was gentle and void of any of the anger it held earlier.

Kia sat up, pulling the covers around her. "It's okay," she mumbled, trying to rid her voice of its just-woke-up-grogginess. "I'm sorry. I didn't mean to fall asleep. I know you wanted me to leave."

Ian's hands came up and cupped her face. "Kia, listen to me. This is very important." When she didn't pull away, he continued. "What I said earlier, I didn't mean it. You have to know that. I would never let anything happen to you."

She stared into his eyes and found nothing but truth in them. No quip. No smoke and mirrors. Only Ian. "I know," she answered. "But that doesn't mean you're not a jackass."

He let go of her face and bowed his head in shame. "God, I know. My mom always said I needed to learn more manners. I kicked a clown once, you know?"

Kia didn't know whether it was because she was half asleep, or if she didn't feel like listening to Ian ramble on about clowns, but she put her hand on his chest cutting him off. "Ian. Shut up." Grabbing him by the shirt, she pulled him forward and pressed her lips to his.

He didn't respond at first. Maybe he was too shocked, but Kia pressed harder, coaxing his lips to open. It didn't take long. In an instant, his lips were moving in rhythm with hers. His hands slid around to the small of her back, pulling her up onto her knees.

Through Ian's paper-thin shirt she could feel his heart beating faster and faster, and she felt hers speeding up as well.

She wanted to forget everything. The gunshot. The magic. The cemetery. And most of all, all the injuries that he had sustained for her. She let herself forget, only for the moment and kissed him. She reached her hands up and tangled them in his still-damp hair. It was getting long, past his ears.

Ian's mouth moved from her lips to her cheek, her ear, her neck, while his hands pressed harder and harder into her back, bringing them closer and closer together. The faint stubble on his face brushed the soft skin of her neck, sending electric jolts through her body.

Pressing her tightly against him, Ian pulled her to the head of the bed, laying her down. He held his body inches above hers. As he pulled back and looked into her eyes, she saw his were burning with an icy fire.

In an answer to the unspoken question in his eyes, she pulled his face back to hers and kissed him again. Moving her hands from his hair, she reached down, pulling his shirt over his head, her hand sliding across the hardened surface of his stomach.

He lifted himself to help her. She felt like his shirt wouldn't come off fast enough, but in her haste, she accidentally raked her fingers across his recently stitched side.

Ian gasped in pain and quickly pulled away from Kia, and sat up, letting his shirt slide back down his torso. He sat there and let his heavy breathing return to normal.

Kia stared in horror. "I'm *so* sorry, Ian. I just...forgot." She sighed because she knew the moment was over, and she wanted to get it back.

"Don't be sorry," he whispered.

She reached for the hem of his shirt again, wanting to check the stitches. "Let me see."

Ian obliged, pulling his shirt the rest of the way off. He scooted closer to her and she bent down to look at the wound. None of the stitches had come apart, but it was bleeding slightly. She needed to bandage it up anyways.

She walked over to her bag that held the medical supplies she brought over. "That was stupid of you, you know?"

He cocked an eyebrow at her. "You didn't seem to mind."

Kia retrieved the biggest bandage she had and started applying it to Ian's side, keeping her head down so he didn't see her flushed face. He was right. She didn't mind at all.

When she was finished, she left her hand resting on his stomach, and he put his hand over hers. "I meant carrying me into your room. You could have easily ripped this open again."

"Can't a man make a romantic gesture anymore?" He pulled her back onto the bed and wrapped his arms around her as she laid her head on his chest.

She listened for a few heartbeats before answering. "Not if it means bleeding to death."

"I'll keep that in mind for next time." His voice had that half-asleep tone that meant he was minutes away from sleep.

"Next time?"

He gave her a quick kiss on the forehead before saying, "Next time. Now get some sleep, kid."

But Kia couldn't sleep. Every time she closed her eyes, she saw the bloody face of the man from the cemetery. The images of what happened in the cemetery replayed over and over in her head. She pushed the blood and torn flesh from her mind.

Ian still had his shirt off, so she lightly traced the edges of the bruising on his side, wishing that they weren't there.

Suddenly, exhaustion wore over her, and she too was asleep.

A beep from Kia's cell phone woke her up.

The sun was streaming in from the only window in Ian's room. From the angle of the light on the carpet, it was probably late morning.

Kia laid on her side, with Ian's strong arm wrapped around her. His chest rose and fell slowly behind her.

Gently, as to not wake Ian, she reached out and grabbed her cell phone. She was right, it was late morning. Ten-thirty, to be exact.

"Oh, crap," she said, springing out of bed.

Ian shot up and grabbed something off the bedside table. He searched around the room with anxious eyes before landing them on Kia. "God, Kia. You scared the shit out of me." He brought his hand up and wiped hair out of his face with the back of his hand. In his hand was a knife. A really big one.

The blade looked to be eight inches long, with the tip slightly curved. The hilt was a beautiful red-colored wood that stretched out and swirled around an emerald the size of a nickel. The sun shone off the blade and Kia saw words engraved where the blade met the hilt. It was the blade that Ian had in the cemetery.

She was mesmerized by it, how it was beautiful and deadly at the same, sort of like Ian.

"What's wrong, kid?" He asked.

Remembering the reason she had shot out of bed the first place, she said, "Look at the time. I've already missed half the school day!"

Ian sat back down on the bed, laying the dagger aside. "That's the reason you jumped out of bed? Because you're missing school?"

"Yes! I've already missed so much. I can't miss much more, or they won't let me graduate."

"What's one more day?" He patted the spot next to him on the bed. "Come see."

She sat on the bed next to him, and he pulled her into his lap. Ever since last night, it was like Ian didn't want to let Kia go. She didn't mind, because she didn't want to let him go either.

She was starting to realize that as a Soulwalker, you had to take chances because life was short. And as a human, you had to take chances, because life was cruel.

She reached up and stroked the now blue-black skin around Ian's eye. She put her lips to the blackened edge and slowly traced her lips down his face. To his cheek. His jawline. His neck. Pushing him back onto the bed, she continued her pathway of kisses down onto his chest, following the line of bruises, touching each one lighter than the last.

Beneath her, Ian's breath grew heavier, his chest moving rapidly. When she got to his ribs, something was wrong. Where last night there had been large purple bruises up and down the side of Ian's stomach, there was now pale, unblemished skin.

"Ian..." Kia said. He could feel her hot breath on the skin of his stomach.

"Hmmm?"

"Your bruises..."

Ian sat up, sensing that whatever it was that had prompted Kia to show affection had passed. It was so strange. The girl was so obviously devoted to her sister, and clearly had some feelings for him, but she hardly ever initiated any sign of affection. Not a kiss, or a touch. He had never even seen her hug her sister. But then last night....

Maybe it was the knight in shining armor bit. Although, typically knights in shining armor don't go home looking as beat up as him. "Am I very badly disfigured?" He joked.

"No." She paused, taking a breath. "They're gone. Completely gone." She had her hand on his stomach, tracing imaginary bruises because the ones that had been there were indeed gone.

He looked down at his side and then up to Kia's face. His own bewilderment was mirrored on hers. Her brow furrowed. Her eyes squinted.

"I don't think your death glare is going to make them come back." He laughed. God, she looked cute in the morning.

She rolled her eyes at him. "This isn't possible Ian. They were here, and now they're not."

"That happens with my keys all the time."

In response, she pushed him up and dragged him into the bathroom, facing him toward the mirror. "You see, this is what the bruises on your stomach should have looked like this morning."

She pointed to the bruises on his face. Ian winced at the sight. His left eye was black, his lip swollen, and all down the side of his face were small scrapes and bruises. But where that jackass had kicked and kicked him was nothing. Not a scrape. Not a bruise. The only thing that remained was the laceration from the tomb that Kia had stitched up, and even that looked slightly better.

He looked closer in the mirror, again not believing what he was seeing. To test it out, he poked his ribs. And nothing. Last night he could barely breathe and now this? Something was definitely wrong. Or right?

"Did you summon the healing fairy last night?" Ian kept poking his ribs, thinking that maybe he would feel a crippling pain any second.

"I thought you said fairies don't exist?" Kia asked, with a note of panic in her voice.

He turned around to face her, grabbing her hands in his. "Of course, they don't."

"Oh. Good." She looked up at him and gave him a quick kiss. It was as if something had changed for her. Something had changed for him, of course. *She* had kissed *him*. Not the other way around. She kissed him!

Now he couldn't go back. He couldn't sit idly by anymore and hope that this girl would figure her feelings out before the worst happened. Okay, maybe he didn't sit *so* idly by, but it was too idle for his liking. Soulwalkers being taken. The man in the cemetery. It was all too much to ignore. Maybe it was a sign from whatever god was up there. Maybe he was saying *Yo,*

Ian. Look at what's happening. Don't be a pussy. He only hoped that God said things like yo and pussy.

"What do you think happened?" Kia said. She still had her eyes on his bruiseless side.

"I don't know. But we better let Samson know about the guy in the cemetery."

"He wasn't some crazy mugger, was he?"

Ian sighed. He knew he would have to tell her eventually. "No, kid. That guy. He was there for one of us."

And then he told her. He told her about the meeting that she wasn't invited to. How Samson and Eugene wanted to experiment with her abilities. The Soulwalkers from the other districts going missing. The check-ins.

"Shit, I missed the check-in." Ian walked over to where he had left his phone. "Samson probably called about fifty times." Sure enough. He had seventeen missed calls on his phone, all from Samson and Eugene.

"I didn't fare too much better myself." Kia held up her phone. "The text that woke me up was from Katelyn. 'In case you're wondering," she read off the screen, "today isn't a national holiday. We still have school, but don't worry, I got a ride.'"

Ian had to go to the Network offices, and he didn't want Kia to be there. Not with Samson and Eugene wanting to *see it for themselves.* "Maybe you should go to school today."

"Change your mind about spending the day with me?" A mischievous smile formed on Kia's lips.

Ian returned the smile with one of his own. "Nope. I just don't want you getting stupid."

It was times like these that Kia was thankful that she carried an extra school uniform in her Jeep. She started doing it after she spilled coffee all down her shirt on the way to school and was forced to wear the coffee-stained shirt and skirt the entire day. But never again, she vowed. So now, tucked neatly under one of the seats was a clean uniform that she would be able to put on before getting to school.

Ian insisted on driving her to school *and* picking her up. Since they had left his car by the cemetery the night before, Ian would have to take her Jeep anyway to pick it up. The whole way he kept one hand on the wheel, but the other he had reached across the center console and entwined his fingers in the back of her hair, absentmindedly playing with her ponytail.

Every touch sent electric jolts through her body causing goose bumps to rise on her arms.

"I'll see you right here after school okay, kid?" Ian said as they pulled up next to the front office. Kia would have to go in there to get a late pass into class.

"Yes, sir." Kia hopped out of the Jeep and walked toward the building. About halfway there she realized that maybe she should have kissed Ian goodbye before she got out. That is what girlfriends did. Was she his girlfriend? She didn't know, but she was something *more.* The classification of their relationship was yet to be discovered.

The school day was amazingly easy considering she was only there for one period, although it was economics, which bored Kia to death. Ian was outside the school as promised when Kia and Katelyn walked out. Katelyn had said nothing more about her skipping the beginning of school or sleeping over at Ian's. Nor did she comment on how Ian—now back in his Prius—was picking them up. Good sister.

"I have to go back to The Network offices," he said as they pulled up to her house.

Katelyn took her cue and got out of the car and headed inside.

"Is everything okay?" Kia asked.

"Yes, only a slap on the wrist for not checking in last night. But I think this," he gestured toward his bruised face, "explained it well enough." He paused. "Do me a favor?"

Kia nodded.

"Do not leave the house, no matter what." Kia opened her mouth to reply, but he went on. "And don't do that thing you like to do and not listen to me, please."

She didn't like the thought of being imprisoned in her own home but considering there was a psycho-Soulwalker-napper on the loose, she would do it. She leaned over and kissed him. "I won't," she said and got out of the car.

It didn't take long after Kia walked in the front door for Katelyn to pounce on her with questions. "You better tell me everything. Now." Or demands.

"Well..." Kia pulled out her ponytail and scratched the back of her head. "We went to St. Louis number one and this guy...jumped us."

"You were in the cemetery? At night? Serves you right. I'm surprised you two are even alive."

Kia was surprised herself. "So, Ian is kind of a badass fighter."

Katelyn stared at her in mock exasperation. "Um, obviously. Have you seen the boy? He's jacked."

"He doesn't look like a fighter. He's...lean."

"Fine. Use whatever adjective you want to use for his muscles. But the fact remains." She paused. "Ian saved your life last night, didn't he?"

"Yeah," Kia said, remembering how Ian told her to run. How he was going to sacrifice himself to keep her safe. "He did."

Kia's phone rang, saving her from answering any other questions. This way, she would let Katelyn believe that guy in the cemetery was just another crazy. Another lie to add to the list.

"Who is it?" Katelyn asked.

Kia looked down at the caller I.D. "It's Riley."

"Well, go on. Answer it."

Kia got up and walked out of the room before answering, and she heard Katelyn give an unnaturally loud sigh. "Hello."

"Hello? Kia?"

"Riley. Hi, how are you?" She sat down on the couch in the formal living room. It was a room they hardly ever used. In fact, she didn't remember the last time they used it since before her dad had left.

"I'm good." He paused, and Kia waited for him to continue. "So...are we still on for tonight?"

"Tonight?" Kia racked her brain for what they were supposed to be doing, and then she remembered. *Oh crap, the date.* "Oh right...umm..."

"I mean, if you don't want to. I totally understand—"

"No...yeah... of course." What had she gotten herself into? She had basically called herself Ian's girlfriend, and now she was going on a date with Riley. She knew she didn't have any feelings for him, regardless of how much Katelyn teased her about "having two boys." But she still needed to know if any of the other Soulwalkers had gotten in contact with Riley. He was clearly a Soulwalker and he needed to know. *I mean, what else could it be?*

"Oh, good. I'll pick you up at seven?"

"Actually, do you mind if I meet you there?" *Then it won't feel so date-ish*, she added silently.

"Oh, yeah sure."

They discussed a couple of different restaurants but finally decided on one of the seafood places in town.

She ran up the stairs to go get ready and hoped that Ian wouldn't call or show up at her house randomly while she was gone. So much for her promise to not leave the house.

✦✦✦

Kia pulled into the restaurant parking lot right at seven o'clock and instantly felt that Riley was there. The connection between them ebbed and flowed, still not as strong as the ones with other Soulwalkers. From across the parking lot, she saw his head snap up as he stood next to his truck. Apparently, he felt her too.

Riley met her at her car, a lone red rose in his hand. He looked great. His jeans had been swapped for slacks and his shirt for a button down. His hair was so short that there wasn't much he could do with it to make it look different. It didn't matter, he still looked polished. It made Kia feel bad for not trying harder, but she had to remind herself that she shouldn't try hard. She didn't need to impress Riley. Not when she had Ian waiting for her.

At the table, Riley pulled the chair out for Kia, which made her giggle. No one had ever done that for her before. Her past boyfriends were growing worse and worse by the second.

Stop thinking about him like that! She screamed inwardly. This so-called date was for business purposes only. But, a voice in the back of her mind asked her how long the business portion of the evening would last.

"How was the rest of your evening last night?" Riley asked.

Unfortunately for Riley, the waitress had sat down a glass of water which Kia had eagerly drunk. But at the thought of answering Riley's question she had spewed the water out of her mouth, all over the front of his spotless polo. "Oh my gosh! I'm so sorry!"

Riley laughed and dabbed at his shirt and face with his napkin. "It's alright. No big deal, promise."

"I can't believe I just did that. I'm so embarrassed."

"It makes for an interesting first date."

She needed to tell him that she wasn't there for a date. "Look, Riley," she began.

But he cut her off, "Kia, it's okay. I promise. I won't melt." He looked down at his napkin. "Though I can't say the same for this."

Riley's napkin was pretty much done for, so Kia got up to go track down the waitress to get another. "At least let me get you another one."

Kia spotted their waitress across the room and started navigating her way through the tables. The food at the restaurant was great, but they liked to pack the people in like cattle.

Kia sucked her stomach in as much as she could to try and squeeze through the space between the tables, but she ended up hitting about every other person.

Before she reached the waitress, Kia stumbled through one particularly tight squeeze and a man sitting at the table stuck his hand out for her to catch before she fell.

She grabbed his hand...

She was on a playground, staring at a group of boys around twelve years old. They stood in a semi-circle around her, they're arms crossed on their chests, scowls on their faces.

"I thought I told you to never talk to my sister again," the one who was clearly the leader said.

"I—I didn't." The words stumbled out of her mouth, but the voice wasn't hers.

"That's not what I heard. And because you disobeyed me, you'll have to pay."

Kia didn't have to look. She knew that although the boy in front of her had four other guys to back him up, she didn't have anyone standing behind her.

Then she was in a living room, feeling younger than she was before. In front of her was an enormous Christmas tree, piles of presents underneath.

And then a man stood in front of her, a terrified look on his face. The front of his pants was wet, and he was pleading. Pleading for his life.

In front of her, a gun appeared, and she realized it was her that was holding it.

Then she pulled the trigger.

Kia shut her eyes, hoping that the screaming would go away. It didn't. She then realized that it wasn't a man's screams but a woman's. When she opened her eyes, it was herself sitting in front of her. It was her that was screaming.

17

KIA PULLED HERSELF out of the Walk. She could feel the tears starting to spill over the side of her eyes. She had to get away.

In her hand, she still held the hand of the man she Walked. The man who would, sometime in the future, do something to her to cause her to be as terrified as she saw herself in the Walk. She looked up into the eyes that had haunted her dreams the night before. Into the eyes of the man from the cemetery.

The cut that Ian had made on the man's face was gone, only a faint pink scar remained. But it was unmistakably him.

"Hello, Kia." His voice came out like slime, and Kia struggled to pull her hand away from his. "My name is Cyrus."

"Let go," she hissed.

A cruel smile played on his lips. "Don't make a scene, darling. I'm not here for you, only for dinner. Although, it is quite a coincidence that you're here. Where is your boyfriend?" Cyrus looked around the room, scanning the faces of the crowd. "Not here? No problem. You two proved to be rather troublesome last night. But don't fret, I got someone else instead, a smaller, less...hostile Soulwalker." He pulled her hand up to her mouth and kissed it before releasing it. "Now, go enjoy your dinner."

Kia watched, stunned, as he got up from the table, leaving a hundred-dollar bill behind, and walked out of the restaurant.

Someone else? Because he didn't succeed in taking Kia and Ian, he had to get someone else? The faces of the other Soulwalker in the city flashed before her eyes. Who could it have been? Samson? Eugene? Ian?

Could he have gone after Ian this evening while she was having dinner with another guy? *Oh my god, Ian!*

She took a breath, calming herself. He said he had to take someone else because he didn't get Ian. So of course, he doesn't have him.

Someone smaller.

Little Ellie? As soon as she thought it, she knew. That was who Cyrus had. Ellie.

Before she knew what she was doing, she was running back to the table to grab her things. She had to go after him.

"I'm so sorry Riley, but something...came up. I have to go." Grabbing her purse from the chair, she turned and ran out the door. Out of the corner of her eye, she saw Riley stand, a bewildered look on his face.

She turned her keys in the ignition, and hastily backed out of her parking spot, determined not to lose sight of Cyrus in his car. He was driving a red Audi coup, so it wasn't too hard to keep her eye on it.

She tried not to follow too close, but once or twice she had to run a red light to keep from losing him. When he pulled onto the causeway over Lake Pontchartrain, she knew it was going to be a long night. The bridge stretched across the lake that bordered New Orleans to the North and measured almost 24 miles long. There was no way off once you got on. And that was exactly where Kia decided that she was doing the stupidest thing possible.

What was she thinking? Driving like a maniac after a man who was a psycho-killer. She had seen him kill someone, and for all she knew, she could be next.

Realizing exactly how stupid she had been, she fished through her purse for her phone. She dug her hand around every inch of the purse but couldn't find it. She cursed to herself. She must have left it on the table.

Now she was following a killer. Without a phone.

"Great. Just great."

She continued down the causeway, keeping the red Audi in her view. She didn't have anything else to do but follow him. She had to finish the mission she started.

"Mission? You call this a mission?" She grunted and threw her hands in the air. "And now you're talking to yourself."

Kia fell silent, looking out over the blackened water around her. The bridge drummed beneath her tires, lulling her into a tired state, so much so that she almost missed the turn the red Audi made at the end of the bridge.

Jerking herself awake, she followed Cyrus as he turned onto another street, this one smaller and darker than the last. Afraid that he would notice her behind him, she turned her headlights off and slowed down to keep a safe distance.

They continued down the road, and Kia's heart started to beat faster as the houses became more spread apart and the trees became thicker and thicker. After what seemed like forever, Cyrus finally turned off the road onto a winding drive.

This was as far as she would go. She had at least enough common sense to not go charging into the house and try to save Ellie all by herself. She would find a way to call Ian and make him go with her.

Turning around at the end of the road, she started the long drive back to the city.

"Come on. Pick up. Pick up!" Kia pressed her body against the outside wall of the gas station, turning her head slightly from the woman whose phone she had borrowed.

"Hello?" Ian's voice came through crackled.

"Ian!" Kia had dialed her house phone, the only phone number she knew by heart, but she wasn't shocked he would be there to answer.

"Kia? Where the hell are you! I've been calling your phone for the past hour!" That came through loud and clear.

"I don't really have time to explain. Listen, Cyrus has Ellie." It wasn't until Kia tasted the salt in her mouth did she realize she was crying.

The storm was growing, and the little protection the roof's overhang provided wasn't enough to keep Kia dry.

"Cyrus? Ellie? What are you talking about? You need to come home. Now."

"No! You don't understand. Cyrus—" Kia was shaking, fear rising with every word. She took a breath to steady herself. "He's the guy from the cemetery."

"Kia, I can barely hear you. It's cutting out."

"Shit," she said, lowering the phone to look at the service bars. *Called failed* flashed on the screen.

"Shit," she said again.

She handed the phone back to the woman, muttering a thank you. Pulling her jacket up over her head, Kia ran out to her car and headed back onto the causeway.

The drive home felt a lot longer than the drive there. Kia looked into her rear-view mirror every few seconds and jumped at every passing red car. She knew that Cyrus wasn't following her, he had better things to do. Like torture and kill Ellie.

"No. No," Kia said to herself. She couldn't allow herself to think that. She—they—would find a way to get her back and stop Cyrus from doing this.

She already knew that Ian was at her house, but the sight of his car in her driveway made her anxious. He never parked in her driveway.

Before getting out, Kia looked at herself in the mirror. She grunted at the girl that stared back at her. She was red and blotchy from crying, and her hair was frizzy from the rain.

Taking a deep breath, she got out and pulled her jacket over her hair, not that it would help much at this point.

She was so focused on the rain and looking down at her feet, praying that she wouldn't slip on the wet cobblestone, that she didn't see Ian until she ran right into him.

He was standing outside the side door. Simply standing there in the rain.

Kia looked up into icy eyes as Ian's strong hands clamped down around her upper arms. He didn't say anything, but a quiet fury burned in his eyes.

Before she had a chance to say something, say anything, Ian's mouth was on hers. His lips met hers with all the passion brewing in his eyes. All the things he didn't say, he told her with the way he moved his mouth on hers. In how he nipped at her bottom lip.

He pulled her toward him, and her jacket fell from around her face, letting the rain wash over her. She could taste the bitterness of the rain as it ran into her mouth and into his.

Suddenly, Ian pushed her away. "What the hell were you thinking?" He yelled over the rain. Not giving her a chance to respond, he continued, "That's right, you weren't. You never do. You just run into this and into that and never care about who you hurt along the way."

Kia looked at him and tried to figure out what had caused the shift. First, they were kissing and then... "Do I get to speak, or would you like me to leave you alone so you can continue yelling at yourself?"

Thunder boomed overhead, but Ian made no move to get out of Kia's way.

It was like they were seven years old, having a staring contest. It was Katelyn who finally interrupted the death stares.

"Are you children coming in by yourselves or do I need to drag y'all's crazy asses inside?"

Kia pushed past Ian into the mudroom, for once aptly named because of the mud that Kia was tracking all over the floor. She took off her shoes and grabbed one of the towels that Katelyn was holding in her hands. Ian ignored both of them and walked past them into the kitchen.

Katelyn called after him, "If you drip your wet hair all over the hardwood our mom will kill you!"

They could hear Ian muttering something as he came back in and grabbed the other towel, but Kia couldn't tell what he was saying.

"Sister, you want to tell me what's going on?" Katelyn asked as soon as Ian had left the room. "Because psycho-lover-boy over there showed up about an hour ago demanding to know where you were. I, of course, had no idea because ever since you've been inducted into this little society of yours, I've had no idea what's been going on with you."

Kia wanted to explain, but she didn't know what to say.

"Kia," Katelyn pleaded, her voice softer this time. "What is going on?"

Ian dried his hair off with the towel. He was waiting in the living room for Kia to come in and explain herself. She promised she wouldn't leave the house. And yet, she followed this Cyrus person to his house? How careless could she be? Look at him. He was a skilled fighter, and he still got his ass kicked last night. Who knew what would have happened to her if...

He shook the thought from his head. Little droplets of water flew from his hair and landed onto the fabric of the couch. He watched as they dried and disappeared, leaving no evidence that they were ever there.

Through their connection, he felt Kia was finally making her way to the living room.

"Well," Ian said. He left the emotions he was feeling out of his voice.

She sat down on the couch opposite Ian and let out a big sigh. Her eyes were rimmed with red. Had she been crying? "I've filled Katelyn in on what happened up until tonight."

"Oh yes, she did," Katelyn said, walking into the room behind Kia. She looked him up and down, and Ian had a feeling that Kia didn't leave anything out.

Kia pursed her mouth to the side, a now-familiar gesture that Ian liked to call, "Kia's thinking face." He waited for her to begin.

"I ran into Cyrus by pure coincidence." She sounded unsure of her words, like she was dancing around something, leaving something out.

"Did he try to hurt you?" Ian asked. He leaned forward to try to take her hand in his, but she was too far away.

160

His hand was left suspended in the air as she stared off at the wall and continued. "No. No, he wasn't mean, just...creepy. He said that because you got away last night, he had to get someone else."

Someone else? Ian didn't think that after the cut to his face, this Cyrus person would have been able to do anything except go to the hospital, but somehow, he was well enough to attack someone else and go out and about on the town. He was worse off than Ian, and even he had a hard time doing the things he did today, unless...

"He has a Warlock helping him. It's the only way he would have been able to heal so quickly."

A thought tickled the back of his mind, but Kia started talking again so he pushed it away as quickly as it came.

"How did you know that he was healed?" She asked.

"I didn't. I guessed. What else happened?"

"I—I," She began, but she didn't continue. He saw the tears in her eyes before she turned away, putting her head and her hands.

Ian looked over to Katelyn, hoping that she knew what to do. He hadn't seen Kia like this before. He could fight with girls like no other but crying ones...he didn't know how to deal. Katelyn shrugged and slowly backed out of the living room.

Kia was sobbing softly, her head still in her hands. He got up and crossed the room in two short strides and sat down next to her. He didn't know what to say—which seemed to be a first—so he sat next to her and pulled her close.

He let her cry for a good while, brushing the back of her hair with his hand. It was nice like that. Neither one of them talking. Yes, he was worried about her, worried that at any moment, in any Walk, something would happen to her. He'd kept his heart cut off and cold for so long, and now he was finally starting to warm up, finally starting to feel like he belonged. It was hard to show her who he was capable of being, who his father knew he could be, bits of his anger would show through. But she...she was doing everything.

Finally, she looked up at him and wiped her eyes and took a deep breath.

"Ready?" He whispered.

A lone tear ran down her face, and he wiped it away with the tip of his thumb. "Yes," she said.

Kia didn't know why she was being so emotional. Okay, that's not true. She did know why. She was whisked away into this fantastic new life, only

161

to find out that there's an expiration date, and that hers is coming up pretty quick. Also, there's the added bonus of not only being a freak among the general population, but also among the people who are supposed to be freaks right alongside her. The perks included a super-hot boyfriend, who then almost gets beaten to death right before your eyes.

Yes, boyfriend.

No wonder her emotions are constantly up and down. At least it coincides with her relationship with Ian. Up and down. Up and down. Up—

"Kia," Ian whispered, bringing her out of her thoughts. He was still stroking her hair and face, catching the stray tears that were still escaping. "Tell me."

And so, she told him. She told him everything. About Riley, meeting him in the park, then again at her school. She told him how everyone was wrong. He was a Soulwalker. She wasn't the only one that felt the connection. He did too. She told him about their date, although she left out the word date.

All the while Ian didn't say anything. He only listened and held Kia as she stared off at the wall and rattled on, but she felt his grip getting tighter and his muscles become more rigid.

When she got to the part about Walking Cyrus, she couldn't help herself, she started crying again, unable to continue. The bullies, the cold, metal weight of the gun, and watching herself scream. It was all too much. She was terrified. She started shaking, and no matter how big of a breath she took she couldn't get enough air into her lungs. She couldn't get the words out to tell him what she had seen.

Ian picked her up from his lap and sat her on the couch next to him. He slid onto the floor in front of her and knelt. He put his hands on her face. "Kia, listen to me. This isn't you. You're better than this, better than him. Don't let him get to you."

She still couldn't catch her breath. Too much air was going in, but not enough going out.

He leaned his face toward hers, letting their foreheads touch slightly. He grabbed her hand and laid it on his chest. "Feel my breathing. Make yours match mine."

He took a deep breath and then exhaled. In and out. In and out. He never let go of her hands or moved his forehead away from hers. Slowly, her breathing started to match his.

He was right. This wasn't her. She was strong. She was always so strong. Strong when her father left. Strong when her mother was not there. Were these the things that someone would see in her Soul? Or would it be this? Crying on the floor unable to even more words. To fight.

Was she strong enough to tell Ian that Cyrus was somehow tied to her future? She wasn't sure.

Before she could stop them, the words flew from her mouth. "Walk me."

Ian's hands instantly fell from Kia's face at her request for him to Walk her. Kia knew that he wasn't taking it lightly, and neither was she, but now she couldn't take the words back even if she wanted to.

"Don't say it if you don't mean it." Ian still sat on the floor in front of her. Every muscle in his body was rigid.

"I do," she whispered.

He looked at her before speaking again, his eyes searching for any sign of regret. "I know why you're doing this, but—"

"Do you?" She interrupted. How could he possibly know why she was asking him to do this? She didn't even know herself. "I'm not trying to even the score or..." The memory of Kia watching herself scream in the Walk filled her head. Soon, she couldn't hear anything else. Not what Ian was saying, although she saw his lips moving, the tick-tick sound the fan above them always made, or the sound of the rain outside. Only her screaming. "There's something I think you need to see," she said finally.

He cocked his head to the side like a dog does when their owner talks to them. She waited for the wall that Ian always had up around him to snap back into place, but it didn't. His blue eyes were huge with wonder, and Kia wanted to see what secrets he kept behind them.

Outside, thunder boomed, and still, she waited for his answer.

"Kia, I can't control what I see in there. You know that," he said.

He hardly ever called her Kia. He always called her his nickname for her. *Kid.* At first it was kind of weird, especially after they kissed, but it gave her a connection to him that she didn't have with anyone else. She didn't want to lose that. Now, him using her full name, she knew he was serious.

He was sitting so close to her that she could smell his faintly woodsy scent, like fresh-cut cedar, and the lines of his hardened muscles were visible through his wet shirt. She involuntarily blushed. No, he couldn't control what he would see. He would see *everything.* Even things she didn't want him to see, like the tingle that his touch gave her, or where her thoughts had been concerning him one night earlier. Her face grew hot.

Luckily, Ian was being a gentleman and didn't comment on it.

"I know," she answered. "But...please."

He nodded in response. Kia slid down off the couch and sat down in front of Ian, the way they had done weeks ago during that first lesson. She put her hands out and he grabbed them.

He leaned forward and whispered into her ear, "Nothing like a stormy night to go for a little Walk." Then he kissed her, a light, sweet kiss, but it was that touch that sent him into the Walk.

Kia knew she shouldn't give in to the urge to Walk Ian simultaneously, but she couldn't help herself. She felt the pull of the Walk. The wind the hummed beneath her skin. She tried hard to resist, but with his lips pressed against hers...

The last thing she heard was the doorbell ring.

18

T HE WALK DIDN'T last long. In fact, Kia only saw maybe one or two images of Ian's. The first was rain so thick she couldn't really see, and the second, well, it looked like her face.

But it wasn't her face that was troubling Kia. It was the face that was staring back down at her from inside her living room.

"Riley," she whispered. "What are you doing here?" The look on his face was that of confusion, anger, and maybe a little fear, as well. She looked back over at Ian, who was coming out of his Walk. She watched as the color in his eyes slowly filled back up. Once they turned back to their normal sky-blue color, he blinked.

Riley cleared his throat, and both Kia and Ian turned to look at him.

Ian took one look and moved to pin Riley against the wall. Ian's forearm was shoved up under his chin, forcing his face upwards. "Who are you?" Ian demanded.

Kia rushed over and tried to pull Ian off Riley, but his muscles were hard as stone and she couldn't move them at all. "Ian, let go of him!"

He turned and looked at her but didn't loosen up. "You know him?"

"Yes! This is Riley!" Kia yelled, still pulling at Ian's arms. "Now let go!"

He did, and Kia stumbled back.

Riley bent over, his hands on his knees, and coughed. Kia went over and put her hand on his back. "Are you okay?"

Riley managed to cough out a "yes," but Kia was sure that his throat would be bruised tomorrow.

Ian was leaning against the other wall, his arms crossed over his chest. "So, you're Riley," he said. He gave Riley a long look up and down. "You're taller than I thought you'd be."

"Just ignore Ian," Kia said to Riley as she helped him to the couch. "He's gone temporarily insane."

"Temporarily?" Katelyn scoffed. She was standing in the doorway, an apparent witness to the events of the past few minutes. She flounced into the room, set down some glasses of water and flopped down onto the big reading chair in the corner and kicked off her heels. They clunked down to the floor. "I imagine that's Ian's reaction to any guy who's more attractive than he is." She winked in Riley's direction.

Kia saw him blush slightly, but across the room, Ian was making *huffing* noises.

Riley spoke for the first time, barely masked anger coloring his voice. "I'm sorry to come over unannounced, but you left your cell phone at dinner. Thought I'd bring it back." He pulled her cell phone out of his pocket and gave it to her.

"Thank you." She said sheepishly. 13 missed calls. Four from Katelyn and nine from Ian. She looked at Ian and mouthed *sorry*, but he ignored her and turned his gaze back toward Riley.

"So, Ry. Mind if I call you Ry?" Ian asked. Riley didn't respond, but he didn't look away either. "Okay good," Ian continued. "So, Ry, do you make it a habit of going on dates with other men's girlfriends?"

Kia nearly choked on her water, but at least this time she didn't spew it across the room.

"So, Ian," Riley said without missing a beat. "Do you make a habit of letting your women go off with other men?"

Ian looked like he was about to launch himself across the room at Riley, but Kia got up and dragged him to the kitchen instead.

"What the hell are you doing?" She hissed as soon as they were out of earshot.

"That guy?" Ian pointed toward the living room. "Really, Kia? *That* guy?"

"*That* guy is a Soulwalker, like you and me. What about *The Family*, Ian? Isn't that important to you?"

He looked shocked, then confused. "Riley isn't a Soulwalker. I've told you that. Samson has told you that. Why do you keep insisting that he is?"

"Because..." Kia felt the pulse of the connection with Riley. How could Ian not feel it too? Riley was getting up from the couch and heading toward them. Kia took the opportunity to prove it to Ian. "He's coming in here."

"What?" Ian asked.

"Riley, he's coming in the kitchen. Right..." She put her figure in the air and pointed to the doorway. "Now."

And just like that, Riley walked in, and Kia had the satisfaction of seeing the look on Ian's face. She raised her eyebrows at him. *Go ahead, challenge me*, they said.

"Kia, I think I'm going to go." Riley took a step toward her, but after taking a glance at Ian stayed where he was. "I'm sorry, but I'm not into that kind of... stuff."

Now she was confused. "What?"

He held up his hands. "I'm not judging, but I'm not into drugs."

"Drugs?" She looked at Ian who shrugged his shoulders and leaned against the counter. She wished he would stop constantly leaning against things and stand up straight like a normal person.

"Yeah, I mean, your eyes... I figured."

"Riley, we weren't doing drugs," Kia said and hoped he would believe her. "I think you should stay. There's something we need to talk—"

"Drugs, right," Ian interrupted her. "They're not for everyone, so you should probably go." He grabbed Riley's arm and started to usher him out of the kitchen.

"No, Ian! Wait!" This time she was able to pull Ian off him. "Riley, when you came in, we weren't doing drugs."

Ian clamped his hand down on Kia's upper arm and leaned into her ear. "I think we have a bit more of a pressing issue right now. In case you have forgotten."

Oh. *Oh.* She had forgotten. Cyrus was out there right now, doing God-knows-what to Ellie, and here she was trying to prove a point to Ian. But Riley was standing in front of her *right now*, and that she could deal with.

"Let me start at the beginning. First, I'm sorry for going to dinner with you under false pretenses, Riley. I should have told you about Ian," Kia began.

"Damn straight you should have," Ian said.

Kia and Riley both ignored Ian. Riley nodded.

"But you remember what we talked about yesterday at the coffee shop? About how it was like you knew where I was, even if you weren't looking?"

"Yeah..." Riley was looking more and more confused as Kia went on.

She took a step toward him. "Well I went to dinner with you because there was something that I wanted to tell you."

"Oh, here we go." Ian hopped up on the counter and settled in.

"The reason you know where I am, that you have a connection with me and with Ian is because you're a Soulwalker."

Riley looked back and forth between Kia and Ian. She could almost see his brain working through his big brown eyes. "I can't...*feel* Ian like I can you."

"Told you, kid. The dude's not a Soulwalker.," Ian said, hopping off the counter. "I'd say it was a pleasure meeting you, but it wasn't. You can go now."

Riley turned toward Kia. "Wait, wait, wait...what's a Soulwalker?"

"Goodbye, Riley," Ian said.

"Ian, be quiet!" Kia said, desperate to sort out what was going on.

Ian grabbed Kia by the arm and pulled her close. He leaned into her ear. She felt his warm breath blowing wisps of her hair. She closed her eyes and almost forgot about everything again. About Riley standing there. About Katelyn in the other room. And let herself get lost in the feel and smell of Ian. But then he spoke, "We need to call Eugene *now*."

Her eyes shot back open.

"A gentleman knows when to take his exit. I believe now is mine, but Kia," Riley said, glancing at Ian, "We'll talk about this later?"

Ian scowled, then took a step toward Riley, dragging Kia alongside him. "About time." And then he stuck his hand out to shake Riley's hand.

Kia's mouth fell to the floor.

Riley returned the gesture, and they shook hands like they were the best of friends.

"Okay, now that's weird." Katelyn said. Kia could always count on her sister to state the obvious. Katelyn grabbed a can of Dr. Pepper out of the fridge, looking questioningly at the exchange between the two men.

"Thank you, Riley," Kia said. "For the phone."

"Thank *you*," said Riley, casting Ian a smirk, "For the date."

Ian paced the room for most of the night. Sometime around three in the morning Kia stopped asking him to lie down and went to sleep. Ian couldn't sleep. He couldn't even sit down. His conversation with Eugene kept replaying in his head.

"Ian. I can assure you. Ellie is fine. She texted me her check-in hours ago," Eugene had said.

"Hours ago! Exactly!" Ian couldn't believe him. "Kia is absolutely positive that this Cyrus character has taken her tonight. And why did she text you and not Sam?"

"Ian. I need to be very clear with you." He paused, taking a breath. "Kia cannot be trusted yet."

He had hung up on his Authority then. If there was anything else that he had to say to him after that, he didn't care. He didn't want to listen.

Couldn't be trusted?

Kia rolled over in her sleep and murmured unintelligibly. She talked in her sleep. That he had learned a long time ago, but tonight her thoughts must be plaguing her more than normal, because the string of mutterings was nonstop.

He hadn't told her what Eugene had said of course. That would have had her storming across the lake to try and save Ellie herself. Hell, *he* was about to storm across the lake to try and save Ellie himself. He would have if Kia wasn't lying there across the room. He couldn't—wouldn't—leave her.

He crossed the room and sat down next to her on the bed. A stray piece of hair lay across her face and blew slightly with every breath she took. She would wake in a few hours and he would have to tell her that The Network had failed them.

19

IAN'S EYES FOLLOWED Kia as she paced at the foot of the bed. Her face turning red in frustration.

"You're telling me that we're not going anywhere?" Kia demanded.

"You're going to school." There were things that Ian needed to do. Well, mostly, he needed to talk to Eugene. There was absolutely no way he was letting Eugene near Kia after what he had said last night. Despite whatever Kia wanted the world to think, people's words hurt her, and Eugene seemed to be saying whatever came to his mind these days. So, school seemed like the best place for her.

She stopped her pacing and turned toward him full-on. Fury burned on her face. "Excuse me?"

Ian, besides not telling her about his conversation with Eugene, also hadn't yet divulged exactly what he had seen in his Walk of her. The screaming. And the blackness. The overwhelming fear. No, Kia wouldn't be going anywhere but school today. He would make sure of it.

He put his hands behind his head and leaned back against the headboard of Kia's bed. "To school. You do remember what school is right? Big, old building. Nuns. Girls in plaid skirts?"

"Yes, you idiot!" She picked up a pillow that was laying at the foot of the bed and threw it at him. Ian caught it easily and threw it back. She swatted it toward the ground. "I hate you sometimes you know," she said as she walked off toward the bathroom.

"What was that? You want me sometimes? Yes, I think I'm rather aware of that." Ian laughed as she slammed the door.

It had been nice that morning. He woke up holding her, smelling that faint lavender smell of her shampoo. *Yes, nice indeed.*

And then reality had crashed back down on him. It was easy to forget things when you're cuddled up next to a pretty girl. Not that he would tell anyone that. Of course, most of his friends had deserted him long ago, and now, even Eugene.

Kia poked her head out of the bathroom door. "Ian?" He could tell that she didn't have a top on from the little amount of skin that was showing out of the door. He let his eyes wander down and then snap back up at the sound of her voice. "What *exactly* did you tell Eugene last night?"

He cocked his head to the side at the sound of the implications in her voice as the door shut again. "What *exactly* do you mean?"

Thirty seconds later Kia walked out in her full school uniform. "It's just..." She took a deep breath and rushed her words. "I know I was doing something I shouldn't have been doing and I know you like to protect me so I thought maybe you didn't want to tell Eugene so that I possibly wouldn't get in trouble." She sighed and her shoulders went with it.

"Oh, is that all?" Ian got up off the bed and made his way toward her. Grabbing her hand, he spun her in a circle, her skirt billowing up as she turned.

She danced along with him, but her smile didn't reach her big, blue eyes. "I know I don't know Ellie all that well, but I want to help her as much as you do."

He stopped the spin as she was facing him. "I told Eugene everything. We will get her." Planting a kiss on her forehead he said, "Now, off to school. Pip, pip!"

Ian dialed Ellie's number for about the dozenth time. He wasn't stupid. If he wanted to prove to Eugene that she was gone, he could leave no stone unturned.

She hadn't answered last night or this morning when he tried calling. So now he drove as fast as he could to her house. If she wasn't there, he would head straight over to The Network offices.

Each turn toward her house and each unanswered ring of her phone diminished any hope he had. He had trusted Kia when she told him Ellie was gone, but there was a part of him that wondered *how exactly does she know that?* He asked her, but she said she didn't know how. It was a *feeling*, and something about what Cyrus had said.

It didn't make sense, but then again nothing made sense when it came to her. Not the way she reacted to a Walk, or how strange everything was surrounding her first Walk, or their relationship, for that matter.

Although, to be fair, a lot of that was his fault. He knew he acted like a complete crazy person most of the time, but he couldn't seem to stop himself.

The driveway at Ellie's house was empty, but that wasn't anything new. Mrs. Kobayashi had been working two jobs since Ellie's dad died last year and was hardly home. Ellie played babysitter to her little brother a lot, and even Ian had chipped in his time to help them out.

He got out of his car and ran up the sidewalk to the door. No one answered on the first, second, or third ring. But then again, no one would answer because everyone was at—

"School." In his rush, he had completely forgotten that even if she hadn't been taken, she'd probably be at school.

"Doesn't mean I can't still look around a bit." He pulled out the spare key that Ellie had given him a couple of months back and unlocked the front door. He didn't like to use it, but desperate times...

Everything seemed pretty much in order, but he didn't really know what he was looking for exactly. He knew he wouldn't be able to get into her room with the number of locks that she normally kept on her door, but he could still look around the rest of the house.

The Kobayashi house was small, but cozy. One wall was covered in pictures of the family. The *entire* family. Great-great-great-grandparents, probably some third cousins, twice removed. Whatever that meant. Painted on the wall behind the pictures was a giant tree—a family tree. Each picture was hung on a branch.

Spread across the living room was evidence of Ellie's genius. An advanced math book, electronics half-put back together, her backpack filled to the brim with even more—

Her backpack?

If, by chance, she was at school, then why would her backpack be here?

Down the hall, a door creaked open very slowly. Ian turned, expecting to see Cyrus dragging an unconscious Ellie down the hall but, to his relief, it was Ellie's little brother.

"Ian?" He whispered. The boy was still in his pajamas and held a stuffed bunny in his hands.

Ian walked up to him and squatted down in front of him. "Joseph, why aren't you at school?"

His hands turned white from clutching the bunny so tight. "Ellie never came home last night."

"You know what I would like to know?" Katelyn asked.

"Why schools can't seem to produce proper food?" Kia threw down her French fry. "This is an insult to fries everywhere."

Katelyn picked up the fry Kia threw down and popped it into her mouth, picking up the conversation as if Kia hadn't spoken at all. "Why exactly can't this school seem to keep a substitute? Seriously, it's like the curse of the Defense Against the Dark Arts teacher."

Kia looked at her sister who was now studiously mixing her ketchup and ranch dip together. "You're so strange."

"Whatever." Katelyn turned to their friend sitting at the table with them. "Sarah tell her."

Sarah opened her mouth but closed it again to finish chewing her food. "There's *another* new sub in French today, and," she looked around to see if anyone was listening, as if whatever she was about to say was a secret, "it's a man!"

Kia wondered why it was such a big deal. "We do have other guy teachers here, you know. In fact, we had one last period."

Katelyn cut off Sarah before she could say anything. "Well, not like this one. He's...*very* pretty."

Kia didn't seem to have an appetite at all so pushed her tray away. "And you know this how? You don't even have French today."

"I told her *all* about him," Sarah answered, making suggestive gestures with her eyebrows. Sarah was in Kia's grade, but because she wasn't in the AP level French class, she had class at a different time.

"This is the big news of the day?" Kia had other thoughts swirling through her mind. Ellie. Ian. What The Network was going to do to help.

"Well, it's a small school," said Sarah. "So yeah."

"Noted." Kia glanced down at her watch. Lunch was almost over.

"You'll see," Katelyn said, finishing the fries off Kia's tray while dipping them in her ketchup/ranch concoction. "You've got French next."

"I'll make sure to create a solid mental image so I can tell you all about him after class."

Katelyn's eyes brightened. "Yeah, you better!"

She obviously didn't catch Kia's sarcasm.

Ian dropped Joseph off at his school before heading straight to The Network offices. Now that he had his proof, he was planning on telling Eugene exactly where he could shove it.

173

He threw open the door, expecting to find the place in disarray. Surely, they had come to their senses by now and were contacting the other Network cities for help. But no. Not one thing was out of order. Helen, their secretary smiled at him as she answered the ringing phone.

"Broussard Incorporated, how can I help you?"

Ian nodded as he walked past her into Samson's office. He would get the Finder on his side first. It would make things easier.

But it wasn't Samson sitting at his desk, or even in the comfy chairs. Instead, Eugene stood by the map on the wall. Staring, just staring.

"Ian," he said. He didn't turn to look at him, but Ian could tell that there were shadows under his eyes. It looked like he hadn't slept all night. *Serves him right.* "I expect you've come here to say, 'I told you so', but you see, you were in fact wrong. It wasn't Ellie that was taken. It was Samson."

"Samson?" That didn't make sense. He had confirmed that Ellie hadn't come home last night. She was a good kid. She always came home. "*You* must be mistaken." He tried to keep his voice even. He didn't want Eugene to think that he had any doubt. *I don't have any doubt,* he told himself.

Finally, Eugene turned around and Ian realized why the Authority was keeping his back toward him. He had a black eye, as big as Ian's.

"No!" The Authority shouted. "I was there! And you would do well to not question me again!"

In the other room, he heard the receptionist stop talking mid-sentence, and for the first time in a long time, he felt embarrassed. This was not the man he knew. "And yet...here you stand." Ian shook his head. "Doing nothing."

Eugene looked taken aback. "If there was anything I could do, don't you think I'd be doing it? I don't know where they've taken him!"

Ian could feel his anger rising, it boiled hot inside of him. "So why aren't you out looking? Why has nobody been called?" He left the question he actually wanted to ask unspoken. *Why did you say we can't trust Kia?*

"I'm not a fighter." Eugene's voice was quieter. Not quite a whisper, but close. It was as if he had no more fight in him, no more energy to even say the words that he was trying to say. He was ashamed.

He walked forward and put a hand on Eugene's shoulder. "But you were once," Ian said, thinking of the trials and tests any Authority goes through to win their place.

It was almost as if the man didn't hear him. Eugene stared off, his eyes glazed over, but Ian could see the fear behind them.

"Ellie was taken as well," Ian said. "Her brother told me as much."

All the color drained from Eugene's face as he slumped down on a chair. "I don't know how to find them."

A smile pulled at the edge of Ian's mouth. "Well, I might be able to help with that."

The screaming woke Ellie up. Her neck ached from the awkward angle she had kept her head, but she couldn't help it. Her right hand was handcuffed to a metal bar that ran lengthwise across the back wall of her room—*no*—cell. Because she was being held prisoner.

The scream came again and for the hundredth time, she looked around trying to figure out some way to help. The place she was being held looked to have been used as a barn to hold animals at some point. The room she was in was a horse stall. Bits of hay still covered the floor, and it still smelled of animals. But that is not what it was used for anymore.

The screams were coming from the stall next to hers. She could hear every moan and every plea. Her spirit broke with every sound, because if *he* couldn't get away, however would she?

She knew who he was of course. She could *feel* him. The cool tingle of their connection. But it was strange, one second there was nothing...and then, there he was, like he appeared out of thin air. At first, she thought he was there to rescue her, and for hours she screamed his name. But he never came for her, instead, he stayed in the stall next to hers.

And then the bad man came. That's when the screams started.

"Tell me where she is!" Ellie heard through the walls.

But the Soulwalker next to her never broke.

"Resist all you want, but in the end, you'll be sorry," he said. Ellie cringed away from the snake-like voice. "Even more sorry than our last Finder."

Kia and her sister had their arms laced together as they walked down the hall to their last class of the day. Kia had French, and Katelyn had math, and they both couldn't wait to be finished with them. Albeit, for completely different reasons.

"I wish I could catch a glimpse of the sexy sub before class," Katelyn whispered. "Why does my class have to be at the opposite end of the building?"

"Ah yes, karma. She's a bitch."

Katelyn pulled them to a stop. "What's the karma for?"

The sisters looked at each other and burst into laughter. "I've no idea."

Katelyn leaned over and kissed her on the cheek. "See ya, big sister." She took off in the opposite direction, her long legs taking her quickly down the hall. For all the craziness that was going on in Kia's life, she could always count on Katelyn to make her laugh.

Her school wasn't large. It wouldn't take Kia very long to get to class. Then she could scope out the new sub, maybe even snap a picture to send to Katelyn before the bell rang. If she hurried, she could do it.

Kia quickly retrieved her French book from her locker and took quick, long strides without looking like she was running. The warning bell had already rung, and the other students hurrying to class were making it difficult.

When she reached her classroom, she realized word must have spread about the "sexy sub" because girls were whispering and giggling as they walked into the classroom. It was strange how one man could turn all these Ivy-league-school-bound girls into tweens at a boyband concert. She smiled at what she was sure Ian would have said to that: *Wait and see how they react when they meet me.* That boy...always so cool and confident. But long ago she had realized that it was a defense mechanism. One more way to protect himself. From what, Kia had yet to learn.

Kia sighed and stepped into the classroom, but what she saw made her stop dead in her tracks.

"Hello, Kia."

She dropped everything and ran. That is what Ian had told her to do in the graveyard. She was stupid to not do it in the restaurant, but it is what she did then. She ignored anyone who tried to stop her and ran to the opposite side of the school and ducked into a bathroom. She tried to catch her breath as she shoved the wooden doorstop under the door to keep it closed.

Cyrus. How the hell was Cyrus in her school? As her substitute? As the sexy substitute? How on earth did Katelyn even think—*Katelyn*!

She should get her out of class and get the hell out of there. Except, it's not like her teacher would let her pull her sister out of class without a reason, and it's not like she could say, *Oh, excuse me, but there's a psycho masquerading as a substitute teacher. But don't worry, he only wants me, so I need to take my sister and go.* Yeah, that would never work.

Ian would be here in a heartbeat if she called him.

She could always call him.

Should she call him?

She should call him.

Kia silently thanked the Catholic-school-girl-uniform Gods for putting pockets in her dress as she pulled out her cell phone and dialed Ian's number.

He answered on the third ring. "Shouldn't you be in class?" He asked, ignoring the conventional pleasantries.

"Ian, he's here. Cyrus is here."

Kia could almost hear the smile go out of Ian's voice. "Are you somewhere safe?"

She looked around the secluded bathroom. "Yes."

The phone rumbled as Ian let out a breath. "Stay where you are. Do not move. Understand?" He didn't wait for her to answer before he hung up.

Kia slumped down on the floor. It wasn't clean, and under normal circumstances, she wouldn't have ever sat on the floor of a public bathroom, but these weren't normal circumstances.

Kia tapped her foot on the pavement waiting for the minutes to pass. Beside her, Ian was just as impatient. He had tried to make her leave as soon as he got there, but Kia wasn't leaving without her sister. There were still five more minutes until the final bell of the day rang and Katelyn would be out of class.

Katelyn had sent Kia a text saying that she would meet her outside, that she had a few things to do as soon as she got out of class. Kia didn't want to alarm Katelyn as to what was going on, so she said "okay." Her foot-tapping wasn't doing much to relieve her stress.

Kia looked over at Ian. He was leaning against the bumper of his Prius, jiggling his leg. It was shaking the entire car. "As soon as she gets out here, we're leaving," he said, without looking over. His eyes, like Kia's, were glued to the exit of the school.

"And The Network? Have they done anything? *Are* they going to do anything?"

Ian glanced over quickly, his eyes flashing a darkened blue before he returned his gaze to the door. "They will."

Then the bell rang, and almost immediately students started pouring out the doors. Front doors, the side doors, masses of girls in plaid streaming out. It would have been difficult to tell when Katelyn came out of one of the side doors, about 50 yards down from where they were standing, if most of the students weren't already out and into their cars or buses.

"There she is," said Ian. "I'll start the car." He hopped into his Prius and started the engine, leaving the driver's side door slightly ajar.

Katelyn was talking to one of her friends, oblivious to her surroundings as always. But not Kia. She was scanning, searching faces. Looking for the one that was seared into her mind. Angular and smooth, except for the light pink scar running down the side of his face.

And then she saw him. He was only steps behind Katelyn, but his eyes were on Kia and that same cocky grin on his face.

She couldn't help it. She yelled, "Katelyn! Run!"

Katelyn looked up and for an instant their eyes met. Confusion was written all over Katelyn's face. Then, everything happened too fast.

Cyrus' gaze moved quickly from Kia to Katelyn, recognition washing over his expression. The sisters, they looked too much alike. He could see it. See it in their brown hair, in the way they moved their bodies. It was all too similar. He didn't have to move much, only a foot or two, to grab her. And he did. Ian jumped out of the car and held an iron-like grip onto Kia's arms, holding her in place. She hadn't realized she was trying to move, but of course she was. Across the parking lot, the man of her nightmares was grabbing a screaming Katelyn, doing his best to hold his hand over her mouth to quiet her.

It didn't take long for people to notice the man shoving a hysterical girl into a car, or for another man to come up beside him, lay a hand on her, and for her to go instantly silent, limp in his arms. Who was that? Kia instantly forgot his face. But no one could do anything. It was already too late.

Behind her, Ian was saying something, but Kia couldn't hear. All she could do was watch as her little sister was driven away.

Ian had already started the car; it was a small miracle. Now, Kia didn't have to wrestle the keys out of his hands. He was stronger than her and she would never make it if she had to fight him on it. She hopped in the car, closed the door, and put the car into drive. Somehow, Ian had made it into the passenger seat before she drove away.

"While I do love a good joyride now and then, driving after a crazy man isn't really my idea of fun," he said, his voice as calm as water. How did he do it? Keep up that facade when the world was crashing down around them. Couldn't he see she was breaking? Or did nothing penetrate that wall of his? When she didn't say anything, he turned toward her. "Kia, what exactly do you think you're doing?"

That was probably the stupidest question she had ever heard. It didn't even deserve an answer.

Kia's eyes scanned the traffic ahead. She knew the car she was looking for. She had followed it last night. Last night? It seemed like so long ago she had driven across the lake. But no, it was last night. Long ago was that first day back in French class. And her Walk with Madam Arson. It was the beginning of all of this...*this madness.*

A few cars ahead she spotted the red Audi. She pressed her foot down on the accelerator.

"Kia!" Ian shouted. "Do I have to yell to get your attention?"

Maybe he did.

"We can find another way." He put a hand on her shoulder, but she shrugged it off, all her focus on the car ahead. She was getting closer. "This," he gestured to her. "It's crazy!"

"No. Crazy is...is skydiving. I mean, come on, who jumps out of a perfectly good airplane?" She didn't know if he had ever been skydiving, but it sounded like something that Ian would do. "Crazy is shooting yourself up with heroin. What I'm doing is what any person would do for their sibling."

Ian's jaw hardened.

She didn't have time to think about if she hurt his feelings. All she had time to do was wish and hope that the car that was now ahead of her would stop. "Please stop!" She screamed. Ian turned and looked at her, unspoken words hanging on the tip of his tongue. She hadn't been talking to him when she had said to stop, but he must have thought so.

Suddenly and inexplicably, she felt this force pushing against her. Nothing concrete, but there was this pressure in her mind, muddling her thoughts, almost like the dull throb of a headache, but more intense. A headache was not something that she needed right now. Right now, she needed to focus on her sister and the red Audi.

Like when she had a headache, she tried to clear her mind of the pain. Slowly the pressure subsided, seeping from her head with each passing moment until it was almost—

Ian's phone started ringing, and Kia lost all her focus. The pressure rebounded tenfold and her vision started to blacken. "Ian..." She whispered, unable to produce a sound any louder. He was on the phone and didn't answer.

Kia lost focus of the red car. Lost focus of everything. Her hands slipped from the wheel just as a truck pulled out in front of them.

20

" I DON'T UNDERSTAND, why is there so much blood?" The voice sounded familiar, but Kia couldn't quite place it.

"Sir, please, you need to sit down. You should go with the other ambulance." Other ambulance? What had happened? Where was she?

Kia heard a laugh. It was pure and sweet and rolled out of his mouth as smooth as ever. *Ian.* "With the other ambulance? You actually think I'm going to leave her alone with you? Not fucking likely."

Kia heard a machine beeping, and it was getting faster. And faster.

"She's going into v-tach. Sir, you're really going to have to go."

Then nothing.

"Are you sure? We'll be breaking about a dozen different regulation rules, so if we take her there and you aren't absolutely sure..."

The beeping from the machine now was at regular intervals. Kia realized now that it was her heart that she was hearing beeping.

"I'm positive," said another voice. This one she hadn't heard before.

Where was Ian? And why could she still not see anything?

The second voice spoke again. "This is definitely Dr. Marie LaStrauss' daughter."

In the end, Ian had to be hauled away by the paramedics. In fact, he was pretty sure he gave one of them a black eye. Under normal circumstances he could have fought them off, but considering he already had a black eye himself, stitches, and scratches up and down his body, he only gave it fifty percent.

Okay, twenty-five percent.

One of the paramedics started pulling up Ian's shirt, he couldn't blame her, since he was covered in blood—Kia's, not his—but he quickly pulled it back down.

"Sir, I need to look. You're not doing yourself any good by resisting."

It was already too much being in the ambulance. He didn't know if they would admit him to the hospital, nothing had really happened to him in the accident. Granted, he looked like he had been messed up bad, but all his injuries were from his encounter with Cyrus.

"Dispatch to 317."

"317, go ahead," Ian heard the driver say through the thin window that separated them from the front seats.

"315 is heading to Ochsner. I've been told you have to proceed there as well."

"10-4."

Ochsner Medical Center was where Kia's mom worked. Smart move. Ian couldn't imagine that Dr. LaStrauss would be very happy if she found out her daughter was in another hospital across the city.

The ambulance made a sharp right turn, and everything swayed slightly to the side. It had been almost four years since Ian had been in an ambulance, which was two times too many if you asked him, and not much has changed since. Fluids hung in a bag attached to the gurney he was sitting on. Other emergency equipment was strapped to the walls, their vivid colors standing out against the white of the inside of the van.

The EMTs righted themselves after the turn, and the woman who had been talking to Ian turned back toward him. "I can give you something for the pain, if you'd like." She pointed to his face. Was it that bad? He had thought that maybe it was healing, but he guessed not.

"Look, I know you're trying to do your job and all, but I'm fine. You people should have let me stay in the other ambulance." Ian pulled his arm away from the other EMT who was trying to stick him with a needle.

The van took another turn, and this time Ian wasn't holding on to anything. He bumped into something sticking out on one of the shelves. It hit him right on his stitches in his side. It wasn't hard, but it was enough to make him cry out in pain.

The paramedics must have made some sort of silent signal to each other, because they both grabbed him and forced him to lie down. And again, he was only at twenty-five percent fighting-back ability. The male paramedic held his arm across Ian's chest pinning him down to the gurney, while the woman paramedic pulled up his shirt, exposing his stitched-up side.

Ian knew that it didn't look too bad. Kia had done a good job on the stitches, which was why he was confused at the look on the lady's face. It was somewhere between shock and pity. "I'd stare if I could see myself at that angle too," he said, still struggling against the guy holding him down. He was buff for a paramedic.

The woman's face flushed red, and Ian smiled. "Mark, can you hand me some gauze please." Still averting her eyes from Ian's, she said, "Sir, you've popped some stitches in your side here."

Mark hesitantly took his arm off Ian's chest and grabbed some gauze from behind him.

"I can stop the bleeding but you're going to need to get this restitched when we arrive at the hospital."

She finished her sentence as they stopped, and Mark opened the back doors. Before anyone had a chance to grab him again, Ian jumped out and ran over to the ambulance that Kia had come in. Doctors were standing by ready to take them.

"The patient is a 17-year-old Caucasian female with an unknown PMH, suffering from bilateral lacerations to the radial arteries and ventricular fibrillation. She was involved in an MVA 20 minutes ago..." The words flew over Ian's head as the paramedic spouted them out, but he could gather one thing: Kia was hurt bad.

He knew she had hit her head hard. Looking back, he wasn't even sure if she was wearing a seatbelt. They had gotten in the car so quickly. Did she hit the windshield? She would be okay. She had to be.

Then Kia's mom ran out of the ER doors. He knew it was her because he had seen her photo before, but more than that, the frantic look on her face was one that only a parent got when their child was hurt.

She stopped dead in her tracks as she went past him and stared Ian in the eyes. He knew who she was, but it was Marie that was looking at him like they knew each other. Like, she was shocked to see him there. But why would she be?

She had stopped for only a moment before she was off talking to the doctor who had received Kia from the paramedics. In a matter of seconds, they were pushing Kia through the ER doors, carrying their voices and diagnosis with them.

182

It was the strangest sensation that Kia was experiencing. She knew she was lying on a gurney being pushed down a hall in the hospital her mother worked at. She was fully aware of what was going on around her. She could hear everything. Feel everything. The breathing device that was over her mouth and nose. The blood that had dripped down her face that was starting to dry. The place where they had used the defibrillator on her was burning. The pressure of the bandage around her forearm. The pain.

But she couldn't move. Not her eyelids to open her eyes. Not her arms. Not her legs. Nothing. For all intents and purposes, she was paralyzed.

She wasn't scared. There was this fog over her mind keeping her from feeling any fear, or any other emotion really.

Kia thought back to what had happened to land her in the hospital, but she couldn't remember anything. The fog that blocked her emotions was also blocking her memories. All she could remember was waking up in Ian's apartment after he had been attacked by...by...she couldn't remember the name of the man that attacked him. She knew she knew it. But it wasn't coming.

"Dr. Houston?" She heard her mom say.

Beside her, she heard a clipboard being picked up and rifled through. "Currently her vitals are stable. Her BP's at 100 over 60, heart rate 110. Respirations 18. O2 Sat 91 on bag-valve mask, Temp 98. She has a GCS of five and EKG currently sinus tachycardia at 110 without ST changes."

Someone picked up her arm and inserted a needle into the crook of her elbow. Whatever it was they connected tugged slightly as they hung it above her.

"Good. Who's doing the surgery?" To anyone else, her mother's voice probably sounded calm, but Kia heard a slight tremor beneath it.

More paper flipping. "Dr. Varin."

"And the boy who came with her?" Ian? She had to be talking about Ian.

The doctor that had been flipping through her file stuttered a bit but was saved from an answer by a scuffle going on nearby.

"And you are?" Her mother asked.

"The boy that came here with her." *Ian!* She felt him take her hand. His long fingers easily wrapped around her small hands.

She wanted to ask a thousand questions. *What had happened? Are you okay? Why can't I move?* But just like everything else, she couldn't get her mouth to open to say the words.

"Mr...?" Kia could almost picture the exact face her mom was wearing.

"Ian." He still held fast onto Kia's hand.

"Mr. Ian. You need to move. Kia is going to the O.R."

✤✤✤

Ian was racking up the black eyes he had given. One to the paramedic. One to the male nurse trying to fit him with an IV bag. And one to the security guard who had, at last, strapped him down the bed with restraints. *They'll come off as soon as you calm down*, he said.

At least he got to see her.

But now, here he was strapped to a table being interrogated about his medical history. Interrogated was the proper word because the nurses clearly had his file in front of them with all the information they needed. Why they felt it necessary to ask him about it was beyond him.

"Are you allergic to any medications?" The nurse was tall and gangly. The poor guy looked to be about 30 years old and still hadn't figured out how to look normal with limbs as long as his.

"Laughter," Ian answered. He tugged slightly at the restraints. They itched.

The nurse looked up over his glasses. "Excuse me?"

"In my case, it isn't the best medicine."

The nurse scribbled something on his clipboard. Ian could only imagine what he was writing. *The patient's cognitive abilities seem off.* Then he walked away.

When the nurse came back, Kia's mom was walking alongside him. "Mr. Ian," she said.

Marie took the clipboard from the nurse, dismissed him, and sat down on the stool next to his bed. Again, she had that look that said she knew him, but Ian had gone through many precautions to make sure that they had never met.

"So," she said, flipping aimlessly through the clipboard, "can you tell me exactly what happened to land my daughter in the hospital?"

Ian opened his mouth to talk, but she cut him off. "Actually, can you tell me *exactly* how you know my daughter?"

Ah, he thought, *so she's read my file.* Ian thought about the times he had been taken to the hospital because of an overdose. Mommies don't like their babies to run in the same circles as drug addicts.

He looked at her and raised an eyebrow. Obviously, he couldn't tell her *exactly* how he knew Kia. "Dr. LaStrauss, is it? I'm sure I could answer your questions a whole lot better if I weren't tied to the bed."

She rose from her chair and leaned across Ian to the restraint on his right arm. But she didn't touch the restraint, instead, she grabbed the

184

syringe laying on the table next to them, lifted his shirt and stuck the needle in his side. "Numbing agent," she said with a satisfied grin.

She retrieved the tools she needed to restitch his side and sat back down. As she looked at his stitches, her face wrinkled in concentration, then smoothed out into a smile. "Kia's work I presume?" She asked.

"I'm not one for hospitals." This time, Ian couldn't feel a thing where Marie was working.

"Your file says otherwise."

"Yeah, I suppose it does." Ian tugged at his restraints again. "This is a surprisingly calm conversation you're having considering your daughter's in surgery."

"This is a surprisingly calm conversation you're having considering your girlfriend is in surgery," she said, then added, "and that you were also in the accident that put her there."

Ian raised an eyebrow at her.

"You think I don't know what's going on in my daughters' lives?" She finished up her stitches with a swish of her instruments, then laid them on the table. "Though I did think it was the tall blonde that she was seeing, but I guess not."

Riley. That bastard, Ian thought.

"No," Marie said. "I know *exactly* what is going on in my daughters' lives."

Did she? The way she said *exactly* made him wonder. If she knew, she would not be having this calm of a conversation. Marie's mention of the plural form of daughter made Ian remember exactly why they had gotten in the accident in the first place.

The person who was terrorizing the lives of the Soulwalkers had Ellie, Samson, and now Katelyn.

21

IT WASN'T THE THROBBING in her head, or the God-awful smell that woke up Katelyn. It was the soft sobbing coming from the girl beside her.

It took a while for everything to come into focus, but by the smell of things, she was in a barn. Who had a barn with actual livestock in New Orleans, she didn't know. But she could smell the livestock, or at least the remnants of some.

One hand was handcuffed to a bar running across the wall, but she lifted the other and touched the place on her head that throbbed. When she brought her hand down it was spotted with blood.

"I wouldn't move too much if I were you," the girl said between sobs. "You hit the ground pretty hard when he threw you in here. You probably have a concussion."

The girl was handcuffed to the same bar that Katelyn was. She turned and looked toward her. Her hair was a black rat's nest, with pieces of hay sticking out every-which-way. Makeup and dirt smeared down her face from her almond-shaped eyes. But underneath it all, Katelyn still recognized her. "Ellie?" she asked.

Ellie gave a slight nod of her head and wiped away a tear with her free hand.

"Ellie, what happened? Why are we here?" Katelyn tugged the handcuff down the bar, scooting closer to the small girl.

"They...they want something from us. I don't know why you're here, but they spent all night trying to find out where your sister was."

"What do they want?"

"I don't know how they found you instead. It doesn't make any sense." Ellie stared off into space. "It was all for nothing then."

"What is it they want, Ellie?" Katelyn asked again. She was confused by what Ellie was saying.

"Unless...they couldn't get to her." She paused. "Of course! They know she'll come if they have you."

Katelyn grabbed Ellie with her free hand. "Ellie! What do they want?"

Ellie looked up into her eyes. Ellie's were so blue, like her sisters. A lone tear escaped and fell before she could catch it. "Our souls," she said. "They want our souls."

Ian was still strapped to the bed even though he had "calmed down." Marie had left 30 minutes ago and the nurse 10 minutes before that. No one had been in to check on him since. Which was really putting a damper on his plans because he desperately needed to call Eugene.

The curtain that created the divider to his little "room" opened suddenly, and none other than Eugene walked in. It looked like he had come from the office, his suit was slightly askew. "Speak of the devil," Ian said. "How did you know I was here?"

Eugene took in Ian's condition, mainly focusing on the restraints and sat down on the stool next to the bed. "I'm still your emergency contact."

"Well, took you long enough to get here. These baboons have me strapped down."

"For good reason, I hear," Eugene said, but he reached over and unstrapped Ian from the bed.

Ian rubbed his wrists, trying to work out the kinks that had developed. "This day could not possibly get any worse."

Eugene nodded his head. At least he understood. "I heard what happened to you and Kia."

"Do you know how she is? How the surgery is going?"

"She's out of surgery. They told me it went fine, and she's in recovery now."

Ian moved to get out of bed, but Eugene put a hand on his chest. "Do not rush out there. You'll get yourself strapped down again, and you staying in the hospital all night is not something The Network can afford."

Ian eased himself back down and sat on the edge of the bed. "What are we going to do? He has Kia's sister now. I know he was going for Kia but..." Ian's face felt hot with anger.

Eugene put his hand on top of Ian's. "I'm scheduled for a call with the Parisian Authority today, then we will decide what our next step is. If she will come here."

"Our next step? Our next step!" Ian pulled his hand away. "Do you have any idea how long the plane ride is from Paris? They could all be dead by then!" He realized he was yelling, lowering his voice he said, "Our next step is to get our people back. And guess who is the only person who knows where they are?"

"Kia," Eugene said with a sigh.

"Damn straight it's Kia." Ian got up out of the bed. "If you'll excuse me, I think I'll go see her now."

Katelyn could handle magic. Everything that was happening, she chalked up to magic. But now, Ellie was sitting here telling her that people could actually lose their souls. It was so.... *television.* "I've seen how Angelus is," Katelyn said, referring to the dark side of the character from *Buffy the Vampire Slayer.* "While I do love a man in leather pants, I prefer Angel better."

Ellie almost smiled. "That's not how it is," she explained. "And don't be silly, vampires don't exist."

Well, at least there was that. "Then, how is it?"

Ellie tried running a hand through her hair, but it got caught in tangles and she pulled it out. "It's like you're not really alive. You're a shell of a person. You're not dead...but you feel nothing, want nothing, and care about nothing." She shook her head. "Ugh, I'm not explaining it right."

Katelyn had this awful picture in her head of herself walking around, caring about nothing. Like a zombie. "I think I get it." She paused. "But why do they want our souls? What do they do with them?"

Ellie scooted closer. "That's what I don't understand. As far as I've read there's no reason to take anyone's soul anymore. It used to be done as punishment or for exorcisms."

"Maybe they're just awful people."

"Yeah, yeah I guess they are."

They both turned their heads as the exterior barn door creaked open. Ellie turned toward Katelyn, pure terror written across her face. Katelyn pulled a finger up to her lips. *Shhh.*

Ian had to ask two nurses how to get to post-op recovery, but he finally found it. Walking in her door, he said, "Don't you ever do that to me again Kia LaStrauss. There are only so many things I can do to keep you—"

Ian skidded to a stop once he saw Marie was in Kia's room.

Kia's mom was standing by her bed, monitoring her vitals. She didn't even look up when he came in, but said, "I see they let you out of your restraints."

Ian ignored her and crossed the room to Kia's bedside. The cuts on her face had been cleaned and bandaged, but she had a purpling bruise running down the side of her eye. Her chest rose and fell normally and the machine monitoring her heart beeped at the appropriate times.

Beep. Beep. Beep.

But her eyes remained closed and she gave no sign of hearing either her mom or Ian. "She's still asleep?" Ian asked.

Marie looked at him and sighed, almost as if she was reluctant to answer. "Yes and no," she said. "She is not asleep, and yet, she cannot wake."

Ian knew his face was saying, *what the hell*, and that would have been enough, but he wanted to make sure Marie knew exactly how crazy she was sounding. "And do, pray tell, how exactly one can be not awake and not asleep at the same time."

"Her brain activity mimics that of someone who is awake, but she cannot talk, cannot move, cannot open her eyes."

"I'm guessing this isn't normal?"

Marie didn't have to answer for Ian to know that it wasn't. They both stared at each other. "I have to go to surgery. I trust that you'll be fine to stay here?"

Ian nodded as Marie walked out of the door, closing it behind her.

"What are we going to do with you, kid?" He sat down on the bed next to Kia and brushed her hair back behind her ear. "I must really love you to be here in this hospital." He looked around the room, images of that night flashing back to him. "My room looked a lot like this. But my parents...they never made it a recovery room. Hell, they never even made it to the hospital." Ian pushed a piece of hair out of her face.

He sighed, leaned over and kissed her on the forehead. "I know you're worried, but don't be. I'll find her. I promise."

22

IAN BANGED on the door as hard as he could. The sun was quickly setting. It was that hour when everything glowed gold. A chill lingered in the air and a shiver went down his spine. He didn't have his jacket, so he wrapped his hands around his goose-bumped arms and waited for the door to open.

"You really should get a phone," Ian said as soon as the door swung open. Dominik smiled and held his hand out for Ian to shake. Ian had this urge to pull him out onto the lawn and drag him to the waiting Uber, explaining along the way, but the Warlock was old-fashioned and reviled in niceties. Shaking his hand, Ian said, "I need your help once again, my friend."

Dominik gestured for Ian to come inside. "What, am I the only Warlock you know?"

Jeanine walked around the corner, joining them, and said, "Yes," at the same time that Ian said, "No."

Jeanine and Dominik laughed. "There aren't as many in the city as there once were, so I can understand," Dominik said. "Please have a seat. Tell me what troubles you this time."

"Kia..." Ian began, not really knowing how to start.

Jeanine leaned forward, her hands on her knees. "How's she doing, dear?"

"At the moment, not so good." Ian got up and started pacing the floor. This was taking too long. "She's in some kind of coma-thing. Her mother doesn't seem too worried, but we don't know when she'll wake up, and there's something that I need to talk to her about."

190

Dominik and Jeanine looked at each other. It might have been a while since Ian had parents, but he knew that look. It was the one that adults gave each other when they weren't telling the children something. "Ian thinks there was a Warlock involved with her accident," Jeanine said, still looking at her husband.

Normally, Ian hated when she listened to his thoughts, but tonight he was too worried about other things to care. "She was fine, and then all of a sudden she was just...unconscious. Someone used magic on her, I know it."

Dominik turned back to Ian. "And you think it was me? No, no that's not it." He thought for a moment. "You want me to wake her up." He said it matter-of-factly, not as a question at all.

Ian nodded.

Dominik looked at his wife. "Jeanine?"

She sat for a moment, thinking. "I see no problem with you helping out our Soulwalker friend."

Dominik got up and shook Ian's hand once again. "I make no promises," the Warlock said. "But I'll see what I can do."

When they arrived at the hospital, the nurses told Ian that there had been no change. Kia still slept. Ian brought Dominik into her room and closed the doors and the blinds. He would have locked the door if there had been a lock. "Right before the crash, it was like she blacked out." He paused as if remembering it for the first time. "That is why we crashed. She wasn't awake to put on the brakes."

Dominik nodded and walked over to Kia. He rubbed his hands together, warming them up. Then, he slowly began to move his hand across her body, starting at her feet and working up toward her head. Close, but never touching. He ran his hand over every inch of her body, slowing down or stopping altogether over places she was injured. He rested his hand over her arm for almost a full minute where the surgeons had repaired her radial arteries.

Ian watched soundlessly as the Warlock worked. He knew that Dominik could feel the disturbances in Kia's body where she was hurt, that to him, it was like reading a report from the doctor's telling him what was wrong with her. Except that, hopefully, he would figure out exactly what was wrong with her instead of Marie's half-assed answer.

Finally, Dominik pulled his hand back from Kia's body. "I cannot wake her," he said.

191

"What do you mean you can't wake her?" Ian's voice grew loud. Realizing that the nurse could probably hear him, he lowered his voice. "What is so wrong with her that you cannot fix?"

"You were right in your thoughts that a Warlock was behind this. The magic is written all over her." Dominik cocked his head to the side. "Only, it is muffled, and I cannot get a good read on who exactly did it."

He looked at Dominik confused.

"When a Warlock does magic, some of their magic is leftover. Almost like a signature." Dominik ran his hand over Kia's head one more time. "The magic was not done by touch, but from far away. But I guess you already knew that." He closed his eyes, concentrating, but he ended up scrunching his face in confusion. "Whoever did this to her is working very hard to cover his tracks."

Ian stepped closer to the bed, wanting so badly to reach out and touch her, but dared not to with Dominik in the room. "You don't know who did it?" Ian said. The Warlock shook his head. "But you do know what he did, right?"

"All of her physical injuries are from the crash," Dominik pointed to her arm, to the bruises and cuts along her forehead, and her chest, an invisible injury that Ian couldn't see. "Except for one." He tapped his temple. "This blackout you mentioned was done by magic. It is a coma that she cannot wake from except in her own time. I can heal all of her other injuries, but I cannot wake her from this."

Ian fell into the chair beside Kia's bed. "How long until she wakes?"

"A couple of hours. A couple of days. There is no way to know."

Ian may not have a couple of hours, much less a couple of days. Kia had the key to finding the Soulwalkers and Katelyn, but the key resided in her memories. She would never forgive him if something happened to Katelyn. But how was he supposed to find her without—

An idea popped into Ian's head, almost as if someone planted it there. "You can't wake her, that I understand." Ian pushed the hair out of his face. "But what I need is inside her mind, and you can go inside—"

"That is not something that Warlocks do lightly," Dominik said with a slight fierceness in his voice, and Ian wondered if he had finally asked too much of the Warlock.

"I know your rules of ethics, Dominik," Ian said, matching Dominik's tone. "But if you only understood what is at stake. If you knew what was going on—"

"Do not think that I am oblivious to The Riven, Soulwalker. I know exactly what is going on."

Ian was on his feet now. Dominik was lucky the bed separated them. He was feeling quite violent today. "And yet you tell me you will do nothing!"

A nurse opened the door and shushed them, quickly closing the door behind her.

Ian turned back toward the Warlock, this time, his voice was lower. "You say you know what is happening. Do you know that her sister was taken?"

Dominik nodded.

"Then you know what is at stake." Ian walked around the bed and laid a hand on Dominik's shoulder. "I know I ask too much of you. I always have. But I must ask you to do one more thing." Ian was pleading now. "Only one thing."

Silence spread out between them and Ian was worried that Dominik would stand his ground and say no, but at last, he spoke. "I cannot guarantee that I can find what it is you seek."

Ian nodded and couldn't help the smile that drew at his lips, glad for his victory.

Dominik spoke again. "I also cannot guarantee that she will be the same afterward."

He looked at the Warlock, confusion written on his face. "What?"

"Digging through someone's mind is like digging for a piece of eggshell you dropped in the meatloaf."

Ian cringed at the analogy.

Dominik continued, "I cannot tell you if her mind will be damaged in the process."

Ian would never risk hurting Kia, but there was this voice in his mind screaming, *Do it! Do it now!* Was this the only way he would be able to find Katelyn? He could Walk her, but there was no guarantee that the memory would show up. If he could even find it, it could take hours. And Kia wouldn't want to waste even a second. "Go ahead," he said.

Katelyn and Ellie didn't dare move. They barely even breathed.

The barn door screeched open. Its hinges protesting at every push. As Katelyn heard the muffled voices of two men walking in, Ellie jumped beside her.

Two men stopped in front of the stall that Katelyn and Ellie were being held in. One began talking. "I thought she would have come by now. I'm sorry sir."

Ellie automatically cringed away from the voice, and Katelyn wondered what the girl had been put through before she got there.

The other man spoke, his voice lower and surer than his partner's. "You were wrong, Cyrus. And now that you have killed our Finder, again, we have no way of knowing how to get to her."

Cyrus paused, then began hesitantly, "Wh—What about the Warlock, sir?"

Katelyn heard someone being slapped and then the retreat of footsteps.

When the door to their stall opened, Katelyn thought that the Devil himself had stepped through.

"Hello, you two," said the man. He was tall and slim, and it looked like almost no muscle rested between his bones and skin. He was wearing a suit on his skeletal frame. Katelyn knew her fashion and this was no cheap suit. It was Hugo Boss. His look said, *don't mess with* me, and Katelyn couldn't imagine that anyone did.

But it wasn't his stature or clothes that scared her. It was the fiery desire that burned behind his eyes. And not the kind of desire that Katelyn had always hoped a man would one day look at her with. It was a desire to see the world and everyone in it burn.

Beside her, Ellie let out a little whimper. Although she wasn't much younger than Katelyn, she was so small and looked so fragile. Katelyn slid her free hand around the girl and pulled her close.

Katelyn put on a brave face. "You're behind this I suppose."

"This," he said, waving his hand in the air, "could mean so many things. Like building this barn or your existence on Earth. But I assume you mean this, as in you being handcuffed to the wall. To which the answer is yes. But where are my manners? I am Preston." He stuck his hand out to shake hers, but Katelyn only pulled Ellie tighter toward her.

Preston cocked his head to the side, genuinely confused as to why they weren't moving. "It's no matter," he said, dropping his hand to his side. "I already know you two so very well. Katelyn." He turned toward Ellie. "And Ellie."

A shudder went down Katelyn's spine when he said her name, but she still didn't move her gaze from his.

"I came to introduce myself," he said. "And to apologize for Cyrus. He's a little rough around the edges, but he can be very...persuasive, and that is an asset to me. It's something you will learn very soon, I'm sure." Preston rubbed non-existent dirt off his suit before looking back up at the two girls. "I see that you are confused." He spoke to Ellie, and Katelyn turned to look at her. He was right. The scared look on her face had turned into one of confusion.

"You have every right to be," He continued. "But you will understand soon enough."

He turned to walk out of the stall, but he turned back around and stared hard into Katelyn's eyes. She noticed for the first time that his eyes were a deep blue...no, blue green. Most people would probably overlook the green and only see the blue, for it was overwhelming, but the green exploded inside the blue, leaving his eyes looking like opal stones.

"Refusing my handshake is the only time that you will disobey me when I ask something of you," he said. "Next time, I won't be so forgiving." With that, Preston turned and shut the door behind him.

Katelyn and Ellie waited a full five minutes before either of them moved. Slowly, Katelyn's shoulders relaxed, and her grip on Ellie loosened.

Ellie still stared out the door where Preston had disappeared. She didn't move her gaze, almost as if she expected him to pop back in at any moment saying, "Just kidding! I'm here to kill you now!" But Katelyn had listened as the barn door closed behind him and thanked the Lord that it was as rusty as it was. It would let them know if anyone decided to make another appearance in the barn.

"I don't understand," Ellie whispered.

Katelyn tugged on her handcuffs and winced as they cut through the raw flesh around her wrist.

Ellie repeated, "I don't understand."

"Ditto," Katelyn said. She saw no point in whispering, so she continued in her normal voice, which as Kia liked to tease her about, was about an octave higher than most. "There are about a million things I don't understand in this world. Take Algebra for example. But this...it definitely tops the list."

Ellie was still staring at the closed barn door, not moving. "Ellie?" Katelyn said, nudging the girl slightly.

Ellie turned and looked at her. Katelyn couldn't help but notice the similarity in her and Preston's eyes. While she hated to compare them in any way whatsoever, both of their eyes, so, so blue, had depth and held secrets.

When Ellie finally spoke again, she looked off into the corner of the stall, avoiding Katelyn's inquisitive stare. "He—he's a Soulwalker."

Kia was screaming so loud inside her head she thought it might explode. While she couldn't remember Katelyn being abducted or what she knew that Ian wanted so badly, she would do anything to help get her sister back.

Do it! Do it now!

Which was why she was screaming for Ian to do it! Of course, he couldn't hear her, she wasn't actually screaming. She wasn't moving, and she still wasn't waking up. Luckily, he didn't change his mind after Dominik talked about the possible side effects.

"Go ahead," she heard him say.

He stood in the corner of the room then, and Dominik sat down on the bed.

"Kia," he whispered as if he was trying to wake a baby.

Nope...still not waking up.

"I don't know if you can hear me."

Yes! Yes, I can!

"But open your mind, let it clear. Resisting would be..." He left the sentence unfinished, obviously not for her sake since he didn't know if she could hear, so she guessed for his. He was a kind enough man, one that didn't want to hurt anyone. She hoped that he didn't have to.

When Dominik put his hands on either side of her head, she let her mind relax. As soon as she had heard Ian say that Katelyn had been taken, her mind had been racing through memories trying to find when it happened, but she couldn't remember. She felt like she would have known that her sister was in trouble. Known deep down, like a twin-sense. Only, they weren't twins, but close enough. Still, she felt nothing.

She stopped trying to remember and let the memories scroll through her mind as Dominik came across them.

It was almost like Walking herself, without any of the emotions. In the other Walks she had been on, images passed before her. Only, these were *her* memories. Dominik slowed down at memories that involved the other Soulwalkers, Ellie and Samson, and luckily pushed through the ones of her and Ian, together. She wanted to blush, but he paid no attention to them.

Dominik got to her very last memory of waking up at Ian's house, but when he got to the part where the edge became blurry, Kia's head erupted as if on fire.

Pain shot through her mind and down the back of her neck. She could feel herself arching up off the hospital bed, but she didn't have control of her body to stop it.

Dominik's hands instantly fell from her face. He sighed, as if he knew that was the end of the road. There was nothing after that.

He didn't say anything, but instead, put his hands along the rest of her body where she had pain. Her arm. Her chest. Her forehead. And slowly...very slowly, the pain was drawn from her body and she felt whole once again.

Ian paced in front of the nurse's station waiting for Dominik to follow him out of Kia's room. When Dominik came out, he almost ran into a nurse. From across the hall, he saw Dominik lay a hand on the nurse's shoulder, and her expression went blank for one full second before returning to normal. When she walked away, Ian asked what Dominik had done.

"I made her believe that she had already checked on Kia during her rounds later." Dominik pulled Ian aside, away from the nurses' station.

The Warlock looked tired, large bags hung around his eyes that hadn't been there earlier, and even his breathing looked labored.

"I have healed Kia of all the wounds I can. If not for the sleeping spell, she would be fit to leave the hospital this minute."

That explained the tiredness. Dominik would have had to draw all the energy from himself to heal Kia. Why didn't he ask Ian to draw from both of their strengths? Ian had known the Warlock for a while and knew that Dominik didn't ask for help very often, but if there was ever a time to do it was this.

"And the memory?" Ian asked, wondering if he was successful.

"There is something blocking all of the memories she has from two days ago. There is nothing since then. If the memory you seek is one from last night, then I'm sorry, but I cannot help you." Dominik scratched his head. "This other Warlock is working very hard to stay hidden."

"But the memory is still there, yes?" If she still had it, and if she woke up, then it might be possible for him to get to them in time. Only, that was a lot of ifs.

"Oh yes," the Warlock exhaled. "The memory is very much intact. It is only clouded with some very powerful magic."

Ian nodded his head, still hopeful that Kia would wake up any minute. Because if she didn't...

"There might be another way." Dominik's voice was quiet, so quiet, almost as if he was talking to himself more than Ian. But Ian had heard and there was no unhearing.

"Well?" Ian asked. "Tell me what it is!"

197

"You're not going to like it." Dominik was pacing back and forth in the narrow hallway. "And we'll need a few things to do it."

"Okay?" Ian said, anxious to hear the rest.

"And there's only one Warlock in the city powerful enough to do it."

Dr. Marie LaStrauss walked toward them, cutting Ian off from his reply to Dominik. "Dr. LaStrauss," Ian said, inclining his head toward her.

She smiled. It was a genuine smile and one that Ian hadn't seen on her yet. But she wasn't smiling at him, she was smiling at Dominik

Then, Dominik said the last thing in the world Ian expected to hear. "Hello, Marie. We were just talking about you."

23

"I'M SORRY, but what the fuck?" Ian looked back and forth between Marie and Dominik. Neither one had heard him. They chatted away like old buddies.

Ian's mind was going to explode.

It couldn't be. Could it? Could Marie LaStrauss. *Dr.* Marie LaStrauss actually be—

No. No. No.

Dominik turned back to Marie. "I wasn't sure, but she looks so much like you. And then I thought, if it was true, how could he not know?" Dominik inclined his head toward Ian.

Marie looked at Ian with what seemed like hatred. "*Him.* I only met a couple of hours ago. If I had known that she was associating with such..."

"Oh, please finish that sentence," Ian spoke up. "I would love to see how imaginative you can be with your adjectives."

Marie's eyes flickered over to the nurses' station. "We should take this somewhere else."

Ian opened the door to Kia's room. "Yes, let's do."

When the door was closed, Ian turned around and stared at the two friends. Marie was by Kia's bed checking on the machines that she was connected to. For a second, it looked like she wanted to reach out and stroke Kia's face, but she pulled her hand back at the last moment.

"So," Ian said, "is anyone going to explain? Or do I need to get Eugene on the phone? Because, even though he's been a huge prick lately, he knows *everything* that goes on in his city."

"Don't be so dramatic, boy," Marie said, waving her hand in the air.

At that moment he hated Marie, but she was still Kia's mother, and his parents had taught him respect. Although, his parents were dead, so maybe it didn't matter. "Boy? That's not what Kia called me—"

"Silence," Marie demanded.

Ian's airway was instantly cut off. He clawed at his throat, willing the air to flow again. It was true then. Marie really *was* a Warlock, and she was choking him to death.

"Marie." Dominik's voice was as calm as water as he laid a hand on her arm. The fury in her eyes burned out, and air returned to Ian's lungs.

Ian regained his breath and choked out, "I don't know what your problem with me is." He stared Marie right in her eyes, but she couldn't hold his gaze. "But whatever it is, it doesn't matter. I'm sure you know that Kia's current situation was no accident. Dominik thinks that you might be able to help."

Marie looked over to her daughter. "I cannot wake her. I have tried everything that I know."

Ian looked over at Dominik, and he took over. "We were talking about a transference spell."

Marie's head whipped around. "Absolutely not."

Ian still had no idea what Dominik was talking about. Transference spell? How would that help at all? "Anyone care to explain?"

"The spell would temporarily exchange one essence for another. In this case, Kia's Soulwalker essence for someone else's," Dominik explained.

"You know then?" Ian asked Marie. "Of course, you know. How could you not?" He cocked his head to the side. "Is that why you look at me with such distaste? Like I am somehow responsible for Kia being who she is."

Marie didn't look at him when she answered but continued to stare at Kia's sleeping body. "Being a Soulwalker is not the only part of her."

He looked at Marie, confused with what she had said, but then it dawned on him. Of course. If Marie was a Warlock, then Kia would be too. A Warlock-Soulwalker. It has never happened before. Kia had always been different. Maybe this could explain it all.

"But this exchange," Ian asked, "how exactly would that give us what we need?"

"During the exchange," Dominik answered, "it is believed that many of the person's memories from right before will come with it. A side effect of sorts."

"But if her memories are blocked?"

Marie cut Dominik off before he even had a chance to answer. "That's what this is about? You want her memories?" Her voice was rising. "Then I stand by my original answer. Absolutely not!"

Ian smacked the food tray, resting beside him. It flung across the room, smashing into the wall spraying its contents everywhere. "That's not good enough! We need to know! Aren't you even worried about Ka—?" He stopped before saying something he shouldn't. Would Kia have wanted to tell her mother about Katelyn? It was strange that Marie hadn't asked about her other daughter yet. Although, maybe not so strange, considering the absent mother she has always been. No, he wouldn't tell. Not yet. He could only hope that Dominik followed his lead.

Ian watched soup slide down the wall for a full second. "Ma—" Ian began, but caught himself and continued, "Dr. LaStrauss, if she was awake, we could ask her for it, but she isn't, so we can't. People are disappearing," Ian continued. "Everyone in The Riven knows it. Stopping it is not something I can do without help...without Kia's help."

Marie's jaw was set, and Ian knew he wasn't getting anywhere with her. He decided to change tactics. "There's a little girl, she's not much younger than Kia, but she's so, so small. So breakable. The place where we can find her is in Kia's memory."

He went on. "We don't know what they're doing to her, but she shouldn't have to go through it. No one should."

The room was quiet for what seemed like hours.

Marie turned back and reached out her hand toward Kia, this time touching her face. "We will need someone for Kia to exchange with," Marie said almost in a whisper. "Someone who is not of The Riven."

Ian knew what he had to do, only there was no way in hell he was going to do it.

But there were no other options, short of abducting some random person on the street. Actually, that wasn't such a bad—

No. Ian shook the thought from his mind before it took hold and became a viable option.

He looked down at Kia's cell phone. *Riley Hewitt.* He cringed as he pressed "send."

It rang only twice before Riley picked up. "Hello."

Ian couldn't bring himself to respond.

"Hello? Kia?"

"Nope," he said. "Ian."

"Ian?" Ian could almost hear the seconds tick by as recognition finally dawned on Riley. "Ian." Riley's voice was hard.

But not as hard as Ian's. "Look, you know I'd have to be bat shit crazy to call you of my own free will."

Riley didn't sound angry, merely curious. "Then why exactly are you doing it?"

Ian could hear noise in the background. People talking and laughing. It was Friday night, Riley was probably out with friends, and yet, he stopped what he was doing to answer a call from "Kia." Ian clenched his fists. "I need you to come to the hospital. Right now." He paused for a split second before saying, "It's Kia."

Riley said he'd be there in ten minutes and hung up.

Ian looked at the clock on the wall, watching the minutes tick by. The sun had set a long time ago, and he was anxious to do this before the night's end.

Then, Riley barged into the hospital room, a wide-eyed and frantic look on his face. He looked like he had come from a rodeo. Maybe he had. He had on cowboy boots, a flannel plaid shirt, and blue jeans that were worn around the knees.

Riley took in the room, the people in it, and then settled his eyes on the motionless Kia.

Ian stood aside as he walked toward the bed, but Marie intercepted him before he could get too far. "Riley!" She said, embracing him.

"Wow, old pals already," Ian snarked.

"Thank you so much for coming to help," she continued, ignoring Ian.

"You're welcome...?" Riley said it more as a question than a statement.

Marie smirked in Ian's direction, then turned to Riley. "You know why you're here then?" She asked.

Riley looked back and forth between mother and daughter, obviously confused. "I'm not sure, ma'am."

His politeness made Ian want to punch him in the face.

"Ian only told me that Kia was in the hospital. I came as soon as I could." Riley narrowed his eyes. "But now that I think about, why would Ian call in the first place?" Under his breath, he said, "He seems like the ulterior motive kind of guy."

Ian laughed. Riley blushed, not realizing everyone had heard.

"That's the thing about hospitals," Ian said, tapping his ear and whispering, "they're quiet."

Riley ignored Ian and, standing up straighter, he turned back to Marie. "What can I do for her?"

Ian paid close attention while Marie explained exactly how the transference spell worked, even though it was the second time he was hearing the process in the last ten minutes.

"The spell calls for an actual exchange," Marie said. "In this case, Kia's essence for Riley's. Riley would lose his non-magical essence, giving it to Kia."

Dominik chimed in. "During the course of the spell, Kia would remain without abilities. Once the spell expired, the exchange would be reversed, both parties returning to their former selves."

"There are different," Marie paused, searching for the right word, "levels of a transference spell. The one we'll be doing today is the lowest strength. There's a time limit to how long Riley will have. Two or three hours at the most."

The time limit didn't bother Ian. He didn't expect to bring Riley along for the ride. He wanted to get what he needed from his head and then leave. There was no way that Ian would be able to keep an eye on Riley while he was trying to save the Soulwalkers and Katelyn. No, Riley would slow him down. Taking one last look at the clock on the wall, Ian said, "Let's get started."

A hundred questions swirled around Riley's mind, but every time he opened his mouth to ask one, another more pressing question popped into his head. He listened, without interrupting, while Dr. LaStrauss explained why he had rushed over to the hospital and what kind of magic spell they were going to do.

The only problem was, no one had explained to him that the people standing in the room were magic. Or that magic really existed. The other night at Kia's house, she had been trying to explain some supernatural force, but it wasn't magic, more like a genetic mutation. She was like an X-Man. Though, he didn't even believe her. Guess the joke was on him. "So..." he began tentatively, "magic is real then?"

Everyone's head whipped toward him and each one wore the same expression. "Stupid question?" Riley asked.

Marie spoke to Ian without turning her head to look at him. She still was staring at Riley, as if he had asked how to spell yellow. "I thought you told me he knew everything?" Dr. LaStrauss hissed.

"That might have been a tad bit of an exaggeration." Ian shrugged his shoulders. Riley hated that guy. He was the same as every other "bad boy" out there. Overly confident, arrogant, and a bully. If there was one thing that Riley hated more than anything, it was a bully.

Dr. LaStrauss looked once at her watch, sighed, and said, "I'll start at the beginning then."

And she did.

It had been hours since Katelyn had given up asking questions to the inconsolable Ellie and even longer since Preston had visited them. Now the two girls sat chained to the wall, quietly accepting their doom.

Katelyn glanced down at her watch. The face was cracked, and she swore under her breath. It was her favorite watch. Her father had sent it to her last year for her birthday. He didn't make an appearance, but a package showed up on the doorstep with a card saying, *love, Dad*.

Beneath the crack, she could make out the time. Three minutes past midnight. "Happy Halloween," Katelyn said with a sigh. So much for her trick-or-treating plans.

Ellie turned to look at her. Her tears had finally dried up, but they had left her face red and blotchy. "What?" She asked.

Katelyn shook her head. "Nothing."

Ellie leaned her head back against the barn wall. "Your sister," She said, "do you think she will come?"

Katelyn thought about her sister. Always the strong one, protecting Katelyn whenever she needed it. Looking under beds and inside closets. Changing the bulb in her nightlight. "Yes. She will." *But probably not in time*, she added to herself.

And then, the scariest sound in the world filled their ears. The barn door screeching open. Both girls cringed back against the wall, but that was as far as they could go.

Katelyn closed her eyes. She would accept her fate, but not Ellie's. If this person was coming to hurt or kill them, she'd put herself in front. She made a vow to herself to try and save the girl beside her. At whatever cost. Opening her eyes, she put on a brave face.

"Hello?" Said a new voice. There was something in the voice that calmed Katelyn. That made her think maybe the man who the voice belonged to wasn't there to kill them. Instead to save them.

The stall door slid open revealing a man who looked quite average. There were no distinguishing marks on him or anything that would make her remember him. In fact, when Katelyn turned away, she almost immediately forgot what the man looked like.

"Hello," the man said again.

Katelyn noticed for the first time that he was carrying a tray with sandwiches and water on it. She narrowed her eyes, wondering what motive was behind the kindness. Was this the good cop to Preston's bad cop?

"I thought you two might be hungry," he said. Again, Katelyn felt a familiarity when the man spoke. He took a step toward them, and Katelyn felt Ellie jump back. He got the message, setting the tray down a couple of feet away and pushing it forward with his foot.

"Please," he said, staring directly into Katelyn's eyes. "Please eat."

Katelyn couldn't hold his gaze and looked away. Out of the corner of her eye, the man became fuzzy, almost as if there was a fog clinging to his body. When Katelyn turned back, he was whole once again.

He nodded once and then left the barn without another word, leaving the girls alone again.

Neither one touched what he had brought them, but he had to know they wouldn't. There was no trusting anyone who walked through that door.

Kia had heard it all. Every single word.

In the cemetery Ian had said, *they are made.* Magic was hereditary. Her mom had it, so she had it.

She was having a hard time accepting it.

Around her, she could hear people shuffling. She figured they were preparing for whatever this transference spell required. Ian had told her once that Soulwalker could temporarily transfer their power to another. At the time, the idea excited her, now she was terrified.

It was one thing for them to look into her mind, but to take the very thing that made her *her.* What would she be like after? Would she be a shell, empty inside? She didn't know.

And she had no way to stop it.

"Riley, if you'd come over here please," her mother said.

She could still *feel* Riley. It was the same connection she always felt when he was in the room, a less-strong version of the ones she felt with other Soulwalkers, but it was there, nonetheless. None of it made any sense. Riley was a Soul—

Oh, she thought. *Oh.* He was never a Soulwalker. His future had always been tied to holding *her* power. She was connected to him because it was her Soulwalker essence that was about to course through his veins.

Kia searched her mind again, desperately trying to find the memory that Ian so longed for. But there was nothing. Only a wall. Unyielding. It didn't matter anyway. Even if she did remember, she was still "sleeping" and had no way to tell them.

"You're going to need to lie down on the bed next to Kia," her mother said.

Ian objected. "Whoa, whoa, whoa. There's no need for that."

"Do you wish for me to complete the spell?" Marie snapped.

Ian didn't say anything, so Kia guessed he had agreed with a nod. She could picture the exact face he was wearing. His lips pursed together. His eyes slightly squinted. It made her laugh. Well, at least it made her laugh inside her head.

Riley tentatively put a hand on the bed beside her. He slowly crawled in and lied down, stiff as a board.

"Now grab her hand."

Ian huffed.

Riley took hold of Kia's hand and again she noticed how rough and worn his hands were.

"I'm going to lay a hand on Kia. Riley, Dominik will lay a hand on you, then we will hold each other's hands. Completing a circle."

"I'll wait right here." She heard Ian say from the corner of the room.

No one said anything after that. Kia wished desperately that she could open her eyes to see what was happening.

Her and Riley's hands grew warm. Wind started to pick up around them. Kia couldn't be sure if it was something that everyone in the room could feel, or if it was between them.

And then she felt it. It was like the draining of a tub; the water swirling around and around until it emptied, except she could feel it. She could feel her power swirl around her body until it left, transferring from herself to Riley through their hands.

And their hands! They felt as if they were lit on fire. Kia wanted to scream out in pain. To pull her hand away. Anything to stop the fire.

Then it did stop. The wind. The fire. The swirling, swirling tub.

Riley dropped her hand and she was left feeling exactly as she had feared.

Empty.

Riley was getting dizzy as images passed before him so quickly. It was like looking into two mirrors that reflected each other. He couldn't see what was real and what wasn't. Then, it stopped, and Riley threw up in the trash can that had been beside Kia's bed.

When he put the trash down, he realized he was on his feet, standing by Kia's hospital bed. The only thing was, he couldn't remember standing up...or anything of the past five minutes.

Around him, everyone was staring at him like he was a lion that had escaped the zoo. They looked at him with caution, afraid to move even the slightest muscle.

But then Ian broke the silence. "Holy shit."

He came up toward Riley and grasped his face in his hands. Riley tried to pull away, but the man was strong. Stronger than Riley.

Ian turned his face from side to side, staring into his eyes. He wore a confused look, and Riley wondered what it was he was so adamantly staring at.

Ian dropped his face and in one stride made it over to Kia's bedside. He took her face in his hands, just as he had done to Riley. Gently, Ian pulled up one of Kia's eyelids, swore under his breath and turned back to Marie, fury burning in his eyes. "What have you done!" He demanded.

"I did what you made me do," she said. Her voice was cold, and Riley wondered what had passed between the two before he had gotten there. She didn't seem to like him much. "They will return, along with her abilities, when the spell expires."

"Sorry to interrupt," Riley said. "But what exactly are you talking about?"

Ian muttered something under his breath and then rummaged through Kia's purse that sat beside her bed. He pulled out a small compact mirror and held it in front on Riley to see.

It took him a second to notice what had changed, but once he did, he couldn't look away.

His eyes. Only, they weren't the brown eyes that he had seen every day of his life in mirrors, but hers. They were Kia's blue eyes in place of his.

Riley went over to Kia's sleeping form and lifted her lids to see what it was that Ian had seen. He had expected his brown to have taken place of her blue, but there was nothing there. Only a black pupil in a sea of white. It was like the color had been stolen from her completely.

"Riley," Marie said cautiously. He didn't know why everyone was babying him, well everyone but Ian. "How are you feeling? Do you feel any different?"

He hadn't realized it earlier, but he did feel a bit different. It wasn't much; he didn't feel powerful or anything. Just...fuller, like there was something else besides muscle and bone resting in him. Something older. Something he didn't quite fully understand yet.

"And the memory?" Ian prompted. "Do you have it?"

Riley thought back to the images that had passed before him minutes earlier. Could they be the memory that Ian so desperately wanted? "This memory...what does it look like?"

"It's of Kia driving somewhere. It was raining." Ian was speaking out loud, but it looked like he was inside of his mind, remembering something himself. "She was scared."

And then the memory was there. Like it had always been there. It was a part of him like his own memories. "I know where it is. I know where you need to go."

24

I AN PAID CLOSE attention to the directions Riley was giving. He was even drawing a map. What a helpful little bastard.

He was having a hard time standing next to Riley. Each Soulwalker had a unique connection with each other. They could identify who was there even if they couldn't see the person, and all of Ian's senses were telling him that it was Kia standing next to him. Her—*Riley's?*— water-like thread, flowed around his body making goosebumps break out across his flesh. It was disorienting, but he would have to deal with it. The transference spell had worked and now they knew where Cyrus was keeping his friends.

Riley finished drawing the map and handed it to Ian as a nurse popped her head into the room. "Dr. LaStrauss, I know you turned your pager off and don't want to be disturbed, but you're needed in the pit."

Marie nodded to the nurse. Turning back toward Ian, she said, "Soulwalker, the rest of this is your business. I ask that you leave my family and me alone once this is done." She walked out of the room before Ian could even respond.

Leave her family alone? Like hell.

"I will leave you to it as well," Dominik said. "It is not my wish to get involved much deeper with Soulwalker business." Ian tried to interject, but Dominik cut him off. "I know you haven't told your Authority what you're doing. I can't imagine that he will be too pleased with you going above his head, but if you succeed, he might forgive you."

Ian nodded, hoping that the Warlock was right.

"As for a car—" Ian was going to have to call another Uber.

Riley interrupted Dominik. "We can take my truck."

Dominik smiled, clasped Ian on the shoulder and then walked out of the door. Ian was left looking back and forth between the door and Riley, wondering how he was going to leave the boy behind.

"Keys?" Ian said, sticking out his hand.

Riley laughed and walked out of the room.

Ian went to Kia's bedside, taking hold of her hand. "That boy is going to be sorely disappointed when I use my ninja skills on him in the parking lot and drive away without him. But don't worry, I'll go easy on him." He leaned down and lightly kissed her forehead. "Be back soon, kid."

Riley was already out in the lobby, anxiously bouncing up and down on the ball on his feet. It was dark outside, but the moon was almost full, and its light was shining through the windows.

He knew when Ian walked up behind him. An iron chain connecting them snapped into place. It was the same way he knew where Kia was, but never feeling it with anyone else it still made him jump when Ian spoke. "Let's go, cowboy."

Riley pulled on his jacket and headed out into the parking lot. "So, what's the plan?"

"The plan," Ian said, pulling on a jacket of his own, "is for you to stay and me to go."

Riley kept walking. "If you think you're going anywhere in my truck without me, then you're delusional. And last time I check, your car was totaled."

"Delusional? I've been called many things. Sexy. Mysterious. Charming. Good in—"

"I've got it, thanks."

Ian stopped walking. "No, I don't think you do. You're only here right now because we needed your mind. Nothing more."

Riley had enough. He pushed Ian up against an SUV in the parking lot. He hit it so hard the alarm started going off. It didn't matter. Riley still pinned him against the side. Ian looked too shocked to fight back. "Look," Riley began. "You're an arrogant asshole...a bully...and I have no idea what it is that Kia sees in you. But she obviously sees something."

Ian choked out, "I wouldn't do that if I were you." He indicated his eyes down. He had opened his jacket slightly. Strapped around his shoulders over his shirt was a holder than held a large knife.

Riley backed away, hands in the air. "I'm here. And I'm going with you," he said, not giving up. He didn't believe that Ian would use the knife on him.

Ian closed his jacket. "Whatever. Get in the truck, Tonto."

Riley unlocked the doors to his truck and climbed in the driver's seat. "Tonto was the horse."

"I know," Ian answered, smirking.

They drove to Ian's apartment mostly in silence. He said they needed to stop the before going anywhere. Riley itched to turn on the radio. The silence was deafening. All around him he could *feel* things. Ian's every move. The pain in the old man's back as he walked the crosswalk in front of them. The light going out in the squirrel that had been hit by a car on the side of the road. He didn't know how Kia wasn't going mad from all the *feeling*. It was enough to make him go crazy. It had all started once he got in the truck, and Riley was dreading that some new "power" was going to pop up sometime soon.

Finally, they pulled into Ian's apartment complex. Ian jumped out of the truck before Riley had even put it in park. Turning the engine off, Riley followed behind him.

"Don't touch anything," Ian said as he unlocked his door.

Riley wasn't shocked at the state of Ian's home. Somehow the guy put off a messy vibe. Maybe it was his hair, always looking like he rolled out of bed or like someone had run their fingers through it. Riley shook his head trying to wipe away a memory of Kia's that had appeared of her running her hands through Ian's hair.

"Stay right there," Ian commanded. He disappeared into the back bedroom, only to emerge one minute later. He threw a large black bag onto the floor and unzipped it. "Do you know how to use a weapon?" He asked.

"I've been skeet shooting," Riley shrugged.

Ian laughed. "Why is it when I say weapon the first thing that comes to your redneck mind is a gun?" Out of the bag, he pulled several large knives and one full-on sword, like one you see at a Renaissance festival. "So, do you know how to use a weapon?" He asked again.

Riley stared, wide-eyed at the dagger Ian handed over to him. The hilt was simple, plain brown that was worn in places where it had been gripped over the years. But the blade itself was what was intimidating.

The steel oscillated cruelly back and forth, coming to a sharp point after about 10 inches.

Riley took the blade in his hand. It was lighter than he thought it would be. He smiled. Maybe he could use this weapon, but Ian's growl of frustration interrupted his thoughts. "No. Hold it like this." Ian adjusted his grip on the hilt, moving his fingers this way and that. When he was finished, the blade felt right in Riley's hand, like it was an extension of his arm.

Ian dug through the bag, looking for a particular weapon. "Why exactly do you have an arsenal of knives hanging out at your house?" Riley asked.

Ian found the knife he was looking for and a sheath that he handed over to Riley. "Martial arts," said Ian. "Okay, let's go." He shoved the smaller blade into his jacket alongside the dagger he had in the parking lot.

Three knives and, apparently, a ninja. Maybe they *could* pull this off.

All Kia could do was wait. It had been, from what she could guess, maybe ten minutes since Riley and Ian had walked out of the door. She still felt empty, like something vital was missing in her, but everything was still there. Except, what mattered most.

She had an itch on her arm, and absentmindedly, reached up to scratch it.

It was a long drive to the North shore of Lake Pontchartrain, and Ian's leg bounced up and down the whole time. He felt like he did when he used to go to martial arts competitions, always anxious, never knowing what to expect.

Only this was no competition. Whatever happened where he was going could end in the death of one of his friends. Or himself. He looked over at Riley. "Did Kia's memories tell you why we are doing this?"

Riley's eyes—Kia's eyes—flickered over to him. "Yes," he whispered.

"Katelyn too?" Ian asked.

Riley nodded.

"Did she go inside?"

Riley shook his head. "She only drove by, then turned around to go home."

Ian nodded. Out the window, water soared by beneath them. The lake would end soon, and they would be there. They needed a strategy. "We don't know where they are being kept, or how the house is set up. Once we get there, we'll park down the street, then split up to look for them. There are three. Samson, Ellie, and Katelyn. I don't think it needs to be said that we need to find them all, but we need to find them all."

Riley nodded again, looking stressed in the pale light. Ian almost felt sorry for dragging him into all this. *Almost.*

He was jolted from his thoughts as Riley pulled off the bridge and took a left on the next road. "We're getting close now," he said.

Ian's heart started pumping faster almost immediately, and when Riley pulled over and parked by the side of the road, turning off his lights, Ian was so wound-up he practically jumped out of the truck.

"The house is about a half a mile up the road. It's big and white and colonial." Riley put his keys in his pocket and caught up to Ian who was already walking down the street.

They stuck mostly to the shadows, although there weren't many streetlights on the road to give them away anyway.

"This is it," Riley whispered.

Ian looked to his right and standing before him was a normal house, where normal people should live. But it wasn't normal people who lived there. Inside, was a kidnapper, a murderer, and God knows who else. "I'll try to get inside," Ian said, his eyes scanning for entrances. Garage. Front door. Windows. "You go around back, see if there's a barn or shed or anything."

"Should we have some kind of signal?"

Ian looked at him and raised an eyebrow. "Signal?"

"You know..." Riley was bouncing on the balls of his feet. "In case we find something, to alert the other person."

"Yeah, sure," Ian smirked. "The signal is to grab them and run."

Riley frowned and muttered something that sounded very close to "jackass" under his breath. He took off along the perimeter of the property, running low to the ground.

Ian took a more direct approach and walked up the driveway. *Let him come*, he thought.

As he got closer, he started to doubt they had the right house. He couldn't *feel* any Soulwalker there...not even Riley. Something wasn't right.

The house was built up high off the ground, like many of the houses this close to the shore. Ian bet when hurricanes blew through this whole area was under five feet or more of water. The bottom level seemed to be a garage, with the main house starting on the second level.

Luckily for Ian, one of the garage doors was raised enough for him to squeeze under. Inside there was a small fishing boat that made the whole place stink of fish. But no car.

"Who is this guy?" Ian said aloud. How could someone have time to go fishing and then abduct people on the side? Or was fishing on the side and abducting was his main gig?

At the end of the garage, there were several doors. Ian picked one at random, he opened it slowly. A bathroom. He worked his way down until the door he opened led to a set of stairs, winding up to the main floor.

He had almost reached the top step when he heard voices.

"Sir, she's here." The voice sounded familiar. But if it was who Ian thought it was, why was he calling someone else "sir?"

Ian scooted closer to try to hear better. But when he stepped down on the top step, it squeaked, and the talking immediately stopped.

Katelyn's head kept falling as she dozed off. She fought to keep her eyes open, but it was so hard. She didn't want anything surprising her in the middle of the night. Beside her, Ellie slept soundlessly, her head leaning on Katelyn's shoulder.

Then she realized what had woken her up in the first place when she heard a noise in the stall beside them. It was someone shuffling around, making the hay rustle together.

Ellie had told her earlier that there was someone in that stall. She never said who it was or where they were now, but Katelyn knew that it had been empty since she had gotten there. Or at least, she never heard any sounds come from it.

Whoever it was slowly opened the door to their stall. It was hard to tell in the dark, but it looked like it was the man who had brought them the sandwiches. Although, Katelyn couldn't recall exactly what he looked like so she couldn't be sure.

The man stepped into the moonlight that streamed through the locked window behind them. It was him.

"What? No more refreshments?" Katelyn sneered.

His eyes glanced down at the uneaten food and frowned. "I'm here to help you escape."

Katelyn hadn't slept and hadn't eaten, so she was worried that she was delirious. The man couldn't have said he was there to help them escape. Could he? "I don't understand," Katelyn said.

214

"Your sister is here and unless she has the spare key," he held up a key, the moonlight shining off of it, "she wouldn't have been able to open these." He knelt and Katelyn shuffled back slightly. She still wasn't sure she could trust this man.

Ellie moved slightly, murmuring in her sleep. How was she still sleeping?

"I know you don't have any reason to trust me," the man said. His face twisted in pain, but in an instant, it was composed again. "But maybe one day you'll understand."

Ellie finally stirred beside her and jumped as she stared up into the man's eyes. He said nothing as he unlocked her handcuffs first, then leaned over and unlocked Katelyn's.

"I'm going to go back out the window," he explained. "Do not leave this barn until your sister gets here."

She stared at him dumbfounded. Right, like she was going to sit still *after* she had been unchained from the wall.

"Do not leave until Kia gets here," he said with more urgency. "Do you understand?"

Kia's arm froze in midair. She had moved. *Moved!* Tentatively, she tried opening her eyes.

Very slowly, as if she had been asleep for a century, her eyes peeled open. She blinked, adjusting to the light. Then she started to move the rest of her body, rolling her shoulders, flexing her toes, making sure everything worked properly.

While her muscle and bones flexed and stretched as they should, she still felt emptier than usual. She didn't feel completely and totally void of what had made her *her*, but there was something off, like eating an Oreo that didn't have its filling. The fog that clouded her brain was still as thick as ever. She sighed.

Across the room, something caught her eye. A little piece of hope on a little piece of white paper.

"The directions," Kia said aloud. She knew that Riley had written them down. She had heard him ask for a pen. Only she had figured he had taken them with him. It was like the gods had come down in her favor after all.

Kia ripped out the wires that connected her body to the many machines behind her. She knew she didn't have long before the machines alerted the nurses something had changed, and someone came to check up on her.

215

Stepping down off the bed, she stood up carefully, keeping hold of the bedrail in case she fell. Her legs held strong, though, and she made a beeline for the door.

She had grown up being in this hospital, waiting for her mother after the nannies had dropped her off. Sometimes it would be hours before her mother finished. She had explored and learned every inch of the hospital. She knew where the nurse's stations were and how to avoid them. More importantly, she knew where her mother kept a spare change of clothes and her car keys.

As Kia has expected at this time of night, there weren't very many people in the hallways. She tiptoed out; her bare feet cold against the floor. Quickly she made her way to the doctor's locker room, ducking behind corners whenever she saw someone coming her way.

The door to the locker room was slightly ajar, and Kia said a silent prayer that no one was in there.

She got lucky again. The locker room was quiet and empty. Kia ran across the lockers looking for the one that read "LaStrauss" across the side. The lockers didn't have any locks on them, so it was easy for Kia to open her mother's and reach inside to grab the clothes.

But all there was were scrub, scrubs, scrubs. "Where are her jeans?" Kia said, talking to herself.

"What are you doing?"

Kia whipped around and stared into the tired face of a doctor in scrubs. He was tall, but his shoulders were slumped like he had gotten off a 48-hour shift.

"I'm Kia LaStrauss," Kia stuttered.

The doctor straightened at the sound of her last name. "As in Dr. LaStrauss, LaStrauss?"

She nodded. "I'm her daughter."

"Why are you in here?"

Kia looked down at herself. Her pale legs stuck out from beneath her hospital gown and Kia crossed her arms over her chest to cover herself up. "I had...an accident. My mother told me to come and get a spare set of her scrubs." She arched an eyebrow at him, daring him to question the Head of Cardio's daughter.

"Oh. Right."

She pointed to the door. "And if you don't mind, I'd like some privacy."

"Of course," the doctor mumbled as he walked out of the door, closing it behind him.

Kia turned back to the task at hand. "Scrubs it is," she said as she pulled on the cotton pants.

Slipping the shirt over her head, she reached for Marie's purse and dug through it until she found the keys to her car.

"Perfect," she said, a grin on her face.

She picked up the directions she had brought with her from her room and made her way to the parking lot.

Riley ran low along the ground around the edge of the wood line. Occasionally, he would duck behind a tree, looking out to see if anyone was after him. He peeked out from behind a pine and saw Ian walking, no *strolling*, up the driveway. *Idiot,* he thought. Riley continued his path to the back of the property.

In the moonlight, he could make out a large building at the very back of the property, maybe 100 yards away. Looking around to make sure there wasn't anyone, he darted across the yard, making his way toward the building.

He didn't get very far before he heard a crash in the main house. It sounded like someone had thrown something out of the window. Looking up, he saw that someone did. Through the now open window, Riley could hear sounds escaping. Grunts, yells, and the occasional curse that sounded like it came from Ian. He looked back toward the building at the back of the property. He didn't know what was in there, but he knew Ian was inside the main house, and from the sounds of it, needed help. Turning around, he headed back toward the main house and slipped under the garage door.

Across the garage there was a door open, leading to some stairs. Riley took them as fast as he could, opening the door at the top. It opened into a living room, ornately decorated in whites and grays. The sounds of the fight were coming from his right. He slid into the kitchen and stopped, staring at Ian who was pinned down to the island countertop. The man pinning him was holding what looked like Ian's own knife to his throat.

Ian's eyes flickered over to Riley for a millisecond. "A little help would be nice, Hewitt."

Hearing his last name brought Riley out of his shock. He grabbed the man around the chest and pulled him off Ian. They both grunted as each fought to overpower the other.

"Cyrus, meet Riley. Riley, Cyrus," Ian said as he deftly grabbed his knife from Cyrus' hand, sheathing it inside his jacket.

Riley had Cyrus around the middle, effectively pinning both of his arms to his side, but he couldn't hold on for much longer. This dude was seriously strong. He knew it was happening, but he couldn't stop Cyrus from breaking free.

Riley was pushed back over the counter. He hit his head on the cabinets and felt blood trickle down his face. Now free, Cyrus completely ignored Riley and went straight for Ian.

Riley watched as they traded a series of blows, each blocking and countering in less than seconds. He didn't know what to do to help. He had never been in a fight before. Well...not a real one. He had messed around with his friends, but it was never serious.

Out of the corner of his eye, he saw a cast iron skillet lying on the counter. Without thinking, he picked it up and hit Cyrus over the head. Riley had expected it to incapacitate him, having put all his strength behind the blow. That's how it happened in the movies, but Cyrus must have had an unnaturally thick skull. He rubbed his head and turned to Riley, fury burning in his eyes and blood running down his face. He looked at Riley like he was an annoying fly buzzing around his head that needed to be swatted.

Ian took this as an opportunity to make a move. Riley watched in awe as he first kicked Cyrus in the head and then spun around and kicked out his legs from underneath him. Cyrus fell backward, hitting the ground hard, but quickly jumped back to his feet and lurched toward the two boys.

Cyrus went for Ian again. He swung his fist wide and caught Ian on the jaw, but Ian hit him right back. Riley jumped in too, getting a couple of blows in when Cyrus had himself unprotected.

Riley and Ian were being pushed against the wall, each hit taking them another step back. Ian seemed to realize this, too, because he suddenly jumped up and kicked Cyrus square in the chest, causing him to stumble back a couple of steps.

All three men were heaving, desperately trying to get enough air in their lungs.

"It's two against one, and you still can't beat me," Cyrus said in between breaths. He smiled, showing his bloody teeth.

"It's not over yet, is it?" Ian growled.

Cyrus arched an eyebrow and opened one of the cabinet drawers, pulling out a gun. "Isn't it?"

Riley held his hands up, defensively.

"Oh, you little cheater!" Ian yelled.

Cyrus shrugged his shoulders, and Riley knew what was coming next. He shoved an irate Ian out of the way as the gun went off.

Ian yelled, but Riley couldn't see if he had been hit or not. His vision started to blacken, and he collapsed to the floor. "You shot me!" was the last thing he heard.

The bullet had hit *him*, not Riley, and so Ian stared in confusion at the boy lying passed out on the floor. Ian was lucky. Riley had pushed him out of the way, so the bullet had merely grazed his leg. It still hurt like hell, but he would survive.

Now, he was pissed off.

Before Cyrus could use the gun again, Ian swung around and, using his good leg to stabilize, kicked it out of the man's hands. It flew across the room, effectively out of both of their reaches. Which was probably a good thing. Ian was losing his self-control and didn't know if he would use the gun on Cyrus if he had the chance.

Adrenaline was pumping through his veins. Ian sent a series of punches and kicks to Cyrus. He aimed one more directly to Cyrus' face.

Cyrus' whole body flew back with the force of Ian's kick. His head hit the corner of the counter and a crack rang out in the kitchen. His body slumped to the floor, unmoving.

Ian didn't have to get close to know. He could see it in the way Cyrus' head was twisted, but he walked up to him and checked anyway. He needed to know if he really killed a man.

25

KATELYN WATCHED as the man who had unchained Ellie and her slipped back out of their stall and silently left the barn. It was strange, what he said. First, he frees them and then demands that they stay. Talk about mixed signals.

"Are we going to do what he said?" Ellie asked tentatively.

Katelyn shook her head. "I don't know."

"What if it's a trap? He tells us to stay when he knows we won't listen, and we leave and then we get blown up and we die?" Her words started to run together, and her voice got higher and higher. "Or what if he wanted us to leave and we stay, and the barn blows up and we die?"

"Looks pretty grim for us either way," Katelyn remarked with a grin.

Ellie punched her softly on the arm. "Shut up," she said.

Katelyn smiled. Ellie had been so full of life the first time she had met her, but here in this barn, she was so...haunted. It was nice to see her smile. "Come on," Katelyn said. "Let's take our chances with the bomb outside."

"Agreed."

They helped each other get up and slowly slid open the stall door. Katelyn walked out and gestured for Ellie to follow. The barn probably had six stalls in total. All the doors were open now except for the one stall that sat next to theirs. Ellie stopped in front of it and gingerly laid a hand on the door. She said nothing out loud, but Katelyn thought she saw the girl mouth *goodbye.* Who was in there?

She didn't have time to look before they headed to the barn door. It wasn't closed all the way. In fact, Katelyn could probably squeeze through it to see if anything outside the barn looked suspicious or bomb-like.

Katelyn fit her head through the opening of the door, and she looked right and left. To the right was nothing but trees. Directly in front was a large white house about a football field away. To the left was—

A man. Walking right toward them.

"Go. Go," Katelyn hissed.

"Go where!" Ellie's voice was high-pitched again.

Katelyn shuffled back inside and pulled the door the rest of the way closed. "Back to the stall!"

They both ran the short distance back to their place of captivity. Katelyn closed the stall door and held on to the handle, trying to slow her heartbeat.

"What was it?" Ellie asked.

"I—I don't know. A man. He was coming here."

"Was it the same guy who let us out?"

Katelyn shook her head. "No. I don't think so."

Ellie nodded. "Sit back down here next to me, like we were before." She sat on the hay covered floor and put her hand back into the handcuff, careful not to close it.

Katelyn did the same as she heard the barn door slide open.

Kia slowed down when she passed Riley's truck on the street, but she didn't stop. They weren't in there. Ian was always where the action was, and according to Riley's map, the action was about half a mile up the road.

She didn't have time to park the car and sneak secretly. She was going to drive her car right up the damn driveway.

The moon was bright so she could see the figure of a man walking toward a large building at the back of the property. He looked over at her for a fraction of a second, before turning around and stepping into the building. Even in the dim light, Kia could tell it was neither Ian nor Riley. Whoever he was, Kia needed to find out.

She started walking toward the building he'd gone into but stopped when she felt the same strange wind picked up that she had in the hospital. Her vision started to darken and before she could help it, she fell to the ground. Everything went black.

When Kia came to, a man was standing over her. His blue eyes piercing down at her. She jerked her body back, trying to put space between them, but she found that she was shackled to the wall. She pressed her body up against it, desperate to get as far away from him as possible.

The man cocked his head to the side. "*Frère de mon âme.*" He said the traditional Soulwalker greeting. *Brother of my soul.* Kia knew what the proper response was, but that greeting was reserved for Soulwalkers, and the man standing in front of her was not a Soulwalker.

She would know. She would have been able to *feel* him, because she could feel everything again. She was whole.

She glared up at the man, wondering if he was working for Cyrus.

He frowned for a fraction of a second at Kia's lack of response before continuing. "I'm so pleased that you are here, Kia." He stuck his hand out and touched her face. She tried moving away, but there was nowhere to go. "Looks like you had a nasty fall outside." When he pulled his hand away, traces of blood were on his hand. He rubbed it between his fingers, but never took his eyes off Kia.

Finally, shaking off her dizziness, she took in her surroundings. She was handcuffed to a metal bar that was bolted into the wall of a stall in a barn.

"Kia!" She heard someone call from somewhere else in the barn.

Katelyn.

The man's eyes flickered toward the voice and a smile spread across his face. "Yes, your sister is here. She's safe," he paused. "For now."

And then another voice pierced the silence. "Kia, help!"

Was that?

The voice sounded again. *Ellie?* But that didn't make any sense, if Ellie was so close by—

"Don't look so confused," the man said, interrupting her thoughts. "It puts a little crease right here." He grazed her forehead with his finger for a fraction of a second. "It's quite unattractive. But if you must know, there are wards all around the property."

Kia's eyebrows knitted together again, not understanding.

"The wards protect me. Protect us. You see, if there is a Warlock on the property at all, then the wards remain intact, allowing us to remain hidden from unwanted eyes." He pointed his finger at her and said, "And you..."

And she was a Warlock. He didn't need to finish his sentence.

"What do you want with us?" Kia hissed.

"I want *you*, of course." He said without pause.

Kia was taken aback by his forwardness. "Me?" She asked. "Why would you want me?"

"Isn't it obvious?" He leaned back against the stall door, completely relaxed.

Kia shook her head at him in response, because, of course, it wasn't obvious.

"It's what you are." He stepped forward, bending down to eye-level with Kia. He grabbed her face in his hands and turned it side to side roughly. "How did you do it? How did you come to be?"

Kia did the only thing that she thought was appropriate. She spit in his face. His hand shot out before the spit even hit its target and slapped her hard across her cheek, with the back of his hand. Kia cried out as her face erupted with pain and the handcuffs bit into her wrists. She felt blood trickle down her chin. She licked her lips, tasting the metallic warmth on her tongue.

He wiped the spit from his cheek and took her face in his hands again. "*Ah-ah,*" he said, like he was chastising a dog. He caressed her face in a grip so strong Kia couldn't pull away.

"Look at you," the man said. "The product of perfect evolution. I have waited a lifetime for you." He dropped his hand from her face, his eyes glowing with desire. "Has your magic bloomed yet?"

She didn't answer, not because she didn't want to, but because she didn't know. She didn't feel magical.

His mouth pressed into a thin line. "You will answer my questions." He squeezed his thumb into the soft of her neck, pressing down until she was coughing.

Kia thought back to the other night with Ian. Was it possible that she had healed his bruises? She didn't know if it was her doing, but it definitely seemed like magic.

There must have been something in her eyes that told him her realization without her having said anything, because he smiled. Still, she kept her bleeding mouth stubbornly shut.

He produced a key from his pocket and leaned over to unlock Kia's handcuffs. "Of course, it has. The wards around the house wouldn't be up if it hadn't." He paused. "There's something I need your help with." His face held a smile of pure joy, like a small child waking up on Christmas morning.

The man dragged her out of the stall, shutting the door behind them and cuffed her to the door handle. He disappeared into another stall down the barn. It was the stall that Ellie and Katelyn were in.

She heard screaming and fought against her cuff, trying to pull out of it. But it didn't work. She only succeeded in tearing open the skin at her wrist.

The man walked out of the stall, dragging Katelyn and Ellie screaming behind him. "Now," He said, "let the show begin."

Ian toed Riley with the tip of his boot. The boy grunted softly but did not stir. Ian toed him again, this time harder.

"What the hell?" Riley muttered. He had passed out at the end of the fight. He looked over at the prone body lying on the floor, his head twisted in an unnatural direction.

Riley's eyes followed his. "What happened?"

Ian looked away from Cyrus and over toward the cuckoo clock on the wall. It had been about an hour and a half since Marie and Dominik had performed the transference spell. It must have worn off. "Well, besides you being a complete and utter waste of space...looks like you're a regular old human again." Ian clasped Riley on the shoulder and pulled him to his feet. "Congrats, mate."

Riley reached his hand up and touched his forehead, wincing when he made contact. In case you've forgotten, I did help you back there. Maybe even saved your life."

"If you think we're going to hug it out, there's an open window right there." Ian looked Riley up and down, taking in his state. When he got to Riley's eyes, he couldn't help but burst out laughing. "Looks like Kia had a lasting effect on you." He pointed to his eyes.

Riley quickly turned around and examined his eyes in the stainless-steel oven vent. "Jesus Christ," Riley swore. "They're...they're..."

"Oh yeah," Ian laughed some more. "They're two different colors." Only one of Riley's eyes had changed back to its natural color after the spell had worn off. The other had Kia's striking blue color.

Ian took a step forward to get a closer look, but he put too much pressure on the leg which had been shot and it gave out beneath him.

Riley rushed forward and caught Ian before he hit the ground. He didn't say anything, instead, acknowledging the man code to not talk about weakness. "So, I take it that Hulk over there isn't just knocked out," Riley asked as he helped Ian over to the counter to lean against.

Ian shook his head. "Humpty Dumpty sat on a wall. Humpty Dumpty had a great fall."

Riley took one more look at the body, then turned and threw up all over the floor. Ian looked back at Cyrus, preferring to look at a dead man rather than the vomit.

"You all done?" Ian asked when he didn't hear any more heaving.

Riley simply nodded, wiping his mouth with the back of his hand.

"Are we going to stand here all day, or do you want to look for the girls?" Ian said.

Riley muttered something under his breath that made Ian wonder if he talked to his mother with that mouth. He smirked after him. Maybe they would get along after all, so long as he kept his vomiting to a minimum.

"Should we call someone?" Riley asked as they left the room.

Ian took one more look at Cyrus lying on the ground. "No."

Light reflecting off Cyrus' gun caught Ian's attention.

He picked up the weapon. It felt foreign in his hands. Cold and hard. Ian's dad had taken him to the gun range once to show him how to use a gun. *Safety first,* his father had said. *But we fight with our hands, we don't cheat by using a gun.*

Ian wondered what his dad would say to him now as he picked it up and tucked it into the waistband of his jeans.

He limped out into the hallway, his adrenaline wearing off, each second bringing more pain to his leg.

Riley was inspecting the contents of a closet.

"Why don't you check upstairs? I'll search down here," Ian said, not expecting to be able to make it up the stairs.

"Can't you use your Soulwalker ESP and pinpoint where they are?"

Ian had already thought of that of course, but there was something wrong. He couldn't feel anything. "No, I think there is some sort of magic here working against that."

"Oh," said Riley. He took off up the stairs without another word.

Ian walked around the entire first floor, looking in every room, but he found nothing.

Riley came down the stairs. "Nothing," he said, reaching the bottom.

"Me either," Ian replied. He ran his hand through his too-long hair and sighed.

Riley began, "I think I saw a—"

"Shut up," Ian interrupted. "Do you smell smoke?"

Kia watched as her sister was dragged toward her. She was bruised and dirty, with torn clothes—something Katelyn was probably having a panic attack over—but she had the biggest smile on her face. "Took you long enough, sister," said Katelyn.

Kia couldn't help herself. She smiled back, but her smile vanished abruptly as Preston threw Katelyn hard to the ground at Kia's feet. A small whimper escaped Katelyn's mouth.

"Enough!" The man screamed.

Despite her bruised and battered appearance, Katelyn grinned. "Oh, Preston. Don't get your panties in a—"

Her bravado was short lived as he backhanded her across the face. Kia screamed at the man—at Preston, but he didn't even turn to look at her.

"My patience is wearing thin," Preston said. He ran a hand through his grey-speckled hair and continued. "I've waited for this for too long."

Ellie spoke up for the first time, her voice trembling. "What do you want? Why are you killing Soulwalkers?"

Preston looked taken aback at Ellie's question. "Killing Soulwalkers? I've done no such thing."

Katelyn interrupted before he could continue. "But you're stealing their souls. Isn't that like the same thing?"

"They are heroes." He looked at them with such intensity that Kia almost laughed. Stealing souls? They couldn't be serious. "Heroes that are losing a bit of themselves for the greater good."

"And what about Samson?" Ellie asked, tears beginning to streak down her dirty face. "Was it stealing his soul that killed him? Or did Cyrus hit him one too many times?"

Preston raised his hand to slap Ellie as well. Forgetting she was still shackled to the door, Kia lunged forward again, only to cry out in pain as the handcuffs bit into her raw flesh. Ellie crumpled to the ground.

Samson couldn't be dead. He couldn't be.

"Whatever you're going to do, just do it!" Katelyn yelled.

Preston took her advice. He smiled and strode toward Kia, producing the key from his pocket. He unlocked her handcuffs.

Kia took off toward her sister. She didn't get very far. Preston grabbed her from behind and with unexpected force, slammed her down to the ground. Kia's vision went black for a full second. He leaned down, whispering into her ear. "I don't have the power you do. That's why I've always needed a partner. You weren't who I had in mind, but you'll do for tonight."

"Let me go!" Kia screamed as Preston dragged her closer to Katelyn and Ellie. She reached her hand out to try and touch her sister, but he slapped it away.

"No touching," he said. "Not yet. It's time to start."

Kia snarled at the man, sounding feral to her own ears. "I'm not helping you with whatever evil plan you've got."

She fought to break free of Preston, but his grip was ironclad. "As I said before, what I'm doing—what *we're* doing—is for the greater good, and each one of you is here for a very specific purpose." His eyes became unfocused, as though he was remembering. "I have tried so many things. So many failed experiments. But this," he waved his hands at them, "this will work. And you," he turned toward Kia, his eyes alight with a burning intensity, "you're going to help, or your sister will die."

A sound escaped Kia's lips, something between a sob and a gasp. She looked over at her little sister, who was struggling to hide her feelings behind a stubborn expression. She had taken care of Katelyn their whole lives, and she would again. "Okay," she whispered. "Okay, I'll help you."

"Very good."

Katelyn started yelling. "Oh no, you don't!" She got up, wobbled a little, and tried to make her way over to Kia. She didn't get very far, though Preston didn't grab her. In fact, he didn't touch her at all. He stuck his hand out and said, "Stop."

Katelyn immediately froze as if she had hit a wall. How had he done that? Was he a Warlock too?

"I can't have you running off and ruining everything," he said. He dragged Katelyn again toward the nearest stall door and secured her dangling handcuff to the handle. He swayed a little, putting his hand flat on the stall to steady himself. "I have been able to give myself the ability to perform a very small amount of magic, though even the smallest spell costs me more energy than it should."

Stepping back toward Ellie and Katelyn, Preston pulled out a large knife from his jacket. A butcher knife, from what Kia could tell in the dim light. The floor of the barn was covered in dirt and pulverized hay, so it made it easy for Preston to draw a circle in the dirt using the butt of the knife, maybe two feet across, between the girls. Kia flashed back to a couple of days ago when Ian was drawing circles in the dirt with his own knife in the cemetery.

After his circle was complete, Preston drew a star inside, creating a pentagram, then grabbed Ellie by the arm. Katelyn twisted into a grimace in her effort to break free of the magic restraining her, but it was pointless. She was still frozen in place.

"What are you doing?" Kia yelled, struggling herself.

Preston didn't answer. In one quick motion, he sliced his knife across Ellie's forearm, creating a shallow cut. He held her arm over the pentagram. She cried out as her blood trickled down, landing in the center.

He let go of Ellie, and in the same breath, grabbed Kia and made the same motion. She winced as the knife cut into her skin. His grip was tight on her as he let her blood fall and mix with Ellie's in the dirt. Preston repeated the gesture on himself.

"The blood links us together. All three of us Soulwalkers. I, myself, with a finite amount of magic. But it is Kia's magic that will make this possible," Preston explained as though he was simply teaching an algebraic equation.

"What?" All three girls said at the same time.

Katelyn said, "Kia can't do magic."

"Oh, that is where you are very, very wrong." Preston turned and looked at Kia, the same desire burning in his eyes that she saw when she first laid eyes on him. He spoke to Katelyn, but his eyes remained on Kia. "Your sister is very unique, and her situation is very difficult to recreate." He paused and cocked his head to the side. "But not impossible."

Kia looked over at her sister. Their eyes met and in Katelyn's eyes, Kia saw a mixture of anger, awe, and fear.

Ellie spoke, her voice quiet and trembling. "Are you going to take my soul?"

He turned around and cupped Ellie's face. She didn't try to move away. "Yes," he whispered back. "Be brave."

Kia still didn't understand. "But why?"

Preston started pacing back and forth. "The Riven has too long stood in balance. Each section holding an equal weight, but history tells us that this cannot last. There must always be a leader, a person on top, and I intend for that person to be me. Soulwalkers have always been the elite, the chosen. But we are held back by our inability to do magic. Imagine what we could overcome if we had both abilities?"

He smiled wickedly then grabbed both Kia and Ellie's hands and starting chanting in what sounded to Kia like French. Or maybe Latin?

Ellie's eyes turned white as they did when a Soulwalker was in a Walk. She seemed frozen in place, as Katelyn was. But Kia wasn't. She was free to look and see the horror on Katelyn's face, mirroring her own.

"We have to do something!" Katelyn yelled at Kia.

Kia tried pulling her hand from Preston's, but she couldn't. Whatever magic he was doing was keeping her hand firmly in place.

And then she felt it. Slowly, very slowly, every ounce of energy she had left was being drained from her body. It became hard to keep her eyes open. To hear Preston's chanting or Katelyn's screams. Everything suddenly seemed less important, and all she wanted to do was lie down.

But she couldn't. Her hand still glued to Preston's, she slumped down against the barn stall. If she could only rest for a minute, then everything would be fine.

Her vision turned black, but there was a thought prickling in the back of her mind. What was it?

"Kia! Wake up!" A voice screamed. "Help Ellie!"

Ellie.

Kia's eyes flew open, all thoughts returning to her mind and with them a wave of hot anger that grew by the second.

She was so angry at everything. She didn't want this life. The constant fear of having to look over her shoulder. Every night since their time in the graveyard she'd been afraid. Hell, ever since that first day of school, in French class. She was a freak. And now she had magic too. No, no she didn't want this.

Her anger grew in her chest, burning hot. It burned through her veins. It felt like her blood was thicker, and her heart was having to work overtime. It expanded, traveling down her arm which she had pressed against the stall. Her hand felt as if it was on fire. Then, as if the thought itself had brought it into being, a fire started in the palm of her hand, igniting the wood beneath it.

26

P AIN.

No other thought could take the forefront of Kia's mind. Nothing else mattered. All she could think about was the searing agony that accompanied sticking your hand in a fire.

Shouts and screams forced her to open her eyes. The whole right side of the barn was in flames, and the fire was quickly spreading. And it was loud. Kia never thought about fire making noise before. It roared and screamed as it consumed the wood in its path.

Whatever magic she had done had not only started the fire but had also opened her handcuffs. They dangled from the door handle. Kia stared at it in awe but was slightly afraid of what she had done. She shook her head and turned around, taking in the rest of the room.

Preston had stopped whatever spell he was performing, but only seconds before. Ellie lay on the ground, motionless, but still breathing. Katelyn was beside her, gently trying to shake her awake.

"What have you done?" Preston screamed. The fire reflected in his blue eyes as he turned his gaze upon Kia, turning them a strange purple. "What have you done?" His voice cracked as he repeated his question.

Just then, the barn doors burst open behind them. All three heads whipped around toward the figures running through the smoke.

"The roof, the roof, the roof is on fire!" It was a cocky voice that Kia knew anywhere.

"Ian!" She yelled, but she sucked in some of the smoke that filled the barn and started coughing violently. When she looked up, Preston had grabbed Katelyn and his knife was pressed to her throat. He stared at Ian and Riley in the doorway.

Kia could see them more clearly now. Ian had pulled out a gun and was aiming directly at Preston. Beside Ian, Riley held a knife that startled Kia. It was long and wicked and gleamed in the firelight. Ian's eyes were focused on Preston, but he spoke to Kia. "What are you doing here, kid? Even comas can't keep you away from me?" His voice was light, but there was an edge to it that Kia thought only she would be able to recognize.

"Enter the little Soulwalker," Preston said through clenched teeth. "Oh yes, I know you as well. First Walk at fifteen. A promising student, so promising in fact, that he could have taken Eugene's place one day."

"Be quiet," Ian said, his voice low and dangerous.

But Preston continued. "But then, something happened didn't it? The Golden Boy's parents—"

"I said, shut up!" Ian shrieked and took a step forward. Kia had never seen him lose his nerve. He got mad, yes, but right before her eyes, he was breaking.

Preston tightened his grip on Katelyn in response, the knife cutting into her enough to bleed. She whimpered, and Kia watched as blood started to run down her neck, turning her shirt red.

"*Ah-ah-ah*," Preston tisked at Ian.

"Ian, stop!" Kia yelled before he could take another step forward. She didn't know what Preston was talking about, or how he seemed to know so much about her and her friends, but she couldn't afford to dwell on the subject.

Ian's eyes flickered over to her for a fraction of a second. He took no more steps, but his gun remained in place.

A smile crept onto Preston's face. "The reckless little boy, who was once willing to throw his life away so easily, tamed by a girl."

"She's not just any girl." Ian's jaw was set. Kia could see the muscles moving beneath it.

"No, no she is not. That is where you and I agree."

Ian cocked the gun. "I suggest you let Katelyn go. That is, unless you feel like dying today. I could make it two for two."

Preston's eyebrow arched questioningly, then dropped as comprehension washed over his face. "Ah, Cyrus. Well, I knew he wouldn't last long. I didn't think you had it in you, Soulwalker, but I've been wrong before."

Kia felt like she was sitting in the background while the leaders of the world discussed whether or not they should release a nuclear weapon. Except instead of dropping the bomb on some unsuspecting country, it would be dropping in this room. Because one of these men would explode, that she had no doubt about. She watched, unable to organize thoughts into words, at the stalemate in front of her.

Around them, the fire was growing by the second. Kia felt it all around her. Not only its unbearable heat, but its energy, growing and flicking its tendrils, consuming everything in its path. Already, parts of the were roof coming down, shattering as they hit the ground.

Riley noticed too. "We need to go! This place is going to come down any second!" He yelled over the roar of the fire.

Preston glanced quickly around the bar. "You're right," he said. "I think it is time to go." He turned to Kia and looked her in the eyes. "You'll understand all of this one day."

In one swift movement, he sliced his knife across Katelyn's throat and turned, running out the door at the back of the barn.

Kia's scream could be heard over the fire and the gunshot, as she watched her sister crumble to the ground.

"Someone help!" Kia cried, but she felt like her voice was a whisper.

She pressed her hand over her sister's throat, desperately trying to keep the blood from pouring out. It wasn't like in the movies where the person died almost instantly. There's a lot of blood in the human body, and it takes some time to all come out. Katelyn's eyes were wide, and her mouth moved like she wanted to say something, but nothing was coming out.

She felt someone come up close behind her and put a hand on her back. She didn't have to turn and look to know it was Ian, he was the only one who's touched warmed her skin. "Call 911. Please, do something!"

His hand stayed on her back, but now his voice had a slight edge to it. "Kia, they won't be here in time. You're the only one that can help her now."

"Me? What can I do!" She shrugged his hand off, maintaining her hold on Katelyn.

Another piece of the barn's roof crashed to the floor beside them.

But there was something. *She* had started the fire, with nothing but her mind. Simply that one thought, *fire*. It was like—

Magic.

Ian continued to stare into her eyes. Something must have changed in hers because he nodded and dropped his hands. "Do it. Quickly."

Kia focused on Katelyn's neck. Faintly, she could feel her heartbeat. *Lub-dub. Lub-dub.* It was slow. Too slow. She pictured the skin on her sister's neck. Together and flawless. She knew where all the arteries in the neck were. How they should fit together. She saw them as they should be. Whole and connected. She pictured her sister happy and smiling. Making one of her inappropriate comments.

And slowly, she felt something move beneath her fingers. But she was getting dizzy and her vision started to go.

Kia put one hand down on the ground to steady herself and felt a surge of energy. All around her she felt life, in the trees, the grass, but most of all in the fire. Beside her, she thought she heard Ian murmur something, but she pushed on. She poured everything she had into her sister. All her energy, all her strength, and hoped that it was enough.

When everything was gone, every ounce of energy given, she slumped down to the ground, closed her eyes, and listened to the absolute silence around her.

27

W HEN KIA WOKE to the sound of her name being called, she was still lying on the barn floor, dirt and hay scattered around her. But more, there was ash. Everywhere.

She sat up slowly, adjusting her tired eyes, and stared into Ian's face. There were trace amounts of worry freckled across his expression, but mostly it was that of pure relief, even giddiness.

"You did it," he said. He pressed his lips tightly against hers and lingered a moment, resting his forehead against hers. He tasted of salt and blood and ash. When he pulled away, she took in the barn around her.

Only there was no barn. The entire thing had burned down. Every stall, every rafter. Where mere minutes ago, the barn had stood, ablaze with fire, was nothing but ash. It floated down as slow as snow, landing in their hair, their eyelashes, their clothes. It was everywhere.

"But—" She began, not knowing what questions to ask. Her head hurt so badly; her thoughts scattered.

"*Shh*," Ian whispered. He brushed away a bit of ash that landed on her face with his thumb.

As the fog on her mind began to clear, her eyes grew wide with panic. "Katelyn?" She tried to scramble to her feet but was held in place by Ian. He indicated his head to the side. Not five feet from her Riley had Katelyn's head in his lap, gently brushing her hair out of her face. "Is she...?" Kia croaked.

"Alive." Riley looked up into Kia's eyes.

Kia gasped. In the hospital, she had heard them talking about their eyes but hadn't realized exactly what it meant. "Your eyes..." She said, unable to look away.

He reached up and gingerly touched the skin beneath his one blue eye. "I hope it's not permanent. I'm not sure how I'll explain that one to the folks."

In his lap, Katelyn looked peaceful. They had cleaned all the blood off her skin, but not much could be done for her clothes. They were ruined. Ellie was sitting nearby. She gave Kia a small smile. Kia smiled back. Whatever spell Preston had been doing, Kia had interrupted it by setting the barn on fire.

She looked around, not expecting to see Preston, and unsure if she would want to or not. Ian followed her gaze, and as if he read her thoughts, said, "He's not here." His body went rigid beside hers. "I missed."

Kia wrapped her arms around herself and clutched her chest. So that wasn't the end of him. Whatever he was planning, he would keep at it. And whatever he wanted with her...

She yawned despite her fear, suddenly unable to control her rapidly falling lids. Ian scooped her up in his arms and said, "Let's go home."

Kia's eyes fluttered open several times on the drive home, but she couldn't bring herself to keep them open for longer than a second. Her entire body was exhausted, but there were so many things she longed to ask Ian about.

His eyes were focused on the road ahead, and every time a car passed by, his face was illuminated. His blue eyes shone like beacons in the dark. Kia turned around toward the backseat where Katelyn leaned against the window, Ellie's head in her lap. Riley followed behind them in his truck.

Kia turned back around to look at Ian. His face was bruised and dirty, but she still thought he was the most beautiful man she had ever seen. Yet, she knew so little about this brave and enigmatic man who had suddenly appeared in her life. Her eyes fell closed again, and she spoke to him. "Ian?"

"Hmmm?"

"Tell me a story. About yourself."

He didn't say anything, and Kia wondered if he wouldn't answer or if he was merely thinking. Finally, he said, "When I was a little boy, before my First Walk, my dad would take me to martial arts classes. I was a small kid, and I got picked on a lot. My dad, he—he wanted to protect me, but I didn't want him to. I wanted to protect myself."

Kia reached over the center console for Ian's hand. He took hers in his and gave it a gentle squeeze, then continued his story.

"Dad was already big into martial arts, so he decided to enroll me. 'It'll help you learn how to become a man,' he had said." Ian chuckled a bit to himself. "He took me every week up until..." He cleared his throat. "Up until he died."

Ian had told her that his parents died while she was in the hospital "asleep," but he didn't know that she could hear him. "You never talk about them."

"I was almost 16 when they were killed in a car accident. I was in the car too, but I guess the guy upstairs decided it wasn't my time."

Kia looked over at him. She remembered the long scar that ran down Ian's chest. The one from open heart surgery. The one that he never liked to talk about, like he never liked to talk about his parents. Did he get it that same night? "Ian, I'm so sorry."

He shrugged. "It was a long time ago. Now," he said, glancing over at her, "get some rest. It's a long drive home."

Kia turned around and checked on Katelyn in the backseat of the car. She was sound asleep, her chest rising and falling exactly like it should. "We can't tell anyone what happened to her."

Ian looked over at her again and raised a brow. "Your mother will just *know*."

Kia sighed. Yes, that she would.

Ian stood in front of the mirror adjusting his tie. It was his funeral tie. It usually hung in the back of his closet like the coffee mug you never used but didn't want to get rid of. He never liked putting it on, but it was the blackest black and today called for its solemnity.

The bruises on his face had almost completely faded, but the little cut under his eye was probably going to scar. Kia offered to heal it for him after she had woken up, but he refused. Once they had gotten home, she slept for 16 hours straight, and Ian agonized over every minute of it. He had been so afraid that she wouldn't wake up. But she did, and then Ian finally rested.

He sat down on the bed in the guest room at Eugene's house. He had been studiously ignoring his Authority since the night of the barn fire, claiming recovery, but he had no choice but to be with him today. Ian was a part of the ceremonies. He didn't want to have to answer questions that even he didn't know the answer to.

How did the fire go out? How did you let Preston get away? What did he want with the Soulwalkers?

Of course, he could explain exactly how the fire went out, only he didn't want to. Ian had watched as Kia had drained the energy of the fire, consuming every piece of wood and nail as it receded. It was a terrifying and beautiful sight to behold, but one that Riley and Ian swore to keep secret. Ian even shrugged when Kia asked what had happened. She was already experimenting too much with her magic, and whatever kind of power she held, it was dangerous. Ian wanted to keep her safe for as long as possible.

Since Eugene still didn't trust Kia, Ian couldn't tell him that she was not only a Soulwalker, but that she also had magic. It would probably give the man a heart attack if he found out. Plus, he had other things on his mind.

Ellie had recounted the entire story of her capture, including the torture of Samson. Ian could barely make out the words that he had been killed through her tears. He had clenched his jaw and pulled the little girl in tight.

Half a dozen of the city's Soulwalkers went back out to the barn site the next day and searched for any remains, but like the barn, Samson's body had burned up in the fire. They had searched the house as well for anything to point to who Preston was, what he wanted, or who was helping him. But the house had been cleaned out. Cyrus' body gone. Not even junk mail remained.

A soft knock at the door jolted Ian from his thoughts. It was probably Veronica, Eugene's wife, coming in to check his suit, but when Eugene stepped through the door, Ian's fists involuntarily clenched. He took deep breaths to calm himself down. These days, Ian could barely look at his Authority without wanting to punch him in the face. "Eugene," Ian said.

Eugene looked like he hadn't slept in days. New, deep lines stretched across his face, and Ian had to remind himself that Eugene was in his 19th year. That any day could be his last. He let his fists relax at his side. Eugene sighed as he slumped into the small reading chair in the corner, unbuttoning his jacket as he did.

The two men stared at each other, letting the silence fill the void between them.

"I never thought I would see this day," Eugene finally said. "It was me that was supposed to go first." It was almost a whisper, but Ian still heard.

He didn't respond. He was afraid that if he opened his mouth, everything that he had kept shut inside would come pouring out. He braced himself for the onslaught of questions from his Authority, but Eugene stared off into space and the circles beneath his eyes became darker and darker with each passing moment.

Finally, Eugene spoke again. "There are things you will have to do. Once I'm gone, and it will be soon, a conclave will be held in Paris. You must try to rise to the top. You must—"

"Whoa, whoa, whoa," Ian interrupted. "That's not for me. Maybe it was a long time ago, but not anymore. I'm a Mentor now."

"Things have changed." Eugene's face grew dark. "Samson is dead. We have no one in line for Authority. It *must* be you."

Kia heard the doorbell ring, but she was nowhere close to being ready. The funeral started in 20 minutes, and Ian, who had insisted on picking her up, was a part of the ceremonies. There's no way they could be late.

She looked down at the three black dresses laid out on her bed. All of them seemingly identical, yet, she couldn't decide which one. None of them seemed appropriate. None of them would accurately display the sadness that she held in her. She needed her sister.

"Katelyn!" She shouted through the walls, as there was a knock on her door. She stuck her head out, hiding the rest of her body behind the door.

"Hey kid," Ian said. He was wearing a dark suit with an even darker tie. Even though he had combed his hair back, the fact that he had several days' worth of facial hair kept his look from being all too put together, something he probably did on purpose. Ian Stalbaum never tried too hard at anything, or at least, he was never *caught* trying too hard.

"Ian," Kia answered back. "Do you mind waiting downstairs? I'll only be a minute."

Katelyn slipped through the door and closed it in Ian's face. "You summoned?"

Kia's eyes flickered down to her sister's throat, not for the first time that day. Ever since that night at the barn, Kia was constantly feeling the need to make sure Katelyn was okay. But, like the past times she had checked, Katelyn's neck remained unmarked and her heart pulsed strong.

Kia looked away before Katelyn said anything. "Which dress?"

"That one." Katelyn pointed to the polka-dotted black chiffon dress that Ian had bought for her. Kia slid it over her head without a second thought. It seemed like so long ago. A lifetime. She had been through so much since that first incident. Drug withdrawal, gunshot wounds, fights in the cemetery, comas.

Without even realizing it, she started to cry.

Kia turned away from Katelyn to wipe her face, trying to get rid of the evidence of her tears. She looked out the window and could see the sun setting. The sky faded into orange, then pink. No matter how hard mankind was on the Earth, it kept on spinning. Day to night. Night to day. Time never stopped. Sometimes people chose to make their time on earth stop. To not watch the sun rise in the morning, or set in the evening. To leave it all behind.

There were so many times in the past weeks that Kia wanted to give up. A voice in the back of her mind had said she was too young for all of this, that she shouldn't have to go through these things. But there were small moments. Little bits of good. Kia smiled as Ian's face appeared in her mind. Then Katelyn's. Riley and Ellie's.

Watching the sun disappear below the tops of the buildings, Kia wiped the last tear from her face and walked past Katelyn and out the door.

Epilogue

MARIE WATCHED the blue-eyed boy pace back and forth in his black suit muttering to himself. By all rights, he was no longer a boy but a man, and yet, she would never be able to call him anything different. Because it was not a man in front of her that she saw when she looked into his eyes, but the small, scared boy from not long ago.

He didn't know—wouldn't remember—that she was the one standing beside him when he had asked, "Where are my parents?"

For years, Marie had wondered what had happened to the orphaned blue-eyed boy. Did he have a family to take him in? Someone that would understand his new ability. Or had he gone to live with the other Soulwalkers in the city? She had never found out until recently.

But now, he had somehow worked his way back into her life. Back into *their* lives.

Her phone started buzzing on the kitchen counter, interrupting her thoughts of the past. The caller ID said "blocked", but she had a feeling she knew who it was.

"Hello," she said in a low voice. She didn't want Ian listening in on her conversation.

"Marie," came the familiar voice. Her body tensed up with recognition. A long time ago she would have relaxed at hearing his voice on the other end of the telephone, but not anymore.

"What do you want?" She hissed.

The man paused, but Marie could hear his breathing. *In and out. In and out.* It was as if he was working up the courage to say what he needed to. "I want what I always do...to make sure they're okay."

Marie's skin started to boil. "She could have died! You don't get—" Her voice was rising. Looking over to make sure Ian hadn't heard, she continued. "I know it was you. It was written all over her. The others, they couldn't see. But you know how deep my power runs, and I could see it clear as day." Her words and sentences ran together as she gave voice to the thoughts that had been plaguing her for days. If he was calling, then they were back together again. He and Preston, carrying on their mission. He would have never risked the call otherwise. Preston had eyes *and ears* everywhere.

He paused for only a fraction of a second, and when he spoke, his voice was firm and sure. "Theirs will run deeper. They are, after all, *our* daughters."

Kia came walking down the stairs, and Marie hung up the phone.

Acknowledgments

When you work on something for over 10 years, the list of people to thank seems never-ending. I dedicated this book to my mother, because it was her dream about people who could *walk* into other's souls that inspired this story. I might have gone a different direction from her political thriller idea, but this story—or myself—still wouldn't exist without her, and for that I am forever grateful. I need to thank my writing partner, Jackie Hook, who spent many an hour by my side, our fingers typing away on laptops. Without her encouragement and presence, this idea would have never gotten off the ground. Katie Heskett-Jones, Anna Jones, Amanda Mueller-Hickler, and Jennifer Horn for edits and feedback. This book is better because of y'all. My beta readers. Colin Green for choreographing the fight scenes, since I know nothing of martial arts or how to throw a punch. Sam Lai for his medical expertise. A special shout out to Sweet Eugene's, the coffee shop where I wrote 90% of this novel. Your Milky-Way latte fueled tens of thousands of words. My dad, my brother, Cole Ryden, Mahssa Chovoshi, Taylor Wagner, Michelle Hernandez, Amy Tolladay, Imogen Tyreman, all of my SOFWAEF girls, and everyone else who never let the light of my dream flicker and die. Thank you all.

CPSIA information can be obtained
at www.ICGtesting.com
Printed in the USA
FSHW010641231019
63252FS